THE PRINCE'S BRIDE

Getaway Bay Romance, Brides & Beaches Romance, Book 3

ELANA JOHNSON

Copyright © 2019 by Elana Johnson

All rights reserved.

No part of this book may be reproduced in any form or by any electronic or mechanical means, including information storage and retrieval systems, without written permission from the author, except for the use of brief quotations in a book review.

ISBN-13: 978-1678723095

CHAPTER ONE

Zara Reddy pulled her dark hair out of its ponytail, the amount of water squeezing out with her elastic making a huge puddle on the floor. She was used to being wet, because she worked as a synchronized swimmer on the island on Getaway Bay, in some of their most popular shows.

This summer's show kept her busy with practices during the week, and nightly shows from Thursday to Sunday. She didn't work the matinees, thankfully. She was grateful for the jobs that always seemed to come her way. That way, she didn't have to go to work at her family's Indian restaurant in downtown Getaway Bay.

They were traditional in every sense of the word, and Zara had made more explanations about her life choices over the years than she cared to admit.

Her phone flashed violently with blue and green lights,

and she checked her texts first as the other swimmers came into the locker room.

"Are you coming with us to dinner?" Suzie asked, taking Zara's attention from her device.

"Oh, uh, I don't think so," she said, lifting her phone. "I think I just got that house-sitting job."

Suzie wrung out her hair and started changing. "That's great, Zee. Up on the bluffs?"

"Yeah. First time." She was an experienced house sitter, and she'd completed a dozen or so jobs now. It was easy work, and she got to stay in some of the nicest houses on the island.

And this one?

This one was the crown jewel of the mansions up on the bluff. She'd been texting back and forth with a woman named Petra for several days now, and Zara had never answered so many questions. It was house sitting, not rocket science.

But Petra wanted a background check, and Zara's references, and if there would be any pets in the house. Zara did have a long-haired white cat, but she'd kept that to herself. Petra didn't seem like the kind that would tolerate felines.

The pay was sky high, and Zara smiled as she tapped out her acceptance of the job. She had a small apartment in a long row of them, and staying up on the bluffs would add to her gasoline bill, but it would be so much better than listening to the thirty-somethings next door try to become Hawaii's next big boy band—at all hours of the night.

The address to the house appeared on her screen, along with the code to the gate and the garage. *Anytime tonight or tomorrow*, Petra said. *Send me your PayMe, and I'll get you the money.*

Zara showered and dressed, throwing her heavy bag full of suits, props, caps, nose clips, goggles, and more over her shoulder and heading out to her car. Hopefully, it would start. It was much too hot to sit in the car without air conditioning, listening to the engine click while she prayed it would turn over.

"With this new job," she muttered to herself as she crossed the parking lot. "You can maybe afford to buy a new car." One that actually started the first time.

Sighing, she got behind the wheel and stuck in the key. Miraculously, the car started with the first turn, and she fiddled with the dials on the air conditioner to make it blow harder. Her phone rang, and she answered the call from one of her best friends, Ash Fox.

"Hey, Ash." Zara put the car in reverse, trying not to let any of the jealousy she'd been experiencing when it came to Ash infuse her voice. See, Ash had been Zara's go-to friend when everyone else had a boyfriend. Ash never did. Ash sat behind her sewing machine almost all the time. Zara could always count on Ash—until Burke.

And now Zara had a huge, empty house on the bluffs to go home to.

"So remember how you said you might be able to help out at Your Tidal Forever?" Ash asked.

"Yeah," Zara said slowly.

"Well, Hope is *swamped*, and she's looking to pick up a few seasonally people this summer. Just until the Bellagio wedding is over in September."

Normally, Zara would've jumped at the chance, because it was work, and she didn't pass up an opportunity to make connections around the island in case she met someone who could open another door for her.

Anything was better than the door leading to Indian Room.

"I can't," she said, infusing the appropriate amount of disappointment into her voice. "I just picked up that house-sitting job I was telling you about. With the show, and now this, I'm not sure I'll have time."

"Oh, that's fine," Ash said. "Hope just said to spread the word. If you know anyone, have them call over to Your Tidal Forever and ask for her assistant, Shannon."

"I will." Zara knew Shannon too, and how she worked so closely with Hope and didn't go insane was a quiet miracle.

"So you got the house-sitting job?" Ash asked.

"Yes." Zara smiled as she turned onto the road that led back to her apartment. She just needed to pack a few things and get Whitewater, her cat, into her carrier. "I'm pretty excited about it. I'm heading up there right now."

"Pool?" Ash asked.

"*Big* pool," Zara said. "In fact, I think there are two pools at this place."

"I have four dresses to make by next weekend." Ash moaned.

"I'll be here until September," she said. "In fact, I think I'm going to give up my lease." After all, it was only June, and she could save three and a half months of rent if she gave up her place. There were plenty of rentals on the island, and she wouldn't have any problem getting somewhere else come fall.

Not only that, but then the boy band wannabes wouldn't be her neighbors anymore. Oh, yes, she was going to give up her apartment, just as soon as she made it back down to town from the bluffs the following morning.

Tonight, she was going to bask in the grandeur of this mansion, maybe sit by the pool, and just *relax*.

AN HOUR LATER, THE SUN WAS NOWHERE NEAR SETTING, for which Zara was thankful. She didn't want to pull up to the house in the dark, but Whitewater would not get in her carrier and it had taken Zara an extraordinarily long time to pack a bag and leave her house with the cat. The backs of Zara's hands could testify of that, what with all the scratches from Whitewater's protests.

The cat yowled from the passenger seat, and Zara said, "Oh, be quiet, Whitey. You're fine." So maybe the words held a bit of exasperation. But some of those scratches were deep, and two had bled a little. So the cat could be quiet as Zara navigated the twisty road up to the bluffs.

All of Getaway Bay's rich and famous lived up here. Okay, fine, not all of them. But all the ones who didn't live in the swanky penthouses on the beach. Beachside didn't exist up on the bluffs. Oh, no. People bought these houses for the privacy and security, as well as the stunning, spectacular, three hundred and sixty degree ocean views.

Zara couldn't decide which she'd rather have. Soft,

white sand right out her back door, or a mansion in the hills. But for the next three months, she'd be taking this twenty-minute drive up to the mansion.

She turned onto the appointed road and went about a block before she met a closed and locked gate. After keying in the code, her excitement grew while the gate rumbled open. A sprawling piece of land sat before her, and she eased her car through the now-open gate onto the driveway.

With the gate moving closed behind her, another sigh passed through her body. She had tomorrow off from swimming practice, as the director was working with the acrobats and the main characters in Fresh Start, the not-to-be-missed show of the summer in Getaway Bay's outdoor theater pool.

Zara had done a few shows at the same venue, and the special effects capabilities were superb. She'd also worked with Ian Granger, the director, several times, and while she'd thought they might have a spark in the beginning, it had fizzled fast.

Just like every other relationship Zara had had. She'd been in the dating pool for a long time, and she was feeling wrinkly and dried out from all the chemicals. She wouldn't care that much that she was boyfriendless if her mother didn't badger her constantly to find that special someone.

As if Zara hadn't been looking.

She gazed at the beautiful Hawaiian flowers, the trees, the black lava rock in the landscaping. This was done by a professional, and Zara loved every piece of it as she drove slowly past.

The house sat down a little hill and it too spread out and up, boasting tall white pillars on the front porch, which faced the ocean. Of course, three sides of this house faced the ocean, and Zara hoped the room where she'd be staying had a walk-out balcony. Or a patio. Something where she could step from inside to out and breathe in the fresh air and hear the waves crashing on the rocks far below.

She pulled up to the front door and peered through the windshield. "All right, Whitey," she said to the cat. "Let's go see where we're going to be living for a few months."

Petra never had to know about the cat. The woman said she and her family would be overseas for the summer, thus the need for a house sitter. So Zara killed the engine, walked around the car and shouldered her overnight bag before picking up the cat carrier.

At the front door, she keyed in the code and the lock disengaged. The alarm sounded once, and she stepped over to the keypad to disarm it. She hadn't gotten a separate code for it, so she put in the same numbers she'd used to unlock the front door.

But that only made the alarm beep at her. The steady, every-two-second beeps made her want to stab something in her ears. She tried the code again, very aware of Whitewater's increased yowling. It was as if the cat was trying to harmonize with the incessant beeping.

"Come on," she muttered when she put in the wrong digit and had to go back.

She became aware of another sound amidst the chaos—

growling. She turned to see a big, black dog standing about ten feet away, his teeth bared.

"Oh," Zara exhaled most of the word as Whitewater started hissing inside the carrier. The dog barked, huge, booming sounds that filled the two-story high foyer.

With the beeping, and the hissing, and the barking, it was a miracle that Zara heard someone say, "Boomer, be quiet," just before a man came through the doorway and stood behind the dog. He paused when he caught sight of Zara, his eyes widening. He lifted the spatula he held like he'd use it to defend himself if necessary.

"What are you doing here?" he yelled over the barking, the hissing, and the beeping.

"House-sitting," she yelled back. "Who are you?"

He looked like he could be a fashion magazine model, what with that dark hair all swept back into a manbun on the back of his skull. He opened his mouth, presumably to yell something else, and then rolled his eyes before striding forward.

"I changed the code," he said, practically pushing her aside to punch in the numbers. The beeping stopped. He turned back to the dog. "Boomer, quiet." The dog stopped barking, and Zara tried not to be impressed.

Tried, and failed.

"Sit," the man said next, and the dog did that too.

Now, if she could get Whitewater to stop hissing....

Their eyes met, and dang if Zara didn't have to jump back at the shock she received. He had gorgeous eyes the color of the black lava rock outside, and his olive skin had certainly been featured in many a woman's daydreams about European beaus.

"Who are you again?" she asked, realizing he'd never said.

"I'm Noah Wales," he said. "And I don't need a house sitter."

CHAPTER TWO

𝒩oah Wales would not be swayed by a beautiful pair of eyes. Or all that dark skin. Or the curves this woman possessed. Oh, no. He would not.

Wasn't that the whole reason he'd come to the island house in the first place? To get away from women like the one standing in front of him?

Yes, yes it was.

He blinked and backed up a step, though this was his house—fine, his family's house—and he didn't have to go anywhere. He gripped the spatula he'd been using to flip eggs, wondering why he still held it.

She blinked too, confusion coloring those dark, chocolatey eyes. He hated that description, as if everything had to be related to food. But when he tried to come up with another way to categorize her eyes, it was related to coffee.

He sighed. "Did my mother hire you?"

"Is your mother named Petra?"

"Yes," he said. "But you said it wrong. It's not Petra, like your cat is a pet. It's Petra, like...peat moss."

"Petra," she said correctly, swinging the cat carrier behind her back as if Noah hadn't already seen it. "Then, yes. Your mother hired me."

Noah's mind raced. He didn't want his mother to know he was here. He didn't want *anyone* to know he was here. He didn't want this woman here with him. He just needed somewhere to lie low for a while until he could figure things out, repair his reputation, and then return home to Triguard.

"What's your name?" he asked.

"Zara Reddy." She extended her hand like they'd be bunkmates. He looked at it for a moment past comfortable and then gave it one pump.

Could he send her away? Would she text his mother?

Her phone shrilled out a few quick beeps in a row, stealing her attention and giving him some time to think. She tapped out a quick response and looked at him. "So, what are we going to do?"

"Well, I really don't need a house sitter," he said. Boomer's claws clicked against the tile as he came closer. "As you can see, I have a guard dog. So I'll be fine."

"I need this job," Zara said, her phone chiming in rapid succession again. "I've already sent your mom my payment info."

Noah nodded. "That's fine. She doesn't need to know." So maybe he spoke the last sentence with a little too much feigned nonchalance, because Zara's perfectly sculpted eyebrows went up.

"She doesn't?" She cocked her hip and put the hand holding her phone on it. "Does she even know you're here?"

"This is *my* house," he said. He didn't have to defend himself to her. An inward sigh practically had him giving up. The truth was, he had to defend himself and his actions to everyone. He had since the moment he was born into the royal family, the Wales of Triguard.

"Your mother hired me this afternoon," Zara said, a definite measure of desperation in her words.

"I'll bet she said no pets." He cocked an eyebrow at the cat carrier, where a definite low meow still emanated.

"You have a dog," she said. "And he's huge, and he's definitely the shedding type."

"This is my house," he repeated, wondering if she'd even heard him the first time.

Her phone rang this time, and she sighed like he was the most annoying man on the planet, and said, "Excuse me a moment, would you?" She lifted her phone to her ear without waiting for him to say anything. "Hey." She turned her back on him and wandered a few steps further into the house.

Noah needed to get rid of her. If any reporters saw her come through the gate, there'd be a dozen cameras watching the place. Where had she parked? Probably right out in the open, and he groaned as he turned to look out the tall, skinny windows that flanked the front door.

Yep, her beat-up sedan sat right there, out in the open for anyone to see.

"Sorry," she said, and he turned back to her. "There's

this huge celebrity wedding on the island this fall, and the owner of the wedding planning place needs extra hands all summer." She shook her head as if she was saying something crazy, but Noah seized onto the information.

"Is she paying or is it volunteer work?" If he could get some volunteer credit, maybe he could start to repair some of the damage he'd caused in Venice....

"I think she's paying." Zara squinted at him. "Why?"

"Why what? Nothing."

"You have a look in your eye."

"What look?" He scoffed. "You met me five minutes ago. I don't have a look."

"Mm hm," she said, nodding. "I know your type. Rich, spoiled, handsome. Living up here on the bluffs like you own the world just because you can see a lot of it. Always looking to play an angle. What is it this time? Knocked up a woman and need to play nice with the press now? Or maybe...maybe you've had a bit of a scandal and need a way to clean up your image."

Noah simply stared at her. Had she crawled inside his mind and rooted around in there until she'd found his exact situation?

"I have not knocked anyone up," he said with disgust. "And I really can't have the press here. So I need you to move your car. Now." Had she said he was handsome?

Yeah, right after rich and spoiled.

"Where?" she asked.

"The garage," he said. "Then we'll talk some more about...stuff."

"Stuff?" She stood there with that strap over her shoulder, her bag bumping her hip.

"An arrangement," he said, the idea swirling around in his mind. "I'll go put coffee on. Unless you prefer tea?"

She blinked at him, and Noah himself was a little weirded out by the way he was whiplashing between polite and defensive.

"Coffee's fine," he said, moving away from her. As he went, he caught the scent of her perfume, and it was part flowers and part something else that he couldn't quite name. As he left her in the foyer and entered the kitchen, the word came to mind.

Chlorine.

She smelled like chlorine. He checked over his shoulder to make sure she hadn't followed him, and relief ran through him when he heard the front door open and close. "All right," he said to himself and Boomer as he filled the coffee pot with water. "Let's just hear what she has to say, okay? Maybe this won't be so bad."

Zara took so long to return to the house that Noah thought she may have left. But she'd left her bag and her cat in the front foyer, so he poured himself a cup of coffee and waited. After all, he was the youngest child of a king, and waiting was practically part of his genes.

When she finally did come in, it wasn't through the front door but the one that led into the garage. "This place is huge," she said. "Did you know there are four doors leading out of the garage? I thought I'd never find my way inside."

Noah smiled at her, enjoying the exuberance in her

expression. "Well, you found the right one at last." He indicated the coffee pot and the ruby red mug he'd gotten down for her. "Coffee?"

She eyed him as she moved closer and poured her own cup of coffee. After putting in a spoonful of sugar and quite a lot of cream, she stirred and faced him again. "So, Noah. You sounded like you had a plan."

"Sort of," he said, his mind still tripping on some of the finer details. "Where did my mother say you'd be sleeping?"

Zara set her coffee mug on the counter and pulled out her phone. "Let's see. She said I could have any of the guest rooms to the right of the main staircase, or I could stay on the main level in any of the three rooms on the west side." She looked at him. "I thought you didn't need a house sitter."

"I don't."

"Then what—?"

"I need the privacy of this place," he said carefully. "I know my parents won't be back for months. I need to...lie low for a while. No one can know I'm here." He didn't know Zara at all, but she seemed like a smart woman. Her quick wit while they'd traded jabs in the foyer told him she might be able to pick up what he was laying down without him having to spell it all out.

"So you want me to 'house sit.'" She made air quotes around the last two words. "To keep people away? So they think no one's here?"

"Bingo," he said. "And you can stay here. Get paid for sitting the house. Lie by the pool. Bring up groceries. Whatever you were planning on doing."

"Bring up groceries," she said. "You mean *your* groceries."

"I might make a few requests," he said as if that were a perfectly reasonable thing for him to do. Then he wouldn't have to go into town. The idea really was coming together. "Everyone will think the house is empty. The paparazzi and cameras won't need to stay or try to find me here."

"Whoa. Paparazzi?"

"They're relentless," he said. "And they know I left Venice." He hoped they didn't know where he'd gone yet. He really just needed some time.

"Oh, of course," Zara said with sarcasm dripping from the words. "Venice."

Noah regarded her coolly. So she was beautiful. Smart. But she had a cat, and he generally disliked felines. Boomer didn't seem to mind, as he'd followed Noah back into the kitchen and now lay panting near the fridge.

"So here's my deal," he said. "You can stay here as you'd planned. Pick any of the rooms on my mother's list, but I am staying on the second floor to the right of the staircase. Use the pools. All of that." He took a step toward her, surprised and even more attracted to her when she didn't back away from him.

"But no one can come up here. So no pool parties or anything like that. You'll get the groceries and other things I might need so I don't have to leave the house. You'll still get your summer here. You'll get paid."

"And you? What do you get from this?" She folded her arms. "Because I'm not one of *those women*." Her dark eyes flashed dangerously.

Noah laughed. "Trust me, Zara. I'm not one of *those men* either. I just got out of a really bad relationship. I'm not looking for another one."

"Or a summer fling," she said. "I don't do flings."

"Great. Makes two of us." Just because she made his stomach flip didn't mean he was going to act on the attraction.

"You still haven't said what you're getting from all of this," she said. "Except me buying your groceries and running your errands and taking care of *your* house."

Perhaps she had heard him when he'd said this place was his.

"I get the time I need," he said. "The anonymity I've never had. And the chance to volunteer on that celebrity wedding."

Her eyebrows went up again, and he wondered if she practiced such a flawless motion in the mirror. "Why would you want to do that?" she asked.

"I have my reasons," he said. He'd been raised to serve others, and volunteer work *was* the best way to repair bad public perception. Now, if Noah hadn't been "the bad boy of Triguard," he definitely wouldn't have logged over ten thousand volunteer hours over the past thirty-one years of his life.

"So what do you think?" he asked, calmly taking another sip of his coffee, the way he'd seen his father do many times.

Zara studied him for several long moments, clearly working through something in her mind. Probably a lot of somethings. Finally, she said, "I think I'm crazy. I can't believe I'm going to say yes to this."

Noah grinned at her and plucked his own phone out of his shorts pocket. "Great. I'm just going to need the number of that wedding planning place...."

CHAPTER THREE

Zara stood in the doorway of Bedroom Number Three, deciding it was the best one. It sat way down at the end of the hall, past the other two rooms. It had its own attached bathroom, and it had a set of double doors directly ahead where the evening sunlight still shone through.

She groaned as she stepped across the threshold, her overnight bag holding hardly anything but weighing so much on her shoulder. Probably because she'd been carrying it for the past twenty minutes as she figured "stuff" out with Noah.

"You must be insane," she muttered to herself as she closed the door behind her. The knob had a lock, which she pressed, and then she could truly relax. Not that she thought Noah would come barging into her bedroom. For some reason, she got the vibe that he'd stay up on the second floor this summer. Even the pool was too out in the open for him, something she'd gathered as the panic from having her car parked by the front door instead of in the garage had rolled across his face.

And yes, there were four doors leading out of the garage, but Zara wasn't an idiot. She'd just needed some time to do a little Google-Fu online. Noah Wales was a prince.

"A freaking prince," she said to the fake flower arrangement on the dresser. It was dust-free, and she wondered if she'd be the maid this summer or if Petra had someone coming in. Because if she did...Zara wanted to be around when Noah met the maid.

She actually smiled thinking about it. With her bag on the bed, she rolled her aching shoulders and stepped over to the double doors. The gauzy curtains billowed as if a bit of a breeze had come in, but Zara knew this house was locked down tight.

She flipped several switches until she found the one that controlled the ceiling fan, and then the curtains really went swish-swish-swish. She pulled them apart and unlocked the door, pushing it open in the next moment.

The warmth from the sun felt glorious on her bare arms, and she drew in another deep breath. This was definitely the best bedroom choice, as it had a small patio with a table built for two and a waist-high railing with a gate in it that led to the pool.

The aqua water undulated and sparkled in the sun, and Zara could think of nothing better than the sight before her.

Oh, yes, she could. She could imagine a situation where

she lived in this beautiful mansion alone for the summer, making a battle plan for her dating game in the fall.

"Nice view, isn't it?"

Horror struck her right between the ribs at the sound of Noah's voice. She shaded her eyes as she glanced around, finally finding him on the second-floor balcony to her right.

"I'm surprised you came outside," she called back. "What if a reporter has a camera on a drone?"

His eyes flew to the skies, and she giggled as he ducked back under the eaves of the house, moving all the way out of sight a moment later. She heard him say, "You think you're so funny," before a door closed.

Zara did think she was funny. And now she knew how to get Noah out of her hair should he ever annoy her.

Ever annoy her? He'd annoyed her from the moment they'd met.

"Playboy," she said to the pool. "A playboy prince." Which was exactly the last thing Zara needed in her life—even if he did have gorgeous hair and eyes and a smile that had probably cost the king several thousand dollars.

And he wasn't going to stop her from having the summer of her life. She owned no less than ten swimming suits, and she went back into her bedroom and changed into one she didn't use for work. Pairing that with a billowy, white coverup, she padded down the hall and around the corner and down another hall into the kitchen to see what Prince Noah had to drink in the fridge.

She'd definitely be getting her steps in just by traveling from her room to the kitchen for meals. The fridge was easily ten feet wide, with huge double doors that swung all the way open. Zara felt like she was standing in front of the refrigeration units at the convenience store as she took in the bottles and cans before her.

"At least he has good taste in beverages," she said, selecting a bottle of pomegranate lemonade.

Down the halls, around the corners, and out the doors, Zara positioned herself beside the pool, her lemonade and her phone all she needed to watch the sun set into the Pacific Ocean in front of her.

And it didn't matter that she'd have to deal with a spoiled prince and his huge dog this summer. This place was big enough for the two of them, and if she couldn't have friends up to the mansion, so be it.

Zara liked being alone anyway.

The following morning, she'd fed Whitewater and shut her in the suite where they'd be living for the next few months. The rainfall showerhead in the bathroom had been divine, and she wound her damp hair around and around into a bun as she entered the kitchen at the same time Noah slid three fried eggs onto a plate.

"Morning," he said like they'd be best friends forever by the end of the day. "Breakfast?" He raised those deliciously thick eyebrows at her, his face a bit less clean shaven this morning.

"You cook?"

"A little," he said. "Coffee, toast, eggs, bacon. The usual suspects for breakfast."

"Then sure," Zara said, sliding onto a barstool. "I'll take an egg."

"Coming up." He set the pan back on the stove and cracked another egg into it. The satisfying hiss of the white and yolk meeting the hot pan sang through Zara's soul. So she liked to cook. It wasn't a crime, and she didn't want to be a chef at Indian Room just because she liked putting a meal together.

"So how'd you sleep?" he asked, turning from the stovetop.

She peered at him, trying to decide if he was really asking or if he knew she'd been awake half the night, wondering if he wore pajamas to bed or not.

"Fine," she ended up saying. "You?"

"Oh, it was a rough night." He ran one hand down his face, flashed her a smile, and plucked a fork from a drawer. He started cutting into his eggs, letting the yolk run out and touch his toast.

Zara almost gagged. "I like my eggs well-done," she said. She got up and rounded the island. "I can do it." She'd just picked up the spatula when he appeared at her side.

"I can do it. My mother called a well-done fried egg a rubber sole." He took the spatula gently from her fingers and carefully broke the yolk, adding a bit of salt and pepper before flipping the egg with the ease of someone who'd done it a great many times before.

"Well then, I need a rubber sole." She inhaled, finding it so unfair that he could smell so good and look like he'd just tumbled out of bed moments ago. She found a hint of pine, something spicy, masculine, and a hint of fabric softener under that. Maybe the fresh breeze scent.

"Are you going down to town today?" he asked.

"Yes," she said. "It's my day off, but I'm going to give notice at my apartment and pack a few more things."

"I was thinking you could drop me off at Your Tidal Forever before you did all that."

Zara backed up a few steps, finally realizing how close they stood together. In the next moment, he turned from the stove too, the pan in his hand. He pulled down a plate with his free hand and slid the rubber sole out of the pan.

"There you go."

"Thanks." She opened the same drawer he had, grabbed a fork, then a couple slices of bacon, and retreated back to the barstool she'd been sitting on earlier.

"So today?" he asked. "I've already spoken to Shannon, and she said I can come in anytime."

"Great," Zara said, though she did not think it was great. "We can go anytime then. Unless, of course, you were planning to shower before leaving the house."

His eyebrows puckered for a moment, and then he dropped his gaze to his food so she couldn't read it. "Maybe I should get your number," he said, ignoring her jab about showering. "Then I can let you know when I'm ready to go."

"I'm not a car service." She bit off the end of a piece of bacon, imagining it to be his head.

"Fine," he said, his dark eyes flashing dangerously. "Then when do you want to go?"

"You tell me."

"But you just said you weren't a car service."

"Because you made it sound like you'd just text me when you were ready, and I should come running out, keys ready." Zara had plenty of her own fire inside too. She tossed the half-eaten piece of bacon on her plate and stood up. "I'm going to go eat in my bedroom."

She'd taken four steps—nowhere near enough to get out of the kitchen—when he said, "Wait." He sounded a bit contrite, so Zara paused and turned back to him. "I'd still like your number, and yes, I need to shower. Maybe we could go in about an hour?"

Ah, so the prince *could* be nice. Zara smiled, hoping it came off as sweet. "Sure. I'll meet you in the car in an hour." She turned and started walking away again. She'd never be able to storm out to make a point the next time they argued. This house was too freaking big.

"What about your number?" he called after her.

"Yeah, I'm still deciding on if you need that or not." She finally reached the hallway and turned left as he started to chuckle, a sound that wormed its way under Zara's skin and into her bloodstream, no matter how much she wished it wouldn't.

An hour later on the dot, she opened the door from the kitchen to the garage to find Noah already there, the huge double-doors already open and letting in tons of sunlight.

"So how are we going to do this?" he asked, peering down through her back door windows.

"Do what?"

He straightened and faced her, and Zara's heart did a

little jig in her chest. So he was extremely good-looking. Handsome. Some might even say gorgeous. *Drop-dead gorgeous*, Zara thought, her own mind betraying her.

No wonder he needed to do some volunteer work to repair his image. He probably had women throwing undergarments at him, and he probably hadn't resisted all that much.

She shook her head, trying to clear the thoughts. She didn't know him, and it wasn't right of her to make such assumptions about him just because she'd read a paragraph off the Internet about him and his royal status.

"I can't be seen coming and going from here," he said. "People have to think you're house-sitting."

"Oh, right." Zara glanced around the garage, but it was like the prince and his family didn't really live here. "Do you have any blankets or anything? We could pile those on top of you."

Inside the house, his dog barked, and Noah looked over her shoulder. "He has to be quiet too. If someone gets too close to the house and hears him, they'll know I'm here too."

"Are you guys like a package deal?" she asked. "Wherever you go, Lassie does too?"

Annoyance flashed across his face, but Zara didn't mind all that much. "His name's Boomer," he said icily. "And yes, he goes everywhere I do—and the paparazzi know it."

"Maybe you should've named him something like Whisper," Zara said.

Noah rolled his eyes and said, "I'll go get some blankets."

She stepped out of his way, enjoying herself a little too much. As soon as he'd gone, a knot of guilt struck her in the gut. She should be nice to him. He was obviously concerned about the media finding him, and something he'd said last night flowed through her mind.

The anonymity I've never had.

Zara's guilt doubled and then tripled, and she sighed under the weight of it. When Noah returned, she said, "Sorry for how I've been acting. I just…I was expecting to be here alone this summer."

Noah blinked at her over the pile of blankets in his arms. "You've been acting badly?"

The urge to roll her eyes was so strong, she almost couldn't stop herself. Luckily, she did, and she stepped forward to take some of the blankets. "I have been. I'm sorry. I'm sure we'll get used to our living arrangements."

Noah put that charming smile on his face, and Zara could definitely see how he'd gotten himself into some trouble with that. "All right. Well, thank you for apologizing. Now let's see how this works."

CHAPTER FOUR

Noah was much too tall and much too broad for the backseat of a sedan. Especially the floor of a sedan. Zara had moved the passenger seat up as far as it would go, and if he put most of his weight on one arm, he could almost fit.

To cover him, though, the blankets would need to go almost all the way to the windows, and he thought that was way too obvious. And how would he get out? Spill out the door and shake off a dozen blankets like he was Boomer?

Foolishness raced through him. Maybe he should abandon this insane plan to be seen volunteering in Getaway Bay. It wouldn't create that much sympathy for him, because everyone would just leave comments like, "Oh, he has to spend his summer in Hawaii. Too bad for him."

Noah had read hundreds of sarcastic comments in his lifetime, and he didn't need any more.

"Okay," Zara said, starting to cover him with the blankets. "Are you ready?"

"Maybe this is stupid," he said. Their eyes met, and in that moment where she wasn't saying something about how he stunk because he hadn't showered or telling him he'd named his dog wrong, there was a tenderness in her gaze.

"You want to volunteer at the wedding, right?" she asked.

"Yes," he said.

"Then this is what we have to do." She started unfolding another blanket to cover his legs. "And you better text me a grocery list so we don't have to do this more than we have to."

"I'll need your number for that," he said, his heartbeat rioting the slightest bit. He wanted her number, and not just to send grocery lists. He'd lain awake in bed last night, thinking about her downstairs and wishing he could talk to her. Tell her some private, personal things about himself that he'd never told anyone before.

Because despite being wealthy and having nearly everything he wanted, Noah was desperately lonely. And sometimes, he made bad decisions just to have someone to talk to. That was all that had happened in Venice, though it certainly looked like something else entirely had gone down.

She laughed, which made Noah smile, and she said, "Oh, you're good, Mister Wales. Very slick."

"Hey, you're the one who suggested it."

She lifted a pile of folded blankets and dropped them

on his head and shoulders. He grunted, but when she said, "Give me your number, and I'll text you," he decided he could handle having the blankets unceremoniously tossed on him.

He recited his number, and a few seconds later, his phone chimed and vibrated.

"That's me," she said. "Now, let's get going. This day is almost halfway over already."

The ride down the twisty, winding road from the bluff to the city seemed to take forever. Every turn put more pressure on his arm, and by the time she parked, his entire left side was numb—and he was sweating.

They hadn't spoken, so when she said, "All right. The coast looks pretty clear," her voice was muted and muffled by all the blankets. "Am I coming to let you out?"

"Yes, please," he said, his royal training kicking in. His tutors would be so proud.

"Oh, there's a couple with a dog."

Noah wanted to scream, but he held still and waited.

"Bicyclists," Zara said next, and Noah started to squirm, trying to find a position that didn't cause agony from his hip to his spine. But her floor in the back wasn't flat, and he felt like a rainbow over the hump that ran down the middle.

Finally, *finally*, the door opened, and she lifted the blankets off his face. It was like breathing for the first time. The sun was too bright, and he squinted as he looked up at Zara. She was haloed in sunshine, and the most beautiful creature he'd ever laid eyes on. His pulse thrummed through his body, and he wondered what it was trying to tell him.

"Come on," she hissed, breaking the vision. "You can't just lie there and stare."

He wiggled his way out of the car and onto the hot pavement, jumping up a moment later and dusting off his hands. She dumped the blankets on the backseat and closed the door behind him. "Very graceful, Your Highness."

Noah froze, his heart racing around his chest for a completely different reason now. "So you know."

"I have a Smartphone," she said. "I looked you up when I was parking yesterday."

Noah clenched his teeth and pressed his lips into a tight line. "Did you recognize me?"

She scoffed like this wasn't the most important conversation on the planet. "Don't flatter yourself."

A measure of relief moved through him, especially when she said, "You gave me your name. I Googled it." She clicked her tongue as she started walking around the car to the driver's side. "You brought up *a lot* of articles, buddy."

Embarrassment heated his blood now. "Which ones did you read? Because you know, not everything on the Internet is true."

Zara laughed, the sound magical as it lifted into the sky. "I read enough to know you're a...." She glanced around and closed her mouth, thankfully. "I'll be back in a bit. You better text me what you want for lunch, and at the grocery store, okay?"

He nodded and looked out at the ocean. It had been so

long since he'd actually touched an ocean despite living beside one. "Okay," he said.

She gave one curt nod like she was his nanny and slid behind the wheel. So Noah watched as her shorts hitched up a little higher on her leg. It wasn't a crime.

Zara was beautiful, with long limbs and miles of that Indian skin. Noah looked away and walked toward the boardwalk that would lead him down the beach a bit to the offices of Your Tidal Forever, hoping that by the time he called his mother that night, he had an action plan in place. Otherwise, the Queen of Triguard would dictate one for him, and Noah was much too old for that.

HOPE SORENSEN BLEW AROUND THE BUILDING LIKE A tornado, and Noah kind of just wanted to stand back and watch. But she had her assistant, a curvy brunette named Shannon Bell—who Noah had communicated with the most—hand out assignments to everyone there to volunteer. Shannon put him to work on the Invitation Committee, which turned out to be the absolute worst place for him.

He didn't care what font was used on the announcements. Then he realized they hadn't even been talking about the actual announcement, but something called the "Save the Date" card that needed to be out in the next three days. Apparently, if it wasn't, the world would end. Or something.

The four women at the table with him kept looking at

him as if he had something to say. So he threw out things like, "I think the cerulean is nice there," and "Honestly, I don't think the seal matters."

They took his advice on the blue, though he had no idea why, but one woman actually gasped when he said the bit about the seal. It was a sticker, for crying out loud.

But Noah had never been married, so clearly he didn't understand the importance of pictures, and colors, and stickers. Oops, seals.

His mother would be all over this, and Noah found himself thinking of her a lot during the two-hour meeting.

Then he got put on something he could actually get behind. Addressing envelopes. It was boring, tedious work. Every time he messed up and had to reposition a sticker, he felt a bit bad at wasting the paper. But at least he could see something getting done.

In Noah's opinion, there was absolutely nothing worse than a meeting. He was convinced the good Lord had invented them just to torture men like him.

Now, his father adored a good meeting, which summed up exactly how different Noah was from his father, the King of Triguard. About the only thing they had in common was the fact that they both wanted the Queen to be happy.

And there was that thought of his mother again. Noah would call her as soon as he got back to the privacy of the house.

With the thought of the mansion, his thoughts turned to Zara. An exasperated sigh slipped from his lips, and he hadn't even seen her for hours. He just wanted some time to himself. Time to figure out why he still didn't know what to do with his life after thirty-one years.

But her being the house sitter would testify that the house was indeed empty. And the mansion was *huge*. Noah could probably go days without having to see her, and he just might.

"Those look great," Hope said when she buzzed into the room. Four long tables had been set up and no less than ten people worked to type in addresses, print them on labels in a font that had taken fifteen minutes to choose.

"You went with Desire?" Hope asked, picking up one of the ivory envelopes. "And are these from our scented line?" She brought the paper to her nose. "Ah, yes. Vanilla crème."

Noah stared at her, sure she was joking. But the small smile on her face wasn't of the kidding kind.

He tuned out the redhead who explained how the decision to use the font had transpired, and instead focused on getting that return address label exactly squared away in the corner of the vanilla crème envelopes.

This wedding was actually the union of two celebrities, one of whom lived right here on the island. Apparently Collin Marsh was a huge action star, and he was marrying a woman from one of those reality TV shows.

So the island would be crawling with reporters. Thankfully, those who wanted pictures of a prince from a tiny island in the Greek Isles didn't usually run in the same circles as those capturing Hollywood stars.

He thought he'd be okay. He hoped. He'd actually prayed for it while he was underneath those blankets, coming down off the bluffs in the back of Zara's sedan.

With only two hundred envelopes left to stuff and label, his phone buzzed against his hip. He pulled it out and checked around the room like he was doing something wrong. But he was a volunteer; Hope couldn't fire him.

Still, all he'd ever done in his life was volunteer. Serve. He'd never had a real job to speak of, and his mother had always taught him to live in the moment. Be present. Put your phone away.

But it was Zara, and she was asking him how much longer he thought he'd be. He glanced around at this pop-up post office, and texted back, *Thirty minutes.*

I'll be straight out from the front doors, on the beach.

Noah acknowledged that he'd come find her when he got done, and promptly slid his phone back in his pocket, glad he'd made it through a four-line conversation without wanting to say something sarcastic to Zara.

Baby steps, then.

Forty-five minutes later, he'd agreed to come back on Thursday to help with the construction of...something. All he knew was that Hope had asked him to be there for something requiring hammers, saws, and a nail gun.

He was all over that, as the castle at Triguard had a crew of six gardeners and four maintenance men, and the closest he ever got to building something was when he tried to fix some stupid misunderstanding between him and the rest of the world.

He left Your Tidal Forever in favor of the hot afternoon sun. It actually soothed him as his dark skin drank it up, and he sighed. He found Zara on the beach all right, wearing a black swimming suit that showed the entire length of her toned, tanned legs.

She carried a beat-up surfboard under one arm as she laughed with another man.

Something hot and spiked roared through Noah, and he paused, still back on the loose sand. Who was that guy? Did Zara have a boyfriend?

Why Noah hadn't thought a woman as beautiful as Zara wouldn't, he wasn't sure. But the thought had never crossed his mind.

It was crossing it now, and Noah didn't like it. Not one little bit.

So he was jealous. Didn't mean he wanted a new relationship with the gorgeous Zara Reddy. It just meant he was a male and had happened to notice that Zara was an attractive female.

After all, they didn't get along, and her having a boyfriend would actually be a good thing. Maybe then, she'd leave him alone in the mansion.

Maybe then, he could stop thinking about her.

CHAPTER FIVE

"Hey, do you give lessons?"

Zara turned toward the man asking the question, saying, "Yeah, sure, all the—" She cut off when she saw it was Noah. She cursed herself for speaking so quickly. Her exuberance to book another job—anything that made money and kept her out of the restaurant—had cost her this time.

"I mean, not anymore." She gave him a tight, closed-mouth smile as he approached. It was wholly criminal how good he looked wearing a pair of sunglasses, his hands all tucked in his pockets like they were.

"Too bad," he said, staring out over the beautiful, teal water of the East Bay. "I've always wanted to learn how to surf."

"You grew up on an island and don't know how to surf?" Zara stared at him, disbelief racing through her. "That's just wrong."

"The water's not exactly the same," he said, glancing in her direction. She couldn't see his eyes, but she was sure he was glaring. The heat of his look seared her, so her assumption had to be right.

He seemed to be focused on Burke, and Zara startled before stepping between him and Ash's new husband. "Should we go?"

Burke edged closer though, his smile wide as he said, "Hey, I'm Burke Lawson."

"Holden Montego," Noah said, shaking Burke's hand. And the name sounded so...true. It had flawlessly slipped out of his mouth as if he'd said it thousands of times before. And Zara wondered if Noah Wales was even his real name.

Probably not, she told herself.

"Are you two together?" Noah asked, and Zara almost choked.

"No." Burke laughed and pointed down the beach a bit. "My wife is down there. She and Zara are best friends." He turned back to Noah. "But she doesn't like to surf, and Zara does, and she's nice enough to let me tag along sometimes."

"So nice," Noah said with a hugely false smile in place.

"Okay," Zara said. "Time to go."

"If he wants to surf, we could rent a board," Burke said, making things infinitely worse.

"Oh, no," Zara said, shaking her head. "No, he's not even wearing swimming trunks, and we need to get...." She didn't know how to finish the sentence. She couldn't say "home," because then Burke would be suspicious about their living situation.

Heat flared in Zara's body, especially when Noah just stood there, mute. If he could make up pseudonyms on the spot, couldn't he come up with a reason they needed to leave the beach? Of course he could.

"Get where?" Burke asked, glancing between the two of them. He took a couple of steps closer to Zara and asked in a near-whisper, "Are you two dating?"

"What?" Zara's laughter was probably too loud. She didn't care. "No." She scoffed and shook her head, looking at Noah just standing there. "No, we are not dating. I'm just giving him a ride somewhere," she said, seizing onto the perfect excuse. "You know how I do that My Car, Your Destination thing sometimes."

A sour look crossed Burke's face. "I thought you gave that up after that guy—"

"Well, I didn't," Zara practically yelled at him, hoping he'd shut up already. The last thing she needed was Noah finding out about the incident that had ended with Zara sitting in the police station, giving statements, until three o'clock in the morning.

She met Noah's gaze, and even through those blasted mirrored shades, and she could feel his curiosity practically sizzling in the air between them.

"And we need to go." She started toward Ash, who lay on her back, a book held up in the sky over her face. She reached her friend and said, "I'll call you later, okay?"

"Okay," Ash said, totally unconcerned.

Zara shoved her clothes in her bag and wadded up her

towel under her other arm. She marched up the beach, away from her friends, without checking to see if Noah was behind her. He was. He had no other way back to the house, and he couldn't stay down in town, out in the open.

Sure enough, she'd pulled on a T-shirt and tossed her beach stuff in the backseat when he joined her. "They seem nice," he said.

"So nice," she echoed back to him in a sarcastic voice, the way he had to Burke down on the beach. She set to work tying her board to the top of the sedan, surprised when Noah helped by securing the lines on his side.

Zara snuck glances at him across the top of the car, finally finishing and saying, "Thank you." She didn't mean to sound so begrudging about it, but she couldn't suck the words back in and try again.

So she got behind the wheel of the car, and then jumped back out. "Oh. The blankets."

Noah groaned as he opened the back door, and by the time she made it around to the passenger side in the back, he was in position.

"I'm sorry," she said. "Maybe you could sit in the front and just lay your seat down."

"No, just put the blankets on, and let's go."

She worked not to throw them with all the force she had in her as she told herself that he probably didn't mean to sound so demanding. So barky, like she better jump to it with a smile on her face.

Probably, probably, probably, she told herself all the way up to the bluffs and into the garage. Then she got out and left Noah in the backseat to get himself out.

THE SCENT OF FRESHLY BAKED BREAD AND CINNAMON urged her awake the following morning. Zara rolled over and breathed in deep, comfortable and warm and still woozy. She'd been having the best dream about lying by the swimming pool at the mansion, a smoothie from The Straw on the ground beside her chaise.

The sun was glorious. The view even better. And then Noah had come out, bringing pizza and chocolate chip cookies for her. He'd put them on the table nearby and taken off his shirt—

Zara's eyes snapped open.

No...she had not just had a summer fantasy about Noah. The man was absolutely maddening, even if he knew his way around a kitchen.

She sat up and pushed the comforter off her legs. She wasn't even that hungry. Her stomach chose that moment to protest loudly about how long ago her last meal had been, and she reached for her phone to see how late she was.

"Only seven-thirty?" she asked as if she couldn't believe the numbers on the home screen of her phone. She had swimming practice that morning at nine, so she'd shower after work. So maybe she had time for a quick bite to eat before heading out.

The fact that she never ate breakfast...well, no one needed to know that. Especially not the handsome man standing in the kitchen, twirling a pair of tongs like they were drumsticks as he sang along with the music blasting through the house.

She leaned against the wall and watched him, a smile tugging at the corners of his mouth. So maybe he was adorable when he let go of his stuffy Prince persona. Maybe he was capable of having a conversation that didn't include sarcastic remarks and barking commands.

He flipped a few pieces of bacon and lifted the tongs to his mouth like they were a microphone.

Zara couldn't help the laugh that bubbled out of her mouth.

Noah stiffened and turned toward her, a perfectly pleasing blush entering his cheeks.

"Oh, go on," she said with a sweeping motion of her arm. "I have a feeling we were just getting to the good part."

He reached up to a speaker on top of the fridge and turned down the music. "What?"

She shook her head and kept grinning. "Nothing. Are you sure you're a prince?" She gasped, but it was obviously fake and over-the-top. "Maybe you're Prince. You know, *the* Prince. They reported that he'd passed away, but I don't know...." She cocked her head. "I think you kind of look like him."

Noah frowned, reached to turn off the burner under the bacon, and twisted away from her as he lined a plate with paper towels. "Who's Prince?"

"Oh, now that's just sad," Zara said as she moved into the kitchen and took her spot at the bar. "You don't know who Prince is?"

"No, I don't." And the barking was back.

"He's a pop star," Zara said, eyeing the cinnamon rolls and enjoying herself entirely too much. "I don't think he used tongs for a mic, though." She giggled, and Noah turned around, half a smile on his face too.

"I'm definitely not a pop star."

"What I heard goes to the contrary." This banter—*flirtatious banter?*—was better than the sarcastic jabs. At least Zara liked it better.

He set the plate of bacon on the counter and asked, "Are you eating or going?"

"Eating first," she said. "Then going. I have practice today." Then she'd bring in all the stuff she'd packed at her apartment. She had another week to get everything out, and she was planning to make several trips.

"What time are you going down on Thursday?" he asked, using a rubber spatula to retrieve a cinnamon roll from the pan.

"I have practice at nine," she said.

"Can I get a ride to Your Tidal Forever?" He looked at her, and for a moment, Zara felt like she was falling.

A breath in, then out, and everything righted itself. She looked away, suddenly self-conscious with him. With her heart beating at the speed of hummingbird wings, she reached for a piece of bacon.

"Sure, yeah," she said, a nervous undertone to the words. "We'll just have to leave a little earlier. My practice facility is in the other bay."

"Tell me what time," he said, the words gentle. "And I'll be ready."

Zara nodded and busied herself with bacon and frosted buns, this new energy between them completely different than before. Had he felt it too? Had she just never looked him fully in the eyes before?

She wasn't sure how she even felt, and her stomach turned over and over as she cleaned up her dishes, gathered her swim gear, and drove down to town. As she pulled into the parking lot at the amphitheater, where they'd be practicing that morning, Zara realized she'd been *attracted* to Noah.

Physically and emotionally *attracted* to him.

"Not happening," she muttered to herself as she heaved her heavy bag onto her shoulder and joined a couple of other women heading into the locker room.

So not happening.

After all, he was a prince in a country several oceans over, and she was a synchronized swimmer with a very traditional Indian family. The very idea of bringing Noah home to meet her parents was laughable—and caused a healthy dose of fear to tumble through her. Her mother would eat Noah for breakfast.

No, she'd house sit for the summer. Keep the paparazzi away from Noah. She'd get to lie by the pool and drink her fruity smoothies and perform in her shows at night.

Noah would do...whatever Noah was doing in Getaway Bay, and then Zara's life would go back to normal.

She took a deep breath, getting quite the lungful of chlorine, satisfied with this new plan no matter how much her heart wailed at her to *please give Noah a chance.*

Do you want to get broken? she asked it as she changed

into her dark blue practice suit and made sure she had her goggles and nose clips. *Because that's what'll happen. Men like Noah...they break hearts.*

Her pulse finally settled after that, and she could focus on what she needed to do that day—master the three-sixty leg kick while wearing heels in the swimming pool. She definitely didn't have room for Noah Wales in her brain too.

CHAPTER SIX

Noah checked all the Internet gossip headlines, and he only found one talking about him and Katya. Nothing he hadn't seen or read before, even if none of it was true. Truth didn't matter on the Internet, nor to the "journalists" that reported on celebrity news.

This particular one had been on his tail for a decade, and Noah was honestly surprised he'd been able to sneak out of Venice without the guy knowing or following him. Tomas seemed to know where Noah was before Noah himself had a plan.

He stood at the sliding glass doors in his suite, looking out at the ocean. He had always wanted to learn to surf, and he'd been doubly excited to learn if Zara would be the teacher.

"And that makes no sense," he murmured to his faint reflection in the window. He couldn't even step out onto the balcony and breathe in the Hawaiian air. No, he hadn't seen any drones out. No one sniffing around the house. Nothing.

Of course, he hadn't left the house for more than the few hours he'd gone down to Your Tidal Forever, and then a few minutes on the beach. No one had recognized him. Of course, all the people at the wedding planning business had been so focused on the tasks they were doing for the Marsh wedding, and people at the beach didn't care who else was there.

Noah had the strangest urge to leave this house. He'd never had a problem being confined to a castle before; he'd done it many times. He'd been late to a few interviews because he was working with the Grandparents Patrol in Triguard. The reporters had been rude, and Noah may have snapped back at them.

It was something no one else in his family would've done. They would've smiled and apologized, answered all the questions, and kept the family's public image through the roof. Noah was obviously the black sheep. The bad boy.

He shook his head. After that incident and the multiple articles that had been printed about his "short fuse," he'd started to work at the library with underprivileged children in the country, as well as keep his hours with the elderly.

That had gone well, and he'd managed to build back up most of his image. He didn't mind the work, but he felt like he wasn't really doing anything with his life. Damien, his older brother, would take over the kingdom, and he was practically perfect in every way. But he didn't spend hours and hours volunteering the way Noah did.

His sister Louisa dealt with a lot of the same pressures as Noah, but she was prim and proper and actually liked it. She had a serious boyfriend she'd been dating for five years, and the wedding plans had been in the works for a solid eighteen months.

Noah hadn't received a Save the Date for his own sister's wedding, which meant it was still months away. He had no doubt Louisa would tie the knot with Eric Newman, because they were a smart match—and they loved each other.

Noah had wondered many times over the years if he'd ever find someone he could love. He'd considered leaving the island country where generations of Wales had been born and raised and going to America, finding a job, and living a more normal life. No one would recognize him, and he'd find someone to live the rest of his life with, the way they did in those romance movies his mom loved so much.

He sighed and turned away from the window. Boomer barked, and Noah rolled his eyes. "Come on, then," he said and opened the bedroom door. Boomer scampered through door, his claws clicking on the tile in the hall. He ran downstairs, and Noah supposed his bathroom needs were quite urgent.

Following, he paused just before the door and opened it a crack. Boomer nosed his way out, and Noah stayed out of sight. If there was someone around and they saw his dog, though, they might as well have seen him.

He could probably go outside just for a few minutes while his dog took care of business. He did, his bare feet touching the grass and found it hot. Of course, it would be hot. It was June in Getaway Bay, in the middle of the day, and everything was hot.

He tipped his head back and looked into the sky, taking a deep breath of the stale, heated air. It wasn't that much better out here than inside, but he somehow didn't feel as caged.

Inside, a door slammed. Boomer barked and headed back in, and Noah turned that way too. "It's just Zara," he said to the dog, but Boomer barked a couple more times and then Zara started giggling.

The sound wormed its way right under his skin, heating his blood and making his pulse accelerate. He stepped over to the door and peered in to see her kneeling down, scrubbing Boomer's back and telling him what a good boy he was.

How would she even know?

But Noah enjoyed watching her, and Boomer obviously liked the attention. He licked her face, and she laughed again.

"How was practice?" he asked as he stepped inside and brought the door closed behind him.

"Oh." Zara quieted and stood up. She picked up her bag, and it looked like it was heavy. He wondered how much swimming suits and swim caps could weigh, but he didn't say anything. What he wanted to say, he couldn't.

If I asked, would you go to dinner with me?

Number one, they couldn't leave the house to go somewhere on the island. With all the modern apps, he could get anything delivered to the house. Well, Zara could. He didn't want to call and order anything, nor answer the door.

So trying to have a romantic dinner with her would be impossible.

The fact that he *wanted* to have a romantic date with her was insane. Completely insane.

"What's your show called?" he asked next, because she hadn't answered his first question and she stood there, staring at him.

"Fresh Start," she said.

"Anyone can get tickets?" He took another step closer, his eyes locked onto hers. Hers were dark with hints of gold, and he wanted to dive in and bask in the warmth of them.

"Well, yes," she said, backing up against the island in the kitchen. "But we've been sold out for a while."

Sold out? Noah blinked, sure he could find tickets somewhere. "Do you get any tickets?"

"Yes," she said slowly, still looking at him. "But my family is using them."

"Of course," he said, backing up and giving her a little space.

"You wouldn't be able to come anyway," she said, tracking his movement as he edged away from her.

"I wouldn't?"

"Am I going to smuggle you down?" She blinked at him. "You don't leave the house."

"I'm thinking I might be okay," he said.

"It's been three days."

"I've actually been here for five days." Noah didn't know why he was arguing this point with her. "And I've worked at Your Tidal Forever. No one even looked at me." He'd been just another body, like always.

No one wanted Noah Wales front and center. He was the throw away. The leftover. The one the C-list reporters wanted interviews with, hoping to catapult themselves up to the King or Queen.

"So you think you can start socializing in town?" Zara gaped at him.

Foolishness raced through him, and he wanted to end this conversation. He'd walked away from a few conversations in his life, but he didn't think he could just turn his back on Zara. She had enough fire to come after him, shouting to be heard if she had to.

"I don't know what I think," he said. "Forget I said anything." He tossed her a look over his shoulder as he left the kitchen. "Come on, Boomer." At least the dog came with him, still knowing where his loyalty should be.

Noah went back upstairs, but there was absolutely nothing for him there. Problem was, Zara was downstairs, and that meant there was definitely nothing for him down there either.

Except a ride back down to Your Tidal Forever in the morning. He could survive until morning. He could.

Couldn't he?

༒

When he walked into Your Tidal Forever, he nearly got knocked back out of the door by the sheer amount of estrogen hanging in the air. He paused, wondering why he'd come here today.

Riley, a cute redheaded woman, stood from her desk in the lobby. "Hello, Holden. We've got the construction crew meeting across the boardwalk at the rehearsal hall." She flashed him a professional smile, her heels clicking as she moved toward him. She stepped past him and pushed open the door. "See? Right there."

Noah could see it. "Great, thanks." He flashed her a smile, and she cocked her head.

"Do I know you?"

Noah kept his royal smile in place. "I don't think so. I'm new in town."

"And you're volunteering here?"

"Yes." He looked over her shoulder. "I'll head over there now. Thanks." He worked hard not to punch his way through the glass door in his haste to get away from Riley. Thankfully, she let him go, and Noah kept his back straight and his strides even as he walked down the sidewalk.

He wanted to bolt as fast as his feet would go. But he also wanted to see what it took to build an altar and a trellis and a custom buffet.

Thankfully, the first thing someone did when he entered the event hall was hand him a pair of goggles. He slipped them on, glad for the extra layer of anonymity.

A man who was clearly in charge came over. He glanced at his clipboard. "Holden?"

"That's right," Noah said.

"I'm Cal." He glanced over his shoulder. "This says you don't have experience with power tools."

"Nope," Noah confirmed.

"Then I'll have you on supplies. This way." Cal wove through the other men working with saws and nail guns, and Noah wished he'd told a little fib. It didn't look that hard to hold a nail gun in place and push a button.

Pop, pop, pop! went the nail gun, and the man turned the two pieces of wood he was holding.

"I'm going to pair you with Ed. He's building the lattices, and he'll need a runner." He pointed to a huge pile of thin strips of wood. "Ed's the big guy with the yellow shirt on. His last name's Lemon, and I've never seen him without the color yellow somewhere." With that, Cal left Noah to find Ed and figure out how often he'd be running back and forth between this pile and the man in the yellow shirt.

Ed was just inside the door, and Noah stepped over to him and introduced himself with his false name. "Ed Lemon." He held a staple gun that looked like a toy in his huge hands. "We're making sixteen trellises." He gestured behind him to where something leaned against the wall.

The thin pieces of wood had been stapled to the frame in a lattice pattern, and Noah was actually surprised he knew such a thing. "Sixteen of these?"

"And then we'll be painting them."

Noah stepped over to the completed trellis and saw all the ninety-degree angles. "Might it be easier to paint them before stapling them together?" He could only imagine how the paint would pool in the creases, and it would definitely be easier to swish color on up and down, up and down, before nailing them all together.

"I suggested that too," Ed said. "But apparently, the bride doesn't want the staples to show." He stapled another thin strip to the one underneath it. "I showed Hope that these staples disappear, but I was vetoed." He nodded to the corner. "We've got spray paint, so it shouldn't be terribly hard."

He stapled again and then again. "So you'll bring me the wood pieces, move the trellises, and once we've got a good system going, you can paint too."

Noah wasn't sure about the painting, but he nodded as if he'd been a construction manager his whole life. "Great. Looks like what? Fifteen across? Twenty down?"

"Twenty-five down," he said, stapling.

"The frame is thicker." Noah hadn't seen any thicker wood.

Ed nodded his chin toward a stack of wood Noah hadn't seen. "That's there."

Noah felt like he knew what he needed to do, and now he just had to hop to it. It looked like Ed had all the wood he needed to finish the trellis on the table, and Noah headed outside to start bringing in the forty lengths of wood Ed would need for trellis number three.

Noah worked up a sweat walking back and forth, and Ed had the trellis built before Noah had all the wood in. He took the trellis and leaned it against the first one. Ed moved with the speed of a Tasmanian devil, and he had the thicker frame put together while Noah had only one more load of wood to bring in.

"What do you do for a living?" he asked Ed.

"Oh, I'm a surgeon," he said, glancing away from his work for a moment. "You?"

"Uh...." Noah had no idea what to say. He had a fake name, but he hadn't thought much farther ahead than that.

Ed stapled and picked up another board, positioning it right along the marks he'd made with a pencil.

"I'm a director," Noah said.

"Sounds made up." Ed gave him a smile that said he knew Noah had just lied to him.

"Why are you here stapling a trellis together if you're a surgeon?" Noah asked.

"The hospital here requires us to donate a certain number of hours to the community," Ed said. "Most doctors do pro bono care, but I do reconstructive surgery. So." He shrugged. "Plus, this gets me out doing something I don't normally do."

Noah left and brought in another load of wood. "You seem pretty handy."

"I've built a few things," Ed said. "A gazebo in my backyard. A tree house for my nephew. That kind of stuff."

Noah could spend time with people, reading with kids or playing chess with someone's grandfather. But he didn't really have any employable skills. Maybe he should spend his time learning how to build things instead of something like surfing.

But then you can't get Zara to help you.

He shook the thought away, but it didn't go far, and by the time all sixteen trellises were finished, he'd decided to see if she'd at least be willing to drive him down to town for a lesson with someone else.

CHAPTER SEVEN

Zara squared her shoulders as she pulled into the parking lot at Indian House. She'd had a long day of practice, and Noah had filled her whole car with the scent of sweat and sawdust, and she was having a very hard time keeping him out of her mind.

He'd asked her to teach him to surf again, and Zara had said she had to get down to talk to her father at the restaurant, and she'd bolted back to the garage.

So now, here she sat, outside the restaurant her parents owned, wondering if she could handle going inside. She hadn't seen her mother in about a week, which meant Zara would need to be ready to defend her single status.

Her stomach grumbled, because Ian had made them work through half of their lunch, dissatisfied with the way the formations on the island that came up out of the water looked. So she killed the engine and headed for the entrance.

It was almost the weekend and right during the dinner rush, which was actually perfect. Then her siblings would be busy, and she wouldn't have to be crammed into a booth for four with all five of her sisters.

The bell rang as she opened the door, and Abi, the hostess looked up. Her whole face brightened, and she said, "Zara." She put the menu back in the holder on the front of the podium, and said, "Mom and Dad just sat down for dinner. You want to join them?"

Zara's heart sank, but she painted a plastic smile on her face and said, "Sure." She gave Abi a big hug, as her older sister was actually one of the more sane members of her family. As Abi led her through the dining room, she caught sight of her youngest sister, Myra, standing at a table, her left hand out for the patrons to admire her new engagement ring.

Zara turned away, her throat dry and her heart suddenly beating at triple-time. Coming here was definitely a mistake.

But her mother had caught sight of her, and she exploded out of the booth, her sari catching as she stood. "Zara." She wrapped Zara in her arms, the smell of fresh cotton and Indian spices meeting Zara's nose. "What are you doing here? You look so good."

"Hey, Mom." She slid into the booth first and another of her sisters asked her what she wanted to drink.

"Just water," Zara said. Swimming in water all day really dehydrated her, and she tried to stick to water during the day and coffee in the morning. While Krisha went to get the drinks, her mom scooted into the booth.

"Still swimming?"

"Every day, Mom."

"We're coming to the show on opening night." She gave her father a look. "Right, Samir. Aren't we so excited to see Zara's show?"

"Of course," her dad said. "Only one month to go." He beamed at her. He'd had a difficult time when Zara had told him she would not be working in the restaurant, though Zara wasn't sure why. All five of her sisters worked here, as well as two brothers-in-law. They didn't need her.

"One month," Zara said as Krisha put her water on the table. "I want the butter chicken, Kris. With extra naan."

Krisha smiled at her and said, "Coming right up."

"So," her mother said. "Are you seeing anyone?"

Zara rolled her eyes and swung her head toward her mother. "No, Mom."

"No one?" Her mom had the best puppy dog eyes on the planet, and they could morph into pool of disappointment in mere moments.

"Well, I met someone," Zara said, the image of Noah entering her mind. She couldn't believe she was still talking. "But I'm not sure about him."

"Not sure?" her mother practically shrieked. "What are you not sure about?"

So many things. "Well, Mother, for one, he's not Indian."

Her mom looked like Zara had punched her. But what Zara was not expecting was the scoff that followed. "Oh, Zara. I gave up on you finding a nice Indian man about five years ago."

"Really?"

"Really. You just need *some*one."

It was Zara's turn to scoff, and she had never been happier to see Krisha approaching with her parents' food. Because now she knew her mom would probably marry her to anyone. After all, it didn't matter if he was a nice man, or employed, or anything.

She just needed *someone*.

Disgust filled her, but thankfully, the butter chicken came next, and Zara decided she could deal with Noah and if he even qualified as *someone* after she ate.

When she entered the mansion, the scent of butter chicken came with her. She put the to-go container on the counter, noting that there was no dog running to see her and barely any lights on. Had Noah gone to bed already? It was barely eight o'clock. Perhaps he'd worked hard at Your Tidal Forever today.

Zara moved down the hall and into her suite to feed Whitewater. The cat wouldn't even come out from her hiding place, but somehow the food disappeared every day.

Back in the kitchen, indecision raging through her. She wanted to see Noah, because he was handsome and someone to talk to. Then she wouldn't have to be alone. She didn't want to see Noah, because they'd probably end up arguing anyway.

In the end, she ended up sending him a simple text.

Brought you some butter chicken from Indian House. If you want it.

She'd barely taken a breath when he responded with *Be right down.* In the next moment, she heard Boomer bark, and the dog made it down to the kitchen a full minute before his owner. And when Noah walked in, his hair was damp and he wore a pair of gym shorts and a T-shirt that was obviously two sizes too small.

He grinned at her and smoothed his hair back while Zara stared at him. "Is this it?" He indicated the container on the counter, picking it up before she could answer. "Mm, smells heavenly."

"Well, Bill is the best Indian chef on the island." Zara took the end barstool where she'd been sitting whenever she ate in the kitchen.

Noah pulled open a drawer and selected a fork before coming around and joining her. He left one stool in between them, but they still sat plenty close together. "Is Bill a brother?" he asked, opening the container.

"Brother-in-law," she said. "A very nice Indian man." She wasn't sure if she succeeded in saying it normally or not. She'd been making sarcastic remarks about how her mother wanted her to find *a nice Indian man* for years now.

She turned when she felt Noah's stare on the side of her face. "We don't like Bill?" He popped a bite of chicken and rice into his mouth.

Zara looked away. "I like Bill fine."

"I detected some sarcasm there."

"My mother's been badgering me to find *a nice Indian man* for a while now," she admitted.

Noah started nodding while he finished chewing. "Oh, I get that."

"Do you?"

"Are you kidding? I'm the bad boy prince. My mother's been after me to find someone 'normal' and 'nice' for years." He chuckled, though it sounded strained around the edges. "No one I date will be good enough for her."

"Do you date a lot?" Zara asked, wondering where the question had come from.

"A little," he said, his voice full of hedging.

"Oh, come on," she teased. "A tall, strapping prince like you? Surely more than a little."

He choked on his food and reached for a napkin. "Strapping?" he pushed out of his mouth.

"How many hours a day do you work out?" she challenged.

"I work out enough," he said, dodging the question.

She laughed, glad they weren't arguing. "I'm sure you do." She stood up, hoping to leave while they were still on good speaking terms. "Well, I'm tired."

"Hey," he said before she'd taken one step. "I signed up for some surfing lessons at the yacht club. Could you drop me off in the morning before your practice?"

Zara's veins filled with ice, and she turned back to Noah. "Surfing lessons at the yacht club?" Oh, no, that would not do. She knew who did those lessons, and Mike Wadsworth wouldn't be able to get someone like Noah to stand up on a board. Ever.

Someone with his height needed a custom board and individualized lessons.

"Yeah," he said easily, forking up more food. "I can hang around until you're done with your work."

"Hang around where?"

"Wherever." He waved his utensil like there were dozens of people he could go visit.

"You're not worried about being seen?"

A flash of worry crossed his face, but he shrugged. "A little bit," he admitted.

Zara retraced her steps and leaned against the counter. "I can teach you to surf."

Noah's dark eyes glinted like stars in a midnight sky. "You can?"

"The yacht club is inferior," she said. "I don't want you to think we here in Getaway Bay don't know how to surf." The fact that she'd mentally labeled herself as part of the local crowd and him as a newcomer to the island didn't escape her.

You're being stupid, she told herself while she waited for him to say something. Even if she taught him to surf, he didn't live here. He was only on the island until whatever storm he'd created for himself blew out.

And then he'd be gone, disappearing as easily as the sun sank into the ocean each evening.

CHAPTER EIGHT

Noah couldn't stop eating the butter chicken. Problem was, Zara was standing there, all curvy and delicious and being so nice, and she was waiting for an answer.

"This is great food," he said.

She cocked her hip and folded her arms. So he would not be telling her he'd found a pair of tickets to her show on opening night. At least not tonight.

"Fine," he finally said. "I can cancel at the yacht club. But when do you think you'll have time to teach me how to surf?" He lifted his eyebrows. "You work a lot, you know."

"Some of us have bills to pay," she shot back. "And the best time to surf is as the sun comes up." She started toward the hallway again, and Noah wanted to call her back. "So be ready at five-thirty, okay?" She tossed him a grin over her shoulder as she reached the arched doorway.

"Zara?" he asked, not sure what to say to get her to stay. He only knew he didn't want to eat alone.

She twisted back to him. "Yeah?"

"Did you...?" His mind blanked, something it literally had never done before. He always knew how to get a woman to come sit by him, smile at him, spend time with him. But Zara was so different in so many ways.

Everything he wanted to suggest required that they leave the mansion. Sit by the pool. Go on a walk. Grab breakfast after the surfing lessons. He couldn't say any of those.

"Maybe we could watch a movie tonight," he suggested, stuffing the last of his butter chicken and rice into his mouth. He watched her eyes widen, her surprise palpable. Honestly, he was a bit stunned he'd said the words too.

He was even more shocked when she said, "Yeah, all right. I just need to go change." She gave him another smile and left the kitchen.

Noah's heart started partying in his chest, and he worked to keep it in check. It was a movie. In the mansion. Still, he could make popcorn, and he jumped up from the counter, tossed his empty container in the trash and his fork in the sink, and started opening cupboards.

Surely his mother kept popcorn in this place. It took him several minutes, but he finally found some in the cupboard above the microwave. It was ninety-nine-percent fat free, but Noah had put butter on his grocery list, and he could spruce up this diet popcorn in no time.

Ten minutes later, with his sweet and salty popcorn in tow, he stepped out of the kitchen and almost ran Zara right over. "Oh, hey," he said, stepping back. "I have popcorn, and there's a mini-fridge outside the theater room. I'm sure there are drinks in there."

She looked from him to the popcorn, her hair hanging over her shoulder. It was the first time he'd seen her with her hair down, and...he looked closer at her. She'd put on a bit of makeup too, her eyes pulling at him until he realized he was leaning forward.

"What kind of movies do you like?" she asked as he got himself moving toward the steps that went down into the basement.

"I'm flexible," he said, which caused her to laugh.

"Is that so?" she asked from behind him. "Because I've seen you sandwich yourself in my backseat, and I gotta say, I don't think you are."

"Ha ha," he said, elated that this conversation was going so well. "You know what I mean."

"So if I say I don't want to watch something where everything explodes, you'd be okay with that?"

"Sure," he said, reaching the bottom of the steps and appreciating the cooler temperatures down here. He hadn't realized he was so dang hot. Had to be the popcorn, and he shifted the warm bowl from one hand to the other.

He glanced around. "Let's see. Movies over there. Fridge here." He stepped over to it, praying with everything in him that there would be something delicious to drink inside, and pulled open the door.

Jackpot. "Yep, there's flavored lemonades in here. And a couple of sodas. Bottled water."

"I'll take water," she said.

"No lemonade?" He tossed her a look out of the corner of his eye to find her examining the shelves holding the movies.

Their eyes met, and Noah felt like he'd been caught in an alien tractor beam. "There's peach and strawberry," he said, his voice almost robotic. "Raspberry. Mango."

She grinned, her white teeth distracting him. "Fine. I'll take the mango." She looked back at the movies, breaking the connection between them. Noah felt like he was on a roller coaster, and he wondered if she had any inkling of the same.

He knew he was attractive, but did *she* find him...attractive? Could she possibly like him?

He slammed the fridge closed and turned away from her, the same way he wished he could turn away from his thoughts. He wasn't a permanent resident of Getaway Bay, and he had no plans to become one. She lived here year-round.

He was a royal, albeit from a small island. Her family had strong cultural values he had no idea about. There was no way they could be together. And yet, Noah wanted to *try*.

It was the strangest thing, because Noah didn't have to try to do a whole lot of anything, especially when it came to women.

"I can't pick," she said, sidling up beside him. He startled, getting a noseful of her unique smell. Almost like being at the swimming pool, but with a definite hint of something like a Hawaiian floral lei.

"So let's play a game," he said, turning away from her

before he could do something stupid, like kiss her. "We close our eyes and pick. We each get a turn, and we have to pick one of them."

Her eyes danced, and Noah felt that sparking attraction in every cell in his body. His hand moved toward hers, and he brushed his fingers against hers. "Deal?"

She settled her weight on her back leg, effectively putting more distance between them. "Deal."

He set down the popcorn and drinks and clapped his hands together. "All right, then. Let's see what we've got here." He moved over in front of the shelves of movies. Knowing his mother, she'd probably had the maid organize them alphabetically.

"No peeking," Zara said, jumping in front of him. She was tall, but not quite to the height of Noah. She grinned up at him and shook her head, her wavy hair swinging with the movement.

"Like you didn't just stand over he and look through them all," he said.

"Close your eyes and pick," she said.

Noah snapped his eyes shut and lifted his hand, almost hoping Zara wouldn't move out of the way. But he didn't touch her, but the hard cases of the movies. He let his fingers trail along them, then moved them down, finally grabbing onto one, slim case and gripping it.

"This one."

She snatched it from him and said, "All right. My turn."

"Wait. What did I get?" He tried to see it, but she hid it behind her back. Her grin could easily be classified as flirtatious and playful, and Noah basked in the warmth of it.

"You'll see. Now step aside."

He complied, and she closed her eyes and plucked a case from the shelves too. She held both films in her hands and said, "Okay, we've got *Sixth Sense* or *Sweet Home Alabama*." She looked up at him, and Noah honestly didn't care what they watched. He didn't think he'd even be able to pay attention.

"I'm not feeling very much like scary," he said, thinking she'd like the romantic comedy better.

"*Sweet Home Alabama* it is," she said, stuffing the other one back into a spot where it didn't belong. He grinned at it, wondering if his mother would notice next time she visited this house. Probably.

Zara took the movie, grabbed her bottle of lemonade, and headed into the theater room. Noah followed, the popcorn and his drink back in his hands. He waited for her to choose one of the recliners right in the middle of the theater, and then he sat right beside her.

"This is sweet and salty popcorn," he said. "It has sugar and salt, and it's *delicious*." He offered her the bowl, and she laughed lightly as she took a few pieces and popped them into her mouth.

A flicker of surprise flashed in her eyes, and she said, "Wow, this *is* really good." She reached over and took another handful and handed him the movie. "I don't know how to put this in."

"I got it." Noah busied himself with getting the movie going, and then he took his spot next to her again. The bowl of popcorn rested on the arms between them, and Noah really wanted to reach for a snack at the same time she did, but he didn't.

Finally, he gave up, quit eating, and moved the popcorn bowl because Zara had stopped snacking too. His pulse thundered in the vein in his neck, and he reminded himself that he'd held a woman's hand before.

Not this woman, he thought, but he employed all the bravery he could and slipped his hand over the armrests and delicately took hers.

She looked at him, but he steadfastly kept his eyes on the huge screen in front of them.

"Noah," she said.

But he squeezed her fingers and said, "Sh. This is my favorite part."

She giggled, squeezed his fingers back, and adjusted herself so he didn't have to reach quite so far to hold her hand.

Noah grinned, this level of happiness something he'd never truly experienced before.

CHAPTER NINE

Zara woke the next morning with the ghost of Noah's fingers between hers. When he'd reached over and held her hand, Zara had no idea what to think. She'd wanted to talk about it, but he'd playfully avoided her.

And in the end, she didn't need to discuss everything to death. He obviously felt the same current between them that she did, and he'd acted on it. Did that need to be hashed out?

After that, though, Zara had barely been able to concentrate on the movie. Her nerves marched through her body like they were on a parade route, and one of her favorite movies had passed quickly.

His hands had been full as they'd gone back upstairs, and she'd lingered in the doorway of the kitchen while he threw bottles in the trash can and rinsed out the bowl. "See you in the morning," she'd said, taking a few steps backward.

He'd grinned and said, "Night," letting her go. She'd been glad for that, as the thought of kissing him both terrified and excited her at the same time.

She finally rolled over when her alarm went off, silencing it and getting out of bed. She yawned, the dawn not that far away, and she didn't want Noah to beat her to be ready to go. When she walked into the kitchen with her swim bag and her beach bag, she found him standing in front of the refrigerator, the door open, and the light spilling onto his face.

"Oh, you're up."

He swung the fridge closed, and even in the dim light, his gaze was powerful and penetrating. "You're late. There's no way we're making it to the beach by dawn."

Zara's shoulder ached already, and her day hadn't even started yet. But she wasn't taking "you're late" from the party boy prince. "Of course we will," she said. "If you're ready to go." She walked past him and toward the garage door.

"Oh, I'm ready."

"Great. The surf shop opens in ten minutes, and if we're lucky, we'll be the first ones through the door." She walked into the garage, Noah catching the door so it wouldn't hit her and all her bags.

He sat in the passenger seat instead of cramming himself onto the floor of the car. "Riding up here?"

"I'm going to have to go into the surf shop, right?"

"Yes. They'll have to measure you."

"Then I think I can—" His voice cut off as she backed out of the garage. "Wait."

She hit the brake, her heart thumping painfully against her breastbone. "What?"

"Pull back in."

She did.

"Close the door."

She pressed the button and the garage door rumbled closed behind the car. "We're really going to be late now."

Noah didn't answer, except to open the door and get in the backseat. "Cover me up."

Zara twisted and started tossing the blankets over the top of him. For good measure, she slid one of her bags over too. He groaned, but she ignored him. "Ready?"

"Yes." His muffled reply reminded her that there was no way she could have a normal relationship with him. The hand-holding felt stupid now, and she wished she'd ripped her fingers away from his.

With the garage open, she backed out again, this time glancing around like she expected a mob of reporters to manifest on the front lawn.

There wasn't a mob, but a single car waited at the closed gate as Zara drove toward it. "Did you see this car?" she hissed out of mostly-closed lips.

"I had a feeling," he said, and Zara kept going toward the gate, even though the two vehicles couldn't pass on this private drive.

The other car backed up and pulled to the side like

they'd have a friendly chat. Zara opened the gate and eased through, indeed stopping beside the other car. She pulled a little too far forward, so her window was nearly past his.

The man behind the steering wheel looked at her behind mirrored shades. He was definitely a reporter, and a tremor of unease ran through Zara. She watched the gate close behind her and then she said, "Can I help you?"

"Do you live here?"

"No," she said, wondering how much to tell him. She had the inexplicable urge to blurt out everything, but she held her tongue and watched this guy right back.

"Do you know the people who do live here?"

"No," she said. "I was hired to housesit, so that's what I'm doing."

"So the house is empty."

"Well, except for me, yes." Something bumped the back of her seat, and she didn't appreciate Noah kicking her. What didn't he like? What did he want her to say? And how was she supposed to know with just a tap?

She inched forward again. "I'm late for work. This is private property."

"Of course."

Zara pulled forward, very slowly, relieved when the reporter made a three-point turn and followed her down the tree-lined lane.

"He's following us," she said, her eyes glued to the rearview mirror and refusing to move her lips.

"Then go to work," Noah said, his voice barely audible.

"I'm about three hours early," she said. Zara wasn't even

sure she'd be able to get in the pool. An idea formed in her mind, and she seized onto it. "I'll go to the community pool. Pretend like I have to do an early-morning workout before my practice today."

Her stomach buzzed with nervous energy, and she didn't like it. Noah couldn't just stay in the car. It was warm already even though the sun was barely starting to rise. No way he could lay under all those blankets for very long.

"Do you think he'll follow me around all day?" she asked.

"What did he look like?"

Zara described the dark-haired man, how combed back and slick his hair was, the neatly trimmed goatee, and the dark olive skin—like Noah's.

"That's not Tomas," he said, and Zara didn't know if that was good or bad. "What's he driving?"

"Sleek, black luxury car."

"Any flags?"

"Flags?" She checked the rearview mirror. "No." He didn't ask another question, and Zara wound down to the stop sign at the bottom of the bluff. She looked both ways and turned left, looking behind her more than in front.

"He turned the other way." She'd never felt such relief in her life, and she almost drove right off the road.

"Where can we go to talk?" Noah asked.

"I don't know."

"You've lived here your whole life, and you don't know where we can go?"

Zara wanted to pull off the road and leave him behind.

Her life was so much simpler when she just had to manage her practice schedule and lay by the pool. Everything had become so complicated the moment she'd entered that mansion and heard Boomer barking at her.

Or maybe the complications had begun when she'd started thinking she and Noah could have a relationship. When had that happened, exactly?

"Zara?" he asked, and she had the distinct impression it wasn't the first time.

"Let me drive for a minute," she clipped out between her clenched teeth, her fingers clutching the steering wheel. She headed out on the highway that led to the cattle ranch, leaving behind the pool and the best surfing spot on the island. But at least that black car wasn't following her anymore.

She finally pulled off the road and into a tiny parking lot covered in sand. Her feet slipped on the loose particles as she rounded the car and opened the back door for Noah. She tossed her bag off and pushed the blankets back. He tumbled out onto the asphalt, his breath puffing out of his mouth.

He stood and brushed his palms down his chest and thighs. "I can't breathe back there." He ran his hands through his hair, exhaled again, and paced away from her.

"The beach down there is private," she said, following him. Down a set of steps, her feet met the beach, and when she glanced behind her, she couldn't see the car. So anyone driving by wouldn't be able to see her or Noah, but they would be able to see the car....

She pushed the thought out of her head. She was

allowed to come to the beach, and Noah could take off running as if he were a jogger. Just to be sure, she mentioned her idea to Noah, and he nodded a couple of times.

Zara paused next to him, both of them facing the ocean as the sun rose higher into the sky. She really hadn't thought this would be their morning on the beach. In her mind, it had been much more romantic, with him shirtless, and both of them getting pushed and pulled by the warm waves. Laughter, and sunshine, and she could admit she'd thought about kissing him before driving him back up to the mansion and then heading to work.

"Do you think that was a reporter?" she asked, deciding she could be as bold and forward as he'd been. She laced her hand through his elbow and leaned her head into his bicep.

"Yes," he said.

Is a relationship between us possible? But Zara wasn't that bold and forward, and she just let the breeze whisper between them as the minutes ticked by.

A COUPLE OF HOURS LATER, ZARA PUSHED INTO THE locker room, her shoulders just as tired as they'd been earlier that day. She and Noah had just stood on the beach for a few minutes, and then he said he'd try to figure out who it was so she'd know what to watch out for.

She wasn't sure why they needed a private place to have that kind of talk, but Zara couldn't figure out a lot about

Noah. Pushing him out of her mind, she opened her locker and started changing.

"Hey," Suzie said, spinning the dial on her own lock. "Another day in the pool." She sighed, and Zara felt like it was a heavy sigh kind of day.

"And Ian seems to be on a rampage this week."

"Right?" Suzie opened her locker and tossed her bag into it with a metallic *clunk!* "We need a fun night away from everything."

"I'd be in on that," Zara said.

"Aren't you up at that house on the bluffs?"

Before Zara could answer, Jill appeared on her other side. "I'm so late." She pulled her bleached hair up into a ponytail and whipped an elastic around it. "Has Ian said anything yet?"

"You're not late," Zara said. "We still have fifteen minutes."

"Really?" She looked at her watch, her dark eyes searching for clarity.

"Really," Suzie said. "And we're planning a girl's night for tonight. Zee has a fancy pool up at this mansion on the bluffs."

Zara froze, her own hair still falling over her shoulders. "What?"

"I'll bring pizza," Jill said. "Can I invite my roommate? She just broke up with her boyfriend, and she needs to get out."

"Sure," Suzie said as if she owned the place.

"Guys," Zara said. "I don't know if we can go up to the house."

"Why not?" Suzie asked, already in her swimming suit, her hair ready for the cap.

Zara avoided her eye and started combing her own hair back into a ponytail. "I'm just not sure the owner would like it."

"How long are you house-sitting?" Jill asked.

"Um, until the beginning of September."

Jill paused, though she'd been sure she was running late only a minute ago. "And we can't come sit by the pool? The owner won't even know."

No, they wouldn't. And this wouldn't be the first time Zara had invited her friends to one of the fancy places she babysat while their rich owners visited their other high-end houses.

Zara had no idea what to say. Could she agree now and cancel later?

"I can't tonight," she said, securing her hair. "I have something at the restaurant."

"When then?" Suzie asked, a bit of a whine in her voice.

"We could try for this weekend," Zara said. Maybe she could talk to Noah and convince him that if she had her friends up to the house, it would convince whoever was watching her that he really wasn't there.

The door to the pool opened, and Ian said, "Come on, ladies. Starting in five minutes." The heavy door swung closed with a thunk, and Zara took a deep breath.

"All right, friends." She looked at Suzie and Jill, two women she'd performed with many times. "If we make it through this, free Indian food on me."

Suzie's face split into a grin. "Deal," she said, and she

practically bounced to the exit. Zara laughed and followed with much less zip in her step, though she was grateful for the friends she saw at work each day.

And tonight, perhaps they could help her figure out what to do about Noah—if she should do anything at all.

CHAPTER TEN

Noah felt like he'd been living underneath a storm cloud for hours. Beyond the curtains and the glass, the sky was a crystalline blue, as was the ocean on the horizon. The trees were bright green, and birds flew through the sky.

But he wasn't part of this world, but some other, alternate world where he just watched the real world pass him by.

"I can't believe this is happening," he muttered to himself. Behind him, Boomer whined, and Noah knew how he felt. At least at home, in Triguard, he could leave the castle for the grounds. Reporters didn't dare come onto the grounds, and he could wander through the trees and stay out of the public eye.

His phone buzzed, but he ignored it. Zara had said she'd check in with him later, but he honestly wasn't sure he should perpetuate anything with her. He sure did like her though, even when they argued.

But a real relationship with her would require a lot from her, and he wasn't sure she'd be willing to give it. She'd have to leave Getaway Bay. Her family. Her job.

And he didn't see that happening. Every one of those was important to her, as he'd picked up from the conversations they'd had.

Could he leave Triguard and move to Getaway Bay? He didn't hold any position in anything important in Triguard, and his mind started down paths it had never been on before.

It had been long enough that he could call his mother, and he pulled out his phone to get the unpleasant task done. He noticed that his brother had texted, which caused a heavy dose of surprise to bolt through him.

Stopped by the house today, he said. *I really thought you'd be there. Can you please check in so Mom won't call the authorities?*

He read and re-read the text, sure the words weren't right. His brother—the next King of Triguard—had flown halfway around the world to Getaway Bay to see if Noah was at the bluff house?

That couldn't be.

Why hadn't Damien pulled through the gate? He knew the code.

Noah half-shrugged. Maybe he didn't know the code. He tapped out *Calling her now*, and then dialed his mother.

She answered after only one ring with, "Noah Sven Wales." Nothing else. No demand to know where he was or when he was coming home. Of course, he hadn't expected one. Just the scathing disappointment.

"Hello, Mother," he said. "As you can see, I'm fine."

"I'm not even going to ask where you are."

"That would be great," Noah said. "And you know that nothing in the newspapers about Venice is true, right?"

"Nothing?"

"Well, I was there with a woman named Katya."

"But you didn't get married." She wasn't asking, which was comforting to Noah.

"Mom, come on. Of course not."

She sighed, and he imagined her sitting at her personal desk, her back straight, the phone held to her ear while she participated fully. She was one of the most attentive people he knew, and a twist of guilt hit him hard.

"Do I want to know what you were doing with her?" she asked.

"Nothing, Mom. She was…in trouble and needed some help. That's what I do, so I helped her."

"You helped her."

He did not appreciate the sarcasm, and honestly, he didn't expect anyone to believe him. "Yes," he said. "She had an abusive boyfriend and needed someone to keep her safe. So she stayed at my place—in her own bed—and she was supposed to leave after a couple of days."

Those days had turned into a week, and then a month, and Noah honestly didn't mind. With sudden realization, he realized he was basically doing the same thing here. Kind of.

Zara didn't need his protection or presence—if

anything, that situation was reversed. But they were living in the same house, and he was thinking about kissing her....

So he'd kissed Katya. Didn't mean they'd slept together, or that he'd proposed, both things she'd either outright said or insinuated. Then the press had descended on his condo in Venice, and he'd denied everything and fled.

So the fleeing had probably canceled out the denials. Noah was used to denying things and then hiding. It was something he was actually quite good at.

"Oh, Noah," his mother said, and Noah recognized the disappointment and acceptance in the words. "So what are you doing now?"

"Just laying low," he said, turning back to the window. The glass separating him from reality seemed so thick, and he looked away again.

"Damien went to Hawaii, but he said he only found the house sitter."

Noah said nothing, not wanting to outright lie to his mother. His long hesitation obviously clued his mother into something, because she said, "Noah," with plenty of warning in her voice.

"What?" he asked.

"Where are you?"

"I'd rather not say," he said. "I'm safe, and I'm going to fix everything that happened in Venice." How, he didn't know. He couldn't retract the articles, and there was no way he could contact Katya and make her come clean.

No, Noah knew he couldn't fix anything. If he waited things out, the story would die, and no one would care what he did. He was an inconsequential prince, and he knew it.

So maybe he could make a relationship with Zara possible....

"Noah," his mother snapped, and Noah startled. He continued his conversation with his mother, but his mind never strayed far from the beautiful woman who was currently staying downstairs.

NOAH MET ZARA IN THE KITCHEN WHEN SHE GOT HOME from work, the sausage and green pepper pizza only minutes away from coming out of the oven. He set the salad bowl on the counter and smiled at her. "Are you hungry?"

Relief crossed her face, and a soft smile touched her mouth. "Starving." She took her place on the barstool on the end of the counter and looked at him. She'd promised her friends free food at Indian House, but Suzie had hit the water strangely during one dive and just wanted to go home.

"You've been gone for a long time today."

"Yeah." She blinked, and it took a second for her eyes to open again. They looked sleepy and Noah leaned toward her.

The timer on the oven went off, startling him back to his tasks. He got the pizza out and set the sheet pan on the stovetop. "Do you like pizza?"

"Who doesn't like pizza?"

"Well, I'm sure there are some people," he said.

Noah cut the pizza into thin rectangles and used a spatula to slide a piece onto a plate for her. He placed it in front of her and slid a fork across the counter too.

"You made this," she said, first gazing at the pizza and then him. "Like, from scratch."

"Yeah." He served himself a couple pieces of pizza and joined her at the bar, keeping that stool between them. "My nani taught me to cook, and some of my favorite times are with her in the kitchen." He flashed her a smile, comfortable with her and glad they'd figured out how to get along. "Surely you learned to cook, what with your family being in the restaurant business."

"Yes," she said. "Plenty of lessons in the kitchen."

"And you didn't like them?"

"I did, sure," she said. "I like cooking, sometimes."

"Just don't want it to be your career."

"Exactly."

Noah nodded like he understood, and on some level, he did. After all, he had an overbearing family who expected him to play a certain role. "And how did your family take it when you became a synchronized swimmer?"

"Oh, my father was livid," she said. "My mother cried and prayed for a week straight." Zara shook her head and cut off a bite of her pizza. "Then she spent the next few years trying to match me up with nice Indian men, hoping I'd see the error of my ways." She put the pizza in her mouth and moaned. "This is *delicious*."

"Well, it's not butter chicken." Noah picked up his pizza with his hands and bit into it. But it was good. The

Alfredo sauce, the sausage, the red peppers. It was like a party in his mouth, and Boomer lay on the floor, gazing up at him hopefully.

"What about you?" she asked. "Is the bad boy prince a disappointment to his parents?"

"I talked to my mother today," he said in response, as that was easier than thinking his parents were disappointed in him. "And that man who came by this morning? He was my brother."

Zara dropped her fork, the sound of metal on ceramic rattling through the whole kitchen. "He was? I talked to a man who's going to be *King*?"

Noah rolled his eyes. "He's just a guy," he said. "Like me. Except proper, and polished, and...perfect."

Zara cocked her head, the surprise gone from her face. "Perfect? Nobody's perfect, Noah." The soft, sincere way she said his name made him once again wonder if they could somehow make their two worlds into one.

"Anyway, you did a great job. He believed I wasn't here. He's on his way home."

"Are you surprised he came?" she asked.

"Actually, yes. But I haven't been in touch with my family for a couple of weeks now, and he wanted to make sure I was all right."

"That's nice of him."

"See? Perfect." Noah finished his pizza while Zara put some salad on her plate. "When we were growing up, Damien was always better at everything. Sports, school, etiquette. All of it. Except cooking. That's the one thing I was better at."

"And what about your sister?"

"Louisa is the best with the press. She works with Damien to make sure he says all the right things, and she's got her finger on the pulse of the country."

"Oh, so we like her," she said.

"I love both of my siblings," he said.

"But Louisa more than Damien."

He looked at her, wondering how she knew. "Do you have sisters you like more than others?"

"Of course," she said easily. "Krisha is my favorite. She's the oldest, and she never acts like I'm the black sheep of the family. And Abi. I like her too. She's the one who told me if I wanted to be a swimmer, I could be a swimmer."

Noah really wanted to see Zara swim, and it had nothing to do with the swimming suit. "That's great. And you have five sisters?"

"Five sisters," she confirmed, going back to her salad. "Our house was crazy growing up. Huge family celebrations, and so much food you'd think my mom and grandmother were cooking for the whole island." She giggled and shook her head. "Our neighbors hated us, I'm pretty sure."

"Oh yeah? Loud music?"

"So loud. So much dancing."

"I'd like to see that," he said, and Zara's eyes darted to his.

"Yeah?"

"Dancing? Definitely." He toyed with the idea of telling her about the tickets he'd been able to procure. But he held onto it, his little secret for now. They were getting along so well, and he didn't want to scare her away.

"They have luau's at the cattle ranch and the pineapple plantation," she said. "We should go sometime."

"That's not Indian dancing," he said.

"No, but it's fun. Food's good too."

"I'll look into it," he said.

She finished her salad and took a deep breath. "I'm exhausted."

"So I guess no more early-morning surfing lessons." Noah watched her stand and take her dishes to the sink. Having her on that side of the island while he sat over here was a new experience, and he liked it.

"We can go surfing," she said.

"You think so?"

"You just said that guy this morning was your brother. Not a reporter. So if you were willing to try this morning, we can go tomorrow."

"You don't mind?"

Zara regarded him, something running through her expression that he couldn't read. "I don't mind."

Noah's temperature lifted several degrees, and he grinned at her. "Five-thirty then."

She groaned, but it was playful. "Five-thirty." She turned and walked away, twisting back at the doorway, giving him a flirtatious little grin before entering the hall and leaving him sitting in the kitchen, wondering how he could make this summer fling into something more permanent.

CHAPTER ELEVEN

Zara met Noah in the kitchen again, wondering if the man ever slept. When she asked him, he said, "Very little, actually."

"Why's that?" she asked, accepting the cup of coffee he handed her.

"My mind never shuts off," he said simply.

"There are pills for that, you know." Their eyes met, and that zing between them was almost familiar now. Hot and quick and like lightning, but familiar.

"I've heard." He nodded her toward the garage exit, and she went that way, fire erupting through her whole body when he put his hand on the small of her back and guided her through the door.

She moved on wooden legs, and he must've noticed, because he said, "Sorry," dropped his hand, and hurried around toward the passenger door.

Zara threw her bags in the backseat and got behind the wheel. She turned on the ignition and sat there, her fingers curling around the wheel. "Noah?" she asked.

"Yeah?"

She stared through the windshield at the immaculate door leading into the house. "Are we just playing a game here?" She couldn't believe she'd asked him, but the question had been rotating through her mind for hours and hours.

He reached over and took one of her tense hands from the wheel, lacing his fingers through hers. Instant comfort spread through her, and she relaxed into the seat. "I'll be honest. I like you, and we'll probably need to take things one step at a time to make something...long-lasting work."

"How many steps do you think it'll take?"

"A lot," he said honestly.

She looked at him, and his dark eyes drank her right up. She couldn't quite get a decent breath, and she had the strangest desire to tell him things she hadn't told anyone else.

"Have you looked up anything about me?" he asked.

"Not much," she said. "Should I?"

He shook his head. "I'd rather you not." He drew in a deep breath and swallowed. "So before I came here, I was living in Venice. I met a woman on my way home from dinner one night. She was crying and her hair was a mess." He squeezed her hand, and Zara liked this soft, vulnerable version of the bad boy prince.

"So I took her back to my condo, and she told me this

big story about her boyfriend. We agreed that she'd stay with me for a couple of days, long enough to get him off her back." He sighed and leaned his head back against the seat. "But she stayed longer than that, and when I finally asked her to leave, she went straight to the press. Told them that we were married and that I'd broken up with her when she'd lost our baby."

Zara blinked, trying to make sense of all he'd said. She came up with, "Baby?"

"None of it was true." He looked at her again, his expression earnest and sincere. "I wasn't married. We didn't sleep together. There was no baby. She was just staying in another room in my place."

"Kind of like me," Zara said, recognizing the similarities there.

"Yeah, but you're not going to go to the press, are you?"

"No." She shook her head. She couldn't imagine a scenario where she'd go to the press and tell them anything about Noah.

He leaned forward, almost like he'd kiss her right then, and Zara's heart tumbled through her chest. But his lips touched her forehead, the gentlest of touches. "Thanks. So can we go surfing?"

She flipped the car into reverse. "Surfing. Yes. Let's go surfing."

SHE PUSHED INTO THE SURF SHOP FIRST, THE RAYS OF

sunlight just starting to paint the sky behind her gold. "Morning, Rich," she said to the man standing a few feet away.

He turned toward her. "Zara." A smile filled his whole face, and he embraced her. Rich was probably ten years older than Zara, and his family had owned this surf shop for generations. They'd been friends since she was a little girl and her grandfather had brought her to the beach to learn to surf.

Her mother, of course, had not approved, but Zara had persisted in her pleadings to her grandfather, and they'd both won the argument.

"I haven't seen you in a while," he said, stepping back. His gaze flickered to Noah, who entered the shop behind her.

"Well, my show starts in less than a month," she said. "The rehearsals are so long." She hooked her thumb at Noah, mentally trying to come up with a way to introduce him. "This is…Holden. A friend I'm teaching to surf while he's here this summer."

The words tasted bitter in her mouth, but she kept her smile in place.

A friend.

She wanted to be a lot more than friends.

Holden.

Not even his real name.

While he's here this summer.

What would happen then?

The defenses around Zara's heart needed strengthening, because she did not want to wander the beach, looking for the broken pieces once Noah left Getaway Bay. And he was the prince of another country; there was no way he could stay.

Still, a nagging part of her brain wondered if he could. That maybe they just needed to talk about it, and make a plan, and everything would be fine.

Fine.

Another word that bounced around Zara's brain as Rich and Noah shook hands.

Nothing in her life had ever worked out to be just fine. She clawed and practiced for what she had, and sometimes she wished her life had been more like Noah's.

"So he needs a board," Zara said. "It'll probably have to be custom-made for his height and all that, but I'm wondering if you have something we can start with this morning."

"Sure," Rich said easily, the way he did everything. If he'd ever been upset or worried about something, she'd never seen it. "I've got something he can use until we get his made."

"Who makes the boards?" Noah asked, and Rich smiled at him.

"I do. Step over here, man, and let's get you measured." Rich worked around Noah, taking notes of his height, his arm span, his weight, all of it.

About twenty minutes later, Noah had paid for a custom board that would be ready in seven to ten days, and he had a rental leaned up against his shoulder.

Zara's nerves pranced around inside her body, urging her to get down to the water and get this lesson over with. Then she could go to work, where the mental and physical requirements of her job would push any fantasies of Noah out of her mind.

They left the surf shop and faced the ocean. A handful of others were already in the water, and Zara set her sunglasses in place. "Let's go down this way a bit," she said, stepping to her right.

Noah came with her saying, "That was great. He was nice."

"Yeah, Rich is great."

"He reminds me of a friend I have in Triguard."

"Triguard?" she asked. "Is that the name of your country?"

"Yeah," he said. "Marco is easy-going too. Always brings me my favorite candy on my birthday. Doesn't seem to care that I'm a royal and he's a mailman."

Zara smiled at the nostalgia in Noah's voice. "When's the last time you saw him?"

"Last year, before I went to Venice."

"What's your favorite candy?" Probably something foreign she wouldn't be able to get.

"Peanut butter cups."

She almost tripped over her own feet, the loose sand half warm and half cold against her skin. "Really?"

He chuckled. "You thought it was going to be something weird, like Turkish delight." His eyes held that flirty, playful glint that had Zara's pulse in a tizzy.

"Yeah, sort of," she admitted, letting a smile touch her

lips as her eyes dropped to his mouth. "I mean, peanut butter cups are so *normal*." As they stood there and watched one another, Zara realized that Noah was indeed normal. And that somehow made him more attractive.

"Yes, well, I'm human," he teased. "And for the record, Turkish delight *is* delicious if done right."

"Isn't that rose-flavored?" Zara made a face and started walking again.

"Yes, and the kind that is covered in powdered sugar and is super soft? It's divine."

"I'll take your word for it."

"Some people cover it in chocolate, but that ruins it for me."

"Anything covered in chocolate is better," she said.

He laughed then, a truly happy sound that filled the sky around them. Zara couldn't help joining in. Something sparked between them again, in this joyous moment with the sun just coming out to breathe life into the day.

Their eyes met, and he slung his arm around her shoulders. "Thanks for doing this," he murmured just before pressing his lips to her temple. "I know your days are long, and I appreciate it."

Zara gazed up at him, wondering if she could kiss him right there on the beach. There were other people around, but not many, and they were dozens of yards down the sand anyway. Her skin sizzled where his touched it, and the insanity of their situation somehow felt...sane.

She tipped up onto her toes and he bent down, brushing his lips against hers almost like he was seeking permission.

But she'd already given it, and in the next moment, he kissed her like he meant to, and everything in Zara turned into that super soft Turkish delight covered in powdered sugar.

She was aware of his rented board falling to the sand. Of both of his hands cradling her face and then moving into her hair. Of the way they moved together, fit together, breathed together.

Zara hadn't kissed anyone in a while, but wow. This was the best kiss she'd experienced in her life, and she felt as if Noah had just ruined her for any other kiss.

He pulled away first, and Zara drew in a deep breath. He kept his face in the hollow of her neck, his breath washing over her bare shoulder and making her shiver.

"So I guess we should probably figure out what steps we need to take," he whispered.

"Probably," Zara said, not wanting to complicate things with steps and talking and plans. She just wanted to exist in this moment with Noah for a while longer.

He kept her within the safety and comfort of his arms for a few more seconds, and when he inhaled as if to speak, she said, "But let's surf first, okay?"

She took a micro-step back and met his eye. He searched her face and finally nodded. "Okay."

Facing the water, the waves she loved, she said again, "Okay."

That night, after her practice, Zara texted Noah to see if he needed anything from town.

Just you came his response, and it filled her with warmth from head to toe.

"Ooh, who's Noah?" Suzie asked, splashing ice water on Zara's memories.

She flipped her phone over and said, "No one. Just some guy I'm working with."

"And he wants you." Suzie sat on the tiny bench and pulled on her running shoes. "So I guess you're not coming jogging with us."

"No." She glanced up at Jill who snapped a headband around her forehead.

"So how are you getting your exercise in this week?" she asked. "Ian will be livid if you say you've laid by the pool for seven straight days."

"I'm surfing in the morning," Zara said, thinking of it on the spot. "So I run a bit there, and then paddle and swim and all that. It's quite strenuous."

Jill looked doubtful, but she shrugged and said, "Okay. Just don't want you to get in trouble."

"I won't." Zara had worked with Ian before, and she knew what it took to earn his approval. She stood with a groan and rubbed her back. "See you guys tomorrow."

"Can't wait to hear about Noah," Suzie said with a dangerous glint in her eye. Zara just smiled and waved at her friends as they left. A pit opened in her gut at the fact that Suzie knew his real name. She probably should've put his pseudonym in her phone, but she hadn't. Suzie had already seen it.

Just you.

She shivered again, hoping tonight would include as much kissing as talking.

She showed up at the mansion with sushi and Chinese takeout, hoping Noah hadn't cooked. Even if he had, she could eat sweet and sour chicken for breakfast. After all, Chinese food was delicious any time of day.

Thankfully, the kitchen was devoid of food when she entered and set all her bags on the counter. "Noah?" she called, and a moment later, Boomer barked...from outside.

She turned that way and found the dog wagging his tail furiously from the other side of the French doors that led into the yard. She walked over to him and let him in, scrubbing him down with a smile and the words, "Where's Noah, huh?" The car he'd obviously driven at some point was still in the garage, but the house felt empty and Boomer's body was hot, as if he'd been outside for a while.

Concern rippled through her, but Zara pushed it back. Noah was a grown man. He could leave the mansion if he wanted to. The gate had been closed. The garage too. Still, she straightened and watched Boomer run over to his water bowl and begin to lap at a speed unknown to other dogs.

So, as she walked down the hall to make sure Whitewater was okay, she pulled out her phone and called Noah, hoping she wouldn't come off as too desperate or too worried.

He didn't answer, and she let her hand fall to her side. What should she do now? She filled the cat's food and water bowls, ready to go find Noah.

Her phone rang, and she practically threw it as she swung it wildly up to check who was calling. "Noah," she said once she got the call connected. "Where are you?"

"I fell asleep," he said, his voice still a bit on the slumbery side. "Are you home?"

"Yep. And I brought sushi and Chinese food."

"On my way down."

She hung up and went to meet him at the bottom of the steps. He swept her easily into his embrace, both of them laughing. "Hey, beautiful." He leaned down and kissed her, and it felt like the most natural action in the world.

"Hey," she said breathlessly when he pulled back.

"So," he said, taking hold of her hand and leading her into the kitchen. "I've been thinking."

"Oh, boy," she said. "Sounds dangerous." She unpacked the white Chinese containers and started popping them open.

"Ha ha." He took out the sushi and got out silverware and plates. "Anyway, I'd need to talk to my parents about leaving Triguard, but I don't see why they'd make me stay there."

Zara's eyebrows went up. "Are you serious?"

"I mean, I'm a prince, but I'm not going to be King. Ever. So why would I need to stay there?"

"I don't know," Zara said, her mind spinning a million different ways. "Family solidarity? United front? That type of thing."

"Yeah, they don't need me. I cause more problems than anything."

Zara watched him take a California roll and then scoop ham fried rice onto his plate. She heard the measure of regret and sadness in his voice. "I'm sure that's not true," she said.

"Trust me, it is." Noah met her eye briefly and went back to the food. "So anyway. I'm thinking of calling my mother tomorrow and talking to her."

Zara let a few seconds go by while she thought about how to phrase her next question. "Will she be...will you tell her about us?"

"Of course."

"And she'll be okay with you having another girlfriend only a week or two after your last one?"

That got him to look up, and when he met her gaze, she found sharp edges in his. "Katya wasn't my girlfriend. Ever."

"Did you kiss her?"

Noah's teeth clenched, and he said, "Yes."

"Ah, well, then she was your girlfriend."

"Is that a rule?"

Zara wanted to sigh and roll her eyes. "I realize different people have different benchmarks for such things," she said. "But to be clear, when I'm kissing a man, he's my boyfriend."

The fire in Noah's eyes changed from angry to something more like passionate. "Noted."

Zara took her food to her spot at the bar, thrilled when Noah sat right next to her instead of leaving an empty barstool there. "So you think you can move to Getaway Bay permanently?"

"I do."

And that was a huge step in the right direction. One that filled Zara with all kinds of emotions she didn't know how to sort through. Happiness, but also a bit of trepidation. Because if he moved here permanently, she didn't have an excuse for why they couldn't be together.

CHAPTER TWELVE

*N*oah paced in his bedroom, the door closed and locked though Zara had gone to work an hour ago. He'd decided to start with Louisa, as his sister could tell him how their mother would react with near exactness.

But she wouldn't pick up the phone. So he hung up without leaving a message. She'd see he'd called, and she'd call him back when she was done with whatever obligation she was dealing with.

His stomach writhed as if he'd swallowed a nest of vipers for breakfast. As it was, he'd sipped a cup of coffee while Zara slathered peanut butter and Nutella on two slices of bread, grabbed a banana, and tucked a protein bar into her purse.

She'd flashed him a smile, kissed him quickly, and left through the garage door. He'd been sealed inside the mansion, but it didn't smother him as much as it had in the past.

His phone rang, and he jumped like he'd been caught on camera doing something naughty. "Hey, sis," he said when he answered. He sounded cool and confident, the way he'd been taught.

"Noah," she said, a brightness to her voice that felt genuine. "What's going on? You called three times."

"Did I?"

"In the span of five minutes. I was dealing with a member of Parliament, and I couldn't even get a text off."

Dealing with a member of Parliament. Noah didn't have to do that either. His mother actually warned him away from politics, citing his short fuse as the reason why. And he didn't even have that short of a fuse. But compared to her, Damien, and Louisa, Noah's temper was downright explosive.

"Sorry," he said. "I guess I'm a little anxious this morning."

"Why?" She drew the word out as if she were preparing herself for terrible news.

"So I'm at the mansion house in Getaway Bay," he said. "I've been here for a week or so." Had it really only been that long? And he'd already kissed Zara? A hint of embarrassment made his blood run hotter through his veins.

"And?" Louisa prompted, and he could just picture her all prim and proper as she chatted with him.

"And I'm thinking I'd like to just stay here." He drew in a deep breath. "Permanently." The word landed like a bomb between them, and Noah waited for his sister to say something. Anything.

"Have you spoken to Mom and Dad about that?" she asked, her voice quiet and downright diplomatic. He'd heard her speak like this before, and he didn't like that she was using the tone on him.

"Not yet," he said. "You're my sounding board."

"So Damien doesn't know either."

"No," he said. "Just you, and I'm just thinking out loud." He'd been doing more than that—in fact, his dreams and daydreams all featured him and Zara in the early-morning waves, surfing. Then doing something around the house. Or building a new children's wing in the library here on the island. Or chartering a jet and island-hopping for a few days. Or weeks. Whatever.

He didn't have a job, and he didn't need one. His inheritance was more than enough to buy a place and live on this Hawaiian island for a good long while. His whole life. Zara wouldn't have to work either, unless she wanted to.

He couldn't wait to see her swim, and he focused on the conversation. If he wanted a future with Zara, he needed to work some things out first.

"I don't know, Noah," his sister was saying. "No one in the royal family has ever left the island permanently."

"Is that true?" Noah asked. "What about that crazy uncle no one will talk about?"

"There's a reason no one talks about him," Louisa said.

"Well, maybe I'll be him," Noah said, though the thought of not being included in family texts and the royal events of the country stung him in a way he hadn't anticipated.

"Noah," Louisa said with plenty of reprimand in the name. "Why would you want to stay in Getaway Bay? To my recollection, you've never liked it all that much."

"That's because we never visit in the summer," he said, turning back to the window. "You should see this place right now. It's beautiful." And he didn't remember *not* liking Getaway Bay.

"And?" Louisa prompted. She really was the smartest of the siblings, and Noah should've anticipated that he'd have to tell her about Zara.

"And nothing," he said, his voice only the teensiest bit false. "Do you think Mother will veto it immediately?"

"Veto outright? No." Louisa paused for a moment. "But, Noah, you should expect to have an iron-clad argument in place. Just this morning, she mentioned she'd spoken to you and you'd be home soon."

"I didn't tell her that."

"You know how she is."

"Yeah." He sighed. "Does she have a parade all lined up?"

"Not yet." Louisa laughed and added, "But she did mention a new charity she wanted you to focus on once you return."

"I'm doing charity work here," he said. "I'm volunteering at a wedding planning place, and I'm donating to the synchronized swimming association here on the island." The last one had just popped into his head, but he seized onto it, determined to do it. No one had to know. His family had made plenty of anonymous donations.

"Mom said she didn't even know where you were."

"No, I didn't tell her."

"So I get the exclusive scoop." Louisa was the last person on Earth who would tell the press where he was. And honestly, he wasn't sure he cared anymore. If he was going to live here permanently, he couldn't take every trip down the bluff concealed under blankets in the backseat.

He chuckled. "Something like that, sis. So you think I need a better argument than it's pretty here in the summer."

"Definitely," she said. "And Noah? It better not be another woman."

He cringed at the word *another*, and he said, "Of course it isn't, Louisa," like such a thing was utterly ridiculous. They talked a bit longer about Damien's quick trip to the island, and if she was any closer to a firm date for her wedding. Then he hung up and returned to his position at the French doors, watching the ocean in the distance.

It better not be another woman.

Well, so what if it was?

He hadn't been in Venice for a woman, nor to run from a scandal. He'd simply been there on vacation. An extended vacation, sure, but not because he'd screwed up again.

Noah was tired of being the bad boy prince. He didn't want to return to his life in Triguard, even if it was somewhat fulfilling to volunteer and serve the people of his country. He wanted a more normal life, with a wife and kids and Boomer. He wanted to go to the beach in the summer, and carve pumpkins at Halloween, and establish his own family traditions for every other holiday.

And when he pictured himself doing those things, it was Zara at his side. So he lifted his phone again, this time calling his mother, no idea what he was going to say to her.

🐚

"You want me to meet your family?" Noah stared at Zara, her hair still damp from the pool.

She unpacked the grocery bags and started putting things in the fridge and cupboards as if she lived in this house. "We've been dating a few weeks now," she said. "My show opens next week. They'll see you there."

He'd told her about the tickets he'd found, and she'd simply shook her head, smiled, and kissed him like she was glad he was so resourceful.

He nodded and swallowed, suddenly so nervous. "And you don't think they'll be a huge roadblock?"

Zara shrugged, but Noah could read her expressions by now. And this one said yes, of course her family was going to be a major roadblock. He still hadn't gotten royal permission to relocate to Getaway Bay, and he'd made a dozen phone calls—two of them conference calls with the whole family—and the job still wasn't done.

His father simply didn't understand why Noah needed to live on a different island. Noah had steadfastly refused to tell them about Zara or the fact that she was house-sitting in the same mansion where he was currently living.

His mother would think that was a scandal, and she'd likely demand her money back from Zara and send someone from her security detail to retrieve Noah. So he hadn't gotten what he wanted yet, because he hadn't been able to give the right answers to his parents' questions.

But he didn't want to jeopardize Zara's job. He didn't want to lie. So he said nothing, and the frustration over the whole thing was starting to take its toll on him.

No, he didn't have official permission to leave Triguard, but he considered himself a permanent resident of Getaway Bay now. He and Zara had fallen into an easy and enjoyable routine. She drove him to Your Tidal Forever. He worked on whatever Hope needed him to do, and then he went to the beach, or hired a pro to teach him more about surfing. Whatever he wanted to pass the time until Zara finished with her rehearsals.

Then they grabbed dinner, went back to the privacy of the mansion, ate, and spent evenings together until one of them fell asleep.

It was almost always Zara, but Noah really didn't mind waking her and then leading her down the hall to her bedroom. He'd kiss her and leave her in the doorway before retreating to his own room on the second floor.

Nothing scandalous, no matter what his mother—or the press—might think should they ever find out how Noah and Zara spent their time.

They'd eaten at a different restaurant every night for the past few weeks, but never her family's. "So maybe we should stop by Indian House this week," he said casually, feeling anything but calm about the prospect.

Zara shook her head as she put crackers on a shelf. "Nope. That's not how it works. Meeting a boyfriend is a huge family affair. My mother will need at least a week's notice, and she'll do an entire Indian festival meal at the house."

Noah almost scoffed but caught himself in time. "What?"

"We've probably waited too long at this point," she said. "Schedules have to be rearranged so all my sisters can come. My aunts and uncles. Grandparents." She sighed as she cleared away the last of the recyclable bags and tucked them in a drawer in the island. "Maybe we should just show up at Indian House."

Noah got up and walked around the island, taking her easily into his arms. "I understand the formality of family things," he said, bending down to touch his forehead to hers. If there was anyone who understood the details that didn't matter, it was him.

"So you tell me what you want me to do. If you want the big meet-the-boyfriend affair, call your mom and set it up. If you don't, let's go to Indian House tomorrow night."

There was no reason they couldn't go tonight, other than the fact that Noah needed a little more time to gather his wits about him. He couldn't even imagine introducing her to his parents, and a slip of fear ran through him. He'd have to do that eventually, and he had no idea how it would go. After all, he couldn't even tell them she was the reason he wanted to relocate.

That's because of her job, he told himself. He knew she needed this job, and his mother would probably hop on her private jet and come to Getaway Bay to get her money back from Zara if she found out.

"Let me call her tonight," she said. "Maybe everyone can meet us for dinner tomorrow."

"I don't want you to think your family can't do their traditions," he said.

"I don't think that." She looked up at him, those honey-brown eyes smoldering at him.

"Good." He gave her a quick kiss and said, "Then let's go get tacos and watch the sun set at Lightning Point. Sound good?"

"Sounds amazing, but you have to bring way more blankets than last time. I got cold."

"I don't even know how that's possible, but okay."

"The wind was wicked," she said. "You were cold too; you just won't admit it."

No, Noah would not admit it. He simply shook his head and went to get another blanket out of the closet in the hall. He really liked spending time with Zara, and while they'd talked a lot over the past few weeks and gotten to know each other, they'd really only taken one step toward a lasting relationship—getting to know each other.

Him moving to the island was a huge step though, if he could get that to go through, and so was meeting her parents. He hoped it wouldn't take as much effort as getting permission to move here, but something told him he better be prepared for anything when it came to Zara's family.

CHAPTER THIRTEEN

Zara cuddled into Noah's side as the sun sank lower and lower into the ocean. The wind really whipped out here, and she was glad she'd grabbed a hoodie from her bedroom before they'd left. At least her hair wasn't flying out of control this time.

She'd decided to start with a text to Krisha, just to see what the family's plans were in the near future. That had turned into quite the texting marathon, and finally Zara shoved her phone in her pocket.

"Krisha knows something's afoot."

Noah burst out laughing, the sound joyful and his chest vibrating with the strength of it. "Afoot?" He snorted as he started laughing again, and that got Zara laughing too.

He kneaded her closer, and she thought back over the past few weeks in the mansion with him. She'd been terrified that Petra—his mother—would ask for her money back. But she'd never asked if Noah had met the house sitter or not. She'd never asked if Zara had run into Noah.

Of course, he hadn't told them about her yet. Every time she thought about that, her chest pinched a little. But he'd explained why, and she didn't want him to be dragged halfway around the world by royal security. Or give back her house-sitting fee.

He'd made every phone call in private, either while she was at work or behind his closed bedroom door. But she believed everything he reported to her. Apparently it was a much bigger deal for him to leave the country than either of them had thought.

The longer the drama dragged on, the more remote the possibility seemed that Noah would be able to move here. He'd said he'd start looking for a place of his own on the island, as his parents still visited Getaway Bay a couple of times a year. He thought that might sway them to allow him to relocate permanently.

To her knowledge, he had not looked for a place of his own, but she didn't care. If she thought the house was huge with him and Boomer there, she couldn't imagine how it would feel if they weren't.

"What else did she say?" Noah asked, bringing Zara back to this moment on the beach. This sunset. This breath. Zara spent so much time thinking about tomorrow—her next show. Her next paycheck. Her next boyfriend.

As she'd gotten to know Noah over the past month, she'd realized that she wasn't living right now. And she wanted to change that.

"She said she thinks everyone will be at the restaurant

tomorrow. As far as she knows, all the sisters are scheduled to work, and Mom and Dad eat there ninety-nine percent of the time."

"So we can go."

Zara drew in a deep breath, admiring the pink and purple among the gold and navy in the sky. "Yes," she said. "We can go tomorrow." She just wished she didn't feel like she was marching Noah up the side of a volcano and sacrificing him to the gods.

It's not that bad, she told herself. Her sisters would be nice, at least. Yes, some were more traditional than others, but they generally supported one another.

Noah ran his thumb up and down her arm, and she tuned in to the fact that he had some nervous energy of his own. "Are you worried about meeting them?" she asked.

"Five sisters and your parents in one go? Grandparents, aunts, uncles, the whole shebang?" He chuckled and added, "Nah. Should be easy. Nothing to it."

"You're such a liar," she said, giggling. "And look who's using outlandish words now. Shebang?"

Noah chuckled too, and Zara melted into the sound of his voice. Several moments passed, and then he said, "Of course I'm nervous about it, Zara," his voice soft and sober now.

She pushed away from his chest and looked at him. "Really? Why?"

"I don't know." He watched the horizon line, and Zara couldn't read the emotion in his eyes.

"You're a *prince*," she said. "If anyone should be nervous

or worried about not meeting expectations, it should be me."

"I'm just a regular guy," he said, something he'd told her a few times over the past few weeks. Zara knew that. Well, deep down inside she knew he was just a normal man. But there was something kingly and royal about him she didn't think just anyone could learn.

"Should I go buy a new suit tomorrow?" he asked.

"Do you even have a suit here?" she asked.

"No."

"Then, yes," she said. "You should go buy a new suit tomorrow."

"Great," he said, seemingly glad for the opportunity. "At least I'll be able to get out of the house."

Zara giggled, but she knew the walls of the mansion trapped Noah from time to time. He didn't go volunteer at Your Tidal Forever every day, and while he rode in the front seat now, he wasn't exactly traipsing all over the island either.

She watched him, this handsome man that had come into her life unexpectedly. No, they had not gotten along in the beginning. But as she learned more about him and as she shared more about her, her heart had opened to the possibility of a real future with him.

"Thanks for doing that," she said, lifting up to kiss him. He received her willingly, and she sent a prayer up to whoever was listening that her family would accept Noah.

That seemed a bit far-fetched, so she amended her plea to just be, *Let them be kind to him,* and snuggled back into

Noah's side to watch the night steal the last breath from the day.

❦

The following evening, Zara twisted and turned and looked at herself in the nicest dress she wore. She should probably be dressed in her nicest sari, but something about it felt false. Almost like she'd be manipulating her mother by wearing such traditional clothes.

She pulled on the hemline of the black fabric, sure it had always fallen a little lower than it currently was. She'd steamed it, and it fell down the lines of her body nicely, but would it be modest enough for her mother?

"I don't know why you care," she muttered to herself. Over the past decade, Zara had blazed her own path, unconcerned about her parents' feelings. But that wasn't entirely true, and she knew it. She did care about them, and how they felt, and her cultural traditions. She simply wanted to be her too, and her family still loved her.

She fluffed her hair one more time and deemed herself as good as she was going to get. Her heels clicked on the marble hallway as she made her way into the kitchen. Noah wasn't there, which meant he was probably twisting to look in a mirror and tugging at something to make it lay right.

She opened the fridge and promptly closed it again. She was starving, but they were eating at Indian House. With the way her stomach vibrated with nervous energy, she wasn't sure how much she'd actually be able to eat.

Noah's footsteps finally echoed off the steps, and he

came into the kitchen a few seconds later. Zara froze, the breath in her lungs absolutely solidifying at the sight before her. If she'd thought he was good-looking before, she now had a new definition for the term.

He wore a suit the color of midnight, and it fit his frame perfectly. His shirt held the color of a pale winter sky, and his tie had pink, blue, and yellow checks among the black.

"How do I look?" he asked, as if he didn't know he was the best looking man on the planet.

Zara stared, sure this man was not her boyfriend. He seemed so far above her, and her self-confidence took a nose-dive.

"Zara?" he asked, stepping toward her. He smelled like musky cologne and soap, with a hint of mint from his toothpaste, and Zara wanted to breathe him in, hold him tight, and kiss him senseless.

He touched her elbow, unfreezing her, and she managed to say, "You look great," in a throaty voice. She cleared her throat and grabbed her purse from the kitchen counter. "Should we go?"

With a curious look on his face, he said, "Sure. Can I drive?"

She stalled in her flight toward the garage. "Do you remember how?"

"Ha ha," he said. "You think you're so funny."

"Well, you never drive, and you said even in Triguard, you'd get chauffeured around." She threw him a playful smile, hoping that would somehow elevate her to his status. But it was hopeless. A synchronized swimmer had no business being with a prince. "I'm just trying to make sure I don't die tonight."

Though she did risk her life with her car every time she got in it, as she still hadn't had a second of time to get it looked at or fixed. It kept starting, though, so that was something.

"You won't die." He put his hand on her back and guided her into the garage, grabbing the keys that had literally hung on the hook beside the door for a solid month.

She sank into his sports car—a rental he seemed to need to take up space in the garage—and adjusted her skirt while he settled behind the wheel. She buckled her seatbelt and cut him a quick look out of the corner of her eye.

He seemed utterly nonplussed, like he remembered where all the important pedals and switches were, and he backed out of the garage just fine.

Zara squinted into the bright sunlight and reached into her purse for her sunglasses. With someone else navigating the twisty roads, Zara simply enjoyed the sunshine and the way it glinted off the ocean in the distance.

Once they made it down to the town, she directed him down Main Street to Indian House. The parking lot was full, and every cell in her body rioted. Neither of them had said much on the drive down, and Zara took a few steadying breaths while Noah parked the car.

"Ready?" he asked, and while every stitch of him was in the perfect place, she could see the anxiety in his eyes. Somehow, it brought her comfort, and she nodded.

"Ready." She got out of the car, and Noah arrived on her side to close the door and link his fingers through hers.

"They're just people," he said as they walked toward the entrance. "We're people. It'll be fine."

"Is this your speech to yourself?" she asked.

"I mean, yeah," he said. "I haven't eaten all day, and I feel like I'm going to faint. My brain isn't working totally, so yeah. This is the best I've got right now."

"Why didn't you eat something?"

"Too nervous." He reached for the door and pulled it open to let out a blast of Indian music. Three or four couples waited in the area in front of the podium, and Abi looked up, a harried look on her face.

When she saw Zara, her smile erased the stress. "Zara," she said as if Zara could cure the crazy currently happening inside the restaurant. But it looked like a tour bus of Japanese travelers had arrived for dinner, and the whole place was packed.

Abi's eyes flickered to Noah. "Let me tell Mom and Dad you're here. They haven't taken dinner yet."

"Busy," Zara said, and Abi ran off. She turned back to Noah. "Maybe we should go. Try another night when things aren't so hectic here." She looked up at him, but he surveyed the restaurant, his dark eyes sharp and taking in every detail.

"Can't do it," he murmured, nodding toward something behind her. "Here come your parents now."

Zara spun around, her heart thrashing inside her chest. Sure enough, her mother and father were navigating through the restaurant toward them. Noah's hand slipped into hers and squeezed, and Zara tried to swallow.

Her throat stuck to itself, but she moved forward

anyway. This was not the introduction she'd envisioned, and she hurried to press her hands together and say, "Namaste." Then she said, "Mother, we can reschedule."

"Nonsense, nonsense," her mom said, her eyes drifting past Zara to Noah. It wasn't like Zara could conceal him.

"You're terribly busy tonight," Zara said, tugging Noah to her side. "Really, we can do this another time."

"Nani and Dadi have a corner booth," her father said, nodding to Zara. "Come with."

"Come with," her mother said, gesturing with her hands. Always the hands.

Zara swallowed, a little moisture in her mouth now, and looked up at Noah.

"Let's go with, sweetheart," he said, barely loud enough for her to hear. And she really had no other choice. She went with.

She bowed to her grandparents, who watched Noah like he was a fascinating film. He was much taller than anyone else, and she finally stepped back and said, "This is Noah Wales, His Royal Highness, Prince of Triguard."

Her words hung in the air, and she could tell her family had not been expecting that. She'd asked Noah how he'd have been introduced in his country, and she'd written down the words and memorized them.

"It's just Noah," he said with a smile, reaching to shake her father's hand. He pulled it back quickly and instead pressed his palms together, his fingertips at exactly chin-level, and nodded. "Namaste. Nice to meet you, sir."

Her father bowed too, and said, "I'm Samir. Please sit down."

Noah bowed to her mother first, and he looked so odd performing the Indian customs she'd grown up with. At the same time, he seemed perfectly natural doing them, and she felt herself falling a little bit farther toward being in love with him.

Which seemed impossible. She'd only known him for a month, and there was still so much to learn about him. But what she did know, she liked.

"Sit," her mother said, and Zara slid into the booth, realizing that once her mother and father joined them, she and Noah would be sandwiched in the middle. No way out.

She kept her smile in place, and spoke to Dadi, her mother's father about her upcoming show.

"Your sisters can't join us tonight," her father said. "But we'll have a celebration at the house soon."

Zara exchanged a glance with Noah. "Oh, we don't need to do that. We're not engaged, Dad."

"Are you really a prince?" her father asked, and Zara's gaze whipped back to Noah's.

"Yes, sir," he said. "Triguard is a tiny island off the coast of Italy. My father's king there, and my older brother, Damien, is set to rule one day."

"So you will not rule," her mother said.

"No, ma'am," he said, taking Zara's hand on top of the table, right in front of everyone. She was surprised her skin didn't incinerate with the way everyone looked at their joined fingers. "Barring an accident where every member of my family is killed, I won't rule. In fact, I'm probably going to move to Getaway Bay permanently." He lifted his arm around Zara's shoulders and smiled at her.

Her mother's eyebrows went up, as did everyone else's at the table. "You can't move?" she asked.

"Not without permission." He reached for the glass of water in front of him and drank from it properly. He'd had some serious training in entertaining or etiquette, and Zara had never seen this side of him before.

He was charming, and dashing, and absolutely everything he needed to be to satisfy her parents. Auntie Tanvi appeared and swept her eyes around the group. "Family tray?" she asked, her eyes landing and staying on Zara.

Her father nodded and said, "Yes, Auntie," and Tanvi left. She wasn't really related to them, but she'd been a family friend for decades, and Zara had grown up calling her auntie. In most social situations, she'd expect her parents to ask Noah questions, but they just sat there, looking at him. She couldn't tell if they were star-struck or just nervous.

"So the show is coming along well," she said to get the conversation started. "We open in eight days."

No one said anything, and Zara felt this evening slipping away from her. Out of her control. And crashing fast. Her mind blanked, and she couldn't think of a single way to salvage this conversation, this meal, this relationship.

CHAPTER FOURTEEN

Noah had never been happier for his lessons about small talk, entertaining dignitaries, and appearing like he was having a grand old time when he really just wanted to go home.

He carried the conversation almost single-handedly with Zara's parents, who couldn't seem to do much more than ask him a question and then wait for the answers.

How old are you?

How many siblings do you have?

Do you have a job?

Zara finally said, "Dad, stop grilling him."

"I am not grilling him," her father said. "I am getting to know him. It's normal to ask questions."

"So you have no job?" her mom asked, as if she didn't believe him the first time.

"Well, I'm a prince," he said. "My job is to volunteer around the country and serve the people." With sudden realization, he realized why his father had been so resistant to letting Noah just slip away from Triguard.

No, they didn't need Noah to volunteer in the country's libraries. But if he left, what would the headlines say? There would be an assumed scandal, and the fact was, Noah's service did keep the royal family in a good light.

So maybe his part in Triguard wasn't completely useless. Every muscle in his body tensed, and he cut a glance in Zara's direction. She hadn't relaxed since they'd left the mansion, and Noah's helplessness had his mood sinking fast.

He was going to call his dad tomorrow, and now he dreaded the task. The only way he could fathom that his dad would let him leave Triguard was if he told him the truth. And that meant outing Zara as his girlfriend, not the house sitter.

"Noah," Zara said, half under her breath, nudging him at the same time.

"I'm sorry," he said smoothly. "What did you say?"

She looked at him with those beautiful eyes, which looked a bit shiny. Glassy. Full of tears? "My dad asked how you'll leave your country if your job is there."

Noah opened his mouth to speak, the perfect answer always right at the tip of his tongue. But he wasn't Damien or Louisa, and he simply sat there. He snapped his lips closed and smiled. "Well, people change jobs," he finally said.

Two of Zara's sisters, Myra and Sai, appeared, and her mom and dad slid out of the booth to make room for them. Myra reached for the lamb and lentils and said, "So, Krisha says you're a prince."

Noah smiled, but he felt like he was about to crack. "That's right."

"Tell us about that." She looked genuinely interested, and thankfully, Zara came to life then, detailing the things he did, based on what he'd told her.

After they'd made it through meeting everyone and driving back up to the mansion in silence, Noah sat on the end of his bed, Boomer's head in his lap. "And it didn't go well," he told the dog after relaying a few other low points of the evening.

He heaved a sigh and finished taking off the suit. With a fresh T-shirt and a pair of gym shorts on, Noah collapsed back onto the bed. "I don't know, Boom. Maybe this is too hard." He stared up at the ceiling, realizing that he and Zara hadn't even cleared one roadblock on the highway toward a lasting relationship.

Her familial customs were so foreign to him. He hadn't expected that they'd fall down and worship him, but he had hoped for a smile at least. Her sisters seemed okay with the relationship, but Zara's parents had definitely been icy.

And he had no idea what to say to his father in the morning. As the minutes ticked by, Noah's mind went round and round, trying to find a solution that he was beginning to think simply didn't exist.

His phone rang before he'd gotten out of bed.

He'd managed to fall asleep at some point in the night, and because he didn't have to go down to Your Tidal Forever today, he'd set no alarm.

He saw *the King calls* on the screen, and was immediately awake. He sat up and swiped open the call. "Hey, Dad," he said, his voice only slightly hoarse.

"Did I wake you?"

"I had a rough night."

"Not sleeping again?" Of course his father knew of Noah's insomnia. Just because he was King didn't mean he wasn't also a good father.

"I...." He paused, the words right there in the back of his throat. He felt like he was standing on the edge of a cliff, and the only way back down to safe ground was to jump.

"I met my girlfriend's family," he said, his voice soft but strong. "And it didn't go well."

Silence poured through the line, and it was amazing to Noah how thick and dense it could feel from halfway around the world.

"So this is why you want to leave Triguard." His father wasn't asking, and Noah would be surprised if he hadn't at least suspected that Noah had met someone in Getaway Bay.

"Yes," Noah said.

"Noah." He sounded tired, and Noah could just see his father rubbing his forehead the way he did when he was trying to find the right thing to say. He never did it in public, but Noah had the privilege of seeing the king behind closed doors.

Noah said nothing. He had no defense for himself. His reputation as the bad boy prince didn't usually extend to women—until Katya. And then the press hadn't been all that surprised. He supposed his father wasn't either, and Noah didn't know what to do with how deeply his dad's disappointment cut him.

He'd once said, "I'm sorry I'm not Damien," to his father when they were arguing. His father had frozen, and all the fight had left his body.

"I don't want you to be Damien," his dad had said. "But you better figure out who you are and be that person."

Noah hadn't known what he meant at the time. He thought he knew who he was.

"Well, are you going to say anything else?" his dad asked. "Who is she?"

Noah pressed his eyes closed. He was not ashamed of Zara. He wasn't. But he also knew she was not the type of girl prince's brought home.

"Her name's Zara," he said. "She's a synchronized swimmer here on the island. She's...nice. She's *normal*, Dad."

"Mm," he said, making that humming noise that drove Noah up the wall. "Why didn't meeting her parents go well?"

"They're Indian," Noah said. "Very traditional. She's already broken ranks by not joining the family restaurant. It was just...awkward."

"But you still like her?"

"Of course," Noah said.

"And when can we meet Zara?"

"Oh, it's too early for that," Noah said with a chuckle. "We've only been seeing each other a few weeks."

"A few weeks?" The sharpness in his dad's voice sliced right through Noah's eardrums. "You only left Venice a few weeks ago."

"So it's been less than that. I don't know."

"I thought you were laying low."

"I was. I *am*." Noah hated how he felt like a child who'd done something wrong. Again. This was why he just wanted a normal life. No titles. No castles. No security detail. No crowns.

"Then how did you meet her?"

Noah hesitated again. "Promise you won't be angry?"

"Noah, you're thirty-one-years-old. Even if I was angry, what can I do?"

"Well, I thought Mom would send Ivan or Vince over here to get me."

"Oh, she's mentioned it."

Horror struck Noah right between the ribs. "She's not going to do that, is she?"

"I've managed to make that plan B or C," his dad said.

"What's plan A?"

"To treat you like you know what you're doing," his dad said, as if it was the most obvious plan of all.

"Dad, I have no idea what I'm doing." Noah didn't want to admit it, but he felt freer after the words left his mouth.

"Well, then, it's time to figure it out. Damien took a while too, but he's getting there. Your sister is days away from being engaged. Your mother wants you here for that Noah. And I do agree with her on that."

"Well, I can come for a party, sure," Noah said. "It's not like I'm never going to come to Triguard again. I just want…anonymity. And Getaway Bay is perfect for that."

"Mm."

Noah turned from the picturesque water beyond the glass in his bedroom. He paced over to the door and back. "Dad," he finally said.

"Louisa's engagement is on Wednesday," he said. "Your mother and I expect you here. We can discuss Zara and everything else then."

"Wednesday?" Noah echoed. "Dad, I don't know if I—"

"It's either you book your own ticket and be here by four p.m., or Ivan will come get you on Tuesday and escort you back."

"Dad, Zara's opening show is on Friday. I can't miss it."

"I don't see why you would."

But Noah nerves were vibrating. Even if he could fly out early on Thursday morning, he wouldn't get back to Getaway Bay until Friday morning, what with the time difference. And a discussion with his mother and father had never gone less than an hour, and that was about which type of china the family should order for their heritage meal.

Something like Noah leaving the country and marrying a synchronized swimmer? That felt like an all-day session to him, and he'd most definitely miss Zara's show then.

"Noah, I'm inclined to grant your request, but I need something from you. A couple of things, actually. I need you here for Louisa's engagement announcement. And I need to know how you and Zara met."

CHAPTER FIFTEEN

Zara pushed herself out of the pool, the sound of Ian's bark coming easily through the water streaming off of her and through her swim cap. Her muscles trembled, and she was starving. They'd been practicing for ten hours, and she had a feeling no matter what happened, Ian would not be satisfied.

She stood on the deck, her chest heaving as she tried to make up for the oxygen she had deprived herself of while underwater. At least she wasn't in Ian's direct line of fire. But she knew she could do her kicks sharper, and she'd run into someone underwater on their last run. So she had some room for improvement too—and the show was only a week away.

Ian finally released them with, "Be here by eight tomorrow," which was an hour earlier than normal. Zara sighed, her stomach roaring at her for something to eat. She stooped by her bag and pulled out a towel to wipe her eyes.

"Is he always this intense?"

She glanced over at the question, asked by James, one of the acrobats who did the high dives.

"Unfortunately, yes," she said with a weary smile.

James watched Ian's retreating back and then looked at Zara again. "A bunch of us are going to dinner if you want to come."

"Thanks," Zara said, a flash of missing hitting her. She usually did spend a lot of time with the cast of the shows she was in, exercising and getting meals. But since she'd met Noah, she'd driven straight back to the mansion to spend evenings with him.

"James," someone called, and he waved to them.

He turned back to her. "So are you coming?"

"Oh, she can't," Suzie said, appearing on Zara's other side and dropping her swim cap into her bag. "She's got a secret boyfriend up in this house on the bluffs." She was practically whispering by the end of her sentence.

Zara rolled her eyes as Suzie started giggling. "But I'd love to go to dinner."

James grinned and said, "All right. We're meeting out front in ten minutes. Everyone's invited." He walked away then, his broad shoulders rippling with muscles.

Zara tossed her towel into her bag. "Thanks for that." She lifted the bag, her shoulder groaning with the added weight.

"Well, it's true." Suzie followed her toward the locker room.

Zara wasn't sure if her friend was upset they hadn't hung out as much as they normally would have, or if she was just stating a fact. And Zara was too tired to try to figure it out. She'd eaten everything she'd brought from the mansion, and there was no way she was making it up the bluff without finding food first.

She opened her locker and saw her phone flashing with both green and blue lights. She was instantly twice as exhausted as she had been previously, but she reached for her phone with her free hand while she dropped her heavy swim bag to the ground.

She had texts from Noah, as well as two of her sisters. She had missed calls from Noah and someone named Petra. She frowned at that name, her slow, calorie-deprived mind taking a few extra moments to try to figure out who Petra was.

All at once, she remembered.

Noah's mother.

The woman who'd hired Zara to housesit the mansion on the bluff.

Her blood felt like ice in her veins, and her heart pumped harder and harder to keep her circulation going.

She sank onto the thin bench in front of the lockers and ignored Suzie when she asked what was the matter.

What was the matter?

Zara was going to lose her job, that was what the matter was. Not only that, she'd probably have to pay Petra back. After all, the house-sitting gig was supposed to go through the beginning of September, and it was barely July.

She tapped on Petra's texts first. Sure enough, her words felt like cannons firing through Zara's system.

I just found out my son has been staying at the beach house, which means I obviously don't need a house sitter.

Zara decided to let the technicalities of what constituted a beach house slide by.

He claims there's been no impropriety, and that you are indeed his girlfriend. However, I don't need to pay someone to be my son's lover. Therefore, I would like you to be out of the house by tonight, and I will need two-thirds of the money back.

Zara's head felt like it weighed hundreds of pounds and she couldn't hold it up. Her neck ached, and her heartbeat wouldn't stop jumping around her chest.

There was no way she could be out of the house tonight. She had nowhere to go. And worse, his mother's words felt full of acid, and Zara feared she'd never please the woman now. The fact that she wanted to was ridiculous, but Noah was her boyfriend….

Not her lover.

Zara's fight and determination flew back into her body. So what if this woman was a queen? Zara had a contract with her, and she had been doing the job she'd agreed to.

Before arguing back with her, though, she swiped over to Noah's messages.

Zara, I just got off the phone with my father. I told him everything. I'm so sorry.

Zara, call me when you go to lunch.

Zara, my mother is livid about the house-sitting. I'm trying to talk to her. Don't do anything yet.

Zara, Zara, Zara.

He'd called twice too, and Zara's head hurt from all the drama. All the swimming. So much hunger. She slumped against the lockers, but all that did was make her back hurt.

She'd known she and Noah were from different worlds, and yet, she'd allowed herself to believe they could build a bridge between them. One step at a time. Wasn't that what Noah had said?

And she'd been foolish enough to believe him.

She shook her head and got to her feet. Petra wanted her out of the house, so she'd get out of the house. She hadn't spent any of the money she'd gotten from house-sitting, so she'd just send some of it back.

Easy.

Done.

But she knew as she walked toward her car that nothing about what was happening was easy. She knew, because her heart was beating strangely. She knew, because she didn't answer Noah's call when it came in. She knew, because she didn't drive up the bluff to the mansion the way she had been for weeks now.

Instead, she drove over to the Sweet Breeze Resort and Spa and checked into a room. No, she couldn't really afford it, but all the performers in Ian's shows got half-price rooms at Sweet Breeze. So she splurged and ordered room service, showered while she waited, and wheeled the cart into her room wearing a fluffy, white robe once she was ready.

She ate, simply going through the motions her body needed to do to stay alive. Her mind whirred constantly, but she couldn't see a way out of the mess she and Noah had created. She shook her head at herself.

"What were you thinking?"

She pulled out her phone to text Petra an apology and that she was out of the house. She wasn't sure when she could go get her things—or Whitewater—but it didn't matter. She had her swim bag and her purse, and she could get her stuff out of storage as soon as she found a new apartment. Maybe Noah would feed Whitewater for her, but she didn't have the mental energy to ask him right now.

Another text from Noah had come before she could text his mother, and she hadn't heard her phone chime. *Where are you? Ian said practice ended over an hour ago.*

He'd called Ian?

A spark of anger ignited in Zara's blood. Of course, Noah had endless resources at his disposal—and she'd used her credit card at Sweet Breeze. So it was only a matter of time before he showed up here.

Instead of waiting for him to track her down, she sent him a text. *Sweet Breeze Resort, room 1215.*

Half an hour later, a knock sounded on the door, and Zara stared at it, trying to decide if she should open it and face Noah, or ignore him. Since she wasn't in junior high anymore, she crossed the room and unlatched the door before twisting the knob and opening it.

Sure enough, Noah stood there, his dark eyes blazing with all kinds of powerful emotions. "There you are. I've called you a bunch of times."

"Three times," she said, as if the number really mattered.

"Fine, three times." He stepped into her personal space,

and she fell back to allow him entrance into the room. "Did you listen to my messages?"

"Nope." Zara let the heavy hotel door swing shut, the resulting *crash!* so loud she cringed.

"Have you texted or called my mother?"

"No, siree."

Noah turned and glared at her. "Zara, this is serious."

"I know this is serious," she snapped. "Why do you think I'm at this hotel I can't afford? Your mom told me to get out of the house by tonight. So I did. I've been off work for a couple of hours, and I was starving. So I showered and I ate, and I'm trying to figure out what to do." Her chest heaved, and tears pricked her eyes. She was so tired, and she just wanted the fun, easy, casual month she'd enjoyed with Noah to be her reality all the time.

His expression softened, and he said, "All right," in a voice made of marshmallows. "All right." He stepped into her and gathered her into his arms, holding her close to his heart while she worked to contain her emotions.

She did not want to cry in front of him. She would not.

"I spoke to my mother," he said. "I convinced her not to take the money back, because you have been taking care of the house. I do nothing there."

"You cook," Zara argued, because she could. Had he really asked his mother to let Zara keep the money?

"And I've moved out," he said. "So there's no reason you shouldn't be at the mansion, taking care of it according to the contract you signed with my mom. You'll earn your money, and you'll have a place to live." He pulled back and held her at arm's length. "Maybe now you can have your girlfriends up to the house for that pool party."

The way he looked at her, all soft smiles and crinkly eyes, and Zara became more confused than ever.

"You moved out?" The thought of staying in that huge house alone—which had once appealed to her greatly—now felt like a threat.

"Yeah. Boomer and I found a little cabin on the beach. It's nice, and he likes the ocean."

"You're such a liar." She could hear the fib in his voice. "Boomer does like the water, so the 'cabin' must not be nice."

"So it's missing a few amenities. I'll be fine."

"What kind of amenities?" Zara narrowed her eyes at him.

"I'll hardly be there anyway," he said instead of answering. "I'm flying to Triguard on Monday."

Alarm pulled through Zara. "You are? Why?"

"My sister is getting engaged on Wednesday, and I need to be there for the event. I'll be meeting with my parents on Tuesday night to talk about...everything."

Zara stepped out of his arms and searched for the bravery she needed to speak.

"What?" he asked when she couldn't quite find it.

"I think this might be too hard," she whispered.

"Zara," he said, his voice full of compassion but also argument. "It's fine. I've worked everything out."

And he likely had. He'd always been able to get what he wanted, even tickets to a sold-out show. But his parents had not granted him permission to leave Triguard permanently, and her parents had not appreciated that he was a prince. Apparently, nice Indian men were higher on the social ladder than royalty.

And she'd caused a rift in his family because of the house-sitting, and she felt dishonest though she *had* been taking care of the house the way Petra had asked her to.

"Did you tell your mom about my cat?" she asked.

"Of course not."

"You said everything."

"Well, I'd actually forgotten about Whitewater." He smiled at her gently. "Okay? Everything is going to be okay."

Zara didn't know what else to do, and she wanted to believe that Noah really could work everything out. So she nodded, let him draw her back into his arms, and bit back the idea of asking him if he at least had running water and a working sewer.

CHAPTER SIXTEEN

Noah knew there were different levels of comfort in a bed. Intellectually. But he'd never experienced it as first-hand as he did that first night in the beach cottage he'd found on a moment's notice.

Sure, he could've gotten one of the condos in the posh buildings near the new Ohana resort, but there wasn't anything available on the first floor. Noah didn't want to take an elevator ride every time Boomer needed to go out and take care of his business.

He'd searched online, and for being touristy, Getaway Bay didn't have a lot available for move-in immediately. Of course, it was the height of summer, and there would certainly be more opening up once autumn came.

He really hoped he'd still be on the island then, but his hopes for getting permission to leave Triguard permanently seemed like a distant dot on the distant horizon.

Like the sleep he was trying to get on this rock-hard

mattress. He finally pushed the flimsy blanket off and said, "Come on, Boomer. The hammock will be more comfortable than that bed."

He could call the furniture store and order the nicest thing they had, authorize them to come in whenever they could, even if he was back home.

Home.

He stared at the dark water, marveling at how it kept coming ashore no matter what. He also liked that it seemed mysterious and a bit sinister in the moonlight as opposed to how joyful and bright it was during the day.

Would Getaway Bay ever feel like home to him? Or would he be a perpetual vacationer here?

His day had been one of chaos. Dozens of texts and phone calls. Desperation all the way up his throat as he tried to find a way to appease his mother while keeping Zara employed. When he'd found out his mother had texted her *and* called her, demanding she move out of the mansion and return most of the money?

Noah hadn't felt that level of anger in a long, long time. Thankfully, he still had access to his bank account, and he'd found this beach house—er, shack—and said he'd already moved out of the mansion, that Zara was doing the job she'd been hired to do, and there was no reason that had to change.

His parents were not happy with him, and Noah wondered how old he'd have to be before they let him make adult decisions for himself. Because he was not letting Zara go without a fight.

As he watched the moonlight glint off the water, he had

the sinking feeling that a fight was exactly what he would get when he touched down in Triguard. He'd booked his own ticket, choosing to go before the engagement announcement so he could return to Getaway Bay in time for Zara's show on Friday night.

He was absolutely not missing it.

Her words from earlier—*maybe this is too hard*—rotated around in his very alert mind. He hadn't liked the sound of them, and he'd promised her that everything would work out. But he honestly had no idea if it would or not.

Her parents hadn't liked him all that much, and the roadblocks they faced seemed insurmountable. He collapsed into the hammock, glad he was right about one thing. It was infinitely more comfortable than that blasted bed.

SUNDAY NIGHT, HE DROVE TO THE AIRPORT, READY FOR his trip to Triguard. It would take a day and a half to get there, and he was already annoyed. He landed in Newark sometime near morning, and had half a mind to wander around the state of New Jersey as if he were a regular man. Maybe ride the subway or visit a park. Maybe carry a briefcase, like he had a job to get to like everyone else.

In the end, he found a hotel that would let him check into a room that hadn't been used the previous night, and he slept for most of his eighteen-hour layover. The bed wasn't the best he'd slept in, but it beat the beach cottage by a large margin.

The sun shone brightly in Triguard when he landed, which totally didn't reflect his mood. Exhaustion weighed him down, and he just wanted to crawl into bed and sleep for a while. Though he'd flown first class, his legs didn't fold right on an airplane, and he was in no mood for the press—or for his family for that matter.

But word had obviously gotten out that he'd be arriving today, because the reporters were five deep as he walked out of the airport. His father had decreed they could not go inside, and there was a special, roped-off area for them.

Noah had never been happier for sunglasses, as he was sure if the photographers caught sight of his eyes, they'd have a dozen speculations as to why he looked so thrashed. As it was, he grinned and lifted his hand in a royal wave, as if he was so incredibly happy to be back in his home country.

He took a deep breath, his grin stuck in place, and a strong pull of happiness did move through him at being home. After all, there was nothing like his mother's hug, and he was suddenly anxious to get on his way toward the castle.

But he knew he had some major public relations work to do, so he signed whatever someone put in front of him, noticing that there were several children with books they wanted him to scrawl his name in.

He took the most time with them, asking, "Have you read this one?"

"Yes," the little boy said.

Noah flipped it over and looked at the front cover. "Oh, I love this one." He grinned at the boy, who couldn't be older than ten. "The ending is a little sad, don't you think?"

He nodded, his eyes wide. His mother kept a grip on his shoulder like Noah might somehow infect him with some sort of bad boy disease if she let her son get too closer. Noah tousled the boy's hair, and said, "Well, keep reading, bud. It's the best way to travel."

He straightened and smiled at the mom, who grinned right back at him. He repeated this process until everyone had been satisfied. The press had taken hundreds of pictures, and once the last person had been taken care of, a reporter yelled, "Where have you been, Prince Noah?"

Prince Noah.

He hadn't been called that for a long time.

"Overseas," he said. "Great for the psyche."

"Are you home for good?" someone asked at the same time someone else called, "Are the rumors about Princess Louisa true?"

Noah waved and hitched his bag higher on his shoulder. "I've been gone for months. I'm sure I don't know what's going on with my sister." He glanced around for his ride, sure his father had arranged something for him. After all, Noah had passed along his flight info, which someone had obviously "leaked" to the media.

He'd been standing outside talking to people for about twenty minutes now, and as he glanced down the busy street, he saw the long limousine with the royal flags. He stepped right over to the curb and lifted his hand as if the driver wouldn't know where he was.

Sure enough, Luc eased to a stop with the back door

only inches from Noah's hand, but he didn't open the door. He never did. He waited for Luc to do it. After all, they paid the man an exorbitant amount of money to drive the limousine and open doors.

He came around and said, "Good afternoon, Prince Noah. So good to see you."

Noah's heart swelled, and he said, "Good to see you too, Luc." And it really was. The servants had never judged Noah, and he'd never been so appreciative of that fact as he was right now. Luc reached for the door handle, and Noah edged to the side, almost desperate to get in the car, get behind those tinted windows, get some relief from this public appearance stuff he wasn't so good at.

But Luc didn't allow him into the car. He stood back as Noah's father, the King himself, unfolded his tall frame from the car. He buttoned his suit coat and looked at the press. He lifted one hand and smiled the same way Noah had before turning to his son.

So many things were said in those few seconds. So much communicated with the meeting of eyes and a few moments of time. Noah's emotions swelled and roared, and he knew his father loved him. Screw ups and all.

His dad took the couple of steps to Noah and embraced him, sending the reporters into a complete tizzy. "Welcome home, son," he said, his voice soft and sincere, and Noah held onto him like his life depended on it.

It was as if thirty-one years of emotions bubbled to the surface all at once. Noah had kept everything bottled up, only showing what he couldn't control in rare instances. He'd long thought his brother and sister were simply better at everything, but really, they were better at blowing off steam behind closed doors, while Noah sometimes erupted when there were cameras around.

He stepped back as his father released him and turned back to the crowd. "Thank you all for respecting the crown," he said. "And don't forget. We have a royal announcement tomorrow evening, at six p.m." With that, he turned toward Luc, nodded, and slid gracefully into the back of the limo.

Noah followed him, ignoring the shouted questions from the media. Inside the car, he found his mother and Damien, and surprise rolled through him that they hadn't gotten out of the vehicle.

"Mom," he said, accepting her side hug, which wasn't nearly as good as the full thing. He glanced at his brother, who wore a completely unreadable look. "What's going on? Where's Louisa?" Might as well have made it a family reunion in the back of the limo, though it was bad enough the King and his heir were in the same car.

Something was really going down, and nerves ran through Noah.

"She's busy preparing for the engagement announcement," his mother said.

"Why didn't you guys get out?"

"Clara said it would be more powerful to have your father welcome you home." His mother flicked something invisible off her skirt. "She said I always forgive you, and you needed to be seen with the King as he welcomed you back with open arms."

Noah met his father's eye again. "And am I welcomed back with open arms?"

"Of course," his dad said, and Noah nodded. Their conversations these past few weeks had been civil. Personal. Familial. Noah had never felt like he didn't belong in his own family—not the way Zara did. He just felt…stifled by the royalty of it.

"What else did Clara say I need to do?" he asked, thinking their press secretary should've come along for the ride too.

"She's lined up a speaking opportunity for you," his mother said, exchanging a glance with Damien.

"Mother, I'm not going to be here long enough for a speaking opportunity." His flight left on Thursday at noon, and with the day and a half trip home, and the eleven-hour time difference, he'd have exactly an hour to spare before Zara made her first dive into the water.

He was not missing it.

His mom said nothing, and Noah looked at Damien too. "What's going on?"

Time seemed to slow as the car continued to move, but no one spoke. Only his mother looked uncomfortable, and Noah realized Damien really was ready to take the throne.

"We need you to stay for a few weeks," he finally said.

"A few weeks?" Noah practically yelled, heat shooting from his toes to his brain. "No." He shook his head now. "I can't do that. I can't."

"We checked on Zara's show, dear," his mother said like he was being petulant on purpose. "It runs all summer. You can see it when you return."

"No, I can't," he said. "It's sold out, and I had to beg, borrow, and practically turn over my inheritance to get the tickets I did." He couldn't miss opening night. It meant a lot to Zara, and he had to be there.

"We're sorry," his mother said, and Noah wanted to rage at her. Sorry? In that moment, he didn't understand his parents or his brother. Couldn't they understand he wanted something different for his life?

"We'd like Zara to come here," his father said, and Noah's gaze shot to him.

"She's working, Dad. She can't just leave the show."

"Of course." He looked out the window.

"Well, Louisa needs an escort around the island as she celebrates with the people, and Clara thought you'd be the best man for the job. It'll repair your reputation and allow you the opportunity to leave Triguard as you wish."

"Why can't Eric escort her?"

"He'll be with you, yes," Damien said. "But it's improper for them to travel alone, and they need an entourage."

Noah scoffed. Of course Louisa and Eric wouldn't be traveling alone. They'd likely have two security guards each, with an additional four undercover, following from a distance.

"This is ridiculous," he said. He wondered what his parents would do if he snuck out of the castle and tried to board the plane on Thursday the way his original itinerary had planned for him to do.

Desperation clogged his throat, and he wanted to text Zara right now and tell her how insane his family was being. But it was two o'clock in the morning there, and he didn't want her to know about any speedbumps.

Then she'd say their relationship was too hard, and when he got back to Getaway Bay—*if* he ever did—she wouldn't be his to kiss anymore.

"I have a plane ticket," he said.

"We'll exchange it," Damien said easily, as if he himself knew how to do such things.

"Louisa needs you, dear," his mom said, and Noah shook his head.

"No, she doesn't."

"No," his father said. "She doesn't. But Noah, you have things to explain to us about Venice, and a reputation with your countrymen to fix because of it. Then we want to know everything about Zara, and how you two met and what's been happening between you. And then, *if* you behave while on this engagement tour, then I'll consider letting you leave Triguard."

Noah heard the threat in his father's voice, definitely heard the emphasis on the word *if*, and absolutely saw the blazing fire in his dad's eyes.

He leaned back against the seat, wishing with everything inside him that he'd never come home. Because it felt like now that he was back on the tiny island where he'd been born and raised, he would never be leaving it again.

CHAPTER SEVENTEEN

Zara shook out her hands, her performance swimming suit on, along with her cap and her goggles. Her nerves zipped through her with the crackling speed of electricity, and she hoped her parents hadn't had too hard of a time parking.

They didn't like coming down to the beach, but the venue was partly outdoors, and there wasn't a lot of parking. If they'd park over by Your Tidal Forever, there'd be a shuttle, but her dad complained about those too.

Hopefully one of her grandparents had just dropped them off.

Zara couldn't believe her thoughts were consumed with her parents and their parking woes. At least they were here. Noah had texted a few times and called once to say that he wouldn't be making it to the show.

Her disappointment still tasted bitter on the back of her tongue, coated her throat as she tried to swallow.

"You ready?" Suzie asked, wearing the same swimming suit as Zara.

"Yes," she said, pushing her parents and Noah and everything out of her mind. She needed to focus and put on the performance of her life. People had paid a lot of money to come see this show, and she'd rehearsed for hundreds if not thousands of hours to give them something to talk about.

"You're up," Suzie said, and Zara pushed out of the locker room and made her way into the pool, securing her nose clips as she went. She dove down to the platform and grabbed on to the handle there. She held her breath and fluttered her feet slightly.

The platform jerked, and she went with it, her feet slamming into it as it moved up, up, up and out of the water. It rose about ten feet, and then a man named Beni joined her, his smile as wide as hers.

Then the platform ascended again, the acrobats and swimmers around them climbing and flipping and creating beautiful, three-dimensional art with their positions.

The music crescendoed, and right at the height of it, she and Beni pushed off and leapt into the air. She flipped and twisted, straightening out about halfway toward the water. She entered the pool cleanly, a definite slap of water against her senses, but she could still hear the applause.

Or maybe she was hallucinating. She wasn't sure.

But when she pushed herself out of the pool and waved at the crowd, they definitely cheered louder for her, the female high-diver that had started the show with a bang.

She slipped back into the water and got in formation

with the other girls, their synchronized movements so familiar and comforting that Zara forgot about the empty house she had to go home to, the lecture she'd probably get from her mother about the high cut of her swimming suit, and the fact that Noah was probably never going to get permission to leave Triguard.

Okay, so that last one didn't get completely forgotten, but at least it took up space in the very back of Zara's mind, leaving her room to focus on the show.

After the show ended, Zara wrapped herself in a robe and went to see her family.

"You were wonderful, Zara," her mother said, drawing her into a hug. "Just wonderful." She kissed both of Zara's cheeks and beamed at her. "How you wear that swimming suit, I don't know, but that dive. Oh." She put her palm over her heart and looked at her husband. "Wasn't she wonderful?"

"So good," he said. "Just so good." He embraced her too and all of Zara's sisters came forward. She appreciated their support, and her emotions swirled and made her choke up a little. Thankfully, she didn't cry, and after all the congratulations and all the hugs, she went back into the locker room to get packed up.

Her body hurt, and all she wanted to do was go home. In that moment, under the bright fluorescent lights in the locker room, she realized she didn't have a home.

Not really.

The mansion on the bluff wasn't hers. She'd given up her apartment.

"Coming to dinner with us?" Jill asked, pulling her swim cap off.

"Yes," Zara said immediately. The cast usually went out together after shows, and she was thrilled she could prolong the solitary drive up to the bluffs. "I'm starved."

Jill laughed and started changing. She and Suzie accepted Zara right back into the group as if she hadn't abandoned them for the past month while she and Noah dated. As she walked with them out to Suzie's car, she couldn't help checking her phone.

Noah knew what day it was, and she expected to see a text from him. A quick note of luck. Something.

Her screen was blank.

Triguard was eleven hours ahead of Getaway Bay, and surely he was out of bed by now. In fact, she'd never known him to sleep much past five o'clock in the morning.

But he hadn't texted, and Zara's heart withered a little as she got in the backseat of Suzie's sedan. She shoved her phone in her pocket when Suzie said, "So, I'm seeing this guy named Ryan...."

Zara didn't hear from Noah in the morning, nor did he text or call on opening weekend at all. She was beginning to think he'd fallen off the face of the Earth, or that he'd been a mirage on this island when she'd needed someone the most. Or that he'd been lying to her this whole time about who he was.

So Monday morning, she sat down with her laptop at the kitchen counter where she'd eaten his cooking dozens of times. She pulled up a search window and put his name in. The results exploded down the screen, and he definitely existed.

Relief sighed through her.

Not only did he exist, but he was also a prince. Double sigh.

And if the pictures and headlines could be believed, he was currently on an engagement tour with his sister Louisa, and her fiancé Eric.

Exactly as he'd told her he would be. He hadn't mentioned that he would be completely unavailable or that he'd forget about her the moment he stepped foot back on his home island country of Triguard.

Zara tried to push away the negative feelings. She slammed her laptop closed with a little too much force, her frustration at his complete silence digging into her in the most uncomfortable way. But he'd known how hard she'd been training for this show, and he'd seemed genuinely upset that he wouldn't be able to use his tickets.

With nothing to do until later that afternoon, Zara suited up and wandered out to the pool. She'd thought this summer would be one of relaxation with fruity drinks, and it hadn't been that way very often.

But today...today, she was going to spend the morning poolside, with that strawberry mango smoothie and the hot Hawaiian sun beating down on her.

And tonight? Tonight, she was inviting all the cast

members to come to the mansion for a midnight pool party. Thinking fast, she swiped open the app on her phone and started tapping to order a few groceries. Soda and chips, salsa and dips, sub sandwiches, and a veggie platter should do the trick.

After all, she couldn't spend all her free time pining away after Noah. The pictures she'd glimpsed on the Internet were enough to know he certainly wasn't shut away in a castle tower, moping about.

No, he'd been wearing expensive suits, and waving to the crowd, and signing autographs. She glanced at her phone. Maybe she could just call him. It would be evening in Triguard, and maybe he could talk for a few minutes. She went back inside and distracted herself by making the smoothie she wanted. But back by the pool, her phone taunted her.

In the end, she sent off a quick text that said, *Opening weekend went great! Hope you're having fun on the tour.*

He didn't answer, and Zara smoothed sunscreen over her exposed skin, knowing the last thing she needed was a sunburn. An hour later, after she woke from her catnap, she texted Suzie about the pool party that night, opened the door when the grocery delivery guy arrived, and checked her phone obsessively.

Noah still had not answered, and her frustrations were starting to morph into worries. Maybe something had happened to him. Maybe he'd lost his phone. Maybe it had been damaged from a stampeding herd of women, chasing after the handsome, eligible prince-bachelor.

Zara disliked the poisonous thoughts in her mind, but

it sure seemed as if Noah had forgotten about her already. And as much as she wished that idea didn't sting her to the core, the fact was that it did.

As she went through her swim bag one last time to make sure she had everything for that night's performance, her phone finally chimed.

The message said it was from Noah, and Zara's heart tapdanced inside her chest.

I am having fun on the tour.

Zara started at the words, trying to make sense of them, when another text came in. *Prince Noah seems to be as well.*

Prince Noah. Zara's fingers tingled and she felt a little removed from her body as the realization that someone else had Noah's phone hit her. *Who is this?* she typed out and sent.

Katya.

Zara stared at the single word. No last name, as if Katya was as famous as someone like Madonna or Cher.

What in the world was Noah doing on his sister's engagement tour with the woman who'd ruined his reputation?

Had he been lying to her this whole time?

She checked the time—she was about to be late—and saw that it was almost two-thirty. So it was one-thirty in the morning in Triguard. And Katya had Noah's phone.

Zara's stomach twisted and turned over, making her feel like she was about to throw up. She didn't want to keep talking to Katya, but she had no guarantee that Noah would ever get his phone back.

She stuffed her phone in her back pocket, shouldered her bag, and stormed out of the house. She had a show to do. A party to put on. And sleep to get.

Then she'd figure out what was going on with Noah and Katya.

CHAPTER EIGHTEEN

Noah pressed his back into the door of the villa, his fingers fumbling to make sure the lock had engaged. He wouldn't put it past Katya to come barging in without knocking, as she'd done it twice on this tour already.

His head pounded with thoughts of Zara and what she must think of him. He had to figure out how to get in touch with her. He knew what he needed to do; he just didn't want to ask his mother for Zara's phone number during the tour. He didn't want to jeopardize his chances of getting permission to leave his country for good.

At the same time, he wondered why he needed permission at all. He'd been gone for several months before, and why couldn't he just relocate and return to Triguard for visits? But he knew that princes didn't always get what they wanted, especially those who wouldn't rule.

Maybe he could ask Louisa to ask their mother for Zara's number.

Always back to Zara.

But Noah felt like he was one breath away from suffocating without being able to contact her. Everything had happened so quickly, and he could barely make sense of it even in quiet moments.

"Ambushed," he muttered to himself as he pushed away from the door. His family had ambushed him with Katya's presence and subsequent announcement that she would be accompanying him on the engagement tour.

Three weeks with the woman who'd lied about him, caused him to flee Venice, and didn't even appear remorseful about any of it. Oh, no. His mother had been busy buying her dresses and getting her hair fixed so Katya could be presented as respectable. So she could hang on his arm and they could pretend to be together.

"Just for a few weeks," his mother had said, looking at Clara. The public relations director had then launched into the insane plan to restore Noah's reputation, at which point he and Katya would have a quiet break-up, and if he'd behaved and played his part well, he might get what he wanted most—Zara and a normal life in Getaway Bay.

He might have been able to go along with the plan better had he been able to communicate with Zara in any way. But his phone had been "accidentally" dropped into the koi pool in his mother's personal suite, and he'd been presented with a new one.

A new one without any contacts in it, and he didn't memorize phone numbers. He'd messaged Zara through the one social media app he'd found her on, but she hadn't responded. She didn't look terribly active there, as her last post was four months old. With every minute and hour that passed, Noah's hope leaked away.

Knocking sounded on his door, and he jumped like a skittish cat. Couldn't he get five minutes of peace?

"Who is it?" he asked through the solid wood.

"Louisa," his sister said. "Hurry up and let me in."

Noah did exactly that, and she darted into the room. He closed the door swiftly behind her and asked, "Who are you running from?"

She patted her hair, smoothing her royal persona back into place along with the errant strands. "Katya."

"Oh, so that makes two of us." He gave her a dark glare and went back into the kitchen. There'd be no alcohol here, and even if there was, Noah wouldn't consume it. He knew better than to drink and try to impress people and reporters at the same time.

He did need an escape though, and the fact that Louisa did too spoke volumes.

"We're at the very beginning of this tour," he said. "Are we going to survive?" He opened the fridge and found soda and water. "Want something to drink?"

"Water, please."

He handed his sister a chilled bottle and took one for himself too. "Why are you doing this tour?"

"Mother thought it would be good for my image," she said. "Damien's not married, and he doesn't have many prospects at the moment. It's quite...untraditional."

"Well, maybe some of our traditions should be changed."

"Noah," Louisa said reprovingly.

"What will happen when you produce an heir first?" he asked, lifting his eyebrows. "I mean, come on, Louisa. Does it really matter if you tour for weeks?" He shook his head as he uncapped his bottle.

"Damien will be King," she said. "And his first heir will be next in line, no matter how many children I have first."

"Exactly," Noah said. "So why does it matter if you tour around, shaking hands and smiling for the camera? It doesn't make a bit of difference."

"It does in public perception," she said.

Noah grunted and drank. After swallowing, he said, "And public perception is all that matters."

Louisa opened her mouth, probably to argue, but more knocking came on the door. Noah knew this rap, and he rolled his eyes. "Katya."

"She really is an interesting woman," Louisa said.

"She really was in trouble that night in Venice," Noah said, wishing it didn't come out so defensively.

"I know." Louisa put her hand on Noah's arm, drawing his attention from the closed door. "Father looked her up. Everything about her. Interviewed her three times. We believe you, Noah. It's just—"

"About public perception," they said together.

"I know," Noah added, a sigh of exhaustion passing through his whole body. "I don't know if I can do this for two more weeks."

"You have to." She straightened and tossed her long, dark hair over her shoulder. "I'll deal with her tonight."

"Thank you," Noah murmured. "Louisa?"

She turned back to him, and the powerful connection of siblings flowed between them. He saw her as a small girl who he used to follow around. She'd pour tea for her animals, and she only ever let him bring one "guest" to the parties—a ratty stuffed elephant he'd gotten from their excursion to Africa when he was four years old.

"Could you maybe get Zara's number for me? Or get in touch with her and let her know what's going on?"

Sadness crossed his sister's face. "I can't, Noah."

"Why not?"

"Because any little leak to the press about how this isn't real could be disastrous for us."

"And you trust Katya to keep her mouth shut?" Because Noah didn't. The woman had already lied and spread rumors once.

"Father does," she said. "So I must."

"So no Zara."

"Not for a few more weeks," Louisa said. "I'm so sorry, Noah. It's obvious you care for her."

Noah nodded, his jaw tight, his teeth clenched, his heart struggling to beat. He wasn't sure Zara would be overly excited to hear from him in a few weeks. In fact, he was quite sure she'd break up with him long before then.

"If she loves you as much as you love her, she'll understand." Louisa ducked her chin and turned back to the door. Noah moved out of sight as she opened the door and said, "Katya, why don't we take dinner in my suite tonight?"

The door closed behind them, and Noah hurried across the room to lock it again.

If she loves you as much as you love her.

Noah wasn't in love with Zara. Was he?

He shook his head, his stomach grumbling for something with more calories than water. No, he wasn't in love with Zara—unless she was in love with him. Could she be in love with him?

The confusing thoughts went round and round, and Noah wanted nothing more than to talk to her. Hear her voice. Assure her that nothing she saw online was true and that he was doing everything he could to return to her and Getaway Bay as fast as possible, for as long as possible.

But he couldn't even text her, and Noah had never been so frustrated.

A WEEK LATER, NOAH'S IRRITATION ONCE AGAIN ROSE TO a level he'd never known. He kept a tight grip on Katya's hand, his plastic smile cemented in place. But he was livid and about to blow. He wished Louisa and Eric would hurry up and finish so he could get away from this insufferable woman, get out of this excruciatingly hot suit, and somehow find relief.

He'd never been overly religious, but he prayed now, harder than he ever had.

Because Katya had kissed him. Right in front of the

reporters, as if they were so madly in love and couldn't wait to be on their own engagement tour. In fact, she may have said those words. Noah's anger roared through him, blocking out other sounds.

The sun beat down. The wind died. Katya's hand in his tried to wiggle away but he squeezed it tighter. And still Louisa talked and nodded.

Finally, finally, she turned and saw him. Alarm crossed her face, and Noah's hope diminished a little more. If she could see his discomfort and annoyance so easily, so could everyone else.

She wrapped up her conversation and waved to the crowd one final time before turning and walking past him and Katya, Eric's hand on the small of her back. Once they were safely inside the library, where Noah himself would be speaking to a group of teens and their parents, Louisa asked, "Will you excuse us?"

The security detail fell back, leaving the four of them to go on alone. Louisa turned toward the door where a woman wearing a name badge stood, and she said, "Noah and I need a moment." She was all smiles and perfection as Noah went past her into the room.

Once the door was closed, he finally released the breath he hadn't realized he'd been holding. "I can't do it," he said, a moan following. "Did you see what she did out there?"

"No, what happened?"

"She kissed me." He braced his hands against a table, trying to get enough air now. "Louisa, this isn't helping. This is only going to make me look worse when we break up." *And what about Zara?* his mind wailed.

Louisa stepped back to the door and opened it a few inches. "Eric, darling, could I have my phone please?"

"What's going on?" he asked, handing it to her.

"Come in a moment." Louisa backed up to let her fiancé in. Noah liked the man. He was charming and good-looking too. A duke from a neighboring island nation. And he adored Louisa and she him, and in Noah's mind, that was all that mattered.

"Oh, no, I just need Eric. Thanks, Katya. We'll only be a moment." Louisa closed the door, dropping her princess politeness as soon as the click sounded. She began tapping and swiping on her phone, and then she gasped.

Her eyes lifted and met Noah's, and she turned the phone to him so he could see what she'd found. Pictures.

Oh, how he hated pictures. And cameras. And anyone who wielded a camera.

"See?" he said. "My name's going to be in even more headlines because of this. And not good ones." He paced away from his sister and her fiancé. "Why did anyone think involving this woman was a good idea? I said it wasn't from the very first mention of her." He shook his head, his teeth grinding together again. It was a miracle he had any enamel left.

"I'm sending it to Dad," she said.

"Who cares?" Noah asked bitterly. "The pictures are already out there." He stared out the window, feeling more lost and alone than ever. Even when he stood at the glass door in the mansion in Getaway Bay, he hadn't felt this low.

Eric stepped next to him. "I got Zara's number," the

man said, so quietly that it took several seconds for Noah's brain to register that Eric had spoken.

"What?" Noah looked at Eric, who steadfastly gazed out the window.

"Sh," he said, his mouth not moving. "Don't look at me."

Noah returned his attention to the glinting sunshine outside.

"Hand me your phone," Eric said. "Carefully now."

Noah moved centimeter by centimeter, finally getting his phone onto the windowsill in front of him and Eric. He wanted to look over his shoulder at Louisa, but he didn't dare. He could hear her sighing, and her phone kept chiming with each message that came in.

Painfully slow, Eric picked up Noah's phone, and then he moved quickly. How he could swipe and tap without truly looking down was a skill Noah needed to start working on. But only seconds later, Noah's phone was back on the windowsill, and Eric had fallen a step or two away.

"Don't tell Louisa," he said in that same low voice before turning back to her. "What's your father saying?"

"He doesn't know what to do either. He's called for Clara."

"That woman won't know what to do," Noah said, leaving his phone where it sat. "Katya is a liability. A loose cannon. No one can predict what she'll do. And now, everyone stands to be dragged into this," he said. "Do you think for a moment she won't tell the papers how Dad paid her to pretend to be with me to smooth over what happened in Venice months ago?" He scoffed. "We're all in very real trouble."

Silence prevailed in the room, and then someone knocked. It didn't sound like Katya, and Eric moved to the door to open it. He was just as fluid as Louisa and Damien. Just as polished, with sandy hair that never sat out of place, and a pair of hazel eyes that observed everything.

Noah hadn't even asked Eric to help him get Zara's number. But Louisa had likely told her fiancé about Noah's feelings for Zara and how she couldn't help him. But that didn't mean Eric couldn't provide some assistance....

"They're ready for you," a woman said. "Should I tell them you'll be another minute?"

"No," Louisa said. "We're ready too." She turned back to Noah. "Don't forget your phone, baby brother." She gave him a smile as she crossed the room toward him. She fiddled and fixed with his tie, though it was absolutely perfect. "I'm so sorry," she whispered. "But let's get through this event and then figure out what to do. Okay?"

Noah nodded. "Okay." Then he picked up his phone and followed his sister out of the room.

Two hours later, he rode in the back of the limousine, his sole focus on his phone as he tapped out a message to Zara. He had so much he wanted to say, but he decided to start small.

Hey, it's Noah. I have a new phone, and I'm sort of under a lot of stress. Can't talk much, but I've been thinking about you and hope your

He didn't know what to put there. He didn't want anyone to know he was texting Zara if they happened to look at his phone. So he didn't want to use her name. Or ask about her show. Or put anything personal that would help anyone connect any dots.

Which made his first communication with her in weeks utterly ridiculous.

He read over the message again, finishing it with *I've been thinking about you and hope to see you really soon.*

Could he put a heart emoticon?

In the end, he didn't, just sending the words across the wide expanse of ocean and continents that separated them.

It was early morning in Getaway Bay, and a weekday, so Zara probably wouldn't have to be up too terribly early. He settled back into his seat, ready to wait a couple of hours to hear from her. Which made the vibration from his phone, indicating that he had a message, all the more thrilling as it moved through his fingers.

His heart beat in the back of his throat as he read her response.

Don't worry about it. Looks like you're having fun with Katya.

His blood ran cold. So she'd seen the Internet stories. What could he say to assure her this was fake without getting himself in trouble with his parents? Without throwing Eric under the bus?

I'm not, he sent.

A picture of him and Katya kissing was her response, along with the dreaded words, *Don't text me again, Noah. I've already moved on.*

CHAPTER NINETEEN

Zara deleted Noah's texts, refusing to save his new number in her phone. He'd been gone for two weeks now, and every minute felt like someone trying to hollow her out the way they would a pumpkin.

You're fine, she told herself as she ran the dry floor mop along the entryway in the mansion. And she was fine. She had a good job. A lead part in a very successful show. Another opportunity as a dancer coming up in a luau this winter. And her friends and family.

She didn't need Prince Noah Wales.

In fact, ever since she'd met him, her life had been turned upside down and twisted inside out. She'd abandoned her friends, and her concentration at work had slipped.

She was better off without him.

Then why didn't she *feel* better? She wasn't sure, but she

knew she could figure it out and then make her text come true. She could figure out how to move on.

She finished the cleaning, packed her bag, and drove down to the amphitheater. She didn't need to be there for another hour, but Ian had asked her to come go over the plans for this new kind of production he wanted to put together. Part luau and part dance party, he actually wanted Zara to participate in the show but also help him direct it.

It was a great opportunity for her to expand her résumé, and she couldn't wait to get started. As she parked, her phone rang, and she really hoped it wasn't Katya again —or Noah. Perhaps he'd been with people earlier, and that was why he'd chosen to text instead of call after so much time had gone by. After all those pictures had been posted.

Did he think she wouldn't see them? That she wouldn't be worried that he'd basically fallen off the face of the planet?

Zara had learned that he didn't know Katya was texting her, and the other woman had never said how she'd gotten Noah's phone with all his contacts. But she was ruthless and relentless, and she made sure Zara saw every little thing going on in Noah's life, emphasizing how Zara wasn't a part of it and Katya was.

It wasn't Katya or Noah, but Shannon, Hope Sorensen's assistant. Zara answered with a very confused, "Hello?"

"Zara," Shannon said brightly. "It's Shannon from Your Tidal Forever?"

Even though her name had come up on the screen, Zara said, "Oh, hi, Shannon."

"I know this is a long shot, but I was wondering if you'd

seen Holden Montego around the island? Someone said you'd dropped him off once or twice while he was volunteering for us."

Someone had seen them. Zara's mouth turned dry, and she wasn't even sure why. "I haven't seen him for a couple of weeks," she said truthfully.

"Oh, that's too bad," Shannon said, her voice definitely deflating. "We've got so much work to do, and I can't seem to get more volunteers in. He was such a good worker. Do you know if he's looking for a job? Hope's hiring a whole new construction crew."

Zara knew Holden was not looking for a job. And a lot more about him. But she just said, "I'm sorry, Shannon. I don't know. I don't think he's even in Getaway Bay anymore."

"Really?"

"I don't know," Zara said, because that seemed the safest answer.

"Okay, well, thanks. Sorry to bother you."

"No problem." Zara hung up and stared out the windshield. The conversation itself wasn't a problem, but the feelings and memories of Noah it stirred up certainly were. She hated that she didn't know if he'd be coming back, and then she reminded herself that she'd broken up with him only a few hours ago.

She didn't *want* him to come back, and his complete lack of response to her break-up text proved he didn't really care that much about her.

With her heart stinging in her chest, Zara got out of her car, shouldered her bag, and headed inside to meet with Ian. She didn't need Noah Wales. Oh, no, she did not. Maybe if she told herself that enough times, she'd start to believe it. Maybe it would even come true.

※

"So he's just gone?" Suzie asked later that week, the cup of coffee she'd insisted on getting before they could drive up to the mansion sitting abandoned on the table beside her.

"I think so," Zara said. She'd shut down every question and conversation about Noah over the past couple of weeks, but Suzie could be relentless in her pursuit of drama and details. She had a flair for gossip and she loved being involved in everything her friends did.

"How are you feeling?"

"Not great," Zara admitted.

"And he was really a prince?"

Zara had told Suzie all about her and Noah's little summer fling over the past couple of nights. Jill had started seeing Beni, and they went out with another group from the cast after the show, leaving Suzie to be Zara's sounding board since the break-up.

Zara knew she didn't mind, and she lifted her hot chocolate to her lips though it was still plenty warm in Getaway Bay. In fact, mid-July could be downright brutal. But they didn't sit by the pool tonight, choosing instead to lounge inside with the air conditioning and the comfy couches in the living room.

"He was really a prince," she said. "I knew him for a

month. I don't know why I'm so hung up on him." She'd dated other guys for much longer.

"There's been no closure," Suzie said simply.

Zara almost rolled her eyes. "You've been talking to your brother about me."

"No," she said, her blue eyes sparkling with mischief. "Though if I did talk to Jeremiah, he'd say the same thing."

"He's a child psychologist."

"And he understands closure," Suzie shot back, the banter between them friendly and so welcome to Zara. She hated coming back to this big house alone, and Suzie had been staying over with her for a few nights now.

A few minutes went by, and then Zara finally said, "Closure," like she'd decided she did need some of that when it came to Noah. He hadn't texted again, but neither had Katya, and while one of those was a relief, Zara couldn't believe Noah had given up so easily.

Two texts, and he was done?

She'd thought he had more determination than that.

"You know, Miah hasn't dated anyone in a while," Suzie said.

Zara stood up with a groan. "I'm not going out with your brother."

"Why not?" Suzie picked up her unfinished coffee and followed Zara into the kitchen.

"Because I don't need to be set up," Zara said. "And he's not a nice Indian man." She smiled at Suzie. "Maybe I should just try to find someone my parents would approve of. I'm sure there's some very nice Indian men I could go out with."

Suzie stared at her, obviously dumbfounded. "Who are you? Where's Zee?"

Zara laughed and shook her head. "Come on. It's late, and we have another show tomorrow night." She stared down the hall, Suzie right beside her.

"Seriousy, Zee, I'm worried about you."

"I'm okay, Suze. Really, I am." She paused outside the bedroom her friend had been staying in. "I do miss him, but it's not like...." Her voice trailed off, unable to say what she wanted to say. *It's not like I was in love with him.*

But they had talked about him moving to the island permanently, and she'd taken him to meet her parents. That in itself was a very big deal, and Zara couldn't just dismiss it. She'd been willing to go through that terrible dinner, and so had Noah.

"Maybe just call him," Suzie said in a small voice. "See what he says."

Zara nodded just so she could escape to her own room. She didn't really think she'd call Noah. After all, she'd erased his texts from that new number, and he hadn't tried to get in touch with her again.

She wasn't the most technical person in the world, but she'd once helped her mother find out who Sai was texting by logging into their cell phone provider's account and looking at the individual texts.

So she knew how to get the number. Instead of pulling out her laptop and doing that, she climbed into bed and stared at the ceiling, wondering where Noah was now and what he was doing.

It would be noon in Triguard, and he'd probably be

lunching with a crowd of adoring fans. Then kissing Katya and laughing about everything that had happened in Getaway Bay with the clueless Indian girl who thought synchronized swimming was a career.

Zara rolled over, bitterness and heartbreak yanking through her hard enough to make tears come. And this time, she didn't push them back or hold them in. She cried, because she missed the man she had fallen in love with.

CHAPTER TWENTY

Noah endured the last week of Louisa's engagement tour alone. It was better than trying to keep Katya's lips off of his, and certainly an improvement from the horrible situation he'd been put in.

But Zara's message had sent him into a tailspin he didn't know how to recover from. He clung to the tiny shred of hope that he'd be the perfect prince his father wanted, and then he'd get permission to leave this wretched island and make a new one his home.

Zara had said not to text her again, and Noah was planning to honor that. But he could call her or show up on her doorstep to talk to her. He just needed to get a few things in order first, and then he would.

The door he'd been sitting outside of opened, and his sister came out. She looked tired, but upbeat, and she gave him a hug after he stood up. "Your turn."

"How is he?" Noah asked, glancing toward his father's private office.

"He's...the king," Louisa said, which did not infuse any hope into Noah's heart. She walked away, her low heels and long skirt absolutely fitting for the princess she was. Noah tugged on his jacket sleeves and entered the office, determined to stay until he'd gotten what he wanted. No, what he needed.

"Father," he said once he'd entered, bowed, and closed the door.

"Noah, come and sit." His father smiled and removed his glasses. He seemed older than Noah remembered, and he took a few moments to really look at his dad. He couldn't even imagine what it would be like to shoulder the affairs of a country, even a small one like Triguard.

"How was the tour?"

Noah cocked his head. "Honestly, Father?"

"Honestly, Noah."

"It was terrible," Noah said. "Katya was a train wreck, and Zara broke up with me."

His father blinked as if Noah had just said it was going to rain later. "I'm sorry to hear that."

"Are you?" Noah hadn't meant to be disrespectful or negative. He drew in a deep breath. "It doesn't matter. I'll make things right with her." Just like he always made things right.

"Katya was a mistake."

"Thank you for saying so," Noah said. He wanted to adjust his tie, but he held very still. Fidgeting showed nerves, and he didn't want his father to think he was anything less than poised and content.

"She won't be causing us any more problems." His father steepled his fingers and watched Noah.

"I'm happy to hear that."

"And now I suppose you want to know how you did on the tour, to see if I'm going to give you permission to live in Getaway Bay permanently."

Noah said nothing. The King had surely received daily reports from one of the people who'd traveled with the royal entourage on the engagement tour. He read six papers each day and spent an hour on the Internet too. He knew everything that happened in his kingdom, almost the moment it happened.

"I'm sorry to say I can't let you do that," he said, leaning back in his chair.

"Dad," Noah started, a whine plentiful in his voice. He cut off the sound and cleared his throat. "Why not?"

"Not for a few more months, at least," he said. "You just returned, and we need time to let the press move on to something else, the way they always do."

"A few more months?" A weight pressed on Noah's chest, making it difficult for his lungs to expand properly. "What's the difference if I hide out here in the castle or on the beach in Getaway Bay?"

He wanted to surf. He wanted to hold Zara and watch her complete that high dive. He wanted to be free from his royal obligations—and that was what his father couldn't grant.

"That's exactly the problem," his father said,

confirming Noah's sudden realization. "You're not a normal man, Noah. You're a prince, and you have certain duties that come with that."

"Then I'll volunteer in libraries in Getaway Bay. They have a great children's hospital wing there. I'll donate money there and spend time there. I've already been volunteering on a celebrity wedding through one of their wedding planning businesses."

"Yes, Your Tidal Forever. I'm aware."

Of course he was. Noah didn't have anything else to say in his defense.

"I need you here for a while," he said. "Damien is launching a new health initiative, and he wants you to be the right-hand man."

"You mean he wants me to attend meetings and make speeches," Noah said. "Stay out of trouble."

"That's exactly what I mean. It will improve your image, and then you'll probably be able to return to Getaway Bay, as you wish to do. But we feel it's simply too soon for you to go now."

"I don't care about my image, Father."

"I realize that," he said dryly. "But we do, and as your reputation reflects on all of us, we've all suffered while you've been learning to surf in the Pacific Ocean."

A splash of shame moved through Noah. "No one cares if I'm learning to surf or if I'm helping a child read."

"You're wrong about that," his dad said. "The child cares, and the child's mother cares, and the library director cares. And they're all citizens of this country. Citizens you're supposed to love and serve."

Noah could see he wasn't going to persuade his father into seeing things his way. He'd never been successful doing that in the past either. "Perhaps I could have a week," he said. "To travel to Getaway Bay, talk to Zara, and come back."

His dad laughed and shook his head. "I don't think so, Noah. I know you, and you're slipperier than an oiled eel. I let you out of my sight, and you'll be off the grid for who knows how long."

Noah stood, the meeting clearly over. "Well, Father, you knew I'd been learning to surf. You knew enough to send Damien on a 4-day round trip to find me. You knew where I was volunteering. Someone as smart as resourceful like you should be able to track me down pretty easily, should I not return." He buttoned his jacket and strode away from the desk though his father called him back.

He was not going to stay in Triguard for another few weeks. Because then it would be something else. Another month for this project. Then another six for holiday preparation. Then Louisa's wedding would be within a year, and there was no way he could leave then.

So he'd leave tonight. True, his father could cut off all of his debit and credit cards, but Noah had allies inside the castle. He just needed to find them and convince them to help him.

Plus, he really needed to see Zara. Talk to her. Make her understand. And he wasn't going to wait another few months to do it.

"Are you sure?" Noah asked Louisa as she sat behind the wheel of a car. He'd never seen his sister drive, and he wasn't entirely sure she knew how.

"Yes, now be quiet." She looked at the dashboard in front of her like all she'd have to do was push a button and the vehicle would start. Noah was once again on the floor in the backseat, feeling too tall and too broad for such things.

His sister got the car started, and she eased it forward a little without jerking. So maybe she did know how to drive. They made it out of the huge shed where all the cars were kept and around the back of the castle before she stopped again.

Noah's pulse felt like it was part of a tennis match, bobbing to the left and then the right with great speed. "What's—"

The passenger door opened, and his brother said, "Are we all set?"

Before Noah could move, Damien looked over the seat. "You didn't even cover him up."

"We drove from the vehicle shed to here," Louisa snapped. "You said *you'd* bring something to cover him up."

Noah's heart warmed listening to his siblings bicker. In the end, Damien ended up running back up to the doors of his wing of the castle, and what felt like an hour later, he returned with one blanket. "It's all I could sneak away from Matzen," he said. "That man is like a bloodhound."

He draped the blanket over Noah, who experienced a strong sense of déjà vu. The drive to the gate happened quickly, and Louisa said, "We're just taking a drive to the seashore," as if she needed the guard's permission to do so. Once free of the Wales Family land, Noah kicked off the blanket and sat up in the backseat. He wanted to tell his brother and sister how much he appreciated them, and that he didn't want to leave Triguard because of them. He said nothing, as the family didn't have a custom of saying what they really felt.

At the airport, she avoided the section where the press were allowed to congregate, and instead, drove around the back of the airport to a place Noah had never been before.

"I've arranged a private flight for you," Damien said. "Straight through to Getaway Bay, with a stop in Toronto for refueling. You won't even get off the plane, though." He turned and looked at Noah, his features serious.

"Thank you, Damien."

"I hope it works out with Zara," he said. "She seems very important to you."

Noah nodded and said, "She is. I hope I'll be able to fix the situation with her." He thought of her stubborn streak and how traditional her family was. But he was willing to do almost anything to be with her, including defying his father and sneaking away in broad daylight.

His sister got out of the car and grabbed onto him. "Be safe, Noah," she said.

"You're the ones who are going to get filleted alive," he whispered. "All three heirs in a car with no security?"

She looked like a scared rabbit as she ducked back into the car and drove off, a final wave from Damien the last thing Noah saw before he faced the jet sitting before him.

Three people waited at the bottom of the stairs, and Noah approached them.

"Prince Noah," the older man said. "I'll be your pilot for the first leg of our journey. My name is Roberto. Antonio will take us from Toronto to Hawaii after we've refueled. And Mary will help you in the cabin with whatever you need." He nodded Noah onto the plane, which was much better than the regular commercial flight he'd taken to get to Triguard.

He was the only passenger besides the three his brother had hired to get him back to Getaway Bay, and he suddenly didn't feel so bad for Damien and his trip to Getaway Bay weeks ago. This plane had a huge bed, as well as two recliners flanking it, and Noah chose one of those for the first part of the flight.

He slept as well as he would've in the mansion, and by the time they landed in Getaway Bay, Noah knew he would never fly on any other plane but this one. He gave all three people a large tip and stepped into the glorious Hawaiian sunshine.

Yes, it was still hot in Getaway Bay. Yes, there were still too many tourists. But as he accepted a flower lei and got in line to wait for a taxi, there was nowhere he'd rather be.

His phone took a few minutes to update to local time, and as he waited, he wondered where he could find Zara at two o'clock in the afternoon. Did she go to work that early, if the show didn't start until seven?

Noah had no plan for how to approach her, or what to say. So when he got in the back of a cab, with only his backpack and wallet, and the driver asked him where to go, Noah said, "Indian House."

He wasn't sure what he'd find at her family's restaurant, but there was no one who knew Zara better than her family.

The moment he stepped inside, a woman gasped and said, "Prince Noah," and he thought he'd been discovered. But it was only Zara's sister, Abi, and she had both hands covering her mouth.

"Hey," he said. "I just need a table in the corner and access to the Internet. Do you think you could help me?"

"What are you doing here?" She plucked a menu from the podium but didn't move.

"I need to figure out how to get Zara back."

Abi grinned like he'd just passed the biggest test of his life and said, "Right this way." She indeed led him to the very corner of the restaurant and he sat with his back to everything.

She put the menu in front of him, and he said, "Bring me the butter chicken, would you?"

"Of course. And the WiFi password is swimmergirl."

Noah looked up, surprised. Abi shrugged and said, "My parents are very proud people," as if that explained everything. Maybe it did.

He nodded and pulled out his laptop, determined to do whatever he could to get tickets to her show. If not that night, then as soon as possible. And he was going to show up and surprise her, apologize until she forgave him, and kiss her until he couldn't breathe.

Oh, and then he needed to go get his dog from the guy

who'd agreed to take him while Noah had been out of town. He'd met Tyler on the beach, and he had two dogs with him that Boomer had really liked. He hadn't been able to text Tyler either, but he seemed like the laid-back type of surfer dude who wouldn't mind keeping a good dog for a few weeks.

He flexed his fingers. "I just need tickets," he muttered to himself. By the time the butter chicken came and he'd consumed it, he still hadn't found even a single ticket for the foreseeable future.

So maybe he needed a miracle instead.

CHAPTER TWENTY-ONE

Zara bounced on the balls of her feet, ready to get this show started. But there had been a lighting glitch, and they'd been delayed for fifteen minutes. She'd sat in the whirlpool to stay warm, and now she just wanted to *go*.

Though she was behind the closed door in the locker room, when Suzie came bursting through it, Zara heard the noise outside. "What's going on?" she asked, trying to get a peek before the door closed. "How close are they?"

Suzie pressed her back into the door, a grin filling her whole face. "They're close. There's just...Maine Fitzgerald showed up, and everyone's making a big deal out of it."

Zara's heart stuttered a little, though she had no chance with quarterback Maine Fitzgerald. He was dating someone, and had been for a long time. But still. A celebrity at Fresh Start.

She'd performed in the show dozens of times now, and

still she felt jittery. A few minutes later someone knocked on the door and said, "Two minutes, Zee."

After snapping her goggles into place, she eased into the pool that would get her out to the arena without being seen. She held onto the platform, she rode it up high, and she and Beni performed their spectacular dives into the pool below.

She usually came up to thunderous applause, but tonight, when she broke the surface of the water, only silence rained down on her. Sliding up onto the edge of the pool as normal, she waved as though they were cheering like they'd just seen her win the Super Bowl.

A man stood up and a spotlight shone on him. Zara's hand froze mid-wave and she felt like she'd just inhaled a lungful of salt water.

It was Noah Wales. Prince Noah Wales.

Right there, just on the other side of the railing. Maybe ten feet from her. He lifted his hand in a wave and called, "Amazing, Zara!" He started to applaud, and his third clap got swallowed by the crowd as they all joined him on their feet, the roof-shaking applause now what she was accustomed to.

She didn't know what to do. The timing of the show was off now, and she still perched on the edge of the pool. Finally, someone grabbed onto her ankles and said, "Come on, Zee. You can talk to him after."

Zara joined Suzie in the water, and she missed the first synchronized move with the other girls but managed to get her leg up on the second one. Her heart skipped every third beat, and she couldn't hold her breath as long as she used to.

Noah was here.

What was Noah *doing* here?

She wanted to go see him during intermission, but she found the exits blocked by James, Beni, and Ian himself.

"After the show," Ian said. "I already did him a *huge* favor by moving his seat, and postponing the show so he could get situated right where you'd come out of the water."

"*You* did that?" Zara stared at him in disbelief. And now she'd have to put her swim cap back on over wet hair and skin, and that was a huge pain.

"Well, the lights were already a problem, so I figured what was a few more minutes?" Ian shrugged and smiled, and added, "He seems like a really great guy, for what it's worth."

Zara wasn't sure what she thought. She didn't really want to see Noah, but he was here. On the island. And she wanted to find out how he'd achieved that. And fine, she wanted to find out if they could have a second chance.

But first she had to finish the second act of her show. As she did, she couldn't help thinking that the name of this production was Fresh Start—and that was exactly what she and Noah needed.

After the final applause, after she'd showered and changed, after she had everything in her bag ready to go, Zara sat on the thin benches in the locker room and stared at her phone. Almost everyone else had left, and her nerves prevented her from doing the same.

"Come *on*," Suzie hissed from the doorway leading into the hall. "What are you doing?"

Zara lifted one shoulder in a shrug and looked at her best friend. "I don't know."

"Don't you at least want to hear how he got here?"

"I don't know," Zara said. She did, but she didn't at the same time. "What if he has to leave again in the morning?" She'd already started piecing her heart back together. It hadn't gone well, and she still had a lot of cracks and wounds to heal, but she'd started.

Suzie entered the locker room, looking like she could eat kittens for breakfast. "Zara, come on. He's all you've talked about for a week, and I know you were suffering in silence before that. So he's here. And he's *gorgeous*. And he's just as nervous as you. So come *on*." She tugged on Zara's hand hard enough to get her to stand.

Zara moved to the door, only because Suzie was behind her and she couldn't turn and flee the other way.

She'd taken one step into the hall when Suzie added, "And besides, your family needs to get back to the restaurant."

"My family?" The last word whispered out of Zara's mouth, because she'd seen Noah. And he was wonderful and strong and everything she held in her memory of him.

He took an anxious step forward, a huge bouquet of flowers in his hands. Sure enough, her family—her parents, both sets of grandparents, all her sisters and their husbands, and her aunties and uncles—flanked him.

Zara could hardly move, but her wooden legs managed

to get her down the hall to a more open area where everyone stood.

"Hey, Zara," Noah said, his warm, deep voice washing over her. Soothing her. So not fair. She wanted to be mad at him, and he'd charmed her simply by saying her name. "These are for you. Your sister said you like carnations the best."

"She does," Krisha said.

"But they smell bad," Abi said. "He should've gotten hibiscus."

"There's some of those too," he said. "Your friend Ash helped me get them. I guess her fiancé owns a flower business?"

Zara nodded and took the bouquet. She did love carnations, and she did like the way hibiscus smelled. "How long have you been back?"

"I got here about noon," he said.

Her eyebrows went up. "And you mobilized my family and met my friend Ash?"

"I was a little late to the show," he said, a magnificent smile touching his mouth. Zara wanted to touch his mouth. Feel him and make sure he was real and not a mirage. "It took *forever* to get a ticket."

"How *did* you get a ticket?" she asked.

"I called Ian."

Of course he did. Only Prince Noah would be able to figure call in a favor to a man he barely knew. Bold. The fact that he'd been able to orchestrate everything so perfectly felt like she'd entered an alternate reality.

"After my lunch of butter chicken," he said. "Things got

really interesting. I wasn't going to do all of this. I just wanted to see you." He took a step forward, his hand reaching toward her like he wanted to make sure she was real too.

"I wanted to apologize," he said. "I'm sure you've seen some things online that have been upsetting. I know I need to explain and earn your trust back." He glanced at her father, who nodded once.

"But I'm in love with you Zara Reddy, and I'll do whatever it takes to make things right between us." He dropped to one knee and took the black jewelry box from her mother in one quick movement.

Zara couldn't breathe. It seemed to take an hour for Noah to crack that lid. When he did, he presented the glittering, diamond ring to her and asked, "Will you marry me?"

Sai and Myra sighed like they were Disney princesses, but tears stung Zara's eyes. She wanted to look to her parents for permission, but their presence meant they'd already given it.

So she nodded, some of her tears splashing down her face, and said, "Yes, Noah. I'll marry you."

He grinned and fumbled a little to remove the ring from the box and slide it on her finger. Then he stood, took the flowers and handed them to someone, and gathered her into the safety of his strong arms.

"I'm so sorry," he murmured just before lowering his head and kissing her. Zara knew there was a lot to talk about still, but it didn't seem to matter all that much. He was here, and he'd fixed a lot already.

So she kissed him back, hoping her actions could convey the three little words she'd yet to say.

Her family and friends cheered, and it was the exact proposal Zara had never known she wanted. She pulled away, giggling, and Noah tucked her into his side while they faced her parents.

Her mother wore a smile and wiped at her eyes, and that set Zara to crying all over again. She hugged her mom, who asked, "You will do the traditional Indian wedding, yes?"

"Nita, give her a few days," her dad said, drawing Zara into his embrace. "Congratulations, Zee. You two will be so happy."

She wondered what had changed their minds, but she decided she had plenty of time to find out. She hugged her sisters, her aunties, and everyone else before returning to find Noah had picked up her swim bag and was holding her flowers.

"Do you want to see where I live?" he asked.

"Don't tell me you found a house since noon too." She looked at him, pure shock moving through her. Was there anything he couldn't do?

He shrugged and said, "You might want to use the bathroom before we go."

CHAPTER TWENTY-TWO

Noah laid on his back, the sand soft beneath him, and stared at the stars, thanking each one for his reunion with Zara.

She lay curled into his side, and neither of them spoke. The slight scent of chlorine mingled with flowers, and it was the best smell in the whole world.

"What did your father say?" she asked to break the silence between them.

"I haven't spoken to him since sneaking away." He'd told her the whole story of his time in Triguard, his horrible experience with Katya, and how he feared his father would never allow him to return to Getaway Bay.

"I'm sure he was livid with Louisa and Damien."

"I would like to meet them," she said.

"You will. We'll go visit my parents, and we'll of course go for her wedding, but that won't be for, like, ever."

"Really?"

"Oh, the royal engagements are ridiculous."

"I would like a short engagement," Zara said, and Noah smiled at the stars.

"That's fine with me, sweetheart."

"I'll talk to my mother tomorrow. See what we can put on the calendar."

"You might need to explain to me what a traditional Indian wedding looks like."

"Oh, we won't have a traditional Indian wedding."

Noah's arm around her tightened. "We won't?"

"I'll wear the traditional clothing, and it'll be loud. Every party we have is very loud. But it won't be full-blown traditional."

"But we can have butter chicken, right?"

Zara giggled, her breath heating his skin beneath his T-shirt. "I suppose we can have butter chicken."

The sky above them held magic, and Noah wanted to stay on this island for the rest of his life.

"Did you know Katya had your phone?" she asked, and Noah flinched.

"What do you mean?"

"I mean, she had your phone and she texted me. She was the one who sent me the picture of you two kissing."

Noah hated the sound of those words coming out of Zara's mouth, and he pressed his eyes closed. "My mother dropped my phone in the koi pond."

"Well, when I texted you to ask you a question, she responded."

"What did she say?"

"I don't know." She took a deep breath. "All kinds of stuff. She was basically bragging about how she was with you and I wasn't."

"You know she was never 'with me,' right?"

"Yes," she said, and it was the best word he'd ever heard. She lifted her head and added, "Come on. You told me you'd show me your place."

"It's too dark," he said.

A beat of silence passed, and then she said, "You don't have electricity?"

"Well...."

"And no running water."

"Nope."

"You're moving back into the mansion."

"No, I'm not."

"Noah." She pushed up on her elbow. "Where do you go to the bathroom?"

"There's a bathroom down the beach a bit," he said. "There's showers and a sink and stuff."

"It's not private."

"I don't mind."

"There's got to be somewhere you can live that has the things you need."

Noah gently drew her back into his side. "I'm sure you're right. I'll find somewhere tomorrow."

"And where's Boomer?" she asked.

"I met a guy named Tyler?" Noah said, like it was a question. "He said he'd take him."

"Tyler Rigby? The billionaire poker player?"

"I have no idea."

"You gave Boomer to a stranger." Zara shook her head against his chest. "I can't believe you."

"He had two other dogs, and he seemed chill."

"Definitely Tyler Rigby."

"Do you have his number then?"

"I'm sure I can figure out how to get in touch with him. I think he's friends with Ash's husband."

"Because I lost all my contacts when I got a new phone, and I don't exactly know how to get in touch with him."

Zara started giggling, and Noah couldn't help but join in. He wanted this life with her, laughing at the moonlight and snuggling on the sand. He wanted electricity and indoor plumbing too, and he decided that tomorrow, finding a functional place to live was priority one.

The next morning, when he finally dragged himself out of bed, he found his phone laden with messages. He read the ones from Zara, Louisa, and Damien, and ignored the ones from his parents.

He asked Zara for Tyler's number, and a few minutes later he was able to text the man about getting Boomer back. While he had Tyler's attention, he asked about a real estate agent, and an hour later, he walked into an office that looked more like a beach hideaway to find a woman sitting behind a desk.

"I'm looking for Jewel," he said.

"Oh, I'm Jewel." She tossed her long, blonde hair as she stood. "You must be Noah." She extended her hand across the desk, and they shook hands.

"That I am," he said. "And I really need a new place as fast as possible." He thought about the hammock he'd slept in last night. No way he could let Zara see where he called home.

"Let's talk for a few minutes, and I'll see what I've got." She settled behind her desk again, and Noah took the chair across from her. "What are we looking at for budget?"

Noah hadn't checked his accounts, and had no idea if they were still operational, but he said, "The budget is wide open."

Jewel didn't blink. "Size?"

"Nothing huge," he said. "Something normal, for a normal person. I am getting married soon, though, so something for two normal people. And maybe a family." He realized he was rambling, and he pressed his lips together in a closed-mouth smile.

"On the beach? A condo? I've got a couple of things up on the bluff." Jewel glanced at him.

"Not the bluff," he said. "My parents have a place up there, and I'd prefer to be down on the beach anyway. Not a condo. I have a dog, and he likes to go outside like, every five seconds."

"Large yard for the dog?"

He could hire a gardener, or better yet, figure out how to push a mower himself. "Sure," he said. "Or not. The yard doesn't matter to me."

"Pool?"

He thought of Zara, and started nodding. "Definitely."

Jewel tapped and clicked and smiled. "I think I have

the perfect place for you." She beamed at him, printed one sheet of paper and said, "Do you want to follow me?"

He nodded, his heart bobbing around in the back of his throat. He'd never purchased a house of his own, and he couldn't wait to see what Jewel had for him. And there was just the one, so he hoped it was available right away.

She drove for about ten minutes before turning into a perfectly normal neighborhood, with completely ordinary homes. She parked in the driveway, which would accommodate four cars, and got out. "Here it is. The house is vacant, so you'll have to use your imagination for where furniture would be." She clicked toward the front porch. "But the whole thing has recently been painted, and there's new carpet throughout."

Noah didn't care about the carpet or the paint. The house screamed normal, and it had five bedrooms and four bathrooms, which was plenty of room for him, Boomer, and Zara, even if they had a family.

It was the pool and yard that sold him the moment he stepped onto the back patio. While the house was in a neighborhood, it sat on the edge of it and the backyard stretched for a good distance before the sand took over.

"Do we own the beach?"

"Unfortunately, no," Jewel said. "But there is access, and not many people come to the beach if they don't live in the neighborhood."

He glanced at the sparkling pool, which a tall, vinyl fence surrounded to provide some privacy. "I'll take it."

"Really?" Jewel asked. "Just like that?"

"Just like that." Noah smiled at her. "Is that not how

people do it?" His grin slipped. "This is my first time buying a house."

"It is?"

"Yes." Did it really show?

"Well, you'll get some incentives for that." She pulled her phone from her purse. "Let me put in an offer." She babbled on about the price of the house and how it really was quite fair, but that the owners had left the island already and were desperate to sell. "So we could probably go in lower." She looked at Noah, obviously asking him.

He had no idea. "I'm fine with the list price," he said. "And I'd love to move in like, tonight."

Jewel's eyebrows went up. "Well, I'm afraid that won't happen, Mister Wales. We have to do the financing, and the inspection, and—"

"I'm willing to buy it as-is," he said. "With cash. Today."

Jewel gaped at him, the hand holding her phone falling to her side. "Cash?" wisped out of her mouth.

"Today," he said.

She regained her professionalism and said, "Let me call the real estate agent for the owners. Perhaps we can work out an agreement that allows you immediate occupancy in exchange for no inspection and a full cash offer."

Noah nodded at her, imagining himself living in this house...with Zara. In fact, he wanted to marry her right there in that gorgeous backyard, with the banyan trees above them and the beach beyond them. He even knew who to hire to make her wedding dreams come true.

He shook away the fantasies and focused on the

moment. He first had to make sure he had the cash in liquid form to buy this place. Then he could bring Zara here and ask her what she thought of tying the knot with him right there in this new, normal place they could call their own.

SIX MONTHS LATER

"Mother," Zara said in a somewhat reproving voice. "Does the music need to be quite so loud?"

She stood in Noah's house—which would soon be her house too—and let her sisters make sure all the pieces of her traditional *lehnga*, which Ash had sewn beautifully, fit and laid right. They wove flowers through her hair, and Sai was currently painting her right arm in intricate henna swirls. Zara's left arm was already done, and the wedding was only an hour away now.

"It is a party," her mother said in response.

Zara rolled her eyes, but she didn't say anything else. She had to live in this neighborhood, and while Noah had been here for a while and said the neighbors were nice, not everyone enjoyed Indian music at ten o'clock in the morning.

There would be the ceremony, and then a huge

luncheon, which Indian House had catered. The restaurant was closed for the day, and Zara had appreciated her parents so much over the past few months as they'd planned the wedding.

No, Noah was not a nice Indian man, but he was a handsome prince. He was *her* handsome prince, and she couldn't wait to see him in his traditional tuxedo and the royal blue and purple tie every man in the Wales family wore to get married.

So they were blending their two worlds, and Zara got a little weepy just thinking about it. She'd flown to Triguard to meet his parents a few months ago, and they were lovely people. Stuffy, as Noah called them, but polite and kind and absolutely accommodating.

They'd arrived on the island about three weeks ago, and Zara had been up to the mansion for dinner with them several times as the wedding approached. His sister and her fiancé were staying in an undisclosed location around the point of the island, and his brother, the Crown Prince of Triguard was staying in a third location with a full security detail.

Noah loved his siblings, and when the three of them were together, Zara could feel the camaraderie between them. Louisa had treated Zara like a sister from the first moment they'd met, and she'd admitted she'd wanted to be the first one to get married, but that everything in Triguard seemed to take an eternity.

"So many details," she said. "And Mother keeps changing her mind."

Zara didn't understand that, as her mother had a set of

rules and cultural traditions that Zara had to continually modify.

"Finished," Sai said, and Zara realized the two of them were alone. "You look so beautiful, Zara."

"Thanks, Sai," she said, smiling at the sister just older than her. "Did Mark come?"

Her sister's dark eyes shone from within. "He sure did. I hope he'll see that it's possible to be normal and be Indian too."

Zara laughed, as Noah had an obsession with being normal, and when she'd suggested they get married in Triguard, with the whole royal affair, he'd immediately said no. He wanted a normal wedding, and he'd somehow gotten it into his mind that the ceremony should take place in his backyard.

Which was fine with Zara, honestly. She just wanted to get married, and she didn't need all the fanfare. However, his parents had asked them to please come to Triguard after their honeymoon so the people there could congratulate the couple.

Noah had said it would be more than a party, but a whole parade with pomp and cheering and gifts galore.

Zara wouldn't be a princess, but his father had declared her with the title of Her Royal Highness, the Duchess of Oceania, and Noah was now His Royal Highness, the Duke of Oceania. She honestly had no idea what the titles meant, but she was happy his family had come to terms with her and Noah's relationship.

"Ready?" her mom asked, bustling back into the room. Shannon came with her, and she looked a little frazzled, which was saying something. The wedding planner rarely looked anything but calm and cool, but she probably didn't know what to do with all of Zara's family's crazy traditions. Or how those were in complete contrast to Noah's family and their demeanor during a wedding.

Zara looked down at her arms, still covered in henna. "No, Sai just finished and this isn't dry yet."

"It can come off," Sai said, collecting a washcloth. She worked quickly, and her mother fussed around Zara for another few minutes before declaring her the perfect Indian bride.

She met her father on the back patio and found the backyard full of chairs and tents. It was windy today, but no one seemed to notice, and the music quieted enough for people to realize she'd arrived and the ceremony was beginning.

She'd asked her dad to walk her down the aisle, which was more of a Western tradition, and they stepped slowly toward Noah, who stood at an altar he'd made himself. Zara kept her eyes on him and let the joy flow through her.

Her father kissed both of her cheeks before passing her to Noah, who looked dashing and dreamy in his tuxedo. His family sat together on the front row, every one of them proper and perfect.

Zara felt perfect too, and she listened as the pastor promised them wealth and health if they turned to each other to work through the storms of life. When he got to the vows, Zara looked at Noah and squeezed both of his hands.

How she'd gotten lucky enough to catch his eye, she'd

never know. But when it was her turn to say, "I do," she did so in a loud voice, glad when Noah repeated the words to her.

Then he tipped her back and kissed her, which caused the onlookers to erupt in cheers. The music blared again, and Zara held onto Noah's face a moment longer, whispering the words, "I love you, Noah, my perfect prince."

He grinned, kissed her again, and said, "I love you too."

THE END

SNEAK PEEK! THE DOCTOR'S BRIDE CHAPTER ONE

"All right, guys." Shannon Bell put her purse over her shoulder and clicked her way toward the front door. "Be good while I'm at work." She flashed a bright smile to her two cats, both of whom sat at perfect attention a few feet away.

Of course, neither of them responded to her, and Shannon went out the door and down the steps. She had a routine she followed each morning, and she was right on schedule to hit Roasted at their slowest time between eight and nine.

She'd tried different times, and eight-twenty in the morning seemed to be the best time to get her daily dose of caffeine before she had to go to work at Your Tidal Forever. She loved her job, though it was a bit intense from time to time.

"At least the celebrity wedding and the royal wedding are over," she told herself as she buckled her seatbelt and started her car. She loved this car, and she lowered the top to let in the spring sunshine as she started toward downtown Getaway Bay.

She hooked her purse over her arm as she walked into the coffee shop, running her fingers through her hair to tame some of the messy curls back into waves. Only four people waited in line, and Shannon smiled to herself that she'd timed her coffee shop visit exactly right again.

Shannon prided herself on the details of things. It was what made her a good secretary, and why Hope Sorensen at Your Tidal Forever had told Shannon she could never quit.

Her body was still recovering from the high-profile weddings over the past couple of months, and she wished she wasn't such a night owl. That, or she needed another job where she didn't have to be to work by nine.

But she had a secretarial degree and a professional certification in organization. So she was well-suited for the many moving parts a wedding planning business required, and she'd enjoyed her last five years at Your Tidal Forever.

Well, most of the time she enjoyed the work. Sometimes Hope could be a little intense, and when they had two of the biggest celebrities tying the knot one month, and then a prince getting married only a couple later, there had been times that Shannon felt like she'd lose her mind with all the tiny pieces that needed to be finished on time.

In the five minutes she waited to put in her order for a large caramel mocha, the bell on the door rang eight more times, and she asked for a cranberry orange bran muffin too, as she rarely ate breakfast before she left the house.

With summer right around the corner, Shannon had

dozens of tasks to complete that day, and she'd be lucky if she got fifteen minutes for lunch. Maybe she could get Riley to get food for everyone, or she'd just run down the boardwalk to the Ohana Resort, which had recently opened a shop that served soups, salads, and sandwiches for the professional lunch crowd. The Lunch Spot promised food in ten minutes or less, and they had dozens of tables in the sand that always seemed full.

She got her coffee and turned to leave. Her eyes scanned the line of people waiting, catching on a tall, good-looking man she'd seen every day for a long time. She couldn't pinpoint when she'd first met Doctor Jeremiah Yeates, or when she'd learned his name, or when she'd realized that he worked in the building just down from Your Tidal Forever.

It seemed like they'd known each other for a while, and she waved to him as she passed.

"You beat me today," he said with a smile, and she couldn't help the little laugh that came out of her mouth. She quelled it by sipping her coffee, because while she and Jeremiah were friendly, there had never been much of a spark there.

She knew his name and where he worked. That was all. They could probably ride to work together if they wanted to, but neither of them had ever brought it up. And Shannon wasn't going to today either.

Yes, Jeremiah was handsome and clearly well-off, as Shannon never saw him wearing anything but an expensive suit, and when he got to Roasted before her, she'd noticed that he bought coffee for his whole office.

Every morning, the man bought coffee for his whole office. Shannon couldn't even imagine Hope doing that, though the owner did sometimes bring in food, but usually for clients and the employees just ate what was left over.

As Hope walked across the parking lot to her car, her purse swinging and the coffee in her hand a bit too warm to really drink. Shannon was more of a lukewarm coffee lover, and she probably wouldn't touch her brew for another hour at least.

She found a couple standing at the front corner of her car, and she glanced at him, a blip of anxiety flipping through her. She clicked her keys to unlock the car, though the top on the convertible was still down and if there had been anything worth stealing inside, it probably would've been gone by now.

The couple moved away, and Shannon glanced at the front of her beloved car. It was fine. Of course it was fine. Getaway Bay didn't have a high crime rate, and Shannon didn't really have anything to be worried about.

Except the flat tire staring back at her.

"Oh, no," she said, the words part of a much larger moan. She opened the door and put her purse inside, as well as her coffee. Then she placed her hands on her hips and faced the tire. Her father had taught her how to change a flat tire, as well as her oil, but Shannon never used the lessons. She had money, and why should she shimmy under her car when Max could do it at the lube shop for thirty bucks?

But Max wasn't here now, and Shannon had a ton to do at work. She opened her trunk and pulled back the roof to reveal the spare tire. She had no idea if she had the right tools to change a tire, but she was going to find out.

She found a X-shaped tool that she seemed to recall her father using to loosen the bolts. Bolts? That didn't seem like the right term, but Shannon literally made appointments, took messages, and tasted wedding cakes for a living.

The tool fit over the bolts, and she twisted. Nothing happened. After several more minutes of straining and trying to get even one of those stupid bolts off, and sweat poured down Shannon's face. Her blouse had come untucked and she had no idea where her heels were.

She crouched next to the tire, frustration about to make her say or do something she'd likely regret later—like calling her father for help.

"Can't do it," she said, and she also regretted her skirt choice, as this one was a little snug along her waist and hips.

"Need some help?" a man asked, and Shannon startled toward the deep, familiar voice. She twisted and peered up at none other than Jeremiah Yeates and the two trays of coffee he held in his hands.

"I have a flat tire," she said, trying to straighten.

Horror struck her like lightning at the sound of a seam *riiipping*, and she spun to put her backside against her cherry red convertible.

To Jeremiah's great credit, he acted like she hadn't just split her skirt open and stepped over to the hood of the car, where he set down the seven cups of coffee. "I think I can change a tire."

"I haven't been able to get off the bolts," she said, wiping her bangs off her forehead. Her hand came away wet, and more embarrassment squirreled through her.

"Let's see what I can do with these lug nuts," Jeremiah said, taking his suit coat off and draping it over the driver's side door. He wore a light blue, short-sleeved dress shirt, and Shannon couldn't help but admire the width of his shoulders and the obvious strength in his biceps.

Shannon looked away, her heart pounding a bit harder than normal for a reason she couldn't identify. So Jeremiah spent some time in the gym. So did a lot of men.

He picked up the tool she'd been wrestling with and crouched where she'd been. With the first yank on the wrench, the bolt—lug nut, whatever—came loose, and Shannon felt another blast of humiliation.

Jeremiah made short work of the lug nuts and pulled the full-size tire off. "Yeah, it looks like you drove over a nail," he said.

"Oh," she said. "I live over in the Cliff Cove area, and they're doing some construction up there."

"Yeah," he said with a big grin. "I live up there too."

Surprise pulled through her. "You do?"

"Yeah, off White Sails Lane."

That was only a few blocks from her, and she said, "I'm off Five Island."

His smile was glorious and beautiful, and why hadn't Shannon ever noticed it before? She tucked her dark hair behind her ear, wishing the sun didn't make her whole head feel like it was ablaze.

"I'm going to be so late for work," she said. "I'm so sorry. Are you—do you have a patient this morning?"

"I'm okay," he said, walking to the back of the car to get the spare tire. "Let me text my secretary real quick." He pulled his phone out and started sending a message, prompting Shannon to do the same thing. Hope couldn't blame her for being late if she had a flat tire. In fact, Shannon beat Hope to the office every day anyway.

"Shannon?" he asked from the trunk, and Shannon looked up from her phone.

"Yeah?"

"I don't think this spare is any good." He glanced at her and back into the trunk.

She shimmied along the side of the car and placed her palm flat against her backside as she turned to stand right beside him. She peered into the trunk too, asking, "What's wrong with it?"

"Look how it's cracked along the side there?" He ran his finger along the edge of the tire. "We can't put this on."

She appreciated the use of "we," but she had absolutely no idea what to do now.

"I can give you a ride to work," he said. "And maybe you can call someone to come tow the car and get the tire fixed?" He looked at her like she had resources to do that. And she did, but she didn't want to call her dad and admit she couldn't change her own tire.

"All right," she said. "Are you sure it's okay?"

Jeremiah grinned at her. "It's no problem, Shannon," he said. "We work right next door to each other, and I just found out you're like, three blocks away from where I live."

He hefted the flat tire into her trunk and slammed it closed. "So it's absolutely no problem."

Shannon couldn't help returning his smile, because it was just so dashing, and he was so good-looking, and he smelled like cologne and sunshine and dark roast coffee.

As she collected her purse and coffee and walked with him over to his car, Shannon wondered why she'd never looked at Doctor Jeremiah Yeates more than once on her way out of the coffee shop.

SNEAK PEEK! THE PRINCE'S BRIDE CHAPTER ONE

*Z*ara Reddy pulled her dark hair out of its ponytail, the amount of water squeezing out with her elastic making a huge puddle on the floor. She was used to being wet, because she worked as a synchronized swimmer on the island on Getaway Bay, in some of their most popular shows.

This summer's show kept her busy with practices during the week, and nightly shows from Thursday to Sunday. She didn't work the matinees, thankfully. She was grateful for the jobs that always seemed to come her way. That way, she didn't have to go to work at her family's Indian restaurant in downtown Getaway Bay.

They were traditional in every sense of the word, and Zara had made more explanations about her life choices over the years than she cared to admit.

Her phone flashed violently with blue and green lights,

and she checked her texts first as the other swimmers came into the locker room.

"Are you coming with us to dinner?" Suzie asked, taking Zara's attention from her device.

"Oh, uh, I don't think so," she said, lifting her phone. "I think I just got that housesitting job."

Suzie wrung out her hair and started changing. "That's great, Zee. Up on the bluffs?"

"Yeah. First time." She was an experienced house sitter, and she'd completed a dozen or so jobs now. It was easy work, and she got to stay in some of the nicest houses on the island.

And this one?

This one was the crown jewel of the mansions up on the bluff. She'd been texting back and forth with a woman named Petra for several days now, and Zara had never answered so many questions. It was house sitting, not rocket science.

But Petra wanted a background check, and Zara's references, and if there would be any pets in the house. Zara did have a long-haired white cat, but she'd kept that to herself. Petra didn't seem like the kind that would tolerate felines.

The pay was sky high, and Zara smiled as she tapped out her acceptance of the job. She had a small apartment in a long row of them, and staying up on the bluffs would add to her gasoline bill, but it would be so much better than listening to the thirty-somethings next door try to become Hawaii's next big boy band—at all hours of the night.

The address to the house appeared on her screen, along with the code to the gate and the garage. *Anytime tonight or tomorrow*, Petra said. *Send me your PayMe, and I'll get you the money.*

Zara showered and dressed, throwing her heavy bag full of suits, props, caps, nose clips, goggles, and more over her shoulder and heading out to her car. Hopefully, it would start. It was much too hot to sit in the car without air conditioning, listening to the engine click while she prayed it would turn over.

"With this new job," she muttered to herself as she crossed the parking lot. "You can maybe afford to buy a new car." One that actually started the first time.

Sighing, she got behind the wheel and stuck in the key. Miraculously, the car started with the first turn, and she fiddled with the dials on the air conditioner to make it blow harder. Her phone rang, and she answered the call from one of her best friends, Ash Fox.

"Hey, Ash." Zara put the car in reverse, trying not to let any of the jealousy she'd been experiencing when it came to Ash infuse her voice. See, Ash had been Zara's go-to friend when everyone else had a boyfriend. Ash never did. Ash sat behind her sewing machine almost all the time. Zara could always count on Ash—until Burke.

And now Zara had a huge, empty house on the bluffs to go home to.

"So remember how you said you might be able to help out at Your Tidal Forever?" Ash asked.

"Yeah," Zara said slowly.

"Well, Hope is *swamped*, and she's looking to pick up a few seasonally people this summer. Just until the Bellagio wedding is over in September."

Normally, Zara would've jumped at the chance, because it was work, and she didn't pass up an opportunity to make connections around the island in case she met someone who could open another door for her.

Anything was better than the door leading to Indian Room.

"I can't," she said, infusing the appropriate amount of disappointment into her voice. "I just picked up that housesitting job I was telling you about. With the show, and now this, I'm not sure I'll have time."

"Oh, that's fine," Ash said. "Hope just said to spread the word. If you know anyone, have them call over to Your Tidal Forever."

"I will."

"So you got the housesitting job?"

"Yes." Zara smiled as she turned onto the road that led back to her apartment. She just needed to pack a few things and get Whitewater, her cat, into her carrier. "I'm pretty excited about it. I'm heading up there right now."

"Pool?" Ash asked.

"*Big* pool," Zara said. "In fact, I think there are two pools at this place."

"I have four dresses to make by next weekend." Ash moaned.

"I'll be here until September," she said. "In fact, I think I'm going to give up my lease." After all, it was only June, and she could save three and a half months of rent if she gave up her place. There were plenty of rentals on the island, and she wouldn't have any problem getting somewhere else come fall.

Not only that, but then the boy band wannabes wouldn't be her neighbors anymore. OH, yes, she was going to give up her apartment, just as soon as she made it back down to town from the bluffs the following morning.

Tonight, she was going to bask in the grandeur of this mansion, maybe sit by the pool, and just *relax*.

\#

An hour later, the sun was nowhere near setting, for which Zara was thankful. She didn't want to pull up to the house in the dark, but Whitewater would not get in her carrier and it had taken Zara an extraordinarily long time to pack a bag and leave her house with the cat. The backs of Zara's hands could testify of that, what with all the scratches from Whitewater's protests.

The cat yowled from the passenger seat, and Zara said, "Oh, be quiet, Whitey. You're fine." So maybe the words held a bit of exasperation. But some of those scratches were deep, and two had bled a little. So the cat could be quiet as Zara navigated the twisty road up to the bluffs.

All of Getaway Bay's rich and famous lived up here. Okay, fine, not all of them. But all the ones who didn't live in the swanky penthouses on the beach. Beachside didn't exist up on the bluffs. Oh, no. People bought these houses for the privacy and security, as well as the stunning, spectacular, three hundred and sixty degree ocean views.

Zara couldn't decide which she'd rather have. Soft, white sand right out her backdoor, or a mansion in the hills. But for the next three months, she'd be taking this twenty-minute drive up to the mansion.

She turned onto the appointed road and went about a

block before she met a closed and locked gate. After keying in the code, her excitement grew while the gate rumbled open. A sprawling piece of land sat before her, and she eased her car through the now-open gate onto the driveway.

With the gate moving closed behind her, another sigh passed through her body. She had tomorrow off from swimming practice, as the director was working with the acrobats and the main characters in Fresh Start, the not-to-be-missed show of the summer in Getaway Bay's outdoor theater pool.

Zara had done a few shows at the same venue, and the special effects capabilities were superb. She'd also worked with Ian Granger, the director, several times, and while she'd thought they might have a spark in the beginning, it had fizzled fast.

Just like every other relationship Zara had had. She'd been in the dating pool for a long time, and she was feeling wrinkly and dried out from all the chemicals. She wouldn't care that much that she was boyfriendless if her mother didn't badger her constantly to find that special someone.

As if Zara hadn't been looking.

She gazed at the beautiful Hawaiian flowers, the trees, the black lava rock in the landscaping. This was done by a professional, and Zara loved every piece of it as she drove slowly past.

The house sat down a little hill and it too spread out and up, boasting tall white pillars on the front porch, which faced the ocean. Of course, three sides of this house faced the ocean, and Zara hoped the room where she'd be staying had a walk-out balcony. Or a patio. Something where she could step from inside to out and breathe in the fresh air and hear the waves crashing on the rocks far below.

She pulled up to the front door and peered through the windshield. "All right, Whitey," she said to the cat. "Let's go see where we're going to be living for a few months."

Petra never had to know about the cat. The woman said she and her family would be overseas for the summer, thus the need for a house sitter. So Zara killed the engine, walked around the car and shouldered her overnight bag before picking up the cat carrier.

At the front door, she keyed in the code and the lock disengaged. The alarm sounded once, and she stepped over to the keypad to disarm it. She hadn't gotten a separate code for it, so she put in the same numbers as she'd used to unlock the front door.

But that only made the alarm beep at her. The steady, every-two-second beeps made her want to stab something in her ears. She tried the code again, very aware of Whitewater's increased yowling. It was as if the cat was trying to harmonize with the incessant beeping.

"Come on," she muttered when she put in the wrong digit and had to go back.

She became aware of another sound amidst the chaos—growling. She turned to see a big, black dog standing about ten feet away, his teeth bared.

"Oh," Zara exhaled most of the word as Whitewater started hissing inside the carrier. The dog barked, huge, booming sounds that filled the two-story high foyer.

With the beeping, and the hissing, and the barking, it was a miracle that Zara heard someone say, "Boomer, be quiet," just before a man came through the doorway and stood behind the dog. He paused when he caught sight of Zara, his eyes widening. He lifted the spatula he held like he'd use it to defend himself if necessary.

"What are you doing here?" he yelled over the barking, the hissing, and the beeping.

"Housesitting," she yelled back. "Who are you?"

He looked like he could be a fashion magazine model, what with that dark hair all swept back into a manbun on the back of his skull. He opened his mouth, presumably to yell something else, and then rolled his eyes before striding forward.

"I changed the code," he said, practically pushing her aside to punch in the numbers. The beeping stopped. He turned back to the dog. "Boomer, quiet." The dog stopped barking, and Zara tried not to be impressed.

Tried, and failed.

"Sit," the man said next, and the dog did that too.

Now, if she could get Whitewater to stop hissing....

Their eyes met, and dang if Zara didn't have to jump back at the shock she received. He had gorgeous eyes the color of the black lava rock outside, and his olive skin had certainly been featured in many a woman's daydreams about European beaus.

"Who are you again?" she asked, realizing he'd never said.

"I'm Noah Wales," he said. "And I don't need a house sitter."

BOOKS IN THE BRIDES & BEACHES ROMANCE SERIES

The Helicopter Pilot's Bride (Brides & Beaches Romance, Book 1): Charlotte Madsen's whole world came crashing down six months ago with the words, "I met someone else." Her marriage of eleven years dissolved, and she left one island on the east coast for the island of Getaway Bay. She was not expecting a tall, handsome man to be flat on his back under the kitchen sink when she arrives at the supposedly abandoned house.

But former Air Force pilot, Dawson Dane, has a charming devil-may-care personality, and Charlotte could use some happiness in her life. **Can Charlotte navigate the healing process to find love again?**

BOOKS IN THE BRIDES & BEACHES ROMANCE SERIES

The Billionaire's Bride (Brides & Beaches Romance, Book 2): Two best friends, their hasty agreement, and the fake engagement that has the island of Getaway Bay in a tailspin...

BOOKS IN THE BRIDES & BEACHES ROMANCE SERIES

The Prince's Bride (Brides & Beaches Romance, Book 3): She's a synchronized swimmer looking to make some extra cash. He's a prince in hiding. When they meet in the "empty" mansion she's supposed to be housesitting, sparks fly. Can Noah and Zara stop arguing long enough to realize their feelings for each other might be romantic?

BOOKS IN THE BRIDES & BEACHES ROMANCE SERIES

The Doctor's Bride (Brides & Beaches Romance, Book 4): A doctor, a wedding planner, and a flat tire... Can Shannon and Jeremiah make a love connection when they work next door to each other?

BOOKS IN THE BRIDES & BEACHES ROMANCE SERIES

The Rockstar's Bride (Brides & Beaches Romance, Book 5): Riley finds a watch and contacts the owner, only to learn he's the lead singer and guitarist for a hugely popular band. Evan is only on the island of Getaway Bay for a friend's wedding, but he's intrigued by the gorgeous woman who returns his watch. Can they make a relationship work when they're from two different worlds?

BOOKS IN THE BRIDES & BEACHES ROMANCE SERIES

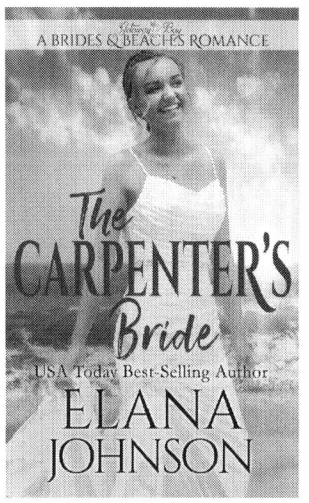

The Carpenter's Bride (Brides & Beaches Romance, Book 6): A wedding planner and the carpenter who's lost his wife... Can Lisa and Cal navigate the mishaps of a relationship in order to find themselves standing at the altar?

BOOKS IN THE BRIDES & BEACHES ROMANCE SERIES

The Police Chief's Bride (Brides & Beaches Romance, Book 7): The Chief of Police and a woman with a restraining order against her... Can Wyatt and Deirdre try for their second chance at love? Or will their pasts keep them apart forever?

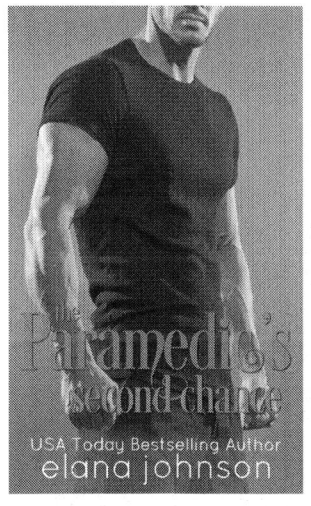

The Paramedic's Second Chance (Hawthorne Harbor Second Chance Romance, Book 1): Paramedic Andrew Herrin delivered Gretchen Samuels's daughter on the side of the road when she and her husband couldn't make it to the hospital in time. When their paths cross again in small-town Hawthorn Harbor, she's a widow and the baby is ten-year-old Dixie.

Dixie gets along great with Drew, and Gretchen finds herself falling in love with the man who's rescued her twice now. But when Drew's ex-girlfriend comes back to town, Gretchen's trust issues rear their ugly head. Can she and Drew find their way toward finding love in the lavender?

The Chief's Second Chance (Hawthorne Harbor Second Chance Romance, Book 2): Janey Germaine is tired of entertaining tourists in Olympic National Park all day and trying to keep her twelve-year-old son occupied at night. When long-time friend and the Chief of Police, Adam Herrin, offers to take the boy on a ride-along one fall evening, Janey starts to see him in a different light. Do they have the courage to take their relationship out of the friend zone?

The Firefighter's Second Chance (Hawthorne Harbor Second Chance Romance, Book 3): Bennett Patterson is content with his boring firefighting job and his big great dane...until he comes face-to-face with his high school girlfriend, Jennie Zimmerman, who swore she'd never return to Hawthorne Harbor. Can they rekindle their old flame? Or will their opposite personalities keep them apart?

The Officer's Second Chance (Hawthorne Harbor Second Chance Romance, Book 4): Trent Baker is ready for another relationship, and he's hopeful he can find someone who wants him and to be a mother to his son. Lauren Michaels runs her own general contract company, and she's never thought she has a maternal bone in her body. But when she gets a second chance with the handsome K9 cop who blew her off when she first came to town, she can't say no... Can Trent and Lauren make their differences into strengths and build a family?

The Soldier's Second Chance (Hawthorne Harbor Second Chance Romance, Book 5): A wounded Marine returns to Hawthorne Harbor years after the woman he was married to for exactly one week before she got an annulment...and then a baby nine months later. Can Hunter and Alice make a family out of past heartache?

The Captain's Second Chance (Hawthorne Harbor Second Chance Romance, Book 6): A Coast Guard captain would rather spend his time on the sea...unless he's with the woman he's been crushing on for months. Can Brooklynn and Dave make their second chance stick?

BOOKS IN THE CLEAN BILLIONAIRE BEACH CLUB ROMANCE SERIES

The Brainy Billionaire (Book 1): A local island B&B owner hates the swanky high-rise hotel down the beach...but not the billionaire who owns it. Can she deal with strange summer weather, tourists, *and* falling in love?

The Brawny Billionaire (Book 2): A car service owner who's been driving the billionaire pineapple plantation owner for years finally gives him a birthday gift that opens his eyes to *see* her, the woman who's literally been right in front of him all this time. Can he open his heart to the possibility of true love?

The Bashful Billionaire (Book 3): A former poker player turned beach bum billionaire needs a date to a hospital gala, so he asks the beach yoga instructor his dog can't seem to stay away from. At the event, they get "engaged" to deter her former boyfriend from pursuing her. Can he move his fake fiancée into a real relationship?

The Brazen Billionaire (Book 4): The owner of a beach-side drink stand has taken more bad advice from rich men than humanly possible, which requires her to take a second job cleaning the home of a billionaire and global diamond mine owner. Can she put aside her preconceptions about rich men and make a relationship with him work?

The Billionaire's Bodyguard (Book 5): Women can be rich too...and this female billionaire can usually take care of herself just fine, thank you very much. But she has no defense against her past...or the gorgeous man she hires to protect her from it. *He's her bodyguard, not her boyfriend.* Will she be able to keep those two B-words separate or will she take her second chance to get her tropical happily-ever-after?

The Billionaire's Boyfriend (Book 6): Can a closet organizer fit herself into a single father's hectic life? Or will this female billionaire choose work over love...again?

The Brave Billionaire (Book 11): A billionaire who has a love affair with his job, his new bank manager, and how they bravely navigate the island of Getaway Bay...and their own ideas about each other.

The Belated Billionaire (Book 12): A silver fox, a dating app, and the mistaken identity that brings this billionaire face-to-face with his ex-wife...

Stranded with the Hidden Billionaire (Stranded in Paradise, Getaway Bay Romance, Book 1): A freak storm has her sliding down the mountain...right into the arms of her ex.

As Eden and Holden spend time out in the wilds of Hawaii trying to survive, their old flame is rekindled. But with secrets and old feelings in the way, will Holden be able to take all the broken pieces of his life and put them back together in a way that makes sense? Or will he lose his heart and the reputation of his company because of a single landslide?

Stranded with the SEAL (Stranded in Paradise, Getaway Bay Romance, Book 2): Friends who ditch her. A pod of killer whales. A limping cruise ship. All reasons Iris finds herself stranded on an deserted island with the handsome Navy SEAL...

Stranded with the Quarterback (Stranded in Paradise, Getaway Bay Romance, Book 3): He can throw a precision pass, but he's dead in the water in matters of the heart...

Stranded with the Cowboy Billionaire (Stranded in Paradise, Getaway Bay Romance, Book 4): Tired of the dating scene, a cowboy billionaire puts up an Internet ad to find a woman to come out to a deserted island with him to see if they can make a love connection...

Boyfriend By Mistake (Carter's Cove Sweet Romance, Book 1): She owns The Heartwood Inn. He needs the land the inn sits on to impress his boss. Neither one of them will give an inch. But will they give each other their hearts?

Accidental Sweetheart (Carter's Cove Sweet Romance, Book 2): She's excited to have a neighbor across the hall. He's got secrets he can never tell her. Will Olympia find a way to leave her past where it belongs so she can have a future with Chet?

Bodyguard, Not Boyfriend (Carter's Cove Sweet Romance, Book 3): She's got a stalker. He's got a loud bark. Can Sheryl tame her bodyguard into a boyfriend?

Not Her Real Fiancé (Carter's Cove Sweet Romance, Book 4): He needs a reason *not* to go out with a journalist. She'd like a guaranteed date for the summer. They don't get along, so keeping Brad in the not-her-real-fiancé category should be easy for Celeste. *Totally* easy.

She Loves Him...Not (Carter's Cove Sweet Romance, Book 5): They've been out before, and now they work in the same kitchen at The Heartwood Inn. Gwen isn't interested in getting anything filleted but fish, because Teagan's broken her heart before... Can Teagan and Gwen manage their professional relationship without letting feelings get in the way?

The Professor's Secret Crush (Forbidden Lake Romance, Book 1): She's about to break her university's rules and date a student...

The Lumberjack's Secret Guest (Forbidden Lake Romance, Book 2): He's about to let in his enemy and call her a guest...

The Owner's Secret Client (Forbidden Lake Romance, Book 3): He knows it's against the rules to date his au pair...he just doesn't care.

The Billionaire's Secret Flame (Forbidden Lake Romance, Book 4): He's her boss and her biggest crush. He's also got secrets that could burn them both...

The Rockstar's Secret Weakness (Forbidden Lake Romance, Book 5): She's about to sign him as a client just to be able to see him...

The Biker's Secret Girlfriend (Forbidden Lake Romance, Book 6): He wants the widow, but she belongs to the rival motorcycle club...

Burn (Sentinels Motorcycle Club Romance Series, Book 1): There's nothing more dangerous than a bad boy making decisions with his heart.

Vice (Sentinels Motorcycle Club Romance Series, Book 2): There's nothing more dangerous than a bad boy giving into his vices...

Crash (Sentinels Motorcycle Club Romance Series, Book 3): There's nothing more dangerous than a bad boy with secrets...

ABOUT ELANA

Elana Johnson is the USA Today bestselling author of dozens of novels, from YA contemporary romance to adult beach romances. She lives in Utah, where she teaches elementary school, taxis her daughter to dance several times a week, and eats a lot of Ferrero Rocher while writing. Find her on her website at elanajohnson.com.

Text SAND to 474747 and get sales, free stuff, and contests from Elana

Made in the USA
Columbia, SC
27 May 2020

*To Nelson again,
I will be forever grateful*

CHAPTER ONE

"ANYWAY, I BANGED him like a screen door all winter. Had to stay warm somehow, you know what I mean?" I line up my shot, aim for the ten-ball, and miss wildly. Whatever. I blow imaginary dust off my pool stick before turning to my best friend, Cassidy, and to the amusement across her face. "But now it's summer and we all know how cruel Virginia summers can be. I let him go."

"You kill me," she says, cracking up and grabbing her own cue. "But he lasted longer than your usual boys, right?"

My usual boys. I consider her words and slide a strand of auburn hair out of my eyes, tucking it behind my ear. Against the wall a few pool tables over, someone changes the jukebox song to some twangy country piece that I instantly hate. "You could say that."

"*You* could say," she bends over the table, taking aim, "that this twelve-ball's about to hit that corner pocket."

Half the pool hall is staring at her ass right now. Not that I blame them—she's got an awesome ass. Wish mine wasn't so flat, but *blah, blah,* self-deprecation's lame and I'm over it. Nobody looks away when Cassidy shoots up with a little victory dance after her ball goes exactly where she says it will. Because of course it does.

But it's my turn to laugh. "Too bad I'm stripes and you totally just sank that for me."

She pauses mid-wiggle. "I'm stripes."

"Nope," I say, grinning. "I sank the nine-ball first. Numbers over eight are striped, under are solid." I've been repeating it to myself all night. "So. Thank you for my point...or whatever it's called in pool."

"Teag. You hit the six-ball in." She walks around the table to the place where balls return and pulls out a...nine-ball. *Ha!*

Nope. Wait. Looking at it the wrong way.

It's the six-ball. Green, *solid*.

Damn it.

"Why didn't you say anything when I was aiming for the ten-ball?" I ask, keeping my tone as light as I can. Because there's no need to get pissed off about this.

"You were shooting for the ten-ball?" she asks, pulling her blonde hair into a messy ponytail that's instantly, effortlessly, annoyingly stylish. "I couldn't tell."

"Oh, fuck you." I smile, forcing it to show in my eyes. *See? Look, I'm not getting heated over something so stupid.*

Even though I am.

Even though *knowing* how stupid it is makes me even more irritated.

Great. And now she's studying my face, trying to tell if I'm actually mad. Because she knows I have...issues, and she wants to help me.

Even though she can't.

And knowing she knows how fucked up I am and can read me the way she does? It makes me furious.

Which is stupid.

And—*here we go again*—knowing how stupid it is, that I'm angry because she cares about me? Yeah. It makes it worse.

God.

My jokes about my sex life might kill Cassidy, but this? This cycle of meaningless anger I can't find my way out of is what's killing me.

Thank the fucking lord, our friend Vera returns from the bar with our drinks.

"Finally." I accept mine and guzzle until the frostiness of the hard cider reaches the pit of my belly, quelling some of the fire there.

"You're welcome," she says, her words short. Pointed. But her dark eyes sparkle in the dim lighting. "If I took too long, maybe next time *you* go wait at the bar."

"Listen. You're on the new side of this friendship, but you should know by now," I say. "You have to accept me for who I am."

"It's true." Cassidy rests her hip against the pool table, taking a sip of her beer.

Vera slides a hand through her short black hair, lifting a brow at me. "Do *you* accept you for who you are?"

Ugh. Why are my friends such *friends?* "I don't know, but your dad did last night."

"My dad is dead." She blinks, and the music over the pool hall's speakers is suddenly sharper in my ears. I hate myself.

"I'm sorry, Ver. I didn't mean it. I didn't know." I'm such an asshole. She stares at me, her eyes all wide and sad, and I want to crawl into a hole in the ground and stay there for the rest of my life.

And then... She laughs. "He's not dead. But screw you for joking about banging him."

My breath shudders out, relief taking its place in my lungs. "Screw *you* for the heart attack."

"You're on the new side of this friendship, but...how the hell did you not know my father was alive?"

"I don't even know who my own father is, so why on earth would I keep track of yours?" I retort. It comes out with more of a bite than I mean it to—*shocker*—and when her face falls, I wave it off. I don't feel sorry for myself about it, so she sure as shit shouldn't either. "Anyway. I'm about to kick Cassidy's ass in this game—you want to take me on next?"

Cassidy blows out an exaggerated sigh, a gesture that reminds me so much of her dead brother it nearly takes my breath away. "Big words for someone who didn't even know if she was stripes or solids."

She's only teasing.

I slice my stick toward her, stopping short of her face. She doesn't even flinch; she knows I'd never hit her.

What she doesn't know is how hard it is to remind myself that she's only teasing, that I don't need to get pissed off at her reminder of what an idiot I am.

She kicks my ass the rest of the game, and I end up on the sidelines, watching Vera give Cassidy a run for her money. It's fine by me because I need another drink anyway. In fact, I'll buy the next round. Only I cringe when the bartender brings me the total. And then I pull out some crumpled bills from my purse and pay it anyway. Soon, it won't matter. I start a new job on Monday.

It's why we're here tonight. There was some snazzy Friday happy hour thing across the street, and I dragged Cassidy with me because it's the company her dad works for, and he said I should come meet some people. *Some people* was an understatement. I met a lot. It was overwhelming and we hightailed it out as soon as it was acceptable.

So yeah. I fight a second cringe and I leave a nice tip when the bartender brings me all our drinks, because I'm salaried as of Monday. Granted, it's an itty-bitty salary with no starting benefits, but it'll still be steadier than what I made at the salon.

Screw that place.

I grab my cider, Cassidy's beer, and Vera's ridiculous and super girlie peaches-and-cream concoction (that I secretly wish I wasn't too cheap to buy for myself, too) and turn—and nearly face-plant into the guy sliding onto the stool beside me.

"Whoa there." His voice is smooth, and he steadies me with his hands on my shoulders, and I can tell before I've even looked up at him he's going to be hot—and cocky. Because his fingers are resting against my skin with that perfect sort of pressure, the kind that says *I touch tons of girls and I know how to make them respond with nothing more than a quick squeeze from my fingertips.* Then I lift my face and... Wow.

He's more than hot. Pretty, but in a rugged way. An angular chin, covered with stubble. Straight nose. Sharp cheeks. Hooded eyes that are somewhere between deep brown and midnight with lashes for freaking miles. And his hair? It's basically fine black silk—a little too long, but in that carelessly messy sort of way that actually makes it the perfect length. There's enough...I don't know? *Practiced casual poise*...in his expression to make me think he's a couple years older than I am.

Plus, he's tall. I'm arching my neck to look up at him and his chest is in front of my face and...his button-up shirt's not so tight that I'd make fun of it—but it sits well enough across his chest that I can tell he works out. And he smells good. Like a woodsy sort of aftershave or something.

I mean, really. Get the fuck out of here with all that.

"*Whoa there?* I'm not a horse." Not my best choice of words, probably, but sarcasm is the best shield against guys who look like this. Plus, the only thing happening in my brain right now is the assessment of how intensely he's staring at me. It's making my neck tingle. Other places, too.

"No," he says, releasing me with one hand to drag it across his sexy mouth. "Horse isn't the animal that'd come to mind... Perhaps a fox. Or maybe a kitten. Though you look like you might bite. Are you feral, little kitten?"

"You don't take your hand off of me, you'll find out real quick."

He waits a second longer than appropriate and, instead of letting go all at once, he slides his fingers over my shoulder and across my collarbone, letting them fall away at their own slow pace.

My skin straight up goose bumps at his touch. So I do what any smart girl would do. I walk away from him without another glance.

Because he's the kind of guy I avoid at all costs. Pretty face, sexy attitude, smelling all masculine and honeyed enough to make my mouth water? Nope. No, no, no. Those guys are to be avoided.

Those guys cost me my mother.

Those guys are assholes.

"That guy's watching you with so much intensity, I'm not sure how you aren't in flames right now," Cassidy says, taking her beer.

I knew it. I knew I could feel that stupid gaze across the backs of my shoulders. "Whatever. Who cares? This is a girls' night, right?"

I definitely am not going to look over my shoulder.

Oh my God, it's difficult not to look over my shoulder.

"Shots," I say, instead. "Somebody go get us shots. Stat." When Cassidy turns toward the bar, I grab her arm. "And steer clear of that dude, okay? He's too slick to be bothered with. And don't bring us whiskey, you weirdo."

She rolls her eyes. "I'm aware I'm hanging out with the girliest drinkers ever. Don't worry."

So we have a round of lemon drops. And then another.

He doesn't do it often enough to be stalkerish, but I feel the guy's eyes on me more than what I'd consider coincidence.

I find my eyes on him almost as much.

The worst is when he catches me and I look away immediately, because I freaking hate looking away, hate giving him that power.

But he's got something in his stare that startles my system. Makes my skin flush and my chin go up, even though I can't maintain eye contact.

I borrowed a blazer from Cassidy for the thing tonight, but it's hanging over a stool now. I'm tempted to put it on though, because I'm too aware of how much skin my tank top flaunts. But the jacket's constricting and it's hot in here. And he's looking at me and I'm *glad* my skin is showing.

Wait. Not that last thing.

"I'd win a game if I could fucking concentrate," I mutter, after Vera schools me yet again.

Whatever. Pool isn't my strong suit. Who cares?

Plus, if the two of them duke it out all night, I don't have to worry whether or not I look dumb leaning on the table with his eyes on me. I may be in professional-looking black pants, but they're a little too small for me—and they get much tighter around my ass when I bend over. And not in a sexy way. I position myself on a stool with my back to the guy I wish I wasn't so aware of.

But after Vera gets us another round of shots, it doesn't even matter that my back's to him, because he comes to us. With drinks. The same ones we've all been drinking. Vera's concoction. My hard cider—which I take without comment. And Cassidy's beer, which he holds out with a smile a bit too wide for my liking.

"She has a boyfriend," I tell him, my tone edgier than I intend.

"Retract the claws, kitten." His voice is silkier when it's not competing with the noises closer to the bar. So silky, in fact, it pairs perfectly with his hair.

"I'm making sure you're aware." I squeeze my fingers tighter around the cider to keep from reaching up and running them through his locks. "Don't try to hit on her."

Cassidy slams me with her elbow. "Dude, *chill*."

"She's not the one I'm hitting on," he says, his eyes on mine for so long my face heats, and Vera and Cassidy giggle.

I'm inclined to make a snarky response, but nothing comes to me when I open my lips—except the thought of how his might feel against them.

Oh. Hmm.

I could be in a little bit of trouble here.

CHAPTER TWO

"HOW DO I know you didn't drug these?" I ask, holding out the cider he handed me.

He takes it, his fingers brushing over mine, and puts it to his lips, drinking it long and slow. Like I'd be able to concentrate on anything other than his throat as he swallows. Like he knows the path the liquid travels, down past his Adam's apple, would appear nearly mesmerizing. So annoying.

"What about theirs?" I ask, my tone coming out completely unaffected when he hands it back to me.

"May I?" he asks, holding out a hand toward Cassidy.

She lifts a shoulder, glancing at me, and gives him her beer.

He drinks, again.

I watch, again.

"Your boyfriend going to have a problem with me drinking on your beer?" he asks her, returning it.

"Considering you've made it clear you're not hitting on me," she says, dryly, "he'll be fine with it."

I open my mouth.

Shut it.

He reaches for Vera's drink, but she's already halfway done with it. "Sorry," she says, giggling. "I guess I trust you."

She's way too trusting. Has been since I've known her.

The guy looks at me.

Oh. Right. "Thanks for the drinks," I say.

"My name's—"

"Nobody asked for your name," I say.

Cassidy sighs. "Don't mind my friend. She hasn't gotten laid in a while and all that pent-up frustration makes it hard for her to remember her manners."

"Are you *kidding* me?" I glare at her because no way can I meet *his* eyes anymore. I want to die. I seriously want to fucking die. "That's none of his business!" Then, I hastily remember to add: "And it's not even true."

"*Anyway*." Vera, always the mediator, sticks out her hand, and it sways a bit in the air before he takes it. "I'm Vera. And this is Cassidy. And this is—"

"Cindy," I finish for her. Because I don't want him to know my real name. Because as a rule I don't get involved with guys like him, but he's so freaking hot and I'm exactly the right amount of tipsy to make an exception tonight. And I'll need an easy way to escape without a trace. Especially if he keeps looking at me like he wants to take a bite of me.

"Cindy," he purrs over the two syllables. "I've always liked that name."

"Funny enough, so have I." At least this part isn't a lie. "Thanks for the drinks, but we're in the middle of a girls' night."

"I figured," he says, smiling. God, even his teeth are beautiful. "I'll leave you alone, then."

"Actually," Vera slurs *this* word into about seven syllables. She holds up a finger to keep him from walking away. "I have to go home—and clean."

I lift a brow. Or…maybe I do. I might be a little drunker than I thought. "You're leaving girls' night to clean?"

"My mom's coming to town tomorrow. She… I can't even try to explain her right now." She doesn't need to, though. I've known Vera almost a year and practically all she ever talks about is her mom and how annoying she is. She sounds like a nightmare. Sometimes I'm thankful I don't have a mother nagging me the way Vera's does.

Most of the time I wish I did. But whatever.

"Fine. It'll be the original two, then," I say, turning to Cassidy. But her expression's way too apologetic for my words to be true. Ugh. "You too?"

"Um... Gage is waiting outside. He's going to drive us home." Her boyfriend. Her sexy, annoyingly perfect boyfriend who would of course wait outside so he wouldn't interrupt our night until Cassidy wants to leave. Which means she called him at some point without me noticing.

What the hell? "I don't want to go."

She glances at Mr. Sex-on-an-Extra-Thick-Stick and then at me, a knowing expression across her stupid face. "So don't."

"I'll stay and play," he says, nodding toward the pool table. And, really, who could say no to his freaking dimples when he grins, all deep and dazzling?

"One more drink," I tell him. "And if someone better comes along, I'm out of here."

"Tea—Cindy." Vera gives me an exasperated look. "Lighten *up*."

I know. I know.

I'm a bitch.

I can't help it. Sometimes, I don't even want to.

But he doesn't seem to mind—especially when he smirks and asks, "If another screen door comes along, you mean?"

"What?" At first I don't understand, even though Cassidy bursts out laughing beside me.

"Someone to bang all summer?" he asks, his smirk widening. "I get it. You find him—or her—and I'll leave you alone."

Who knew cheeks were made of kindling? Because his words spark mine and they erupt into flames.

"I don't get it," Vera says. "What am I missing?"

"Were you *spying* on me? On us, I mean," I demand, aiming for an indignant tone regardless of how neon my face must be. Damn red-haired complexion...

"I was walking past your pool table," he says.

"Right." I don't believe him. I would've seen him.

"He was," Cassidy says. "He walked behind you. I...noticed." Her cheeks go a pretty light pink color that is so unfair.

"You sell screen doors?" Vera asks, still confused.

I'd laugh as hard as *he* does at her question, but a different thought suddenly turns my stomach sour. "So what? You thought I'd make an easy mark? Because, trust me, I'm not going to—"

"Nothing about you seems easy to me," he says—and it wins him some points, to be honest. "But you're pretty, and you're feisty—and I'm into the combination."

"And that's our cue," Cassidy says, her tone full of approval. She glances at her phone and links her arm through Vera's. "Let's go, V." She looks at me. "You cool?"

"As ice," I say and sip my cider, even if my blood's heating more and more every second this dude's standing beside me. "Tell Gage I say he sucks. And also hi. I'll call you tomorrow."

"I have a feeling you've never been cool as ice," the guy says to me while my friends walk away. "You're too fiery for that."

"You're smooth." I roll my eyes to keep from looking at his face for at least one second longer, wondering if he actually *sees me* already or if this is his game. Then I study his hand when he holds it out toward me.

Trim, even fingernails. Long fingers. Big palm. He clears his throat. "Guess I should tell you my name now, if I'll be keeping you company until someone better comes along."

I wrap both hands around my cider. "I don't want to know your name. In fact, I'll choose one for you. How about…Frank?" Because I don't like the name Frank. Because maybe if I call him Frank, I'll find him less attractive.

This is what I tell myself as I drag my eyes to his face, and…

Ha.

Ha ha.

Eyes as dark as his should appear soulless. But nope. Staring into them is like peering into an endless night sky. Filled with stars you can't see but know are there, waiting to be unveiled if you focus long enough.

"…game of pool?" Frank's question comes through a second too late. I didn't even catch his reaction to my name for him, damn it.

"No. I suck at pool. Let's drink." Which is probably a stupid decision, but everything in me seems to be click-click-clicking into doing something even more stupid (stupider?) (ugh, who cares?) with this guy. With *Frank*. And I need a little more liquid courage to grease the gears that will wind me into being confident enough to do it.

"You're at a pool hall and you don't enjoy pool?" he asks. "Odd choice. Or did your friends drag you here?"

"I had a work thing nearby," I say, loving the way the words glide through my mouth. *A work thing.* Like I have a real job. Even if I had to beg for it from my best friend's father. Still. I'm working a real nine-to-fiver.

I'm tempted to brag about the company, Chambers & Britt. But I don't know enough about the equity firm—or about mergers and acquisitions—to answer any questions if he asks. And even if I'm proud of the company's name, I'm still only starting as a second assistant. Not super impressive to someone like this guy.

"Apparently this is the area happy hour hotspot strip," he says. "This row of bars and restaurants is always slammed right at five."

"You just get off?" I ask, then my cheeks heat all over again. Damn, this guy makes me jittery. "Of work, I mean?"

He nods. "Figured a drink or six might wash the day away."

"Want to talk about it?" Wait. I don't want to get to know him. What the hell am I asking for?

Thankfully, he says, "Not really. My boss turned down a proposal I've been working on."

"That sucks." But on the inside, I'm all *cry me a freaking river, dude. You're too hot to have real problems.*

"Sucks even more that the boss also happens to be my father. But the less I talk about it, the better."

"Good," I say. "Less talking, more drinking."

"Well, Cindy," he says, purring my fake name again. Now I kind of wish I'd given him the real one, to hear him stroke it like that with his tongue. "If drinking's what you're after, there are two seats at the bar."

I step toward where he motions, and he places his hand flat against the small of my back, and for a moment everything slows down. My heart pumps my blood in heavy glugs, like the fluid in my veins is actually molasses. My ears go a little fuzzy. The sudden excess of saliva pooling in my mouth takes eons to travel down my throat.

The warmth from his palm is seeping through my top and into my skin and igniting an entirely different sort of heat everywhere else.

Shit, shit, shit.

Or maybe...

Finally, finally, *finally*.

That's probably the alcohol talking, though. Which means I should have some more.

I let him lead me to the bar, which I lean against instead of grabbing a stool so he'll keep his hand on me a little longer. And while we stand there, waiting for the bartender, he traces little paths back and forth with his thumb, and even though I don't look at him, his presence is everywhere, all tall and muscular. His scent—aftershave or rainy pine tree forest or whatever it is—keeps wafting over to me and my entire body is completely *aware* of his and every time I inhale I get tingles in my lower belly and by the time we order drinks, I kind of want to jump him.

But with a guy like this? I don't even know where to begin.

Not that it's going to keep me from trying.

CHAPTER THREE

FRANK DOESN'T DRINK nearly as much as he should, which I continue to tell him every time I order another round for myself. He laughs and sips on his stupid Jack and Coke.

"Oh, I get it," I say (or maybe slur). "You're worried about getting it up later?"

Yep. Liquid courage is in full effect.

But this guy, this *Frank*... He's too much. Too hot. Too smooth. Too...just...*standing here* already making my entire body flush.

He laughs again, but this time he wipes a hand across his face, like he's embarrassed. His words say otherwise, though. "Believe me, that wouldn't be an issue. But I don't know if I want to be an addition to your screen door collection."

Maybe it's from the fuzziness that comes with alcohol, or maybe it's because it sometimes takes me a split second longer than other people to get things, but his remark sits between us for a moment before it sinks in. And then it burns.

"One," I say, holding up a finger, "fuck you. And two, why?" I can't believe I asked. I don't want to hear that I'm not pretty enough or funny enough or smart enough. Not that he knows me well enough to know the last two yet. Which means—oh, *great*—he isn't attracted to me. Story of my life.

I think of Vera and Cassidy and my stomach twists. Vera's stick-straight, jet-black satin-otherwise-known-as-hair, her slender build, her beautiful, flawless skin. Cassidy's annoyingly perfect blonde hair, her level-headed intelligence, and her sexy-as-sin curves... Next to them I'm a lump. Bland. Next to them, I'm—

"Hey, where'd you go?" Frank nudges me.

"Nothing. Never mind." I sip on my cider and watch a couple of guys taking shots at the end of the bar. I can't bring myself to look at Frank. Instead, I say, "I'm going home."

"Oh, no, you're not getting out of this one." He puts his hand over mine on the bar, grabbing it when I try to slide my fingers away. "You are the first reason I've had to smile this entire shitty day."

Now I look at him. It's easier when I'm pissed. "You're gonna keep me from leaving? I'd like to see you try."

Yeah, I actually would like to see him try. But guys like Frank don't beg girls like me to stick around.

Then he says, "You can leave if you want to. But I want my chance to answer your question first."

Again, I try to slide my hand from the bar. He tightens his grip, but not so much that I couldn't break free if I truly wanted to. Which is annoying because if I let him keep my hand in place, it tells him that I want this.

I do want this. I'm just not partial to being so open in my admission.

His palm is rough against my skin, scratchy. Hmm. How would it feel against other parts of my body?

I keep my hand where it is.

"I'm not interested in being someone's disposable screen door, Cindy." He watches my face. I temper my expression, glad he doesn't know my real name—but also full of regret over my lie. "You're sexy enough to be tempting, but that's not the kind of guy I am."

"So you're saying it's not me, it's you?" I lift a brow again, pretty sure I make it happen this time. And then, I realize he called me sexy. And there's this glow that slides softly through me, making my bones all melty... "Are you reverse psychology-ing me?"

He studies me over the rim of his glass, taking a sip before answering. "So we're clear, what exactly are you talking about?"

"Telling me you don't want to sleep with me while mentioning in the same breath that you think I'm sexy. Like you're trying to get me to bang you to beg me." Or...that didn't come out right... "Wait. No. Like you're trying to get me to beg you to bang me. Which I won't be doing," I add with a smug tilt to my mouth.

Which slides away when he leans in until his lips are at my ear and says, "I never said I didn't want to sleep with you. But I don't enjoy being used and tossed aside. Trust me, kitten, sleeping with you? My imagination roars just thinking about it."

"Oh." Needing to steady myself, I grab a stool, finally, and slide into it, though his face stays close to mine. In fact, I'm pretty sure if I were to angle my head to the side, his lips would find their way to my neck.

I tuck my hair over my opposite shoulder to free up some skin, and I...chicken out. I lean away from him, turning my face toward his but with a safe distance between us. "I'm pretty choosy about my screen door selection, anyway. I'm not sure you'd make the cut."

"Maybe we should find out." A smile plays around his mouth, and I can't help admiring his very soft-looking, very kissable lips. There's a perfect little dip on the upper one and I kind of want to lick it.

"And how would we do that?" I ask instead, keeping my tongue from doing anything embarrassing. I grab a few napkins from a stack on the bar and wipe up a leftover spill in front of where I'm sitting.

"We'll play a game." He moves smoothly into his own seat and motions the bartender over for another drink.

The bartender looks at me, expecting me to order another shot probably, but I ask for water. Because any more liquid courage right now risks souring into liquid puke...

"What sort of game?" I'm tempted to run a finger along the line of his jaw, over his stubble. I'm drunk enough to do it, but I pop the finger in my mouth instead. He watches, his gaze following my finger, lingering on my mouth...and I start to think maybe he meant what he said about finding me sexy. And I'm not exactly sure what to do with the feeling.

"Two truths," he says, raising his voice when someone turns up the music, "and one lie." And when I stare at him, puzzled, he says,

"Oh, come on. You've never played this before? It's the standard corporate icebreaker."

"I must've missed that day," I say. "And if it's so *standard*, it's probably boring anyway."

"Not the way we're going to play." He tilts his head toward me. "Tell me three—no, actually let's make it harder—four secrets. Two truths, two lies. If I guess something true, you take a shot. If I don't, I take one."

"Why do they have to be secrets?"

"To keep it from being boring."

Hmm. Yeah, okay. This sounds kind of fun. And like something I'll kick his ass at. Whether or not the room's spinning a little bit around me.

"Ready?" I scoot further into my stool and wait for him to nod, truths and lies filtering easily through my mind. "My mother's famous. My father's a baker. I can tie a cherry stem in a knot with my tongue in less than five seconds. And," I bite back a laugh, "I'm a virgin."

Frank doesn't hold in his laugh; his eyes dance, all delighted. His dimples flash all deep and lickable. "That makes things a little easier..."

"I thought you said nothing about me seemed easy?"

"That's still true. But you made the game easier. I'm going with option B as one of the true statements. Your father's a baker—even though that doesn't count as a secret."

"Maybe he's a *secret* baker." I run my fingers up his sleeve, my stomach jumping at the hard muscle they encounter underneath it, and flick his shoulder. "But no. Drink up, bitch."

"Really? He isn't a baker?"

When I shake my head, he slides his face along mine, toward my hair, and takes a long inhale that sends goose bumps running down my body. "Then why do you smell so sweet? I had your whole story in my head, picturing your dad as a baker with the big white hat and everything. You as a little girl with flour on your nose. Growing into something this red-hot... It made sense for baking to be in your bones."

His tone is teasing, but his words push a wave of longing through me. I shake it off and motion the bartender over again. "Tequila," I say, pointing at Frank. "For this guy."

"You're looking for some trouble if you want me drinking tequila tonight."

"You made the rules," I remind him. "Plus, it's your turn."

"Oh, I don't think so. If your father's not a baker, that means your mom's famous *and* you can tie a cherry stem into a knot with your tongue in less than five seconds. I can't decide which I want to focus on more at the moment." His eyes fall to my lips. "You think our bartender will give you a cherry if you ask?"

"Maybe," I say. "But I won't ask."

"You're going to leave me to my imagination? Picturing you tying knots in stems, over and over again?"

"Just because I say I can do something doesn't mean I will. Sorry, my friend."

"Are we friends then?"

"I don't know. Tell me your truths and we'll see."

"Fine, but if we're friends, I expect the full story about your mother."

I laugh, because yeah freaking right.

"I'm serious," he says, straight-faced. "And...I want an example of your knot-tying talents."

"I don't need a cherry stem to show the talents of my tongue." The words slip out, and my face bursts into flames *again*. Here's yet another reason I avoid guys like Frank. He's too pretty, too smooth. The second I open my mouth around him I feel like an idiot.

However, there's a sweet sort of power in the way he takes a deep breath, and the look in his eyes grows hungry. He opens his mouth to respond, but the bartender brings over the shot and he takes it instead, shaking his head when the tequila hits his mouth and sucking the lime immediately after.

Lucky, lucky lime.

There's a drop of lime juice left over in the corner of his mouth, and this time I don't stop myself from touching him, from wiping it off with my finger.

"Your turn." I slide my finger over my own lips, letting the sweet and tart aftertaste sink in. But he's staring at my mouth again, and I don't think he hears me. Pretty sure I've upped the stakes of our game... I let one corner of my mouth rise. "Frank?"

"Right." His eyes shoot to mine. "Let's make this more interesting. If you guess wrong—you take a shot, as promised. If you guess a truth, though, you come home with me."

"This...feels slanted in your favor," I say.

"It's slanted in both our favors," he counters.

I pretend to consider, even though I know exactly what I'm going to say. "I'm in."

"Good." He weaves a rather intense promise through the one word that I can't quite define—but it makes me really, *really* hope I can guess a truth. He taps the sharp line of his jaw. "Let me think..."

I sip my water while I wait and, sneaking peeks out of the corner of my eye that he continually catches, I wonder what his secrets are. Plastic surgery to have a face like that? Or maybe he's a model, but secretly a lumberjack on the side, chopping trees down for extra money and that warm woodsy scent?

Perhaps a teeny tiny penis to compensate for the rest of his perfection?

"I have a brother who's getting married in a month—"

"That is not a secret," I say, shaking my head.

"Yeah, but I was about to say he's marrying the wrong girl. Better?" He lifts his brows, pleased with himself.

"Definitely." And I can tell it's true by his tone. Usually, I'd dig for the story, but tonight's not about getting to know Frank's mind. It's about getting my hands on his body—and being able to walk away after—so I keep my mouth closed.

"Okay, that's one. Two: I love comic books. Three: I grew up with a bad stutter—it still resurfaces once in a while. And...four: Every bone in my body, and not only the obvious one, is dying for you to come home with me tonight."

If that last one isn't true, this guy's a total asshole, because my body is *revving* at his words. I should probably run. Right now. Out the door.

But really, who am I kidding? This is where the night's been heading since I first saw him. There's not a person alive who's attracted to guys who wouldn't say exactly what I'm about to.

I slide my stool back and hook Cassidy's blazer over my elbow. "I'm picking your brother marrying the wrong girl as a truth—and if the one about your bones is truth too, let's get out of here. Like, five minutes ago."

Frank stands, throwing up a hand to catch the bartender's attention, again. "We need our check. Now."

CHAPTER FOUR

FRANK PAYS THE tab, over my protests. We both stick out money—me cash, him a card—but when the bartender pauses, Frank gives him some stupid intimidating stare and my bills are ignored. Annoying.

I roll my eyes. "This isn't a date. I can buy my own drinks."

"So you're automatically assuming I'd pay if we were on a date? That's rude."

"No, I mean..." I can't bite back a small smile. He's winning with sarcasm, beating me at my own game. "Fine."

"Don't smile at me that way," he says, his tone full of warning.

"Why?" For some reason his words make me grin even wider. I shove my money in the pocket of Cassidy's blazer so I won't forget it. The blazer, that is. I never forget where I have cash.

"Because I'll never be able to say no to you if you do."

"What if I ask you to be a screen door?" Another set of words that fall from my mouth, like I'm this brazen thing who will bang anyone anytime. From what he knows, I am.

Oh, well. Clearly it doesn't bother him.

Plus, he isn't *anyone anytime*. Not that I plan to see him after tonight, but I have a feeling he'll be memorable.

His expression falters. "I asked you to come home with me, didn't

I?"

"So you're automatically assuming because I'm coming home with you we'll be...banging like screen doors? That's rude."

He laughs and scribbles his signature on the receipt when the bartender drops it off. "I don't expect anything. But I find myself hoping."

"I make no promises, but what sort of person would I be if I stomped all over your hope?" My tone says I'm sure of myself, but as we make our way toward the exit, nerves shoot through me so fast and so sharp they create a hole for my stomach to fall out of. It hits the floor, splattering everywhere, the stupid-ass nerves hopping and dancing around down there to the beat of the music in the bar.

Can I do this? Am I really going to do this?

"Why the change of heart?" I ask, stalling near an empty pool table, running my fingers along its edge. "Twenty minutes ago you were *so* against becoming a screen door."

"I don't want to be a screen door," he says. "But I do want you." He trails his fingers down my arm and runs them against the small of my back again, and my heart freaking *seizes*. From his touch—but even more from his words, which keep coming. "And maybe I can convince you in the meantime that I'm more than"—another short laugh slips through his lickable lips—"a piece of wood."

Don't look down. Do not *look at the space below his belt.* My eyes sting from all the effort to remain pointed toward his face.

His thumb moves in an arc over my lower back, and I almost jump. I need him to remove his hand. I need him to put his other one on me. I need to take another shot.

I need to get a damn grip. "Maybe you're a collection of smooth words with no substance."

"Maybe I want the chance to show you you're wrong."

"Maybe I can't figure out why." Oh shit. Too much. Didn't mean to admit that. "Or, you know, maybe I don't want to find out. Maybe I only want your hot body."

"Maybe I want yours, too."

Okay, this is definitely too much. "Whatever, this game's getting old. You got the drinks, so I'll pick up the cab."

"I have a driver." He says it casually, like an afterthought, like *everyone's* got a driver.

"Oh, right. It's a good thing, too, because my pilot's home with a cold." I pull off the sarcasm, but on the inside doubts are forming stronger than ever. This guy has a driver? God. The closest I've ever come to having a driver is when my freaking car breaks down *again* and I have to ride with a tow-truck driver to the repair shop.

Actually, that's not true. I won VIP tickets to a concert last summer, and the experience included a chauffeur. I took Cassidy with me—and spent the night giving her shit for taking an internship at her father's company, like a complete asshole.

Because it was supposed to be her brother's internship, but he died. And his death soured me.

Well. It made me more sour, anyway.

But the tables have changed this summer and now I'm the one working for Cassidy's father's company. Thank God she's a better person than I am, because she hasn't said "I told you so" even once. If I were in her shoes? I'd be merciless.

"I drive a ten-year-old Toyota with a broken taillight." I don't know why I have to make sure he knows this, that he gets we come from different worlds, but I do.

"Cool." He doesn't flinch, doesn't stutter—so that one was obviously a lie.

"It's so old you can't even tell what color it used to be." My guess has always been red, but that's probably because of all the rust.

"Do you think telling me you drive a beater is going to change my mind about wanting to take you home with me?"

Am I that transparent, or is he that good at reading people? I nibble at a fingernail, my expression as composed as I can make it. "Do you have alcohol at your place?"

Now he pauses, and then slowly nods. "But we can go to yours if you'd prefer."

That's laughable. I can imagine Gran's reaction to this guy setting foot in our place. I can hear her now, telling me I'm no better than my mother, leaving with someone like Frank. Spreading my legs for a pretty face and a bank account.

"Hey, where'd you go again?" He lets go of me, waiting for me to turn my face toward him. "I can have my driver take you home—by yourself—if you're having doubts. All you have to do is tell me."

Sometimes in cartoons a character finds herself with a devil on one shoulder and an angel on the other, battling it out over a questionable decision. For me, on one shoulder my Gran's calling me a whore, and on the other my empty shot glasses from tonight are telling me I shouldn't even wait till we get to his place to wrap my legs around him.

I cross my arms over my stomach, my hands in fists, because I'm starting to get annoyed. Not at him, but at myself. At life in general.

Ugh. Why can't I ever get out of my own head?

Okay, Teagan. Get your shit together. Let's not scare off the guy who's going to be The Guy tonight.

Deep breath.

Another.

Nope. Not working.

"Give me a second," I say, pretending to check my purse for something. Blindly, I grab my cell phone—there's a text from Cassidy. *You okay? I feel bad for leaving you with a random. He's hot and seemed nice, but still. #friendfail*

She has a point, but I can't even count the amount of times I've failed her in ways much worse. If I'm honest with myself, I'm a pretty shitty friend.

Oh, good. There's more irritation. Yep, and now it's slithering right into red-hot anger.

God.

Stop.

This has to stop.

I close my eyes and take another breath. I smell the bar, a little sour like old alcohol—because, duh—but I also inhale Frank's scent again. It's kind of calming this time.

Mentally, I shove everything away from my shoulders, and then there's only me. Standing next to a guy who's smoking hot and wants to take me home. One who's not commenting on my standoffish behavior, who's letting me have a moment to myself even though the heat of his arm is sinking into my own. The heat of his stare is searing the side of my face.

I'm starting a new job on Monday, and I want a better life to come with it. I need to learn to loosen up—and maybe the best way to do it is with a bang.

With Frank.

Who, when I turn my face toward him, is looking at me with these *come play with me* puppy-dog eyes and a charming little grin—like he knows his expression is exactly what I need to make up my mind. The last drop of irritation rolls away. I wonder how many girls he's used it on.

I don't care.

"I want your place," I say, starting toward the exit again, pulling him with me. "And liquor. And you."

CHAPTER FIVE

FRANK'S DRIVER IS a guy named Miles. He's ancient and bone-thin and smells like cigars. I like him immediately, and when he tells me to be sure to *buckle up back there* with a smarmy double eyebrow raise—as though he's maybe talking about using a condom instead of a seat belt—it's clear he and Frank have a relationship outside the realm of just driver to passenger. And also that maybe Frank gets around...

Then Miles closes the door behind me, and I'm alone in the back of a town car with Frank, with one tiny seat between us, and there goes all the ease, right out the closed car window. In its place is something cutting, something spicy. Nerves on top of nerves on top of the sizzle of attraction.

Frank, however, seems calm, leaning against his seat and glancing at me with a grin as the car starts to move. "I'm glad you decided to come."

"Yeah," is what I attempt to say, but it comes out strangled and unintelligible and I'm forced to clear my throat and repeat myself.

"Water?" He slides toward me and reaches across my seat—*across me*—to grab one of the (chilled, sparkling, and, of course, *glass* bottled) waters Miles set out for us on this little platform near the door. He pulls back, and this time he moves a little slower in the space that should be mine and, for a moment, the top of his shirt, unbuttoned, is eye-level and his scent sweeps across me like a breeze and my blood rushes through my veins like it's revived with a second wind.

I stare at his throat, at his Adam's apple, because if I lift my gaze to his face... I might be tempted to run my nose along the scruff lining his chin. Which is a weird thing to want to do, but knowing that doesn't keep away the impulse. But, also... I think if I look up, he'll kiss me. And the thought makes me panic.

And then the moment's over and he's in his seat, unscrewing the top of the water and pouring it into a thick-stemmed glass, while I sit still as a statue and try to slow my breathing.

He holds the water toward me and I take a second too long to grab it. My fingers accidentally slide over his in the exchange, and he maneuvers until mine are trapped beneath his. I can *feel* his smile widening, but I can't take my eyes off of the water. Off of his fingers—they're big, covering mine.

But I break the moment and take the water from him because damn if I don't need a sip of it with the way my mouth goes dry.

I'm so out of my element. I want to take back control of the situation.

"Tell me, honestly," I say, wrapping both hands around my glass. "Why did you want to leave with me? Why me, when you look...the way you do?"

He studies me, half a frown tugging at his mouth. "I don't know how to take that. Is it a compliment to me, or an insult to you—which would make it an insult to me too, actually?"

"Just tell me." I stare at him, unblinking, trying to keep my expression serious, even if my cheeks and my eyelids are a little heavy, like gravity's pushing harder on them than usual. He's slightly blurry in my vision, but that only means the water I drank at the bar didn't kill the swing of my buzz.

"I overheard you talking about your screen door—"

"And thought I'd be easy to bang your way into?"

He shakes his head and leans toward me until his face is tantalizingly close to mine, and even though my tone makes me an asshole, his eyes are dancing, like his own mood won't be deterred.

"Didn't we already have this conversation? I'm not in the business of sex with no emotions, remember?"

He takes away the cutesy screen door metaphor and lays the truth of it bare and I wonder how I've managed to find someone—a guy—who's so sincere. It feels...weird. And it turns me on so much I have to cross my legs. He watches my movement and amusement highlights his features. "I approached you because you sounded sure of yourself—"

"And you're using this as a way to somehow knock me down a peg?" I'm being a jerk. He's not trying to knock me down; I can spot that shit from a mile away after growing up with my grandparents. Basically, what we have here is another example of me being a bitch for no reason without the ability to stop myself.

Before I can blink, he's in his own seat and the charming twinkle in his eyes is gone. "Do you want me to have Miles take you home? Because I'm getting a hell of a mixed bag of signals from you, Cindy." I cringe. Both because of the name and that I've already managed to push him past his tipping point. "I don't want to do that, but if you're this uncomfortable with me, or this certain you have me pegged as whatever type of guy you think I am, I have some pretty strong doubts you'll be happy to wake up next to me tomorrow."

He's wrong, though.

I do want to wake up next to him tomorrow.

I want to wake up with a fresh perspective and a new me.

I want it every morning, to be honest, but...tonight could be the exact jumpstart I need.

"Will you answer my question?" I place the glass of water in a cup holder and grab Cassidy's blazer, draping the fabric over my pants, spreading it out with my hands. But Frank doesn't say anything and I think he's waiting for me to meet his eyes again. So I look up.

"You're pretty," he says. "Maybe I'm shallow, but I like the way you look. And when I walked past your conversation, you sounded sexy and confident—and I liked that even more. It made me want to know you."

"Oh." Heat pulses under the skin of my face, and yet again I wish I was a pretty blusher, all tawny pinks instead of balloon reds. But he's given me one of the best compliments I've received in a long time. Maybe ever.

Then it hits me. He heard me boasting and acting like I didn't have a care in the world. He's attracted to my fake personality, the one I wear for everyone else. Guess it goes well with the fake name. Tonight I'll be Cindy. I like her better, anyway. "I don't want Miles to take me home."

"Thank God." His tone is back to light and the mood between us shifts again, less intense now. He glances down into his lap and then at me with a huge grin. "Because there are two of us in this seat who would've been really fucking disappointed. You didn't think I was unaffected when I slid across you for the water, did you?"

I follow his gaze, because of course I do. And his pressed gray slacks are extremely tented. Because of course they are.

Of all the reactions I could possibly have in the moment, I put my face in my hands, and I giggle like a fucking schoolgirl.

CHAPTER SIX

"ARE YOU GIGGLING at my boner?" Frank asks, and when I uncover my face, his eyes widen. "You are."

The urge to keep giggling fills my stomach like a balloon. I glance toward Miles in the rearview mirror, but he's focused on the road, giving no indication that he heard Frank. *Don't giggle. Don't giggle.*

"I'm not... I mean..."

"Come on, kitten. You're kinda killing my ego."

"I didn't even touch you," I say. "You...surprised me, that's all. I don't think you're...small, or anything." The opposite actually, if the rise in his khakis is any indication. *Not* that I'd tell him that.

He winces. "Well, now his pride's pretty much nonexistent."

"Well, now *you're* speaking about your..." I clear my throat and another giggle slips out. "...*thing* like it's an actual person with actual feelings."

"*You* couldn't even use the word dick."

I'm hit with the blush of the fucking century. He's right. *What am I? Thirteen?*

Oh, but that thought pushes my mind into a better comeback. "*You're* the one who's rock hard when we haven't even kissed yet. What are you? *Thirteen?*" There. Point, me.

"I like that word...*yet*," he says. He's still smiling, but his focus is

31

on my mouth now, and all of a sudden we aren't in a game anymore. Or we are. But it's not the kind with silly insults and childish blushing.

This is more like...a dare situation.

I just don't know how to go about stepping up to the challenge.

Or I do, but it turns out I'm a coward. I look away first, out the window at the trees that line the parkway and streetlights that flash by. Then the trees are gone and we're passing Springs Corner—an outdoor shopping center, all lit up with restaurants, local boutiques, a huge movie theater, and even bigger pavilion in the center of it all. I pretend to be fascinated by the place, staring so hard out my window, it's a wonder the glass doesn't crack.

I tap my fingers on the seat beside me, trying to drum up the nerve to turn and kiss him. He already thinks I'm forward, so why am I feeling shy?

Because I really want him.

Because I *super* want him.

Because sitting in the back of a town car with him feels too good to be true. These things don't happen to me.

But then he covers my hand with his own, and I drop my gaze to watch, and I realize they do happen to me. Right now. This is happening. Finally. And it's perfect. One night of a fairy tale.

Granted, a fairy tale where the prince doesn't know the princess's real name, but maybe that makes it better.

He rubs his thumb over the back of my hand, trailing heat across my skin, and finally I lift my heavy eyes toward his.

"Hi," he says.

"Hi." I breathe.

"You don't need to be nervous." Another stroke of his thumb. Thank God it's over the top of my hand, because my palms are getting damp. "I won't bite."

I wipe my free hand across my lap. "Just wondering where you live."

"Oh. I thought you might be thinking about whether or not I'd bite. But you have my word I won't."

"What if I want you to?" Seriously, I'm getting whiplash. Ballsy Cindy or gun-shy Teagan. I can't keep track of myself.

"Then that's a different story." He flashes those damn dimples again. "Here we are."

Miles pulls into the circular drive-thru of a sky-high condominium complex, a sign naming it *The Grands*, to drop us off. He opens the door and I step out, craning my neck to scan up the length of the building. Floor-to-ceiling windows in every unit make the whole tower look as though it's made of glass. "Whoa."

"Wait till you see the inside," Miles says, a smile in his voice.

I turn toward him as Frank unfolds himself from the car, all long legs, long torso, long body in general. Wide shoulders. Muscular neck—this dude definitely works out. Face like…well, I've given his face more than enough attention tonight. It takes me a moment to remember what I was going to say. "Miles, thank you." I dig through the pockets of Cassidy's blazer and pull out the rest of my crumpled wad of cash. A whopping fifteen dollars. I hold it out to him.

He grins and—adorably—blushes in the bright light of the overhead archway, gently pushing my hand to the side. "I couldn't take that, but thank you."

The thought of ever brushing off a tip is foreign to me. I push the money toward him again. "But you gave such nice service."

"That's why I'm paid a salary," he says, ignoring the money. "But again, thank you."

I guess he doesn't work on commission, but still. Who turns down free money?

Then again, he works for Frank, who I'm beginning to think might be kind of loaded. This condominium building is fancy. Like, there's a doorman waiting for us. In a polished black suit. And there's a row of chandeliers hanging above us—outside—that look like they're made of diamonds. I mean, probably not though, right? Because that'd be ridiculous.

"You're sweet, you know that?" Frank chuckles as Miles drives away.

"You're probably the first person in my life to accuse me of it," I tell him, honestly.

"Accuse you? I meant it as a compliment."

When we're close enough, the doorman opens the door for us, saying, "Good evening, sir, miss."

"Good evening." Frank motions for me to go ahead. "Where's Matthew tonight?"

"Family emergency, sir."

"His daughter?" Frank sounds so genuinely concerned that I turn to him—and his expression matches his tone. "Is she back in the hospital? I thought she was feeling a little better?"

"I wouldn't know, sir." The doorman's stiff as a board and staring straight ahead. Clearly, he takes his job as seriously as the Queen's guard in England; all he needs is a red outfit instead of his all-black, and one of those tall fluffy hats. The thought has me stifling a giggle.

Frank takes the man's hint and wishes him a goodnight, and then puts his hand against my lower back to guide me into the foyer. Like last time, his touch sends sparks shooting up my spine, and I resist the urge to arch like a cat against his palm.

"Is Matthew your regular doorman?" I ask.

He nods, his eyes far away for a moment. "His daughter's been sick a lot the past year."

"I'm sorry."

"So am I."

There's a *huge* bronze light structure attached to the high-rise ceiling above us; my eyes follow it to the end of the foyer, where it slides down into an extravagant marbled water fountain. The walls are painted in vertical stripes of mint and white, and the entire space feels polished—and so spacious I bet my voice will echo when I speak. Which I do as casually as possible, like this is nothing new. "Nice place."

He glances around, his expression impassive. "My father picked it."

"You live with your parents?" The thought hadn't even occurred to me.

"God, no." He mock-shudders. "They foot the bill."

"Oh." How one single word can come out as judgmentally as mine does, I have no clue. I clear my throat. "I mean, must be nice." Nope. Not any better. What is *wrong* with me? "Are you close with your parents?"

"We participate in each other's lives." For the first time, he seems uncomfortable, so I let him lead me toward the glass elevators against the wall without asking him any of the follow-up questions I'm dying to ask. Instead, I focus on the way the palm of his hand keeps the spot on my back warm against the chilly air conditioner of the lobby.

I focus on the way that heat's keeping me warm everywhere else, too.

"You could get very naughty in these," I say—or, rather, evocative *Cindy* says—with half a smile, gesturing to the elevators, making the tension in his eyes drain away.

"If you're into letting people watch." His hand slips a little lower, right above my ass and my skin's starting to burn, hoping he'll slide it all the way down. "Let's see... So far, you're into biting and public shows of affection..."

"Maybe with you I will be." I'm not sure if I'm teasing or serious, but there's a wild energy rushing through me because every step we take gets us closer to the moment he's inside of me, and I'm starting to imagine how it might feel. How he might feel, his body over mine, the grunts he'll make, the bend of my knees when I wrap my legs around him...

Movie sex. That's what tonight will be like. Sheets wrapped around us. Sexy sweat raised on our skin. Perfect, sexy lovemaking. Someone like this guy? I bet it's how he does everything.

Oh, God. Why didn't I bring that water in from the car? My mouth is parched now. And as the elevator slides down the glass shaft, Frank studies me in the reflection. Even in dimly lit glass, he's gorgeous. His eyes appear darker than the night and just as intense.

When the door opens, I step in and try to look casual, leaning against the back glass wall.

He follows me, but stands directly in front of me instead of to my side, like I figured he would. Like, *directly* in front of me. I doubt there's room for even a ruler between us.

I can either stare at his chest, or look up at him. I choose the latter, even if it takes a few seconds to make it happen.

No turning back now.

Not that I'd want to.

Not that *any* girl would want to.

"You have very nice hair," he says, his breath washing over my face. It smells like mint, somehow, and citrus, like the faintest hint of the lime he bit into at the bar. I have roughly 0.06 seconds to process it though, because then he's twirling a strand of my hair through his fingers and the sensation of his skin brushing against my neck is dizzying. "Makes me think of summer strawberry fields, and it's so soft, I can't stop playing with it."

"I have good conditioner." *So* smooth. But somewhere on the inside, I'm beginning to shake. Little vibrations that promise to turn into epic earthquakes.

Okay.

Okay. I can do this.

I trail a hand up his stomach—*holy shit his abs are freaking tight*—and over his chest—*and yep, equally muscular pecs*—and wrap it around his neck. I run my thumb over his stubble. His breath catches, which makes mine speed up. Cassidy's brother was the last guy who affected me this way. I've waited almost two years to meet someone who excites me as much as Frank has in just a few hours. Finally, I don't have to fake it. Something tells me I won't have to fake anything with this guy.

Well, except my name.

Frank lowers his head, slowly, his eyes on mine the whole time. The air is so tense around us, it's like snapping elastics *everywhere*. So I open my mouth to whisper against his.

"You didn't press the button."

CHAPTER SEVEN

"Y-YOU'RE RIGHT." FRANK blinks after I break the spell of our almost-kiss. "Damn it."

Yes. Damn it. Why did I have to say anything?

Nerves are so *unbelievably* annoying. I need to figure out how to slice away the ones making me jittery while protecting the ones making me as aroused as I am.

There are so many areas of my life where my body has trouble differentiating between good and bad emotions. So many areas of my life in which I wish I could get the fuck out of my head for a little bit.

Frank turns to press the button for his floor—followed by a code on a keypad beside the regular numbers.

"Fancy security," I say.

He shrugs, returning to me, sliding one hand up my side and around my back, placing his other palm against the wall beside my face. "Now. Where were we?"

But this time we're interrupted when someone slams a hand in to stop the door. Behind Frank's shoulder stands a tall, thin, leggy blonde. She ignores me, but speaks to the back of Frank's head.

"Alex." The word—*his real name*—cuts through the air and he turns around like a shotgun's gone off.

"Kelly." For the first time, there's zero warmth in his tone. In fact, as the door closes behind her, all the air in the elevator suddenly feels frosty—from the chill between them, not the air-conditioning.

The ground falls away and Kelly slices her eyes over me and back to Fr—Alex. "New one tonight, huh? Not your usual fare."

"Back off," he says, warily. "Don't be so—"

"Um, excuse me?" I cut in, using what many might call my typical Teagan tone. God, it feels good to slip into me without feeling awkward. Bitch is easy. "Not his usual fare?"

"I wasn't speaking to you, sweetie." She doesn't bother looking at me, just drills holes into Alex.

"But you were speaking about me, *sweetie*. And I'm standing right here." I wait until her focus is on me. "I don't know if you're some scorned ex or whatever, but I do know your loss is going to be my gain tonight—probably multiple times. So maybe you should keep your snotty little mouth shut and get the fuck over yourself."

"Well, well," Alex murmurs, sliding closer to me. "You do have claws. And some very high—and, I promise you, very attainable—expectations for our evening. And you," he says to Kelly, "should probably do exactly as my friend says."

With perfect timing, the doors open onto her floor and she shoots us a scathing look before turning to walk—or glide, rather, with her annoyingly long, slim legs—away.

"Yeah. That's a story I'm going to have to hear...*Alex*," I say.

"About my name—"

"Nope." I put a finger to his mouth. I only wanted to say it once, to let it travel along my tongue like an indulgence. "Tonight you're Frank."

I can tell he wants to say more, but the moment passes and he nods, smiling against my finger—then he wraps his tongue around it and takes it into his mouth. And he uses his tongue to do things to my finger that make my panties wet, and the trembles from earlier are starting to echo outwards from the center of my belly, in rings of vibrations running through my arms and down my legs. Up my neck... Heat following their path.

He pushes me until the glass is at my back and his body's pressed against mine and holy hell *he's so hard*. I moan, imagining more than my mind can handle.

And I get a little nervous, too.
Okay. A lot nervous.
I slide my finger out of his mouth.
"You taste salty," he whispers in my ear, with a low hum. "Delicious." He runs his hands up the sides of my legs, over my hips, wrapping around my waist. "But I bet I can discover where you taste the sweetest."
Oh.
My.
God.
How should I respond? Why won't my brain work? Why am I turning to mush everywhere?
The elevator dings, opening, and I sigh.
"Damn we've had bad timing so far," he says, right as I think, *saved by the bell.*
"S'okay." I clear my throat, trying to hide how relieved I am. "I'm thirsty anyway."
Then I step off the elevator and discover why he needed the security code to get here. Because I've stepped into a foyer—*his* foyer. Right off of the elevator.
"Wait. Is this the penthouse?"
He walks past me—*breezes past me*—and simply says, "Yeah." Like it's no big deal. "What can I get you to drink?"
The ceilings are so high in his entryway, Frank couldn't even touch them if he jumped, and he's *tall*. Hell, not even with a ladder could he jump high enough. There's a staircase spiraling up to a second level and, I'm assuming, his bedroom. He probably has a fluffy king-sized bed, tucked in every day by personal maids. I bet the entire room is ostentatious.
Fucking awesome, probably, my mother's voice flows through my mind, and, after the shock of hearing her wears off, I shiver. On TV she always speaks with a bland sort of forced-casual manner, and in my mind, her tone stays the same. I imagine she'd look at this place and start drooling. So I refuse to.
There's space for miles past his foyer, and all the way across from me, past sets of dining and living room furniture that probably cost more than...well, more than anything I've ever owned (and let's not even mention the TV the size of a damn planet), there are walls made

of glass between us and the outside. I stare out one of the panes, watching the lights from Springs Corner—and places farther out—twinkle in the night like multicolored stars.

He's waiting for me to answer him, having made his way to the open kitchen around the corner. But maybe I should walk backwards, right onto the elevator and out into the night. Back to my grandparents' rundown place. Back to real life. Because this? No matter how fun a one-night fairy tale sounds... This is almost too much.

But just *almost*.

Instead of walking backwards, I step toward him. "What's the strongest thing you have?"

"The strongest thing that you might actually like, you mean, Miss Sweet Hard Cider?" His teasing unfurls some of the unease in my chest.

"Yes." I smile to show him I appreciate the humor.

He makes us vodka tonics with a dash of sugar and a twist of orange. It's not quite sweet enough for me to love it, but it's not so bitter that I can't drink it either.

In fact, I lean against his tall kitchen island and I down it and I ask for another.

We move into his living room, which is half the size of a football field and contains a TV with corresponding proportions. And of course the furniture is fitted to him. I practically have to climb onto his couch—though it's actually comfortable once I'm settled. I could fall asleep easily with everything I've had to drink. Except for the adrenaline spiking through my veins over what's about to happen, like a both bitter and delicious drug... But maybe one more drink first.

"You keep this up," he says, when I ask for another, "and I won't feel right about taking you upstairs."

"I'm a big girl," I slur. "I can handle my liquor." He looks unsure, so I study the shape of my next words before they exit my mouth, making sure they're not as messy: "I tell you what... Make it a fresh glass and a *smaller* one, if it'll make you feel better. And anyway, I wanted to come home with you the moment I first saw you. I'd only had two drinks then."

Thank God, he turns away from me for the kitchen and misses the way I hold in a hiccup—and the way I bend over and drink the rest of my current cocktail upside down to get rid of the rest of them. But it *works*. And the fluid path my hair takes through the air when I flip myself upright again makes me feel like surely it's all sex kitten-ish now. I glance around for a mirror, but he doesn't have any out. Not even in the foyer.

I sigh. I'm sure it was wishful thinking anyway. Pretty sure my hair's never had a sex kitten moment in all its life. The wave of confidence passes as quickly as they ever do, and I'm more than ready for the new drink when he brings it to me.

"So." I gulp half the vodka down. Huh, it doesn't even burn anymore. "Should we do this?"

"Are you flirting with me?" he asks, his expression serious. "Because if you are, I'm not getting it."

Shit. My words ring between us still, sounding like I want to get it over with. Which isn't true. Not all the way, anyway. "What do you mean?"

"You've seemed on the fence all night. I'm trying not to be blinded by the way my body reacts to you and walk you upstairs into something you'll regret in the morning."

"Are *you* sure *you* want to do this?" I slide toward him and rise on my tiptoes to whisper as close to his ear as I can get, which is basically his sexy, delicious-smelling neck. "Because you keep giving me ways out, when I'm very clearly not taking them."

"Cindy," he says, still serious. "Tell me the truth."

Why the fuck did I give him that name?

"I'm nervous, okay? *God*." Great, and now I'm prickly and giving him some of the truth I'm doing everything I can to keep buried tonight.

"Why?" he sounds genuinely confused.

"Um, look at you. Look at your place."

"So?"

"So you're a fucking GQ advertisement, and it makes me anxious." Maybe my *poor* is showing, but I'm too jittery to keep it so bottled up. I *want* him. So much I can barely breathe. Or maybe part of that is my nerves. And this much alcohol makes it harder to keep my Cindy mask on straight.

"Come here, little kitten," he says, demand in his tone. Usually, I'd balk at his bossiness. At the moment, though, I let it make my decision for me and I go to him. He grips my shoulders, firmly enough to hold me in place. Sensually enough to make me shiver. Especially when he leans in and breathes against my neck with his whispered words. "My place is amazing; I'm not a liar, and I won't try to pretend it's not the truth. But as amazing as it is? You're the only thing in it I can't take my eyes off of. So what does that say about *you*?"

Okay. *Swallow, Teagan.*

"I'm not a thing." My words are automatic, and they make me cringe.

Thankfully, he leans back, nodding. "You're right. But you are gorgeous. And I think you might need someone to show you that you deserve whatever you want. And I want to take you upstairs to get a head start on it."

It feels like a culminating moment. Will I, or won't I?

I've been wavering all night, but only because I'm nervous. The one thing that hasn't wavered is how attracted I am to him. It's time to be Cindy for real. It's time to do what I want.

I take a deep breath to steady my nerves, inhaling him, letting his scent wash over me before I answer. "It's about freaking time."

His bedroom is...perfect. Huge, yes, but far from ostentatious. Yes, his bed's king-sized, but it's otherwise simple and it looks really comfortable. The rest of the room is clean, but there's a misplaced sock in the corner and a crumpled shirt on the floor by his bed. And the entire space smells faintly like him, a lingering reminder of whose room it is while he's gone.

"What is that?" I turn to him and have to catch myself when the room tilts a little beneath me.

"What is what?"

"That scent. *Your* scent. It's enough to drive a girl mad."

He glances down and sniffs himself, making me giggle, and puzzles his brows when he looks at me again. "I don't smell anything."

"Oh come on. It must be a cologne if I can still smell it in here." I trail across his room, using the excuse to check out some of the things on his desk, on his dressers. Also, holding on to the furniture helps keep the ground steady.

"I'm not wearing cologne."

"Uh-huh. Sure." There isn't much to run my fingers over. A pair of cufflinks and a watch. A signed baseball. A black and white photo of a younger Frank surrounded by a group of people, friends. And that's pretty much it.

"I get it now." I spin to face him, smiling. "You're hot and you're rich—but you're *boring*. What a *relief.*"

Now his brows shoot up, along with the corners of his mouth, making those dimples pop out. "Boring? I've been accused of many things in my life, but not that."

"Yeah, maybe not to your *face*."

"Oh, you think?" He's in full grin-mode now and takes a few stalking steps toward me. I back up until the foot of his bed hits my ass. I swear to God there's a look in his eye that says he wants to tickle me, and I can't keep yet another giggle from slipping up from my belly. He pauses, considering something.

"What?" I can't keep from asking. "What are you waiting for?"

"I want to get my hands on you—all over you…but I also want to show you something." He reaches his hand out, palm up. "Come here."

I hesitate. "Are you gonna get your hands all over me, or show me something?"

I'm not sure what I want his answer to be.

Both, maybe.

"Both, maybe." He says the words directly from my mind, and I'm so shocked I put my hand in his. I let him pull me out of the room and halfway down a hardwood hall before I'm ready to speak again.

"Tell me you've got a foot fetish and a hidden closet full of Jimmy Choos and I'll be yours forever." Truly, I don't care about shoes. But maybe Cindy does. And the brand is something rich people are aware of—Cassidy's mom has more pairs than I can count. So maybe he'll think Cindy's a bit closer to the level of his world than I actually am.

"Not quite," he says, laughing. "Though I do think you have pretty toes." He glances down as we walk and my feet suddenly feel very naked in my open-toed heels. Thank God I let Cassidy talk me into pedicures this afternoon.

We come to a stop in front of a closed door.

"Okay, but I have to tell you… If this is some room full of tied-up ex-girlfriends, I'm a master of jujitsu. I know enough to take you down like that." I snap my fingers.

"That might be fun." He laughs again, shaking his head, and opens the door. "But this'll be better."

CHAPTER EIGHT

THE ROOM IS completely dark, but before my eyes can adjust to make out more than a few structural shapes, Frank reaches in and flips a switch.

There's a whirring noise and then the room is filled with lights. Lots and lots of lights.

Regular ones, to brighten the room—but game lights, too, spinning around arcade games and scoreboards. Little *beeps* and *boops* and other game-type noises softly fill the air while I take it all in.

"Whoa."

And, also, thank God, because I actually don't know jujitsu.

There's a plush poker table in one corner, surrounded by leather seats and a white-cabineted wet bar behind it. A shuffleboard along one wall, which, if I wasn't in so much shock, would make me grimace because Gran loves the game. One of the only things in the world she loves. That and Gramps, for some reason. And making sure to point out every single thing wrong with me, which is basically everything. But my eyes are too busy darting all around for those thoughts to take over. An ancient-looking row of arcade games—Pac-Man's the only one I recognize. A red pool table toward the back of the room and two huge flat TVs in the upper back corners.

"This room is every teenage boy's wet dream." I step inside.

"Most grown men's, too," Frank says, following me. "And a ton of women's."

"This is...just... You're a nerd!" I spin toward him to see if he'll admit it, but my attention's drawn to the long rows of built-in shelves spreading out from the doorway behind us—and filled to the brim with comic books. Half in plastic casing, half well loved. And a few face out in glass boxes, also in plastic casing. "Like, nerd with a capital N."

He turns too, grabbing one at random and flipping through it, peeking at me over the cover with laughing eyes. "But I'm not boring."

"Definitely not." I wish he'd drop the stupid thing and put his hands back on me.

He's an undercover comic book geek. It makes me like him even more. He's not some perfectly suave GQ sort of guy.

Shit. It might be harder than I thought to leave in the morning...

"Do you like comics?" he asks, hope in his voice.

"You mean the things people need with pictures when they can't handle real books?" God, I'm such a dick sometimes. Most of the time. "That was rude. Someone said that to me once, in high school, when I thought maybe I could get into comics. Turns out I've been waiting years to use the line on someone else. So what does that say about me?"

He shrugs, carefully placing the comic book on the shelf. "It says I need to reintroduce you to comics."

"Reading's not really my thing in any form, to be honest." This is part of the fairy tale. I can tell Frank anything I want because I won't see him again.

"That's too bad," he says, honesty in his tone making me regret my words. "But I guess that means we'll have to find another way to pass the time."

Now I grin, sliding further into the room, feeling his eyes on me like feathers trailing my body. I shiver. Because every minute we're getting closer and closer, the circle's closing in. And sex is at the center. "Whatever did you have in mind?" I head to the wet bar behind the poker table, grabbing a glass. "Wanna take some shots?"

One shot of chilled vodka later—all he would agree to, the jerk—I turn toward the poker table, opening the metal case holding poker chips. The clicks of its snaps fill the room, sharp. And a moment later he's right behind me, his hands at my hips, his body pressed against mine.

His erection at my butt.

Oh, boy.

Oh, big-penised *man*.

Go big, or go home, right?

A soft laugh escapes from my stomach, up my throat, out my lips.

"Do you like this?" he asks, laying a soft kiss against the side of my neck.

I can't find my voice to speak, so I nod.

"And this?" He slides his hands up my sides, making my breath constrict in my lungs, and over my breasts.

I nod again, my nipples tightening under his touch, and he presses his mouth to the side of my neck a second time.

And oh, God, I want his lips on mine. He's moving them along my skin in sweet, tender trails, and... I start to tremble again.

He lifts his hands to fiddle with the straps of my camisole, sliding them down, whispering against my skin, "We could play cards for clothes, make it interesting."

"I suck at cards." I take a deep breath—*this is it*—and I turn, sliding my body against his, to face him. "And there's no need for strip poker if you want to get me naked."

He lifts his head and his hands slip around my neck and a rumble comes up from his throat. "I've wanted to do that since I first saw you." His gaze drops to my mouth and slowly, slowly rises to mine again. "This, too."

He's going to kiss me now. I know it.

I wet my lips, and I slide my hands up his stomach and over his chest, wrapping one around his neck. I stand on my tiptoes.

And I kiss him.

I wanted to make the first move my own, I wanted to make sure he knows—and that I know—I want this. I want him.

But it doesn't matter that I moved first because within a breath, he's dominating the kiss. His lips are smooth against mine and he concentrates on my lower lip and then my upper and I try to match him, but he's so smooth, so well-practiced. I sigh something like a purr and he slips his tongue into my mouth.

My fingers curl into a fist, gripping his shirt. I slide my tongue past his to take in his mouth as he tastes mine.

My eyes are closed and the vodka's starting to sink in, making me feel a bit like we're on a rocking boat, rather than solid ground leaning against a solid table. But I must do something right, because he groans, a soft little roar, really. His hands fall to my waist and he lifts me—like I'm featherlight, which I very much am not, which makes it really fucking hot—and presses me onto the table. He pushes between my legs until his erection is...*right there*, and he groans again, into my mouth this time.

Fuck, why am I still wearing pants? *Why is he?* The kiss stretches on, sensual and perfect, and I unbutton his shirt, yanking it from his pants to finish the last few. I slide my hands beneath his undershirt, feeling the warm, soft skin covering his oh-so-fucking-hard abs, and *this* is what's going to be above my body tonight? All night?

Yes, please.

He gives one slow lick inside my lips, making my skin stand on edge, and then his mouth is gliding over my chin and down my neck, his tongue fluttering against my pulse point and it's my turn to moan, because my insides are melting into hot caramel. I slip a hand between our bodies to stroke him over his pants, and he nips my skin with his teeth and a little growl. "Careful. I want to take this slow."

But I don't want to be careful. I don't want to take this slow. I run my fingers over the fabric, tracing him and massaging him until he grabs my wrist, stilling the motion and saying, "You are so fucking sexy, you're making it hard for me to take the time to explore you as thoroughly as I want."

My hand is still, held captive by his, but the room is not. When I open my eyes to grin at him, the poker table suddenly seems to be the world's slowest carousel ride. Slowly, slowly, slowly spinning to the side.

I steady myself against his chest and wrap my legs around him, pulling him closer to me, his erection pressing against me. "We have all night. Take it slow later. On the next round... Take *me* now."

He grabs my face and kisses me, fast and hard. "Here?" he asks, his mouth a whisper away from mine. "Or the bedroom?"

Poker table sex would be memorable for sure, but he has that comfortable-looking king-sized bed, and maybe it'll be steadier under my unsteady body. Maybe a more traditional start will be...easier. "Bedroom," I slur out the word and the next few, too. "This time. But I expect you to bring me back in here before the night is over."

I take his hand and pull him toward the door, but I stumble a little—so he swoops down and picks me up. Again, like I weigh nothing. I twist in his arms to face him and wrap my legs around his stomach and I take my turn now, tasting his neck, running my tongue along his skin, rubbing myself against his body while he walks. I slide a little lower along him until his erection is pressing against the very center of my thighs, making me moan. Making me so wet that if he doesn't have my pants off in the next few minutes I may be nothing but a fucking puddle by the time he tries.

He's making noises too—half pained, half something sexy—and I want to taste the sounds as they fall from his mouth. I let my lips travel along his sandpapery chin and I squeeze myself tighter around him when our lips meet again.

"This might be my new favorite way to walk anywhere," he says against my mouth and I kiss him harder in agreement, letting him carry me into his bedroom.

CHAPTER NINE

I'M IN FRANK'S bedroom.

I'm in Frank's bedroom and he's hard as a rock, pressing through his pants and mine.

I'm in Frank's bedroom and he's hard as a rock *because he wants me*.

We're standing here—actually, *he's* standing here, holding me up with my legs around him and his erection begging to find release, and he's starting to grind against me and all these warm sensations are shooting like fireworks through the lower half of my body.

We're really going to do this.

Holy shit.

I push myself away from him and slide down his body, stepping back.

Panic. Panic is lacing through those streams of fireworks.

I need a moment. I need a moment to gather myself. To gather *Cindy* and her super forward takes-what-she-wants ways.

"Can I use your bathroom?" I ask and then blush because what if he thinks I have to...do something embarrassing. I scramble to clarify. "To freshen up first?"

I don't even know what that means, to freshen up, but I know people say it in movies.

He's watching my face, amused. "Sure." He points to a huge set of double doors that I figured led to a huge walk-in closet. They're covered in thick, intricately carved wooden panels over panes of frosted glass. Or at least I think they are. All the vodka's definitely catching up to me now, and the maze of wood almost seems to be moving in my vision.

Still, I manage to push through the doors and let them swing shut behind me. I make my way to the sink and lean on it, dropping my head between my arms, breathing huge gulps of air.

I cannot believe I'm this nervous.

It's ridiculous. I'm a fucking adult. Kind of, anyway. I need to stand up, march out there, and take what I want.

I turn on the faucet and pause right as I'm about to splash water on my face. One, because I remember I'm wearing makeup, but two, because his bathroom is unreal. His shower's big enough to be a sauna and there's a huge, footed tub on the other side of the room. A new sort of longing blossoms between my ribs, sharper than the heat of the fireworks. One that tells me this'll be the closest I come to a tub like this. Oh, what I wouldn't give for a soak in there...

There's a dresser against the wall and I want to snoop through it so badly my fingers itch. But that'd be me getting to know more about Frank. And I already know too much for a one-night fling.

Instead I wash my hands, and I lift my eyes to study my reflection, maybe to give myself a mental pep talk—but there's no mirror. I find a small circular one, face down, on top of the dresser. A shaving mirror, but that's it.

I dry my hands and wipe them under my eyes to catch mascara smudges—and am filled with pleasure as Frank's scent hits my nose. It's his soap. A simple bar of soap has had my senses tingling every time he's been near me tonight. I almost laugh.

Instead, I take another deep inhale, and I turn and head into his room. Back to him. Back to exactly what I want.

He's sitting on his bed, looking at his phone. His shirts are still untucked, his button-up unbuttoned, his undershirt bright white and tight across his chest. I can't keep my eyes from dropping to his lap for a very, very brief glance. And he's still hard. Very, very hard.

He looks up when I pull the doors all the way open.

"What's with the no mirrors policy?" I ask.

"What do you mean?" But his tone is too carefully blank, so I know there's a story here.

"You know what I mean," I say, sauntering toward him. I step out of my shoes, kicking them to the side. I unbutton my pants, slide them slowly down my hips, past my knees, stepping out of them, too. Loving the bob of his Adam's apple when he swallows, watching my movements. Wish I'd worn sexier underwear, but at least these are black. That's kind of sexy, right? And I will not think about the shape of my legs. Not even for a second. "Who doesn't have a bathroom mirror?"

I climb into his lap, sighing when he wraps his arms around me. And...oh wow. Without my pants in the way, his erection is much more pronounced. *There.* I rock my hips back and forth, needing more friction. It's time for his pants to go. Like, now.

He groans, tightening his arms and angling himself against me in a way that has a noise I don't recognize slipping from my mouth, but he says, "Sorry, kitten, but you've reached your truth quotient from me for now."

"Please," I say, my tone as teasing as I can make it—because it takes most of my effort not to slur. "Two truths from a game we played hours ago? That's all I get?" I think back to what he said... "Your brother's getting married, and you wanted to take me home. That's it?"

"Four truths, actually." He confesses with a guilty little smile. "I wanted you to guess right."

"*Right.* The comic books thing. I should've known. You are such a cheater!" I shove his chest and he falls onto the bed, bringing me down with him. I giggle, loving the way his erection presses against me, but when we land, the world's tilting at an angle adjacent to where we lie. I have to roll off of him and I scoot myself backwards until I hit his headboard, needing it to steady me.

It helps, but not that much.

"You do not stutter," I say, focusing on his face. Even kind of blurry it's the sexiest face I've ever seen.

"Oh, believe me. I do."

"I think you're a cheater *and* a liar." But I smile and so does he.

"My next stutter is always at the tip of my tongue," he says, his lips still curved up, but the truth lies at the center of his tone.

"That must be hard." I fiddle with one of his many pillows, running the fabric through my fingers.

He shrugs, his smile gone now. "I had an excellent fluency coach for a lot of years. Perks of parents who accept nothing but the best." There's a sour note buried under his words and I wonder if he means his parents expected the best of him, rather than the fluency coach, but we're falling into that trap of getting to know each other more than I'm comfortable with.

I lean toward him and I channel my inner Cindy, and I say, "I can think of something else you can do with the tip of your tongue."

"Is that so?"

I tilt my head. "Or there are a few things to do with the tip of *my* tongue..."

"I think I love the way you think." He stands, sliding his shirt off his shoulders. His arms, beneath his undershirt, ripple with tight, toned muscle. "But I want my turn now. I've been dying to taste more of your skin since the first sweet tease I got earlier."

"I thought you said I tasted salty?"

"That was before I sampled your pretty neck... Your tempting mouth..." He means what he says, I can tell, and it freaking *thrills* me. Like, literally, thrills are shooting through my veins. But it's hard to give in to the sensations when there's a shadow in his expression. I wonder if it's because I made him think of his stutter, of his parents. And he still isn't moving toward me.

And I'm still dizzy.

And I'd like for him to steady me.

Or unravel me altogether.

"Are you..." I swallow around the lump of nerves in my throat. "How often do you do this? Sleep with random girls?"

There's a bit of a pause before he answers. "I'm not a priest. But I'm very careful. And I'm clean."

If I can trust what he says—and I do, oddly, trust him, or want to, at least—maybe we won't have to do the awkward condom dance when things really get started.

"I'm on the pill," I say, pushing the conversation toward what we're about to do. Plus, it's probably the type of conversation you should have before sleeping with someone. "And I'm clean, too."

"Good to know." He's watching me, musing stretched across his features, and I have a feeling my own thoughts have been stretched across mine.

"Anyway, you gave me four truths," I say, hastily. "I must owe you a couple more. Here. I'll give you three. Three truths, no lies. Ready?"

He nods.

"First...my mom actually is famous. Well. Half-famous, maybe." The words trip right over my tongue, falling out easily thanks to all the alcohol coursing through my system.

"Really?" Curiosity replaces the shadow across his features, and I feel like I've achieved something awesome. "Who is she?"

"Nope. Nuh-uh. That's a truth I'll never share." It's been years and years and years since I've spoken her name out loud. I don't plan to ever do it again.

"What if I kiss it out of you?"

"You'd have to kiss me for a very, very long time," I say. "I mean, I still wouldn't tell you. I'd just like for you to kiss me. For a very, very long time."

"I have no problem with that." He crawls toward me, *finally*.

I scoot down to let him rise over me.

He takes his time.

Dropping kisses along the tops of my feet, my ankles, my legs.

Trailing his hands and then his tongue along my inner thigh, first one and then the other, and my entire body flashes with heat.

Oh my God did I shave this morning?

Wait. Is it tomorrow morning now? What time is it? My mind is so tired, but my body... My body is so alive.

His tongue is silk against my skin and my blood is rushing, magnetized directly to the lines he's licking like arrows, up, up, up my legs. His hands are calloused. Why are his hands calloused? What will they feel like when they're... *Right there.*

Slipping under my panties, drawing a line through the very center of me.

"*Oh my God, that feels so fucking good.*" Wait. Did I say that out loud? Shit. I did, didn't I? My mind is shutting down; I can't keep track of my thoughts. I can't keep track of anything except the way it feels to have his finger sliding through me, into me. Twisting, turning, curving until he's hitting a spot that makes me want to fucking sing and has all that heat shooting straight to where he's touching me. Liquid heat—I feel myself soaking into his hand.

I think I say something again. I think I repeat myself. I wonder if I should be embarrassed. Am I reacting the way I should? It doesn't matter; I can't control myself, not with what he's doing to me. And Frank doesn't seem to mind. In fact, he tugs at the skin of my inner thigh with his teeth, sending tingles everywhere, muttering, "Jesus, you really are sweet."

And then another long, slow lick along my leg, and when I force my eyes open, he's watching my face and I've never lived through a hotter moment in my entire life.

"Kiss me, please," I hear myself say, not sure where the words are coming from. "I need you to kiss me. Right fucking now."

"Where?" he asks, slipping in another finger and making me swallow so hard it's a miracle I don't choke. "Where do you want me to kiss you?"

"My lips."

"Which ones?"

And my toes fucking curl.

"My..." I struggle to get words out because of the pressure he's suddenly applying. With two fingers. And his thumb. I can barely breathe. "My mouth."

"As you wish." He plants one more kiss against my thigh and slips his fingers out of me—smoothly enough to make me shiver. He guides his hands under my tank top, trailing a bit of my own wetness along my skin. "I wanted an excuse to take this thing off of you anyway."

He lifts my shirt higher, trailing kisses along my stomach, until his hands are sliding over my breasts, his thumbs rubbing my nipples through the sheer fabric of my bra until they're so tight under his touch I might explode.

"I haven't told you all three truths yet," I say, starting to ramble as a pressure in my stomach quivers and expands, warm and fluttery. "It doesn't seem fair. It's not *even*. You know?"

Ramble, ramble, ramble. I can't shut my mouth.

He lifts my shirt over my head and runs his mouth up my neck and along my jaw.

I don't know what to do with what I feel. It's too much. Too intense.
And I'm too dizzy.
So I keep talking.
I keep talking; I keep talking; I keep talking until I lose track of every word that falls from my mouth.
And then I pass out.
And then I wake up with the sun hitting my face and I can't recall a single damn thing about anything else from the end of the night.
Fuck.

CHAPTER TEN

NOTHING. NOT A thing. I remember Frank kissing up my neck. I know I was jibber jabbering. And that's it. That's all I've got.

Oh my God, *Frank*.

I force my sandpaper eyes to open wider than their current narrow slits and I roll to my side.

And there he is. Sleeping. Snoring softly on his inhales.

How can I wake up so attracted to someone who snores?

Maybe because even with his mouth slack, slightly parted, he looks like a damn Greek god.

A Greek god I came home with. To have sex with.

Oh my God, *sex*.

Did we?

I gently roll onto my back and run a hand over myself. Over my underwear. I don't feel touched, or tender. Or stretched. Or...who knows what it'd feel like after sleeping with this way-too-beautiful guy beside me?

The point is, not me.

We didn't do it. He's still in an undershirt, and—I slowly lift the covers to peek—his boxer briefs. Holy shit he's got morning wood, though.

Yeah. No way that thing was inside me last night. I wouldn't be able to walk the rest of the day. Probably not tomorrow either.

Yeesh.

Frank sighs—and I freeze, but he only closes his mouth and settles more deeply into sleep. One of his arms is strewn out toward me, palm down like he's holding the covers in place, though he gave way easily enough when I lifted them. A strand of morning sunlight flows across his skin, highlighting an odd pattern of jagged scars across the top of his hand. I didn't notice them last night, though maybe I never looked. Plus, let's be real, every time he touched me with either hand, I lost a little focus. But I wonder what caused the scars. They're healed now, but the skin's still raised and whatever happened looks like it was painful.

My eyes catch on something a few inches from his hand—my tank top. I quietly rise and reach for it, holding my breath—and he clears his throat, shifting behind me. Panic pushes me out from under the covers. I move slowly, carefully, and once I'm free, I dart into his bathroom to get dressed.

At least from the waist up.

Not sure where my pants are.

No, wait.

The memory slams into me like a physical blow. I remember sliding them down my legs last night, stepping out of them, straddling him... His lips on my neck, his hands riding up the skin of my stomach.

How am I *this* turned on all over again from a memory—and while the dredges of a hangover are beginning to sink their claws into the sides of my skull? But the very skin of the very stomach he ran his hands along last night is quivering. And that is very much not from my hangover.

Okay. It was one night. It's over. And now I need to get out of here. And the point is that my pants are at the side of his bed. I must've walked right over them, and now I have to go out to get them and he's probably wide awake waiting for me. For my pasty, freckled legs in the light of day. And without the aid of alcohol to give them any sort of faux-confident swagger.

Plus my knees are wobbly from remembering all the heat from last night.

I splash water on my face and thank God there's an elastic around my wrist for me to tie my rat's nest hair up with. I find a tube of toothpaste in a drawer and squirt some onto my finger, rubbing it over my teeth and then rinsing some of the dried saliva out of my mouth.

Hoping I'm at least halfway presentable, I pull the doors open like I'm not at all intimidated.

And I nearly pass out with relief when Frank's no longer in the room.

I finish dressing in privacy, and try to figure out if I'm glad we didn't sleep together, or disappointed. But it's the sinking weight of disappointment winning in my belly, because when will I ever have a chance like this again? Last night was unreal.

Literally. Not real. He doesn't even have my name. He doesn't know anything about me, really. Everything he learned, he learned from *Cindy*...

And now I have to figure out how to get out of here without making it worse.

I should slip out. I should sneak down his stairs and let myself out the door.

But I want one more glance. One more peek at what might've been. One more mental snapshot of the most beautiful person who's ever wanted me. I'll say goodbye. That's it. A quick goodbye, and then I'm gone.

I sling my purse over my shoulder and tiptoe down the hall the best I can in last night's heels. I spiral myself halfway down his staircase, pausing when he comes into view.

He's sitting at his kitchen island with a tall coffee mug in his hands. There's a second one in front of the seat next to him. And the air smells like cinnamon rolls, making my stomach grumble. I choose to think it's my step down onto the next wooden stair that makes him look up, though.

"Good morning." Good. I'm the first one to speak.

He clears his throat and waits until I'm all the way down to respond. "Hi."

"Smells good." I walk toward him with a confidence I don't feel. It's exhausting. Especially hungover.

Mostly because the sight of him stirs things up in me I don't want to deal with, especially sober.

"I take mine black," he says, sliding the second mug toward me. "But I made yours extra sweet."

"Please, please don't tell me it's as sweet as I am or something similarly lame." I'm so proud of my careless tone right now I want to take it out for ice cream.

"You liked sweet drinks last night. I made an educated guess." He smiles, but it doesn't reach his eyes and that makes me a little nervous.

"Well then." I stop across the island from him, reaching to grab the coffee. "Your reasoning paid off. I do like my coffee extra sweet." And with the first sip I have to keep from moaning. It's perfect and creamy and smooth. Hot enough to burn the roof of my mouth, but I don't need taste buds after this anyway.

"We should talk," he says, his tone serious enough to cancel out the pride I felt for my own a few seconds ago.

"About?" I keep my gaze on his for approximately half a second before I can't take it anymore and I study the mug in my hands instead. Tall and blue, ceramic. Probably not dishwasher safe.

"About last night."

My chest tightens. He doesn't strike me as the kind of guy who'll be pissed we didn't bang... But I don't strike him as the type of girl who's named Teagan. We all have our secrets.

"Listen," I say. "About that... Sorry I passed out. I don't usually make promises I can't keep."

"You didn't make me any promises last night." His voice is sharp, and I can't help but look up. There's a muscle clenched in his jaw, his sexy, sexy shadowed jaw. "You don't owe me—or anyone else—anything."

"No shit." I don't get where he's going with this, or why.

I'm not sure he does either, because it takes him a few moments—and a few sips of coffee—to speak again.

"You told me—wait." He breaks off, shaking his head, and nervousness swirls into panic in the pit of my stomach. I told him what? A fake name? *Does he know?* When he looks at me again, his gaze is so direct it's startling. "You don't even know my real name. Let's start there."

Oh my God, he does want to discuss names. He knows I lied.

Should I tell him the truth? Laugh it off like I thought he knew I was joking?

He walks toward me and my stomach clenches for too many reasons to name.

I grip my coffee mug like it'll shield me from any awkwardness.

It's not working.

At all.

And then he's in front of me, watching me so studiously I slide a hand across my face in case there's something stuck there.

"I'm Alec," he says, sticking out his hand. I check for, but don't find, any scars on this one.

Don't tell me, is what I mean to say. But what slips out is, "I thought the girl last night called you *Alex*?"

"Probably to irritate me. We hold no particular fondness for one another." He says it casually, like it weighs nothing in his mind. Still, I wonder why—and am tempted to ask—but then he continues with, "Anyway. I'm *Alec* Chambers."

And his full name echoes through my brain, bouncing around and, instead of fading, growing louder with every iteration.

It's officially worse.

So. Much. Worse.

I know his name.

I know who he is.

"Cool." I take his hand, offering the limpest shake of my life and letting go as soon as possible. "Do you have any headache meds or anything?" I gulp my coffee so fast it scalds my throat. "Got a crucial hangover."

Got a crucial hangover? What am I? Some teenage surfer? Why don't I throw up a hang ten sign while I'm at it?

But he takes the bait. "Probably somewhere upstairs—I'll go check."

I don't even wait for the relief to hit. I get the hell out of his condo the second he's far enough away not to hear his door shut.

The glass elevator seems so much more appropriate this morning. Almost like the universe is handing me a dose of the snide sarcasm I use so spectacularly on my own. Everything I wanted to keep hidden is about to be made clear, whether I like it or not.

Fuck.

I went after a fairy tale, but I didn't get it—and the stupid fucking clock just struck twelve anyway. Here's my Cinderella moment, fleeing before I return to tatters before his eyes.

But this time, the prince won't need a glass slipper to find me.

Because Alec Chambers?

His father is the CEO of Chambers & Britt.

I know this for a fact because my starting position at the company is to be the second assistant to the CEO's son, while he's home for the summer, studying for his MBA from fucking Harvard. And that son's name? Yep. It's Alec Chambers.

I'll see him again on Monday.

CHAPTER ELEVEN

MAYBE I SHOULD quit... But I shake my head before the thought's finished filtering through my mind. I shove myself out of the apartment complex, squinting in the bright morning sun. I'm desperate for this job. Considering I was fired from my last one—and especially the reason for it—makes getting hired anywhere else pretty much impossible.

When Frank—or, no, *Alec*—figures out who I am, I'll probably be fired all over again.

This is bad. This is so, so bad.

But, like I'm being granted some sort of respite to the rest of this shitty situation, there's a cab waiting out front. The driver looks up when I exit, and I dash straight to him.

I open the door, breathless and nervous. Every second that ticks by gives Alec one more second to come after me.

"*Go,*" I say, slamming the door. "Please. The faster, the better."

I don't care that I'm stealing someone else's cab, but karma is a total effing bitch and we don't even make it out of the long driveway before I'm yelling for him to stop.

Because my cash is in Cassidy's blazer.

And Cassidy's blazer is somewhere in Alec's place.

The cab driver is not pleased and, understandably, refuses to even drop me off at Springs Corner right up the street. So I hoof it. In last night's wrinkled outfit, wearing a mangled wreck of a bun in my hair. And after the third honk from a passing car, I want to murder someone. Anyone. Maybe Alec. Mostly myself. Humiliation is hot and unforgiving in my veins.

I call Cassidy over and over and over again.

Finally, Gage answers her phone, his voice all groggy like I woke him up. Boo-freaking-hoo. He tells me Cassidy's in the shower. I tell him I don't care, get her out. She, at least, responds like a friend, telling me she'll throw on clothes and rush to come get me without even needing an explanation.

"I can't tell if this means things went well with that guy or not," she says before I've even gotten my seat belt on. "I'm thinking maybe not?"

"*That guy?* You mean the one you *had* to tell I hadn't gotten laid in a while?" I glare at her when she snorts. Her hair's wet, flung up in a bun, and I can tell she didn't stop to put on a bra under her T-shirt. I should be nicer to her. But I don't have anything nice in me at the moment. "Yeah. I went home with that guy. And guess what? Turns out he's my fucking boss for the summer." I'm suddenly furious all over again that she thought it was funny, then or now.

She pauses mid-giggle. "Are you kidding?"

"Why the hell would I kid about something like this?" Why the hell would I get myself into this situation? "He's your dad's CEO's son. Working for the summer until he returns to his Ivy League MBA program. I was hired by his dad's secretary to be *his* second assistant for the summer. Because apparently one isn't enough." Then it hits me. "*How could you not tell me who he was?*"

She blinks. "How would I have known?"

"Your dad is his dad's second-in-command. You can't tell me you've never met Alec before."

Understanding dawns across her face. "I haven't, Teag. I swear. Not once. There aren't, like, company family functions all the time. I've been to Mr. Chambers' house for dinner before but I've never met his kids. They're all out of the house, I think. Maybe if I'd paid better attention to pictures, or—oh my God, he does look like his father. There was something familiar about him, but I didn't place it. Because he's hot and I've never thought of his dad that way. But I should've re—"

"Whatever. It's fine," I cut her off, because she's spiraling into self-doubt when it's really not her fault. Not that it keeps me from being irritated with her anyway. "But what the fuck am I going to do?"

"Did you sleep with him?"

"Who cares?" I can't bring myself to lie to her about it. "He's my fucking boss and I lied to him about my name. And instead of coming clean, I split while his back was turned."

"Teag!" She shoots me a sympathetic glance, which would maybe mean something if her stupid lips weren't quivering to hold in her laughter. "What *are* you going to do?"

"Not talk to *you* about it anymore." I stare blindly out my window, hating how bitchy I'm being, hating how she's not grasping the seriousness of this.

Hating everything, basically.

Myself most of all.

"I'm sorry. I'm not laughing at you—just at how ridiculous this situation is." The sincerity in her apology makes me feel even shittier. "Is there anything I can—?"

"It's fine." My tone says otherwise, but it'll have to do. "Can we not talk about it for a while? I need some time to process." To stew.

No. To get over myself and this *thing* that lives inside my stomach, the one that has my hands in tangled fists across my lap, squeezing as hard as they can to try to keep some of the fury at bay—because this is my fault, not anyone else's. Not his, and definitely not Cassidy's.

"Okay." She says the word quietly and now I loathe myself. But it doesn't keep me from staying silent the rest of the drive. From muttering a thank you before letting myself out of the car and not looking back, even when she halfheartedly calls out to me that she'll see me later.

Angry or not, I can't look back, though. I never can, not when I'm this close to where I live. If I were to look back, I might go running after Cassidy's car, begging her to take me with her.

My house is two seconds away from looking like one of those rundown, boarded-up, peeling-paint shacks visible from the side of the road in bad neighborhoods. It's one more falling shutter away from being dilapidated, a word I know because it's been flung in my face several times. I got over the teases a long time ago, though, because the outside is such a perfect representation of the inside. And the people within.

My key is in my hand, but I can't bring myself to use it. I don't have it in me to deal with my grandparents on top of everything else. And… I can't stop flashing back to this morning. Frank's face. Alec's face, I mean.

Why didn't I laugh and confess who I was the instant I realized he was my freaking boss? Why did I flee? All I did was make things *so much* worse.

And before he even said his name…he looked so serious. What happened to the sweet and charming guy from the bar—from his game room…his bedroom?

Damn it. I wanted last night to mean something, to give me something to hold on to. A memory to cherish, to pull me through until I can afford my own apartment, to push me into a newer, better, more experienced me. Instead, all I have is anxiety and fingers itching to call Chambers & Britt to quit before I've even started.

Alec. I shape his name on my tongue. The name suits him way more than Frank ever did.

And that's as far as I get because Gran opens the door, in her uniform, anger in her eyes and the still-lit butt of a cigarette hanging from her lips. She doesn't speak, stepping aside to let me pass. I don't speak either, slipping through the doorway, holding my breath to escape the worst of the smoke.

And then I figure, fuck it. And I breathe it in. This, at least, is familiar; it goes all the way to my bones. Dirty house. Stench of smoke. Gran's contempt. These things bring me back to myself.

"You look like yesterday's trash." She's looking for an argument and my throat tightens. I pause on the bottom step to the upstairs and turn to face her. We've lasted weeks this time without speaking to each other. Guess this means Gramps fell off the wagon again. He's probably still sleeping it off. I bet if I inhale deeply enough, I'll smell the rank scent of cheap booze underneath all her cigarette smoke. I choose not to try it. I also choose not to give her the fight she wants.

Six more months, I remind myself, instead. If I save for six months, with my salary—even as small as it is—I'll be able to afford almost a year of a cheap apartment on my own. Clinging to this knowledge, all I say is, "You're right."

If it shocks her that I'm agreeing for a change, she doesn't show it. "Gonna turn out like your mama, knocked up before your time."

Maybe if I turned out like my mother, I'd be the one my grandparents taped once a week on a cheap TV tape player. The one on a reality series to be the next top LA socialite, pretending not to have a family anywhere.

Maybe I'd be the one who managed to escape this house and everyone in it. Sometimes I almost understand why she did it.

But, "I'll never be like her," is what I say. Because no matter what other path of hers I might follow, I would never abandon a newborn. Especially if it meant leaving her with my grandparents, people more likely to laugh when a child falls down than to help her up.

Gran cackles, a hacking sort of cough disguised as a laugh. "Keep telling yourself that, chub-doll."

"I'm going to shower." My voice carries no emotion. It's deadened and that same deadness creeps through the rest of me, weighing me down like my limbs and my stomach are full of wet sand.

She pulls on the last embers of her cigarette. "Hot water's off, but you look like you could use a cold one, anyway. I work a double at the grocery today, so make sure you feed your grandfather this evening."

"He can fend for himself," I say without much bite, heading up the stairs before she has a chance to respond.

My feet automatically skip the third and eighth steps; one's splintered, the other close to joining it. And I hold on to the wall instead of the railing, which is also splintered in spots. I dump my clothes in my bedroom, wrap myself in a clean towel, and head straight to the bathroom. I need to wash off this morning's humiliation, but more than that, I need to rinse Gran's words down the drain with it.

I turn the water on to mute my voice, and then I turn toward the full-length mirror hanging on the back of the bathroom door. I hesitate a few moments, but I know I have to do it, so I drop the towel. And I study myself. Hard.

"You are not a chub-doll." I glare at my reflection so that maybe the truth will sink in. There are bags under my eyes and my cheeks are a little gaunt. I force my gaze lower. My boobs are medium-sized and perky and *almost* symmetrical. There's pudge around my belly, and some cellulite on my thighs, but not a ton. *Not* a ton—the thought needs some extra force behind it. My feet are slender, my toes thin and pretty. I tell myself the truth every day. I'm honest with myself about my appearance, sometimes brutally. But I have to be. If I tell myself no lies, her criticisms won't sink all the way in. Not the way they used to.

"I am not fat. I am average. And sometimes even passable as pretty." I've said these words a thousand times, so I don't know why my voice is quivering this morning. I don't know why my eyes sting with tears, or why I find any of it so hard to believe now. "Even Alec thought I was attractive enough to take home."

Oh, God. Alec.

I wait for the surge of embarrassment to swell through me, but it doesn't happen. I'm too…heavy to feel anything with much force.

This is worse.

This is so much worse than all the anger.

Sadness has no outlet, no fury to unleash and relieve.

Even ice-cold shower water doesn't do anything to shock it out of my system, try as I might to scrub it all away.

I let my wet, sandbag limbs carry me to my bedroom. I let them crawl me onto my thin old mattress. I let them weigh me down into sleep.

CHAPTER TWELVE

CASSIDY CALLS ME all weekend. I ignore her.

Vera tries me, too. Same goes.

Clearing their calls makes me hate myself. But I hate the thought of speaking with anyone even more than that.

Gran doesn't bother trying to speak to me—neither does Gramps—the few times I stumble downstairs to grab water and the occasional snack. I think they prefer me out of sight.

I know I do.

When I'm not sleeping, I'm curled tightly as I can be on my side, squishing any feeling that tries to rise, wanting to be asleep. It's easier during the days. The nights? Nights are always the worst.

Nights bring the stomach ants. Anxiety. When I was younger, I only understood the tight, crawling sensation that circled in my belly to be ants. Marching nonstop. Biting the inside of my tummy. Making my breath come faster and my mind swirl.

All the things I've done, the ways I've acted. I never get to forget them; they're just around the corner of my mind, every time. External reminders. Internal guilt. The weight of it all is crushing.

And it's always there, a river of gasoline through my veins.

Plenty of times, it goes dormant. There, but manageable. Not forgotten—but abated. Happy days. Happy weeks. Happy months... Well, not *happy*. But not miserable, at least.

The thing about gasoline, though... It only takes a spark to explode. And every single time I fail at something, there's a flame.

When I let my friends down. When Gran's digs manage to get to me. When an inch of my belly hangs over pants that shouldn't be too tight.

When I can't understand the things everyone around me seems to find simple. When Gramps spends the money I pay them for bills every month on something other than what it's intended for, and our hot water gets shut off.

When I feel fat. Ugly. Bad skinned. When I notice my plainness compared to my friends in pictures. When my pudgy stomach's the first thing I focus on.

Such vanity. I wish I could let it all go and be happy with who I am.

But I can't.

And all that gasoline in my veins? And all those sparks?

They meet way too often.

Ka-fucking-*boom*.

I spend both weekend nights unable to sleep, tossing and turning and lost in thoughts that grow darker with each minute until I'm crying without tears.

Because tears would give me release, and apparently my chub-doll body hates me too much to let me have it.

Then, somehow, it's Monday morning and I don't have a choice anymore. I'm sleepless, disheveled, *gross*. And I have to get out of bed.

I reach in my closet and pull out a tilted old picnic basket. I made it in middle school home ec, and it was the first thing I'd ever created that wasn't a total disaster. Yes, it's crooked. And the paint's not thick enough to cover some of the newspaper print from the pages I cut up and rolled into tubes to weave into the basket.

But it's functional. It gets the job done. And that's what I have to do today. Be functional. Get the job done.

In the basket is the only other thing I have of value. A blanket I made, also in middle school, out of scraps of cloth—and sewn into the center is my baby blanket. The thing I came home from the hospital with, tattered and threadbare. I found it when I was younger, thrown in with dust rags. Gran laughed about it when I asked why it was different colors than the other white rags. Then she told me what it was, and when I got mad that she'd used something that was mine to collect dust and dirt, she laughed again.

Sometimes looking at these things, touching them, remembering the way it felt to make them, helps when I'm in a bad mood. Today is no exception, but the little rise in temperament they give isn't nearly enough to push through the weight of the fog holding me down.

CHAPTER THIRTEEN

ANOTHER COLD SHOWER—and the bite of anxiety coming through over seeing Alec again—helps to clear some of my fog.

At first, it's almost nice to feel something other than overwhelming nothingness. Little nips and jolts along my nerves... It's like remembering I'm alive. It's enough to push me into actually attempting to style my hair, which I'm sure I'll appreciate later. It's also enough to have me squandering away a few precious dollars for a drive-through coffee on my way to Chambers & Britt.

But once I'm there, my poor car sputtering her way into the parking lot, past the company's three towering glass buildings? Suddenly, as hard as I've been trying to avoid it all morning, Alec's face is in my mind. So in focus that everything else blurs away. So sharp I can practically *smell* him, that woodsy soap scent.

If my face wasn't numb from lack of movement for two days, I'd cringe. As it is, I schlep into an empty space and bury my face in my hands anyway. God. Right now, in his mind, I'm some girl who disappeared like an asshole. Big deal. But the second he sees me this morning? I'll become so much more than that. *A way bigger asshole. A huge liar.*

Possibly fired.

I wish I hadn't left.

I wish I *had* slept with him. Not that it'd make this situation any easier, but I bet the memories would be worth it.

I wish I'd been honest.

I wish—*shit*. The time on my dashboard tells me I really can't be sitting here making regret-filled wishes right now. I wish I wasn't about to be late for my first day of work.

I'm out of the car and halfway through the lot before I notice all of the sleek and fancy cars lined up around me. If I wasn't still so *blah* about everything, they'd make me feel so inadequate I'd turn around and sputter my little Toyota right the hell out of here. I don't have that option though. I need this job.

I need to figure out how to convince Alec not to kick me to the curb the second he sees me.

I want to pause for one last deep breath before stepping through the doors, but there's a woman rushing beside me and she pauses to hold the door, offering a halfhearted smile.

So in I go.

And, when I check in to ask for the badge that's supposed to be waiting for me, the receptionist at the front desk tells me I'm half an hour late.

"What?" I almost lean forward to grip the jutting top of the counter he stands behind.

"You're half an hour late." He says the words slowly, like he's speaking to an idiot. Which maybe he is, but his tone still pisses me the hell off. Another nice burst of *feeling* shoots through me.

"The email said—*confirmed*, actually—my start time was nine a.m. every day except Thursdays." I have to come in half an hour early those days to help set up for a weekly all-hands meeting that starts at nine sharp. I read that line ten freaking times to make sure I had it right—in a magnified print. I point to the clock on the wall behind him. "I'm exactly on time."

"For the record, exactly on time would mean you're in your desk at nine a.m., which you aren't." He's so smug I want to pinch him. "And the email also said that on your first day, you should arrive thirty minutes early for a brief orientation follow-up."

"Where?" My one word is full of enough attitude to make him blink, but I'm getting irritated. Or maybe it's the panic clawing at my throat at how much worse Alec's first—or, actually, second—impression of me will be. "In fine print?"

"It's in the line immediately after your regular schedule is listed." He waves to someone walking past me.

"How would you know that? Did you send the email?" It came from someone in human resources, so I don't understand. I also don't understand why he's being such a dick.

"It's the standard format for all new employees." He doesn't roll his eyes, but he might as well have.

And, fuck. I always do this shit. I try so hard to focus on what I think is important that sometimes other important things slip right past my eyes. I swear I read the email start to finish. The problem is, sometimes words blur over each other if I'm not really looking for them.

"Listen, if you're waiting for me to apologize, it's not going to happen," I say, because his expression's so impatient that now I want to pinch him and twist the skin. "So may I *please* have my badge?"

He pulls it out of an envelope, handing it to me without comment.

"Thank you. And now what do I do because I missed this morning's orientation?"

He shrugs. "Ask your boss."

Right. My boss. I turn, making my way toward the elevators, and just like that Mr. Way-Too-Much-Gel-in-My-Hair Receptionist is out of my mind. Replaced by Alec. And his dimples. And his hard, hard chest. And the knowledge of what I've done to make this situation so incredibly shitty.

Fake name? Check.

Run out while his back is turned? Check.

Late for my first day? Check.

I can't do this. Nope.

As the elevator door opens, I swivel around, weaving through the group of people waiting with me, and I head toward the exit.

Right as Mr. Evans—Cassidy's dad—walks through it. Damn it. His face lights up when he sees me and he waves, calling to me as he comes closer. "Happy first day, hon."

I nod, unable to find my voice.

"Nervous?" He walks right past the guy in reception, who's watching us like he's confused I associate with someone this high ranking. It makes me feel a little better—but not enough to stay.

"Mr. Evans, I—"

"Please. We're colleagues now. Call me Brad." He throws an arm around my shoulder, leading me toward the elevators again. "You'll let me take you to lunch today, won't you? First day celebration?"

How do I refuse?

Last summer, Cassidy was supposed to intern here, but she changed her mind at the last minute to work at a rock venue. He was furious. Like, *kick his own daughter out of the house* furious. Granted, his son had died six months prior and he was a wreck with grief. They all were. *We* all were. He seems to have come a long way in the past year, but still. I can't let him put his neck out for me and be the second hire to fall through after he's vouched for them.

Damn it.

"Walk me to my desk?" I ask, hating how timid my voice comes out, but if I'm staying, I can't go up there alone. I *need* someone by my side the first time I see Alec again, and Mr. Evans is almost as high up in the company as Alec's own father. Maybe it's dumb, but I think he gives me a little clout.

Still, it's not enough to keep my hands from shaking the moment we step onto the elevator. It's not enough to give me the incentive to press the button for my floor. Mr. Evans pushes the nineteen absentmindedly while jabbering on about restaurants in the area.

I zone him out because the thought of food turns my stomach.

Then the elevator doors open on the nineteenth floor and I think I'm going to puke anyway.

Because Alec is standing in front of me, waiting for the elevator I'm about to step out of.

CHAPTER FOURTEEN

I VAGUELY RECOGNIZE that there's a man standing next to Alec, but I can't force my gaze from the guy in front of me. Shock etches into his handsome face, in every dazzling feature. I'm pretty sure a similar shock is marring my own freckled expression. Because even though I was expecting to see him, my memory of how pretty he is did nothing to prepare me for the sight of him in a suit.

Sharp. Tall. Slender, but somehow overpowering. Hair swept away from his face, still destructured enough to make me want to run my fingers through it, but styled in a much more professional manner than the last time I saw him. It looks soft. He must use wax instead of gel.

So. Fucking. Hot.

After a moment that stretches out eons, his brows go down. "Cindy?" The disbelief in his voice is matched in strength only to the burning heat that floods my face.

"This is *Teagan*," Mr. Evans says, beside me, stopping the door from closing in our faces and pulling me forward, out of the elevator. Closer to Alec. "Your new assistant, I believe."

This time the pause lasts at least a millennia. Alec's face filters through so many emotions it's dizzying. Confusion, more shock, more disbelief, and back to confusion. And then...nothing. His expression goes carefully, purposefully blank. Guarded. I'm surprised what a difference it makes. I hadn't realized how easy he'd been around me, how free.

He sticks out his hand and, *yet again*, I take it. One quick shake and he lets go. His words are brisk, toneless. "Nice to meet you." After a pause, like an afterthought, he adds, "Teagan." My name is an accusation.

"And this is Philip Chambers." Mr. Evans motions, palm up, toward the man next to Alec. He's unfazed by the crackling tension in the air between Alec and me. I pull my gaze from the son and put my hand out to meet the father. Who, I notice with an extra little jolt of shock, is nearly identical to his son in features. Gray hair and a bit of a belly, but otherwise the resemblance is jarring. Fucking Cassidy. How she missed it the night we met Alec, I'll never know.

"Pleasure," he says. "I'm making your job a little easier this morning and taking Alec out for coffee." He squeezes my hand before dropping it. "But don't worry, I won't have them take it out of your paycheck." He laughs. I do, too. Mechanically. I'm still too lost in the aftereffect of everything going on to make it genuine—and, anyway, is he mocking me?

Yes, part of my job is to fetch coffee. It's been grating on me since I was hired. "Let's really turn the tables, then. Grab one for me, too."

There's a hesitation before his laughter this time, and the humor doesn't quite reach his eyes. I wonder if I took it too far, or if my tone was bitchier than I intended, rather than the playful I was shooting for. Mr. Evans, on the other hand, is cracking up. He puts his arm around my shoulder for a quick squeeze. Alec, I notice in my peripheral—and with every nerve ending in my body—doesn't respond at all.

"You go on ahead, honey," Mr. Evans says. "I've got to speak with Philip for a moment, but I'll come by in a few to help you get settled in." And to my absolute horror, he pulls Mr. Chambers aside, leaving me alone with Alec.

My eyes make it as far as his neckline, to the very neat knot in his very expensive-looking tie, tucked into the very crisp collar of his very pressed shirt under his very sleek suit jacket. I can't look higher than that. I can't. "Where do I go?"

"Take a left at the end of the hall." He points and my gaze tracks the motion of his arm like a lifeline. "My office is in the back right corner. There's a desk set up for you in front of it. There's a note with your name so you won't miss it. Unless you're confused about what your name is." He waits for me to look at him.

Well. Keep on waiting, buddy, because my eyes are statues pointed straight at the ground.

"You'll see Sam at the desk next to yours, if you need help getting settled in."

"Sam?" I ask, finally forcing myself to look at him. At his blank expression. The one twisting my stomach into one gigantic hangman's noose.

"My other assistant."

"Oh. Right. Because you need two people to get you coffee." My sarcasm makes him wince—which, in turn, makes me wince. Why do I have to be such a bitch?

"Is that the tone you want to set for this...working relationship?" Still impassive, but there's a muscle clenched in his jaw, and under the facade I sense his growing anger.

"I'm sorry." I hate apologizing, even when I know I've done something to make it necessary. Especially when I have so many other things to apologize for—which I should probably do now. Damn it. I take a deep breath and endure another jolt to my senses when his woodsy aroma floods through me. Double damn it. Now I'm turned on while mortified and the conflicting senses are making my stomach twist. "Listen. I should probably tell you—"

"I'll speak with you when I return." He's so brusque, so short, it's almost physically painful.

"Right. I'll just find my desk then." I wait for him to nod, but he's already turned toward his father and Mr. Evans, like I'm not even here anymore.

My senses have never been so awake, so completely aware of every little detail as I make my way down the hall. At least the fog of the weekend is gone. That's a good thing.

Isn't it?

Maybe not. Because holy shit feeling like this big of an asshole is not fun. And this is coming from someone who feels like at least a little bit of an asshole most of the time.

Sam. Samuel or Samantha? I have no right to feel a pending jealousy if his other assistant is female, but I do.

Plus, the air is heavy with the mixed scent of pencil shavings and stale coffee and for some reason it reminds me of high school, adding to the dread pulling my stomach into a black hole. Every step I take pushes my nervous system into something more appropriate to a teenage girl. Especially when I turn at the end of the hall and find myself in a huge open-space work area, the size of a miniature stadium, filled with desks and people on phones and the soft whirs of printers and...just...too much busyness to take in all at once.

I'm so far out of my element I don't even know what an element is anymore. But I plaster on an expression that says otherwise, like I did in high school—like I do most days of my life—and I step further into the space.

The deep timbre of Alec's voice plays back for me, my mind putting a friendlier twist on his shortness this morning, because *Frank* wouldn't speak like that—and in the farthest right corner, there's a glass office where he said it'd be. In fact the entire back wall is a row of beveled, frosted-glass offices, but the one in the corner is the biggest. Of course it is. Nothing but the best for the son of the CEO.

There are two desks in front of the door. One empty, the other occupied by an Asian guy who looks about my age. Maybe a little younger. He's typing furiously at the computer on his desk, completely in the zone. So professional-looking. I can't type half that fast.

I should glance around and try to force my numb lips into a smile as I make my way through the office for what seems like hours in a maze, but I don't. I can't. I'm too rattled, too out of place.

Too tempted to turn around, sprint back toward Alec, and jump him.

Or ditch him altogether and get the hell out of this office, out of this life.

But I don't want to return to the other one, to the old me. This is my step forward—I can't afford to look back.

"Samuel?" I ask when I'm finally close enough to get his attention, stopping in front of the desk I assume will be mine.

"Sam, actually," he says, looking up, his fingers pausing over the keys.

"Oh, sorry."

"No biggie." He lifts a shoulder like maybe he's used to it. "Sam's short for Osamu. My mother had high hopes."

I'm missing something, but he speaks so plainly, it's like I should know what he means about his mother. If I'm not born smarter in my next life, I'm giving up on coming back at all.

He must see the confusion I'm trying to hide because he offers a smile. "Osamu means ruler."

"Oh." Relief is a small thing compared to everything else going on inside of me, but at least it's something. I *wasn't* supposed to know. "And yet, here you are, an assistant."

"And here *you* are," he says, his words calm, his eyes narrow, his smile gone, "below even me. A kid fresh out of high school. And you must be what? Thirty?"

"Twenty-two," I say, rankled. I don't look thirty. I *know* I don't. This is off to a *great* start. I drag a finger along my new desk, admiring how sleek the wood is, how unsplintered. Trying to smile, and halfway succeeding, I start over. "Where are you from?"

"Delaware."

"No—I meant—"

"I know what you meant." He stares at the flat screen of his computer, fiddling with the mouse. "My parents are American, too. In case that's your follow-up."

"I'm not trying to be offensive." For once in my damn life.

"Doesn't mean you aren't." He starts typing again, saying coolly, "Anyway. Let me know if you need help logging in. Otherwise I have a ton of shit to do."

And I stand here with my mouth wide enough to let an airplane land. Great. I'm an asshole even when I don't mean to be. Everyone I have to work with hates me already. I search my mind for what I said to offend Sam. "Listen, I—"

"*Teagan.*" Alec's voice is a whip cutting through the air behind me, the force strong enough to whirl me around. "My office. Now."

My mouth grows wet at the sight of him striding toward me, all angry and sexy—and wearing his suit like it was tailored to highlight his height, the width of his shoulders, the narrow slope of his waist. I can't do this. I can't face him. Not now. Not every day.

People are staring at us. Sam's snorting behind me. My ears have cotton in them, and my blood is no longer flowing beneath my skin.

"Aren't you going for coffee with your father?" My question comes out barely a whisper, and still somehow he hears me, coming closer and closer and closer, until he's near enough for me to catch a whiff of that soap I love.

"I told him to go without me. I thought it'd be a better use of my time to meet with my new assistant." He storms past me, straight into his office.

"Jeff Santos called from Berkeley Group earlier—and Piper left a message for you," Sam says after him. "She wants you to turn your damn phone on—and that's a direct quote." Alec doesn't even acknowledge him, and Sam whistles, muttering under his voice, "In trouble already?" I'm pretty sure there's admiration in his tone. "I will need details of this as soon as you're done getting reamed a new one."

"Pretty sure I'm getting fired, so don't hold your breath." I smile at him, sweet as a lemon. "Or, maybe, do."

But my smile drops the second I step past Sam toward Alec's office. My stomach, too. He's standing in front of his desk, waving me in with a short jerk of his hand and a look that says the longer I keep him waiting, the more trouble I'm in.

I lift my chin and I meet his gaze and I force myself through the door into his office.

CHAPTER FIFTEEN

"SHUT THE DOOR." His tone is calm, and he's leaning against his desk oh-so-casually, but his knuckles are white where they grip the wood, and that same muscle is clenched in his jaw as before.
I shut the door. "You're mad at me."
"I'm confused." He doesn't sound confused, though. He's short, pointed, *pissed*. "Start explaining."
I try to smile, but I can't get the corners of my mouth to work. I aim for humor instead. "There are so many things I could start with... Hard to pick one..."
It falls flat.
Like a pancake-on-the-floor flat.
Not even a halfhearted amused twinkle passes through his dark, dark eyes. Not even the slightest hint of one of his dimples. Just his angular face, all stiff...and smoldery...and *lickable*.
Fuck. That last one is totally inappropriate.
"Try your name."
"Right." I swallow around the ball of nerves bunched at the base of my throat, glancing around the room. Rectangular table in the corner. Bold splashes of color in abstract paintings hanging on the two non-glass walls. One windowed wall looking clear out into the city. What am I doing here?

"Any time now."

Shit. Okay. "I'm Teagan—"

"Walker, I know." He shakes his head—and then starts to laugh.

"*What?*" I'm in no position to snap, but his laughter is directed *at* me. And I don't do well with that shit. "What's so funny?"

"Just… Walker?" His brows go up. "You sure it isn't Runner?"

I roll my eyes. "You're a trip and a half."

"And you're lucky I'm laughing instead of—" He cuts himself off, his eyes flickering away. He swallows heavily when they travel back to mine.

"Instead of *what?*" I shouldn't push him like this, but he's swallowing a second time and… I think he's not thinking about professional things right now. His stare is so intense, it gives me a total rush, and his cheek muscle's working overtime and his hands are gripping that desk harder, harder, harder until he lets it go completely, stretching out his palms.

I swear to God I think he was going to say I was lucky he didn't spank me.

And I get the oddest urge to giggle. It grows and grows and grows until I have to clear my throat to cover the noise that slips out.

A war battles its way across his face and in the end, a professional mask slips over his expression. He pushes off of his desk and walks around it, sliding into his chair. "Why'd you leave without saying anything on Saturday morning?"

I tuck a strand of hair behind an ear. "I—"

"Sit." He points to one of the chairs in front of his desk.

"I'm not a dog." I'm also not somebody who will ever learn to bite her stupid tongue, apparently.

"Are you always this defensive?"

"Yes. Since apparently me telling the truth is the point of this whole meeting."

It's gone so fast I almost missed it—but the side of his mouth undeniably quirks up.

Now he wants to smile?

The nerves making loops in my stomach unwind a fraction of an inch. I sigh and take a seat in front of him, conceding.

"I'm sorry I lied to you about my name," I say. "And I'm sorry I left without saying anything. But until you told me who you were, I never thought I'd see you again—and then I panicked."

"What do you think I did when you disappeared?" He flips the page of his desk calendar, running a finger over the paper, tapping it a few times without even looking at it. "And it's pretty fucked up you thought we wouldn't see each other again. I thought we had a connection."

We still do, I want to say. But this is about the truth, so that's what I'll give. "Come on, Alec. We come from two totally different worlds."

"Yeah." His agreement somehow both hurts and relieves me. Until he says, "One where I tell the truth and you're a total liar."

"I'm usually an honest person, actually," I say, my words clipped.

He laughs again and I want to punch him. Or kiss him.

Both, if I'm honest. "Fine. Maybe I haven't shown you that yet, but if you don't fire me, I will."

"Pretty sure I can't legally fire you for what we did—and didn't—do on Friday." He straightens a frame on his desk, a silver, square thing—and I'm suddenly desperately curious about who's on the other side. His mother? Fraternity brothers? Love of his life? Then he's looking at me again and there's so much fire in his expression, I almost start to sweat. He crosses his hands on his desk. "Pretty sure we shouldn't be having this conversation at all. But tough shit."

He waits, watching me intently, but... I didn't hear a question. Did I miss something? "What am I supposed to say?"

"You aren't finished explaining yourself."

"You know my name—and that I'm sorry. That's all I have to say at the moment."

"I told you, I didn't want to be some swinging screen door, and you—"

"We didn't even—"

"And *that's* the worst part." He clenches his jaw, that same muscle in his cheek flexing like he's trying to hold back—but doesn't succeed.

"That I didn't sleep with you?" If that's the case, it seems out of character for the guy I took him for. Granted, I probably shouldn't make assumptions about anyone's character when I can't keep track of the ones I play.

He shakes his head in short, sharp motions. "Are you playing dumb on purpose?"

"Fuck *you*." It's my automatic response to that sort of question, and rage funnels through my veins so swiftly I'm not even embarrassed to have said it. Barely, only *barely*, do I keep my voice from raising loud enough for it to filter out through the office walls. "I don't care if you're my boss. Go ahead and fire me. But don't you ever—*ever*—call me dumb."

"I know you aren't dumb, Jesus. You've got to be smart to be as slippery as *you* are." He drags a hand through his hair and focuses somewhere behind me for a moment before bringing his eyes to mine.

"Then what is it?" I'm actually grateful for my anger now; it makes this conversation easier. "I said I was sorry for misleading you and disappearing. And I am. But can't we laugh this off and move on with our lives?" Even if I'll spend the rest of mine regretting not sleeping with him because being this close to him is doing horrible things to my hormones. Through all the anger. Through all the embarrassment. Through all the *everything*.

If he were to pull me across his desk right now and have his way with me… I would have mine with him even harder. Without giving the slightest fuck that the entire office might be able to watch our blurred forms through the frosted glass walls of his office.

That won't happen, though, because there's no desire in his expression. Only anger.

"If you're worried I'll tell anyone I duped you or laugh about it behind your back, don't be. If this is some rage over your hurt masculinity, put it away."

"You think this is about my masculinity? Trust me, doll, with what I'm packing, I never have to worry about that. You think I'd be upset because you might hurt my *fragile* ego?" The sarcasm dripping in his words comes close to schooling the best I've ever had to offer, and he studies me so hard I instantly want to check myself over to make sure nothing's out of place. "Are you for real?"

"I am for real. But that girl you met on Friday? *She* was a figment of your imagination. Can we start over from right here, right now?" I should heed my own question. But he brought up what he's packing, and now the glimpse I got of his hard-on under the covers on Saturday morning is frozen in my brain.

"Do you really not remember?"

Do I really not remember what? I open my mouth but the question doesn't come out, because suddenly I'm nervous about what I might not be remembering.

"You were going to let me be your first and then you were going to walk out in the morning."

"Stop." My hand flies up to block his words, but they find their way to me anyway. Like a sledgehammer to the gut, stealing every last breath. It takes all I have not to double over. And I have to respond... Finally, lamely, I come up with: "That's bullshit."

"You told me the truth that night, so drop the act."

"What are you talking about?" *Oh my God. Oh my God. Oh my God.* "Nothing I told you on Friday was true—that's why we're here having this very conversation, remember?"

"You're the one who needs to stop." He says it patiently, like his anger with me is suddenly gone.

However, for me, panic is a rabid tiger with foot-long claws, slashing through my insides. "Alec—I don't know what you're getting—"

"You're a virgin."

And I drop dead.

Or at least I squeeze my eyes shut and wish I could. Because what he's accusing me of?

It's the truth.

CHAPTER SIXTEEN

"YOU'RE A VIRGIN," he repeats, making the entire world crash down around me a second fucking time. "And you weren't going to tell me before I fucked you."

He watches my face, scrutinizing me so closely he must be looking for any chinks in the armor of my reaction. But his words spin me around so roughly, I'm too dizzy to gather anything to protect myself with.

Virgin, virgin, virgin. The word echoes through my mind, through my limbs.

It's the biggest truth I've never told anyone.

Except, apparently, for him.

Fucking alcohol. I'm never drinking again. Like, ever.

"I... That's not true." Breathe. Why can't I breathe? "I've had tons of sex—ask my friends. Ask *anyone.*"

"So if I had *fucked* you—and trust me, Teagan, that's what we were building toward—something fast, something hard, something unrestrained..." Naked desire weaves through his expression, making my breath catch—it stays stuck even when he wrestles control over his features, contorting them into anger instead. "If we'd done that, you wouldn't have bled? It wouldn't have hurt you to be taken so roughly your first time?"

I should not be picturing him above me, *fast, hard, unrestrained... Rough*. Oh, God. I need to stop. I need to cross my legs to ease the fluttering happening between my thighs. Focus, Teagan. *Focus*. Now I can breathe, go figure, but it's happening too fast, too heavy. And he's watching my mouth. And, very, very deliberately, I'm biting my lower lip to keep his attention there.

Virgin, virgin, virgin.

The fact that he knows this thing about me should hit me like a freezing cold shower, should get rid of this damn attraction. But the way he's speaking to me, so rough, so purposefully graphic... It's heating me in a way a splash of water could never cool off. Hell, an entire tub of ice couldn't chill the rush burning through my veins. Even if he's using the language to try to freak me out. *Wrong route to take, buddy.*

"I don't think you're supposed to speak to me this way," I say, my voice *almost* steady.

"You're right." He breathes deeply, trying to rein himself in.

"I'm not saying you should stop. Just pointing out that you aren't perfect either." What am I doing?

"What are you doing?" *His* voice is strained, and for some reason it makes me want to giggle again.

"I don't know." But I do. I've dipped my toes into the quicksand of this attraction and instead of pulling my feet back, I want to dive in all the way. "I've regretted Friday night from the moment I opened my eyes on Saturday."

"If you'd told me, I wouldn't have been so—"

"So what? So aggressive? So demanding? So *hot*?" I almost smile when he starts to nod, but stops short with my last question, confused. "I don't regret any of that, you moron. What I regret is not sleeping with you."

His beautiful cheekbones stand out a little sharper when he presses his lips into a line before speaking. "Why?"

"Um, look at you." I let my eyes slowly drift down his face, his neck, his chest...and just as slowly, back up, my own body tingling with desire.

"Who cares how I look?" he asks. "You're beautiful, and you're funny. You deserve something spectacular. Something gentle for your first time. Not some drunk guy from a bar."

"You're clearly more than a drunk guy from a bar," I say, glowing too much from his compliments to stem the words falling from my mouth. "And I get the feeling you might actually be a semi-decent human being. Maybe the perfect kind of guy to be somebody's first. And if you ever tried to give me less than what you started to on Friday night? Something slower, something more *gentle*? I'd be so...not pleased."

"You'd be surprised by all the ways I can think of pleasing you, kitten, and if I were to go slow? You'd love it." Instantly the air between us is pregnant with something I'm not sure I can name. A mixture of hormones and nerves.

Or maybe that's just me.

Virgin, virgin, virgin...

"Fuck. That was insanely inappropriate." He slides a hand down his face. "I can't believe I fucking said that. I'm sorry."

"Don't be." I want to wipe his words away. The apology is dampening the rest of the mood. "I told you I didn't want gentle. I still don't..."

He clears his throat. "Are you asking me to—"

"No." I laugh, interrupting him before he can finish the question. *Completely chickening out.* "Get over yourself."

He smirks. "Really? 'Cause it sounded for a second like you actually wanted me over *you*."

He's giving me another chance to do it. Or maybe he's trying to ease the tension with a joke. Either way, I should go for it. Deep breath. "Maybe we could—"

"It's probably best we keep things—"

"What?"

"No, go ahead."

"Aw, you're such a gentleman," I say, letting my lip rise in a sneer. I know what he was going to say—which was the opposite of what I was going to say. Which makes my stomach close in on itself, and which means no way am I saying what I wanted to say in the first place right now. And if I keep thinking in these circles I'm going to get a freaking headache. "Friday night was a onetime thing for us. It'd be a mistake to try again."

"Right. Because now I'm your boss, and sleeping with you would be breaking a ton of ethical rules," he says, adding almost as an afterthought, "but mostly because I don't trust you."

"Because now you're my boss." I sigh, the tightening in my stomach turning sharper, more sour. "And you don't trust me." I pause, hoping he'll say something to make it still seem possible, but he doesn't. "Then I guess we've said all we need to say on the matter. Unless you wanted to sit there and judge me for a few more minutes."

"I'm not judging you," he's quick to say. "But you sell yourself short."

"I landed a job at Chambers and Britt. I'm doing all right."

He cringes at the name of the company, and I wonder why, but I won't ask. "I don't mean professionally, Teagan."

God. Why is he pressing this? Forget attraction. Forget regret. That slithery snake of anger is starting to stir in my veins. I stand, pushing my chair out with the backs of my knees. "No shit. But guess what, *boss?* It's none of your business."

He stands, too, his hands pressed flat on his desk, tension leveling his shoulders. "You want to play boss and employee? Fine. Start by speaking to me with a little more respect."

"Respect? After you basically call me a slut? Good luck with that shit."

He stares at me, his mouth agape. "That's not what I'm saying. Do you always put words in people's mouths? Jesus."

"My name's Teagan," I deadpan, too pissed to be proud of the quick retort.

"Could've fooled me. Oh wait, you did."

"We're back on that? Because if you're going to talk in freaking circles all day, I should sit down. These heels aren't comfortable enough to stand in for that long." I don't sit, though. Neither does he.

He sighs, loud, hard, his shoulders relaxing a few degrees. "No. That's...behind us. I don't know why I'm being such a dick. I can't keep myself in check around you."

"Actually, most people have that reaction," I say, shrugging off some irritation of my own. It's easier because he did it first. "Probably because I'm such a bitch."

TRUTH & TEMPTATION

I wait for him to tell me I'm not, but all he does is offer a small smile, and his honesty—or at least his lack of a lie—loosens more of the tight emotion in my chest. I'm out of breath, like I've run a mile while standing here. He's breathing heavily, too, and for a moment we watch each other without speaking.

And gradually, the rest of the tension—from the anger, at least—fades. His mouth quirks and, this time, mine follows.

"We'll start over," he says.

I want to say no. I don't want to start over—I want to finish what we already started. But he knows my truth. And more than anything, I want to return to a place where he didn't. Which means we're starting over. From scratch. So I stick out my hand, across his desk. "Hi. I'm Teagan. Your assistant. And I think we should discuss the proposal your father rejected on Friday. Put me to work and maybe we can get him to change his mind."

"I'm not sure how you'd know about that if this is our first time meeting," he says, a smarmy little smile across his mouth. "But I like your line of thinking."

I'm both relieved and disappointed when he doesn't hang on to the handshake longer than professionally necessary.

Mostly disappointed, though.

CHAPTER SEVENTEEN

ALEC'S PROPOSAL IS...well, basically I'm way out of my depth and suddenly beyond thankful I'm starting at such a low position because I'll have time to build up my understanding of the industry. But his proposal *sounds* smart, at least. Shit, the guy goes to grad school at Harvard. I'm pretty sure he knows a thing or two...

Chambers & Britt—built from the ground up by Alec's grandfather—is a family equity firm, and both Alec's father and grandfather have kept the firm's focus on financial and industrial markets. Alec has an idea to move toward investments in tech startups and small businesses. He wants to give dreamers the chance to build companies. (His Cinderella-style words, not mine.)

"My father always shuts me down," he says.

And, finally, here's a spot where I can be helpful. Thank God for my natural bitchy inclinations. "So?" I keep my tone aloof, kind of catty. "Don't let him."

"It's not that simple. There are a lot of considerations. My father—who's basically remote-operated by my grandfather—is old school. They want the focus on traditional assembly-line industries. They—"

"You're making my eyes glaze over," I say. "I don't know enough yet to help with the technical aspects, but I do know about getting what you want. Look where I am. I want to be here. I made it happen." Okay, it's not all that easy, but he doesn't need to hear that part of it right now. "I do know that you can either whine about your father rejecting what you proposed—or you can fight harder for what you want."

Alec blinks. Maybe he's never considered it. "I always go after what I want," he says. "I went after you, didn't I?"

Not hard enough, I almost say, biting my tongue at the last second. "And for one night, I went with it, didn't I? Because you were persuasive."

"You were pretty persuasive yourself," he says.

There's this sudden jolt of candy-coated tension sending shockwaves of sugar through the space between us. I bite my lower lip again, accidentally on purpose, to see if his eyes will drop to it.

They do.

He swallows.

I pull sweetened air into my lungs.

"This is not going to be easy, is it?" he asks.

"I don't know what you're talking about," I say. "Considering we decided to start over."

"Right. Starting over."

"And on to your daddy issues." I wonder if I've gone too far, but thankfully he laughs.

I probably have the bigger daddy issues of the two of us, all things considered, but I'll keep that little nugget to myself. Instead, I bring us back to his proposal.

It's a much, much safer ground.

Later, at Alec's instruction, Sam gets me set up on my computer—giving me the side eye the entire time. I don't have time to set him in his place though, because I have to mentally prep for my next official task. Note-taking.

Of all the fucking things I'm supposed to do, keeping notes at meetings is my number one priority for Alec.

I knew this this coming in—it was explained very clearly in my interview. I may have fibbed about my note-taking skills. Truth: They are abysmal. I can never read my own handwriting. I figured I could fake it, like I've always done—but I didn't realize I'd be working for someone like *Alec*. For someone I don't want to look like an idiot in front of. For someone who seems to see through anything I try to fake.

So that's great.

"Do you have a notebook I can borrow?" I ask Sam, who's at his own desk, typing away.

"If you ask me nicely."

I want to scream. "Please."

"Come on." He stands and motions for me to follow. "I'll show you the supply room. Might as well get familiar with it, as we have to keep it clean. Break room, too."

I enter the conference room armed with tools that'll do me absolutely no good, but make me appear to have a clue, anyway. Paper, pens, and freshly applied lip gloss.

Sam and I are the first to arrive, as we're supposed to be, to set everything else up. We un-lid platters of pastries and lay out napkins and plastic cutlery. We stack disposable coffee cups and fill containers with sweeteners and stirrers. We lay out pens at each seat around the long oval table and connect the dial-in contraption speaker things for people who call in to the meeting from off-site. We do a lot of other boring, mindless tasks that somehow still make me feel like I've accomplished something when, at the end of it all, the room is set up. Neat and professional looking.

I smile at Sam. "It looks awesome in here."

He blinks, surprised at my good mood. "Yeah. So?"

"Feels good to actually get something done," I admit, guilt bringing me down to reality already. I fucking hate how shocking it is when I act like a decent person. And I hate even more that I do it to myself. It's all my fault. Why did I start off like such a bitch to him?

"Got the new job jitters?" he asks, grabbing a muffin and shoving half of it in his mouth, speaking through it all. "I had those, too. But Alec's chill and nothing we have to do is ever really hard."

The corners of my mouth fall to their usual spots, the rest of my good mood disappearing. How nice for him to think the job's easy. He probably has legible handwriting. He probably takes in emails on the first read...

"Here." He shoves out the chair beside him. "Sit next to me. I'll show you the kinds of things that we have to make sure to catch in our notes during meetings."

Relief is instantaneous and I work my way around the table to drop down next to him. "You're taking notes, too? Mine are only backup?"

"For the first few meetings, then you'll take over full-time and I'll be back to other stuff."

Yep. There goes all the relief. But maybe I'll figure something out, some sort of system, before Sam stops.

People wander in, greeting Sam, introducing themselves to me. I smile. Or I try to, at least. I write a panicky note to Sam on my pad asking for help remembering names. Usually my memory's great for names, but today my mind's blanking. He squints at the note, unable to read my handwriting.

Great. That makes two of us.

"Are we supposed to get everyone coffee?" I whisper.

"*Oh.*" He shakes his head, whispering back. "Just Alec, in the morning. And sometimes he wants one after lunch, too." He doodles something on his own notebook, adding a second later: "He takes it black, so it's easy."

"I know," the words slip out before I realize my error. How on earth would I already know that? "I mean, he seems like the type to take..." But I trail off because Sam's not paying attention. He's drawing some intensely detailed patterned thing. It's impressive. And distracting him.

Then Alec walks in and Sam's not the only one distracted anymore. He zeroes in on me almost as immediately as I do him. My palms start to sweat at the heat in his gaze—and then it's gone, replaced with the professional mask that hopefully mirrors the one I'm attempting to wear, too.

Yeah, right. There's no way to hide my attraction, or the things he stirs up in me. Plus...

Virgin, virgin, virgin.

Ugh.

Of course, he sits directly across from Sam, effectively right in front of me, too. He's messing with his phone, not looking at me, but still. I need to stop staring at him, except he's like a damn magnet for my eyes. He's all relaxed and gorgeous and sharp and *almost* close enough to reach out and touch... How am I supposed to pay attention to anything, much less attempt to take notes?

The woman in charge of the meeting makes it easier. Her name's Denise. She's beautiful, she's black, and she commands the room by stepping into it. She sits at the head of the table, smiling and shooting the shit for a few. Asking about one guy's kids, another woman's upcoming vacation... And then she starts the meeting and it's all business.

She's clear and concise and it's obvious everyone respects what she has to say. Even me. Not that I understand half of it, but the calm way she speaks and her clear enunciation makes it easier to record her words about financial contracts and client management in my notebook. And when anyone interrupts her, or disagrees, she listens and considers and answers with her own thoughts in a totally levelheaded manner.

I want to be her when I grow up.

By the time the meeting's over, I have pages of scrawl to sort through. People are laughing, grabbing the last few muffins, and exiting together. Alec sticks around to speak with Denise, not that I'm watching him or anything (yeah freaking right), and I make it to my desk still in one piece.

I can't believe I pulled that off. I managed to sit in that meeting, to follow it, like an actual responsible, capable person.

My hands are shaking.

Why are my hands shaking?

Why is my breath coming so fast?

Oh God. Is this a panic attack?

I sink into my chair, staring at my computer screen until it blurs.

This should feel good. This should feel *incredible*. Instead, I feel like a complete imposter.

"Uh, are you okay?" Sam asks, and when I turn to him, hoping for... I don't know what, but some sort of kindness, instead I find that his brows are furrowed, not in concern, but something more like half a sneer. The kind only a teenager can pull off.

I don't even have the energy left to try to match it. "I was fine until you started talking to me."

Now those brows shoot straight up. "You are the most hostile person I've ever met."

"Should I clear off space on my desk for that trophy?" I bite my tongue, a second too late, reminding myself he *is* a teenager, after all. And he helped me before the meeting. We even had an almost friendly start-over back in the conference room. "I'm..." I cough, choking over the next word, irritated that I have to say it even though I know I'm in the wrong. "Sorry. I don't mean to be such an asshole."

"You're failing." His dry tone and complete honesty makes me laugh, crumbling one of the bricks of tension in my chest.

I hold my breath, clicking on the little email inbox icon on my computer, sighing in relief when there isn't anything new. "I'm kind of overwhelmed."

"Really?" His voice rises in surprise. "But you're on break from college—isn't this a million times less overwhelming than that?"

Right. He assumes I'm in college. Because that's where I *should* be at my age.

According to the rest of the stupid world, anyway.

Alec must know I'm not in college.

I don't want to care. I usually don't.

School's not my thing. Hell, I spent my senior year in my high school's cosmetology vocational program—which boosted me almost all the way to my hairstylist license. Six months after graduation, I had the certification in my hands. I stood in the moment with absolutely zero intention of considering college. Nothing's changed since.

But... Alec's in grad school at *Harvard*. I mean... Let's just add another checkmark to the tally of things that make me feel small.

I stare at my monitor and press my fingers into my mouse so hard something flashes across the screen and disappears so fast I have no idea what file I opened. Or deleted. Or whatever.

Who the fuck cares?

"Where do you go again?" Sam asks, apparently caring.

Ugh. I cannot be a bitch again. No matter how much I want to.

No matter how hot anger boils in my veins.

"Levels of being overwhelmed are different in different situations." I don't know what I'm saying, but it's either talk nonsense or snap his freaking head off. Plus, out of the corner of my eye, he nods, so maybe I made sense after all. I'm the only one too dumb to get it.

Super fucking awesome. I sound smarter when I spew shit I don't understand than I do when I speak like myself.

Little prickles, both sweet and stinging, nip the sensitive skin of my neck and when I look up from my computer, Alec is striding toward me, through the office. The instant our eyes meet, he looks away, saying something to the guy he's passing, pausing to laugh at whatever his response is. He doesn't glance at me again, only stopping to ask Sam for any messages when he passes between our desks.

More awesome. Now he won't even look at me?

Sorry, he says in an email that pops up a few minutes later. *I was rude walking past you. Still trying to figure out how to treat you as a coworker. Forgive me?*

I almost reply with, *I get it. How can I think of you as my boss when I know what you look like with a huge erection?* But I don't have the guts to do it. Instead, all I come up with is, *Moonwalk into the office tomorrow, and we'll see.*

God, I'm lame.

But a hint of his laughter echoes through the glass walls of his office—I'm not sure I'd even hear it if I wasn't listening for it—and it melts like warm honey along my skin, making me resist the strongest urge to giggle.

Or stride right into his office and kiss some of that laughter right out of his perfect mouth.

It's enough to distract me for a good half an hour, thinking about doing that. Who knows how many times Sam has to say my name until I notice? He asks if I want him to walk me around and make introductions.

Obviously, I don't. Even if I enjoyed making small talk, I've met most of them, either today, or at the happy hour. But I do let Sam ramble on, telling me about his high school baseball team (he pitched) and the various scandals that happened over his senior year. It helps to keep my mind off of Alec, but not for nearly long enough.

Later, Mr. Evans drops by, reminding me of my promise to go to lunch with him. It's a relief to leave, and it's hard not to turn and glance at the shadow of Alec in his office as I walk away, but I manage.

When I'm back, stuffed with more pasta than I've ever eaten in one sitting, Alec is gone, out with clients for the rest of the day.

I hate it.

But damn if I don't find it a lot easier to do even the simplest of things without him in his office behind me.

CHAPTER EIGHTEEN

THE NEXT MORNING, after a restless night of sleep—with only Alec and the word *virgin* spinning through my mind until they became so connected I doubt I'll ever be able to separate them—I walk straight past the reception guy in the lobby. Pretty sure he rolls his eyes at me, but I refuse to look his way. Today's going to be a better, less insecure day.

I'm going to read things carefully. I'm going to finish transcribing what I can from my notes yesterday.

I'm going to convince Alec to sleep with me.

It's the perfect situation. He knows my secret. He's fucking gorgeous. And he leaves at the end of the summer to head back to grad school. So I don't have to worry about wanting more than a fling, if my mind's already aware of how unavailable he is. There's no way I'll end up like my mother, because he'll be gone, far enough away that I won't be able to cling to him.

Even if the thought of him leaving tightens muscles in my stomach with the anticipation of some longing I definitely have no right to.

But that's easy enough to ignore.

Or, at least, I'm sure it will be.

Sam's already at his desk—and there's a steaming cup of coffee waiting on mine. I look from it to him. "Did you poison this?"

He rolls his eyes. "It's a peace offering."

"A poisoned cup of coffee disguised as a peace offering?" But I smile when I ask, and this time he laughs.

"Ty—my boyfriend—thought maybe I should've been nicer to you yesterday."

This surprises me. "Why? I was the asshole."

"My grandparents were Japanese." He says it like an explanation.

"Okay?" I grab the coffee, wincing with the first sip—not sweet enough. And, when he doesn't elaborate, "So?"

"Both my parents were born in America. So was I. When you asked where I was from… People ask those questions to make me feel different. *Other.* But I'm not. I'm American."

I need more coffee to process what he's saying. I take another bitter sip. "I didn't mean to—"

"I try to believe that most people don't *mean* anything intentional with questions like that. But when you've been asked it your entire life, every time ends up a dagger, slicing me away from the ability to feel normal, like I belong." He sighs. "And now my instincts are to apologize to you for being a jerk about it, but that would be more—"

"You shouldn't." I shake my head. "Don't apologize. I'm the one who's sorry." I am, too. I don't mind offending people—but only when I do it intentionally.

"So you get it then?"

"Yeah." I'm tempted to admit that I feel out of place all the time. That when people say things they assume I'll understand, I either have to ask for clarification like an idiot, or nod along like I get it, feeling more and more isolated the longer the conversation goes on. It's a totally different situation from what Sam goes through, but the end results are certainly similar. All I say, though, is, "Thank you for explaining. I never would have understood that on my own."

"Now you can." He starts to say something else, but the phone rings and he sighs. "Here we go."

The rest of the morning he's busy. I try to appear busy, at least. I open my email, not expecting much yet. But there's a message from Alec. *Thought you might like to know…* is the subject line. Instantly, I'm nervous. Or maybe excited. Sometimes I have trouble telling the difference. Either way, my face heats, and I hesitate before opening the rest of the email, mentally counting down from three first. And then reading slowly to keep from missing anything.

Teagan, it begins, as I wrongly interpreted your two truths and two lies from the game on Friday, I thought you might find this video to be educational. On the other hand, I personally found it distracting.

A bit like I find you.

Alec.

On my first read, my stomach tightens painfully. I see the word *lies* and everything plummets. He's still upset with me. All I want to do is close it out, delete it, and leave. But I can't, and I need to pay attention to anything else he wants me to do, in case there are instructions here that I've missed.

On my next read, I'm interrupted because Sam laughs at me and I realize I'm sounding words out—not just in my mind. Shit. But I don't stop, because I don't want to make another mistake like I did yesterday, missing key information and showing up late on accident. I angle my face away from Sam, though, and keep the mouthing silent on the next read.

This time, his other words sink in. *The game on Friday. Distracting...like you.* I swivel in the spinning seat of my chair, biting back a smile, though its lightness makes the muscles in my face lift anyway.

He thinks I'm distracting? Like, *still* distracting? Like, even after everything he now knows about me?

A little thrill rushes through my veins.

Okay, that was a lie.

It was a huge thrill, and it's still rushing. And it grows fiercer when I notice the time stamp of the email and discover he sent it at ten p.m. *He was thinking about me at ten p.m.*

Or some educational video reminded him of me, at least.

What sort of person watches educational videos that late? I guess guys who have entire game rooms full of comic books and video games; the thought has me smirking.

Then I click on the link, and it's a fucking instructional video about how to tie a cherry stem into a knot with my tongue. "Oh my God."

"What?" Sam looks over and I click out of the video with almost superhuman speed. He laughs. "Watching porn on your second day? Ballsy."

"It wasn't porn," I say, my face boiling, an annoying smile forcing my lips apart.

"Right. Because that's why you're grinning like an idiot."

"Your sarcasm is on point today," I say, trying to get my expression under control, a weird giddiness making it impossible to get all the way back to my smirk, so I settle for half of that, half of the smile. "Dry enough to make me thirsty."

"Good thing I brought you a coffee then."

"Could've used some sugar." I hold it up in thanks, though, before taking a sip. Sam rolls his eyes, turning his attention to his computer.

I want to open the video again.

Badly.

Maybe something between us really isn't off the table after all.

Maybe he can take me *on* a table. Or over his desk.

Yum.

I might not ever have actually had sex—but I've definitely participated in the preceding events a time or two. And, regardless, not having done it doesn't mean I can't vividly imagine what it'll be like. Especially with Alec. If I close my eyes, I can *feel* him. His chest against my back, his thighs pressing my legs into his desk... His warm, soapy scent. His stubble rubbing the skin of my shoulder while his lips travel my neck...

I force my eyes open, sliding them toward Sam—thankfully, he's typing something and not paying me an ounce of attention.

I'm at work.

I'm at work and I should not be this turned on.

I should not be shifting in my padded mesh desk chair to ease the fluttering between my legs.

This is inappropriate.

I stare out at the rest of the office, zeroing in on a guy who's old enough to be my grandfather at the far end of an aisle. Wrinkled face, huge nose, receding hairline...

There. I no longer feel the need to shift back and forth.

So that helps.

But the universe is laughing at me, because behind the old man, Alec freaking appears, striding toward me. Gray suit this time. Hair slicked back. Stubble-less, but still sharp jawline.

He's looking at a paper in his hand, not at me, but I appreciate the private moment to...appreciate him.

A woman I recognize from the meeting yesterday steps in his path, drawing his attention to something at her desk. He leans down to study her computer screen. I shift to my side, wondering if there's any way to get a better view of the way his suit shapes his ass while he's bent over.

"Neck cramp?" Sam asks.

I snap upright, rubbing my neck, staring at my computer screen. "Yep. Slept funny last night."

"Are you sure it has nothing to do with our super hot boss?"

"Eh." I shrug—and then wince, like it hurt my sore neck. "He's all right."

"You're definitely lying about your neck, then." He's all smug.

"Does your boyfriend care that you check out your boss so hard?" There. My turn to be smug.

But he laughs. "Ty crushes on Alec harder than I do."

I lean back in my seat, smirking. "That's weird."

"*Eh.*" He shrugs, mimicking me. "He's straight. Alec, I mean. Obviously not my boyfriend."

"No shit." My tone's dry, though the kid's kind of starting to crack me up.

"Who cares? It's like thinking a celebrity's hot. Doesn't mean there's anything real to it."

I make a noncommittal response. That's the thing. My attraction? Oh, yeah. There's something real to it.

And if Alec's sending me cherry stem tying videos, if he's thinking about me outside of work—enough to imagine me tying a cherry stem with my tongue... It's maybe not a one-sided thing, either.

I probably shouldn't be excited about this. It's probably a recipe for destruction. He's the son of the CEO. He's my *boss*, for fuck's sake.

But I'm excited, anyway.

Because... I can't help staring as he closes the distance between us, striding, striding my way, his eyes on mine this time... He's so, so pretty.

I've got it fucking bad.

"Sam, Teagan." He nods to each of us, his eyes lingering on me, my face. "You get your email set up all right?"

I nod back through my blush. "But I got the weirdest spam message last night. With the most random-looking link. I didn't click it, so don't worry. The company won't get a virus because of me."

"You didn't click it?" He shakes his head. "That's too bad. I thought you might enjoy clicking it. A few times."

"Well..." I bite my lip, my heart jumping into my freaking throat when his gaze drops to it. "Okay, I might have clicked it a little bit."

He snorts, clearly biting back a harder laugh. "Me too."

I have to look away or I'm going to die laughing.

Sam clears his throat, and Alec's gaze jumps straight to him, like he's late to remember we have an audience. "Any messages?"

Sam shakes his head. "A few meeting confirmations."

"Thanks." And then he's gone, past us, into his office. Not even a glance back.

But I don't need one. Because I got everything I wanted with our one little exchange.

Holy hell, it's freaking electric, flirting this way.

With the guy who knows more about me already than anyone I've ever known.

The one who knows all of it—and still seems to want me.

God.

Back to shifting in my seat again.

Damn it.

This is going to get uncomfortable, real quick.

"Uh, what was that?" Sam asks.

"Nothing. You're crazy. I mean, what do you mean?" But I say it all with a smile, because Sam already knows there's something going on.

"Holy shit, is your crush more than a crush?" He leans forward, toward me, his hands on his knees. "There's definitely some sort of leftover sizzle in the air right now. I want details. Spill 'em."

"What crush? No idea what you're talking about."

"*Sure...*" He studies me, clearly biting something back.

"What aren't you saying?" I really need to quit this grin. "Jealous?"

He laughs. "Maybe a little." Then his face grows a little more serious. "Be careful, okay? Because I kind of think you might be fun to have around...but Piper'll skin you alive."

"Piper..." I hesitate to ask, my throat suddenly thicker than a moment ago. "Who's Piper?"

"Piper's his fiancée."

I blink.

I wait for his words to make sense.

It takes too long.

My smile turns brittle and cracks into pieces. Surely if the floor wasn't carpeted, we'd hear them crinkling like shards of glass when they land. "Alec's engaged?"

"Unless the definition of fiancée's changed, yeah."

CHAPTER NINETEEN

"OH, SHIT. YOU didn't know." Sam hasn't moved, but his voice is tinny and far away. "Whoa—are you okay? Your face is really white."

"Funny," I say through gritted teeth. "Because I'm seeing a whole lot of fucking red."

I am, too. I never fully understood that expression until now. My vision is literally blurry and I'm so furious that a red-hot sort of film is webbed over my thoughts, stretching out, reaching its way to the outer corners of my eyes.

I'm standing, somehow. My chair shoved back. And I'm turned toward Alec's office. Sam's saying something, or telling me to wait or... I don't know. Don't care.

And then I'm in Alec's office, without really even telling my feet to move me there. I shut his door and then I'm at his desk and he's glancing up at me in surprise—a fucking smile on his perfect, stupid lips. "Are you here for a knot-tying lesson?"

Like he's pleased to see me standing here.

Like I'm such a fucking idiot, I'd run in here over a cherry stem to flirt.

"You think that's what I'm here to use my tongue for?" I ask, my voice scathing.

But he doesn't get it. Dumbass. He's still smiling. Like maybe I'm being suggestive. Yeah. Let's nip that shit in the bud. *"How could you send me that fucking video?"*

"I thought you enjoyed it." His eyes dip in confusion—which is almost more infuriating than anything else. He's playing dumb, because he thinks *I'm* dumb enough to fall for it.

I take a few steps back, sliding behind a desk chair, needing to distance myself from him. Deep breath to keep from screaming. And to keep the swelling in my throat from closing it completely. "That was before I found out you have a fiancée."

Yep. That wipes the stupid fucking gorgeous smile from his face. "Piper."

"Piper," I repeat. The girl I should feel bad for, for being with an asshat like Alec—but I can't because apparently she'd eat me alive for flirting with him—and that sounds like a challenge and I never back down from one of those. So, instead, I want to hate her. And I hate girls who hate girls for that sort of reason. *Ugh.* Alec's watching my face, calmly, like I didn't just bust him on being a huge hypocrite. "You asshole."

"Now wait a second." He lifts a finger, his face stern. He's going to lecture me? Yeah. No. Fuck that.

"No. You made me—"

Sam's voice buzzes through the phone on Alec's desk. "Um, Alec?"

"What?" Alec snaps, his gaze hot on mine.

"Sorry to interrupt your...um...meeting, but Denise is on the phone."

"I'll call her back." Alec slams his palm against the phone, effectively hanging up on Sam, still not dropping his eyes.

I glare at him. "You made me feel like such shit about Friday. For lying to you. But you? You sleaze on strangers in bars when you're about to get *married.* Who's the bigger dick now?"

"You have no idea—"

"If I had any other options, I'd walk the fuck out of here. I'd quit. But I can't. Nobody will hire someone who got fired from a fucking hair salon." I'm too pissed off to be embarrassed about it, but that'll probably come. So that's great. "Get me transferred. I want to work for someone else, be someone else's assistant." *Like Denise,* I almost say. But everything I felt yesterday? Thinking I wanted to be her when I grow up? What a joke.

I'll never be her. I'm not smart enough. Not nice enough.

And it's too late, anyway. I'm already grown up. I'm already who I'm going to be. The fucking fool who's dumb enough to get fired from a hair salon. Who's dumb enough to fall for lies that come out of the pretty mouth of a pretty face.

Exactly like her dumb mother.

"Are you done?" he has the total effing gall to ask.

"Just getting warmed up, actually. Unless..." I pause, the tiniest glimmer of hope flaring. "Unless you're letting me make a jerk out of myself because you aren't actually engaged. Are you?" I ask, my voice steady. "Engaged?"

His jaw goes tense and his eyes drill into mine. "Yes, but—"

"Nope. No *buts*. I'm out. Find me a new boss."

"There's another side to this." His voice is annoyingly placid. His expression is too.

"Alec?" Sam buzzes in again.

Alec suddenly cusses under his breath, and his expression slips. He's closer to losing it than I thought. Well, good. "I said to tell her I'll call her back."

"It's Mr. Chambers. Your dad, I mean."

"Give him the same fucking message." Alec's snarling now, and there's a quiver in Sam's intake of air before the line's disconnected.

"You should treat your assistant a little nicer," I say. "Considering he's the only one you have left."

"You don't get to come in here calling me names," Alec says, standing, his voice rising in a way that makes my heart jump. "You don't get to come in here throwing accusations around when you don't know the entire story."

"You're engaged. You took me home. You got mad at *me* for lying to you. These are all the things I need to know. I'll be out there, at my desk. Waiting to hear from you who my new boss is. Unless you want me to do this through HR."

I turn to storm out, happy with the last word, but the steel in his tone spins me back around. "You don't get to play this both ways."

"Excuse me?"

"You want to make this an HR issue? I'll walk you there myself. But I think you're this pissed because you feel something for me and you're hurt. And if that's the case, you need to step off your high horse and listen to what I have to say."

"My high horse?" The words sputter out of my mouth and I search for something else to say, but I can't find anything. I'm too mad.

"Just listen," he says. "I'm not... I can't tell you certain things, but I can assure you, I wasn't *sleazing* when I brought you home on Friday. Or when I sent you that video last night. I have every—"

"Does she have cancer? Is this some thing where you're still with her because dying? Because that still makes you a huge douche canoe." I grab the chair separating me from his desk, squeezing—and, frustratingly, not even making a dent in the leather.

Alec jerks his head to the side once. "She's not dying."

"Then what is it? How the hell are you so okay with what you've done?"

"I can't tell you, but I s-swear, Teagan, I'm not doing anything dirty or...douche canoe-ish." He's pleading with me, but there's an underlying anger making him stiff and his words short. His stutter tugs at me, which is so fucking annoying. So does the clench of his jaw, and the way his hands are pressed so hard against his desk that his knuckles are white.

Why do I find him attractive still? Why do I want to press his buttons until he snaps completely? This is so messed up.

"I'm supposed to stand here and say, what? *Oh sure. Tell me there are things you can't share, but it's cool. Flirt with me, send me videos. I'll eat that shit right up.*"

"No, it's—"

"Girls who are always doing that in movies? They piss me the hell off. *Oh, yeah, keep secrets from me. I'll go along with it.* Uh, no. I don't fit that mold, never will. You can go screw yourself."

Of all the reactions he could have, laughter is not one I expect. But it's what he does. I frown. "This isn't funny."

He wipes his mouth. "It isn't. I know. But you're so fierce in your conviction."

"And that's laughable to you?"

"It's respectable, honestly." He sounds surprised. Surprised I'd be respectable in this situation? Fuck that.

"What the hell do you know about respectable?" I'm seething, staring at his stupidly calm face.

"Alec?" Sam's voice cuts through again.

"Goddamn it, Sam. Give everyone the same message." Alec hangs up on him again.

A moment later, Sam's knocking on the door. Quietly, tentatively peeking his head through.

"You seem determined to try my patience today," Alec says. His voice is mild but irritation tightens itself in the set of his jaw.

"I'm sorry, Alec. But your dad…"

"What?" Alec barks. "Out with it."

I turn as Sam steps into the room. He closes the door softly, not coming closer than he has to. "Your dad wants you to meet him at the hospital. Your grandfather had a stroke."

I spin toward Alec and the change in him is immediate. The anger is gone from his stance, the humor from his eyes. He looks…hollow. In shock, maybe. "Is h-he…" He clears his throat. "Is he still alive?"

"Yes," Sam's word comes out almost in a whisper. "But he was unresponsive when he arrived. Last night."

"Last night? Jesus." Alec sinks into his seat.

My own anger droops; it's still there, but hidden under the weight of Sam's message. I can't believe Alec's dad didn't demand to speak to his son. His son who, somehow, looks very much like a little boy right now. Lost and confused.

I should say something.

I should open my mouth and say something.

But what? A second ago I was telling him to fuck off—how will anything that comes from my lips seem sincere now?

"Should I call your driver?" Sam asks.

Alec starts to nod, but words push themselves through my mouth, finally. "I can drive you."

He looks at me.

"I mean, if you don't want to be alone. Not that you'd be alone because Miles is great, but I—"

"Yes. You drive me. Please." His voice is shaky. It makes my heart hurt in an entirely new way.

CHAPTER TWENTY

I AM SURE forgetting that my car's a total piece of shit until we're in the parking lot is some sort of karma biting me in the ass. I stop short half a row away. "Maybe we should call Miles."

"Just take me, please." Alec keeps walking, heading straight for the hunk of junk.

Right. Because I already told him about my car, and he knows it's the fugliest thing in the lot without my having to point him in the direction. I hurry after him, my face in flames, and slide into the driver's seat. I reach over to unlock his door, doing my best to ignore my embarrassment when he ducks into his side. "Sorry for the complete downgrade."

"I've always dreamed of riding in a ten-year-old Toyota with a broken taillight." He tries to crack a grin, fails pretty epically.

"How do you remember *every* little detail of everything like that?"

He closes his eyes, resting his head against the seat, though he's so tall he nearly misses. "I remember every little detail when it comes to you, it would seem."

"I..." Don't know what to say to that.

"Turning out to be a pain in my damn ass, though."

"I'm a pain in your ass?" I pull out of the parking lot, shaking my head. "Funny. You're the one who's—" I cut myself off. His grandfather's in the hospital. This fight can wait.

"Oh, no. Please, let me have it." His eyes are still closed, a whisper of a smile still trying to happen across his lips. "I know I deserve it, and the distraction will be nice."

"There's nothing nice about what I want to say to you." But it's hard to be furious with someone who looks so damn vulnerable. Especially someone who's usually more aggressive. Now, though, he has these little blue veins running across his eyelids and they...I don't know...make me want to make everything better.

Which is fucking annoying.

Literally every person on Earth has veins in their eyelids. His should have zero effect on me.

His eyelashes are almost long enough to rest on his cheeks. He seems so innocent.

He's engaged.

Okay, there. A little of the anger comes to a simmer. That helps. "Which hospital am I taking you to?"

"Riverview."

"Are you sure? Do you need to check with your dad?"

"My grandfather funded a wing of the hospital—it's named after him. He only lives about a mile from it."

God. These people live on a level I couldn't even dream of. I know where it is, so I keep quiet and I drive, thinking he might want silence to process his thoughts or feelings or whatever. Until he says, "Talk to me. I can't stand sitting here in the quiet."

"What do you want me to talk about?"

"I don't know. You. Life. Keep telling me off about Piper. Anything."

Hearing her name makes my chest hurt, makes my blood rage. "Your grandfather had a stroke. I can wait on all the yelling I have left to do."

He doesn't respond, sitting there with his eyes closed, his face drawn.

"Are you close with him?" I ask.

"Sometimes." His fingers lace together in his lap, a casual gesture but there's tension in his grip. "It's complicated. He's complicated."

"Why?"

"I'd rather not get into it right now, until I know if he's going to be okay."

"Right. That makes sense. God. I'm not very good at this distraction thing."

"Um…" What do I talk about? Why is my mind blanking? "I love movies. Do you watch them?" *Does he watch them?* I'm a moron. "I mean, obviously you do. Otherwise you're an alien."

He nods. "Mostly during summers. School keeps me too slammed."

"Have you seen *The Great Gatsby*?" I watched it two weekends ago. Stuck with me. I didn't cry, but that ending hit me so hard it still makes my chest feel tight—not that this is something I'll ever share with him, or anyone.

"Awesome score. The book is better."

Ugh. Books. "Okay—what about…" Think. What sort of movies would Alec be into? "*Fight Club*. Tell me you didn't love that movie."

He halfway unshutters his lashes to focus on me. "Good movie. Still not as good as its book."

"Get the fuck out of here. No way the book was better than that masterpiece."

"Read it and you'll see."

"Wow. You're a tough crowd."

Something kind of sort of resembling a laugh rumbles in his throat.

"No digs at my all-time favorite… *Interview with a Vampire*." I watch it at least once a year. There's something so horrible and sexy about it.

Finally he offers a real smile that has me grinning in return even if I'm still mad at him, even if after this I'm still done working for him. Done speaking to him.

"You're missing out," he says, "on some awesome books. I have all three—I'll lend you one, or all. Though *Fight Club* is so dog-eared, I should probably buy you a new copy."

"Reading's not my thing." I shrug, like it doesn't bother me. Like it hasn't always bothered me. "I can't lose myself in a book the way I can in a movie."

"But you miss so much of the story with movies." Great. He's ruining one of the few things I actually love.

"Music, then," I say. "Tell me your favorite artists—and I'll pull an Alec, systematically telling you why you're wrong to enjoy them."

I'm rewarded with a full laugh this time, and we spend the rest of the ride arguing over Franklin Charles and Castle Zero. Spinster Malady and Demi Jade. The merits of my favorite drummer, Norris Marshall, and why I wish he'd leave Gold Rush Standard. I might be a little biased. I know, personally, what a complete twat the lead singer is—via Cassidy and her mistake of a fling with him last summer.

"I met Norris last summer," I say, pulling into the hospital's parking lot. "He's incredibly sexy and genuinely nice and... I might love him a little." He's also very married and his wife is cool as hell, too.

"No kidding?" Alec asks. "I saw him solo once in Virginia Beach—one of the best shows I've ever seen."

"Get out." My heart does a funny little tripping thing.

He smiles, though there's tension etched into his face. "I'm not James Bond. You need to park first."

"No. I mean I was there. At that show." Norris was in Virginia Beach for one night, randomly, and threw together a last-minute solo gig.

He studies me and I can tell he wants to ask me about it, about the strange coincidence of us both being there. But a second later, he looks out his window and I can also tell his mind's splitting—weighted much heavier toward the fact that we're at the hospital. Because his grandfather had a stroke.

I want to talk about it, too. But he's engaged. And I shouldn't want to know him any more than I already do. The memory of that concert is something I cherish, and I don't want to weave Alec into it. Plus, we're here. I'm parking. We have to go in. Or, at least Alec does.

"I'll wait here," I say. "Or, I can drive you up to the entrance, if you want."

"Come with me," he says.

"I'm not sure that's appropriate." I hate how much I long to ease the anxiety in his eyes, in his shoulders.

"I get it." He opens his door, turning to me before stepping out. "I'll call Miles for a ride after. I don't know how long I'll be. You don't have to stick around."

I nod. And a minute later, I cuss, throwing my own door open, chasing him down the parking lot. "You don't have to walk in there alone," I say, halfway reaching out to take his arm, dropping my hand instead.

"Thank you." We catch eyes for a moment and I swear in his I see a world of conflict, a world of destruction. He's feeling things deeply enough to travel straight from him into my own heart, where it twists and aches and makes me wish I had the words to take away all the pain.

But I walk silently beside him into the building, and that will have to be enough for us both.

CHAPTER TWENTY-ONE

ALEC'S PHONE IS in his hand and when it buzzes he glances down, reading from it to me. "My brother's on his way. He spoke with my dad, and Grandfather's in a private room on the third floor in the family wing."

We head straight past registration because Alec knows exactly where he's going. Thank God, because I'm too blown away to think about asking for directions. *The family wing.* The casual way he threw the term out there is a shock to my system all over again.

The only wing my family's ever had is fried. And from a greasy, cardboard bucket.

While we wait for an elevator, a short black doctor walks toward us, a still-steaming cup of coffee in his hands.

"Dr. Greenwald," Alec greets the man, who smiles somewhat tersely before speaking.

"Alec, good to see you. Sorry for the circumstances."

We stop right inside the doors and he waits patiently for Alec to respond.

"How's m-m-my..." He shuts his mouth, swallows, and starts over. "How is he?" He shakes the doctor's hand without pause, but his expression shows what the stutter cost him, and I want to squeeze him. There's something about this beautiful man looking so broken that tugs at me in a way I haven't quite experienced before.

This must be compassion. I wasn't sure I had it in me, before this. Which is really freaking sad all on its own.

But then Dr. Greenwald says, "He's up, actually. Speaking, even," and the relief in Alec is palpable. He exhales a long breath, as though maybe he's only been taking shallow ones for a while, and his shoulders lose some of their tension. Without thinking, I wrap my arms around him, feeling little vibrations in his body, the excitement of relief, maybe, and only a moment later do I catch Dr. Greenwald's frown. Which reminds me that this is totally inappropriate.

I apologize, pulling back. "Lost myself for a second. I'm happy for you... For him, I mean."

"Hello. I'm Charles Greenwald." The man shifts his coffee between hands and sticks one out to me.

"Teagan Walker," I respond, taking it.

"And how do you know Alec?" He's not asking unkindly, but there's a wariness in his expression.

"Teagan's my..." Alec trails off, glancing at me.

"I'm his assistant," I finish. Because it's still true. For now, at least.

"Right." Dr. Greenwald's tone is as weary as his face, but thank God the elevator opens right then, and we all step through, the conversation halted.

We walk down a long hallway, my skin feeling tighter and tighter by the second. I don't have good memories of my own hospital visit a few years back.

Obviously, my plan is to wait outside Alec's grandfather's room— no way do I want to interfere with the family. Problem is, I don't realize we're getting close to the right room until the door beside us is opened by an exiting nurse, and Dr. Greenwald pushes me through in his haste to get by.

Fucker.

I keep my back against the wall, trying to keep a pleasant expression, not quite sure how to manage it. The room—bigger than my entire living room at home—smells astringent, and everyone's faces match the scent. Tight. A little sour. Two women—one clearly Alec's mother, the resemblance is spot-on, minus the just-bit-a-lemon twist to her features—and Alec's dad. Plus, his grandfather. In a bed by a huge bay window.

Dr. Greenwald heads straight to the chart at the foot of Alec's grandfather's bed, studying it without comment.

Alec strides by me, but grabs my arm for the briefest of moments, squeezing it. Thanking me, maybe, for sticking around. "Grandfather," he says. "How are you feeling?"

"As though I've been in the hospital all night and am going to rescind every one of my donations if they don't let me out now." He glares at Dr. Greenwald, who seems to be impervious to the sudden chill in the air.

"Glad you finally made it," Mr. Chambers—Philip, Alec's father—says, his voice booming toward Alec. He looks at me for a moment, until recognition replaces his puzzled expression, and then his eyes slide away, much like they would over a piece of furniture.

Alec's grandfather's eyes are dark like his grandson's, but cold, like he's looking straight into me and finding me lacking. "Who are you?"

For someone who just had a stroke, he looks very out of place in a hospital bed. He's too commanding. Thick white hair, square jawline. A set to his mouth that says he owns the world and is not to be fucked with.

I want to cower, and it pisses me the hell off. I stand a little straighter. "I'm Teagan, Alec's assistant."

"Get out." He doesn't even have to snap his words to make me jump. So much for standing tall. "This is a family matter."

"Grandfather," Alec starts, but I shake my head, telling him it's fine.

"I'll be in my car." It really is fine, too. Hospitals make my skin crawl. And no way do I want to spend another second in this room.

So, instead, I spend thirty minutes in my car developing an ulcer.

I should hate Alec. He's engaged. He's a liar.

He's sexy. He's sweet. He's vulnerable right now.

I beat my hand against the dashboard until the radio kicks in.

Of course it's a stupid Gold Rush Standard love song.

I beat the dashboard again until it shuts off.

My thoughts chase each other like crushes on the playground for the next thirty minutes, until I'm actually glad when Alec shows up again, even if they've all been about him.

"Sorry he was such a dick to you," Alec says, sliding into his seat. "I'd say it's a side effect of his stroke, but that's all him."

"It's fine."

"It isn't." He drags a hand over his face.

"Will he be okay?"

"It was a mini-stroke," Alec says. "That's why his speech wasn't slurred or anything—but a few minutes in I swear his face turned gray from the effort of speaking. Naturally, he was even nastier than normal for as long as he could be before falling asleep. Weakness in any form is unacceptable. He has it in his paperwork that next of kin isn't allowed to be notified unless he's dead or unresponsive. He was in there, all night, fighting. But he'd rather struggle alone than let anyone see him defenseless. That's why he was such an ass to you. Because he's depending on other people to live right now."

"I needed a reason to leave anyway."

"Hate hospitals?"

"Nah, but being in one made me feel like my barely there bank account was about to deplete completely."

His brows dip when he looks at me, asking what I mean.

"Not having health insurance costs a whole lot of money if you end up in a hospital. I broke my arm when I was eighteen. I'm still paying it off."

"That's shitty."

"Yup." I back out of the spot. The last time I was at the doctors was...when I broke my arm. Not counting Planned Parenthood for birth control a few months ago, because I swore I would find a way to lose my virginity at some point this year, not that it's gone so well... Which I am *not* going to think about with Alec sitting next to me. "Anyway. Do you want to talk about your grandfather?"

"No."

"Well, there's not much else I'd like to talk about," I say. *Because I don't want to know you any more than I already do...* "Mind driving in silence for a bit?"

"If that's what you want," he says. But a after a short stretch of quiet, he speaks again. "Piper's wearing a ring I gave her, but—"

"Nope." Seriously. Nope. Can't go down this road. I'm conflicted enough as it is. "I don't want—"

"But we aren't getting married." He cuts me off, dropping that bomb, letting its explosion eat all of the oxygen in the now quiet air, until I turn to him.

"Explain."

"I'm helping her to keep her family happy. But we have an agreement, and I can still date—privately. And if things get serious, we break off the engagement."

"That...sounds like one of Gran's soap operas," I say, waiting for his words to sink in. They have an agreement? "And it also sounds like bullshit. I need you to clarify."

He sighs, his eyes still closed. "Piper's set to inherit a lot of money, but part of the stipulation is that she marries a...guy her family approves of. She has no interest in that, but to keep her family happy—to keep that inheritance on the line—she plays the role. Hell, she created the role."

His voice gives away how tired he is. How exhausted, how defeated. The anger gripping my spine begins to loosen—but not all the way. "What do you get out of it? Sex without strings?"

"I love her." Now, he opens his eyes, waiting until I meet them. "Like a sister. No sex. We grew up together. I owe her a lot." He flexes his palms, one at a time, in his lap. "And it makes my parents happy—my grandfather, too. He's stuck in the old way of thinking that a pedigreed—which is his word, not mine—coupling is good for business."

"So they can tout you around like dogs at a show?" It comes out sharper than I intend, but *God*.

"Pretty much." His eyes are closed again. He's resigned.

"Is she hideous?" I ask. "Because looking at you—I don't know why she doesn't go for the real thing."

"She's gorgeous," he says. "But I'm not her type. And I don't feel it for her, either. We tried years ago, ended up laughing the entire thing off."

If she's gorgeous and he's gorgeous, it doesn't make sense that they wouldn't live their perfect little money-filled lives together. Though I should know better than anyone that you can't force someone to love you if they don't. Romantically or parentally... Not grandparentally, either. Ugh. Not going down that particular slip-and-slide right now. But there's no good direction for my thoughts to go, because I'm jealous that this gorgeous Piper had him for real even for a moment. Which is stupid. He's not mine to claim.

But...maybe he could be. For the summer.

If he's really not engaged. Which is the real question. Do I believe him? He's rich. He's cocky. He carries himself like a typical playboy. This feels like something I could regret later.

But...

I'm good at reading liars, and there's nothing in his expression, in his tone, in...*him*, that feels off about what he's saying.

"I wasn't sleazing on you," he says. "I wasn't cheating on her. I was trying to get to know the girl who sparked my interest from the first word I heard her speak."

"Screen door?"

This earns me a small laugh. "Yeah, but not because you were talking about banging. Something about you stood out to me. Not just the way you look—everything. Your stance. Your voice... I had to know you. And now, you're so fierce in your conviction about how wrong it is to cheat—something I actually agree with one hundred percent... I think I like you even more, if that's possible."

"Why didn't you tell me right away? You could've saved yourself a lot of yelling..."

"This is more Piper's secret than mine. I promised her to keep it, unless I got serious about someone."

"I mean, we've known each other less than a week..." I'm not delusional enough to think he's serious about me. "And most of that time, you didn't really know who I was."

"The thing is, kitten, who you are shines through regardless of what name you gave me. You've got claws and they're hooked under my skin and, for some reason, I don't want you to extract them. I want the chance to know you. I want the chance to see where this could go. So maybe this isn't serious, but it was coming down to telling you or losing you, and you see which one I picked."

He didn't want to lose me.

He picked me. This is a total first. I'm not sure how to respond—but my body feels like it's made of air. Or cotton candy. Or something else sweet and light and totally foreign. "But I've been such a bitch."

"Yep."

"And you haven't deserved at least half of it."

"Nope."

"And you still want—"

"Everything."

CHAPTER TWENTY-TWO

"EVERYTHING?" I REPEAT Alec's word, my blood beginning to swirl, beginning to *long*. He wants everything with me. And he's not engaged. Not really, anyway.

And then that big neon sign starts flashing in my mind... *Virgin, virgin, virgin.*

He doesn't mean *that* everything. But still...it's out there. "What do you mean, everything?"

"A date, at least," he says, opening his eyes, one corner of his mouth lifting in a lazy smile. "How's Friday?"

"I have plans." The words shoot out of my mouth and I don't know why I'm pushing back.

Wait. Yes, I do know why. *Virgin, virgin, virginnnnn.*

He blinks. "Plans with your girlfriends again, or plans with someone giving me some competition?"

"Plans with..." I sigh, shaking my head. "You make me nervous and I made it up. I'm free Friday."

He laughs. "I make *you* nervous? Pretty sure you've got that mixed up."

"I mean, obviously I can demolish you with my well-sharpened bitch. I get it. But you make me nervous, too."

"I wouldn't say *demolish*."

"How would you define what I was doing this morning in your office after I found out about Piper?" Saying her name brings a sour taste to my mouth. Not toward her specifically, but maybe I'm not all the way over Alec's secret yet.

"Fair point. But you're making *my* point at the same time. You're the one who makes *me* nervous." His lazy smile evolves into something cockier. "And pretty girls very rarely make me nervous."

"Right. Because you're God's gift to women?" I stop at a red light, lifting a brow.

"Maybe." He watches my face, his eyes dancing. "I'll take you to dinner on Friday so you can find out for yourself."

"I haven't said yes yet." I'm going to, obviously. But this teasing, this back and forth, it's pushing him out of the shade of sorrow he's been cocooned in since learning about his grandfather. Now that I know the truth about Piper, all I want to do is make him smile.

"Why do I make you nervous?" he asks.

"Oh, that."

"Oh," he deadpans, "that."

"You know things about me," I say, deciding on straight honesty, realizing how freeing it is to have someone who knows my truths. "One thing in particular that makes me a little…unsettled."

"That you've never…" He clears his throat. "That you're a—"

"Yep. That one." No matter how he says it, the virgin status of my vag isn't suddenly going to get sexy. Just awkward. I mean, not that my vag isn't sexy. Just that… God, now I'm even embarrassing myself in my own thoughts. "And, you know… You had morning wood on Saturday and I got a glimpse and… I can't quite compute how all of that will fit in—" Someone behind me honks because the light's green, and the blaring horn jolts me out of my ramble. "Never mind. Forget it."

I throw my hand up to flip off the driver in my rearview. Alec laughs and grabs my hand, tugging it into his lap. "One date on a Friday night won't lead to me asking for more than you're ready to give. One million dates on one million different days won't lead to that either."

Oh God. He's being sweet. And he's rubbing the pad of his thumb over the back of my hand and I'm suddenly super close to either giggling or...I don't know...moaning. "Pretty sure I made clear what I'm ready for. I would've done it if I hadn't passed out."

"Last Friday worked out exactly how it should have," he says, rub, rub, rubbing. I'm not sure how he's able to use his thumb here on my hand to send shivers all the way up my spine. But he does. "Maybe you're ready." Stroke, stroke, stroke. "But maybe I'm not. Maybe I want to take my time. Maybe sex on Friday is off the table."

He flips my hand palm-side up, tracing spiraled circles over the inside of my wrist, making my breath come a little faster, my shivers dance a little lower. "Maybe I want to touch you, tease you...taste you first." He lifts my arm until my wrist is against his mouth and his tongue takes a turn circling my skin and somehow he's taking this conversation and spinning it into a sensual realm I've never visited before.

"Oh..." Yeah, awesome response. But come on. Like I should have to be able to think about anything while he's doing what he's doing... We're lucky I haven't crashed the car.

"And if you're worried about my size," he breaks off, a cocky little chuckle, like he's aware of how worried any girl—virgin or not—might be. Which, fine, I won't even snark about because seriously. "If it gets to that point, I'll be gentle. You, kitten, aren't the only one with a talented tongue. I'll have you ready, wanting, needing." Another dart of his tongue against my pulse point. "Begging."

"Sorry, Charlie. This girl doesn't beg." I pull my hand away, placing it carefully on my steering wheel, before I make a liar of myself. Talented tongue? Yeah. Triple check that column. "And you might want to speak with someone about those self-esteem issues..."

"I'm being honest. Isn't that our thing? Honesty? Unless your name isn't really Teagan and you've got a whole different life you're hiding from me. Because that would be impressive."

A laugh pushes itself out of my mouth, but accidentally, "Trust me. I'd give anything for a different life," slips out behind it. "I'm me, I mean."

He doesn't respond until I stop at the next red light. And he tugs my chin toward him first. "See? Complete honesty. You be you. I'll be me."

"A pessimistic bitch and a guy whose ego almost matches the size of his..."

"Thing?" he says, his eyes laughing the same way they were when Miles was driving us home on Friday night.

"I can say *dick*." Even if my face bursts into flames when I do it.

"You see yourself much differently than I do."

"The pessimistic bitch thing? Don't worry. You just met me. You'll come around. Everyone always does."

"We'll see," he says in a tone that really says he doesn't believe it.

"Guess we'll see about a few things," I say in a tone that really says hurry up and make me beg like you've promised...

"Why were you fired from the hair salon?" he asks.

"I—wait. Are you asking as my boss or as my...something more personal?"

"This will have zero impact on your job. Though your resume didn't mention that you were fired. Funny, that." He gives me a look sarcastic enough to have my lips curling up. If I tutored him only a little, he could have the whole Teagan impression down in less than a day.

"Well... Mr. Not My Boss..." I glance at him, waiting to continue until he nods, confirming that this is off the record. "I had a client who was a total piece of work. I mean, nasty. Judgmental. Bitchy. Rude—and yes, I know, I'm practically describing myself—but she was on a whole other level. Cruel—and loved it about herself."

Casey Cantrell. I can picture her clearly. Probably will be able to forever. Especially the last time I saw her. "She thought her husband flirted with me when he came in to pick her up. Didn't happen, but she told my boss all these lies. Like that I was texting him, sexting him—never mind that I didn't have his number, even when my boss took my phone to check."

"Your boss took your phone?"

"Yup."

"And fired you even when she found nothing?"

"Not exactly... That wasn't when I got fired." Here's the tricky part. "The client made me keep doing her hair. Weekly blow outs. Monthly dyes. All the while spreading rumor after rumor about me. She did it to make me squirm. But I don't squirm that easily."

"Wanna bet I can change that?"

"Do you want to flirt—or do you want my story?" Oddly, I want to tell him what happened. Another first for me.

"I already told you. I want everything."

Thrills. Up and down my belly. His words—and the sincerity behind them—make me feel light in the middle of a story that usually brings me down.

"She wanted something different the day I got fired. She wanted to go from brunette to platinum blonde. And... I... At the end of the appointment, chunks of her hair were so ruined they crumbled into mush. Burned her scalp, too."

"Jesus."

"My boss asked if I did it on purpose."

"She's an asshole." There's no pause before his words. He doesn't think for a second before assuming I didn't do it, and those thrills melt into a gooier sort of happiness.

"The thing is... I admitted to it." I watch his face carefully, testing him in the most unfair way.

But—literally, the first person ever—he passes, and says, "So, it's not just me you lie to."

I can't remember the last time I cried, and I'm sure as shit not about to start because he has this sort of faith in me.

My damn eyes need to stop stinging. Immediately.

"What makes you so sure?" I ask, staring out the windshield now, avoiding his gaze. Blinking like a fucking madwoman.

"You're a kitten," he says. "Not a scorpion. You've got the tools to hurt people—but not the drive to really fuck them up."

"Not a scorpion," I repeat. "That's the strangest compliment I've ever received. But I'm not sure you know me as well as you think you do. Plenty of people would disagree."

"Because you lie," he says. "Because you present a version of yourself to push people away."

"Whatever you say, Dr. Shrink Man." I mock him, but the truth is—he scares me.

He forces a sort of...not happiness, exactly, but something closer to excitement through my veins. He gets me and I don't know why. One part of my mind whispers *finally*. But another is screaming *run*.

"Anyway," I say, my voice flat. "Whatever. No. I didn't do it on purpose. I mixed up the instructions. Added too high a level of peroxide and kept her under the lamp for too long. I told you, reading isn't my thing. So, for the record, if you could stop shoving books down my throat, that'd be great."

Slipping into asshole-mode is like rediscovering my skin, keeping my insides from feeling so exposed.

It also makes me hate myself.

He's quiet for the rest of the ride, but when I park, before he slides out of the car he turns to me and says, "Push me away all you want. I'm still taking you out on Friday."

"Can't you get in—I don't know—*huge* trouble for sleeping with your assistant?"

He lifts his brows. "Who said anything about sleeping with you?"

"Alec, come on." I'm not sure his answer will change anything, but I'd like to know what we could be up against.

"My father owns this company," he reminds me, though it doesn't really reassure me. "And I told you. I like you. I'm not a random sleazy boss trying to get in the hot chick's pants because I have some sort of power over you. You like me, too—even," he holds up a hand when I open my mouth to contradict him, "if you won't admit it. So I'm taking you out."

I was going to protest the hot chick comment, but I'm glad he stopped me. There's a flush in my veins making me feel way too light inside to ruin it by dismissing his compliment. Still, "I still haven't said yes."

"You will."

"Really, that self-esteem. Try to think a little higher of yourself, okay? Or maybe you should try talking to a professional." I laugh and he does too, and we get out of the car like nothing's changed, but I can't help wondering if he hears the tiniest bit of longing that slipped into my voice. He seems so observant about every little thing.

But it's weird, isn't it? That a girl might fantasize about affording professional help. Like, screw fancy cars. Forget designer clothes. I'll spend my adulthood in a one-bedroom apartment, if I have to.

Someday, I will have health insurance.

Someday, *I* will be the one to speak with a shrink.

Someday, I will stop hating people for no reason. I will stop being so goddamn angry over nothing, ninety percent of the time.

Okay, ninety-five, if I'm being honest. And that's the new goal, isn't it?

CHAPTER TWENTY-THREE

"YES, BY THE way, to Friday night," I say as we walk into the building. My voice is steady, as though my heart is beating at its regular pace instead of like it's chugged a gallon of coffee. "One condition, though. I meet you out. You aren't picking me up." Not in a million years is he laying eyes on my grandparents' place.

"No," he says. "I'm driving, like a real date. You don't need a car to make an escape. If you want to go home at any point, I'll take you."

Oh, God. He doesn't get it. It's almost laughable.

But maybe I can let him grab me at Cassidy's house. "Fine."

"Good," he says. "I like when you let me have my way."

"Don't count on it becoming a thing."

"I've been very clear about my...thing." He says it with a straight face and a low tone, and I explode into a firework and burn down the building around us.

Now how am I supposed to make it until Friday? How am I supposed to stay professional around my very sexy, very commanding boss?

How the hell am I supposed to stop thinking about his *thing*? Or the way he might use it to make me beg? Or his tongue? Or... God. I have to get a fucking grip.

It's just that he doesn't make it easy.

On Wednesday, I find a wrapped gift on my chair, hidden under my desk. And when Sam gets up to grab coffee, I tear into it, finding a fancy set of headphones attached to two cards: one in an envelope, the other face up with instructions written on it.

Download an app called AudioVectorEase on my phone. Enter the code listed on the instructions. Then read the second card. I do it all—a bit hesitantly, though I'm not sure why.

The second card reads: *I know books aren't your thing. But I think audiobooks could be. The code you entered pre-downloaded one of my all-time favorites. Figured you might enjoy it, given your love of vampires and violence. And trust me, you won't need a movie to enjoy this one. Alec.*

At first, I'm confused.

At first, I think, books? Reading on my phone will suck even more than reading across a page. He doesn't get me like I thought he did.

But a second or two later, I put it together. Not reading. Listening. *Audio.* Plus headphones.

Interesting...

And sweet.

Then stupid Sam returns with coffee and even though he has one for me, I hate him a little. I want to listen right away, but I want to do it in private. So I'm stuck in a workday with hours and hours to go until I can use Alec's gift.

Alec, who smiles when he sees me and asks if I *liked my assignment*, like he's trying to speak code in front of Sam—though Sam's expression says he knows there's something else going on.

"We'll see," I say, noncommittally. His smile turns smug, like he's so sure I'll love it. Which kind of makes me not want to—which is totally fucked up. "How's your grandfather?"

"Released last night," he says. "Home. Dr. Greenwald's staying with him for a few days."

A live-in doctor. It must be so weird and so amazing and so… I can't even come up with the right word, to have that much money.

It turns out, I do love Alec's gift. Listening to a book—all I have to do is close my eyes and soak it up. No actual reading. And the one he chose for me is perfect. *The Passage.* Post-apocalyptic vampires created in a government experiment gone wrong? Game freaking on. I'm up all night listening to it—to the point that I have to stop at a drugstore on my way to work, to find something to cover the bags under my eyes that are threatening to eat my cheeks.

I'm sluggish and dreading seeing Alec because I'm also all crumpled and not put together. I have half a mind to tell him it's all his fault, but he'd probably get a kick out of keeping me up all night. He's not in today, though. His grandfather is back in the hospital.

"He left a message this morning," Sam says. "And requested you set up your voice mail. Guess he tried to call you first?" His voice rises on the last word, like he's fishing, like he's hoping I'll tell him what's going on.

I'm tempted to, too. But my secret infringes on Alec's secret, which isn't mine to share. Instead, I nod. "Can you show me how?"

I email Alec with my cell phone number when Sam's done. It's on my resume, but I guess he didn't look there. Makes sense since he's not the one who hired me. It's weird we've never texted or spoken on our phones before—but it's also not, because we've known each other a whopping six days. It feels like a hell of a lot longer than that though.

Which makes me wonder if my mother's genes are starting to surface.

Am I letting myself get swept up the exact way I've always sworn I wouldn't? With a rich guy and a pretty face?

My heart tells me this is nothing like that. I do enjoy his pretty face, but I don't care about his money. Hell, had I known how wealthy he was when I met him, I'd never have bothered speaking to him. It's more of a deterrent than a turn-on. But my mind's too used to seeing the darker side of…well, pretty much everything, and I've all but convinced myself to cancel when he texts me.

Kitten, Looking forward to tomorrow. Wear something sexy to work. To our date, too.

How's your grandfather?

A cranky old man. Still kicking.

I'm glad.

I miss your face. Send me a picture.

I snap a shot of my desk.

Not what I meant.

    I let the conversation taper off here, because his flirting makes me smile—and, annoyingly, that makes something inside of me go sour. I'm not my mom. I know I'm not. And I'm not backing out. Alec has substance to go with his pretty face and sky-high bank account. I'm not even interested in the latter, anyway. *Wouldn't it be nice, though*, a little nagging voice—my mother's voice, again, what the fuck?—whispers in my mind, *to let him take care of you. Pay away all your worries. Buy you fancy things and*—
"Earth to Teagan." Sam interrupts my brain spew.
"What?" I snap even though I'm grateful for the interruption and immediately draw in a deep breath to chill out.
"I asked if you could cover for me if I leave thirty minutes early."
"Hot date?"
"*Maybe.*"
    Taking on Sam's responsibilities might help me pass the time a little faster—until I get to go on my own hot date. "What do I need to do?"
    He spends the next while showing me how to work Alec's calendar in case anyone calls regarding meetings. Then, I spend the rest of the day trying really, really hard not to snoop through it. Even when I find a few times blocked out with Piper's name across them.
    She's not his real fiancée.
    I repeat the line so many times to myself it stops holding much meaning.
    But God, I wonder what they do when they're together.

Shit. Between his fake engagement, and my goddamn mother in my mind, this is pretty much doomed from the start. Even if it's only a summer fling—there's no way for it to end well.

I miss your face, he said. I stare at the text until my eyes blur.

Stupid. Every thought I've had today is stupid. I need to relax a little.

Ha.

Ha ha.

Because that's so freaking easy.

Sometimes it's like I'm only a projection of myself. Like the real me actually lives inside my brain, rattling around in there, pounding to get out. Some different, more positive version of myself. She's in there somewhere. *I'm* in there somewhere. But my brain's got a tight-twisted deadbolt and I don't have a fucking key to get out of it.

On Friday, I don't dress sexy.

First of all, I mentally prepare to tell Alec, *it's not appropriate.* He might be leaving at the end of the summer, but I want to keep working here. I don't want to get a reputation based on how I dress. Which is a bullshit thing to be judged on, but if my grandparents are any indication, that's how the current world works.

And, second of all… I can't help it, something in me rebels at the thought of following orders, even of a sexy variety.

I do, though, wear a black lacy bra and undies set under my blouse and skirt, which I have every intention of hinting at to Alec, to wet his tongue.

I forget all about it when I open my inbox and discover an email from HR telling me there's been a mix-up and that I'm eligible for company-sponsored health insurance.

And I clap so fucking loud a handful of people turn to stare. And then I drop dead right in my seat.

Because *health insurance.*

CHAPTER TWENTY-FOUR

"ARE YOU ALIVE?" Sam asks a few minutes later, when I'm still sitting frozen, my head tilted against the back of the chair, my eyes closed. Who knew so much relief would be like sugared air in my veins?

I take my time and then I smile so wide it's his turn to look shocked. "I'm fucking great."

"O-*kay*." He stretches the word out, and it makes me laugh.

"How was your hot date?"

He grimaces and I'm about to ask what's wrong, but Alec turns the corner into the room and the world goes a little off-kilter. God, he's fucking hot.

"He looks like a magazine ad," Sam says, pretty much reading my thoughts.

"Yup."

But by the time he's closer to us, both Sam and I are busy working at our computers like we haven't even noticed him.

"Sam," he says, his tone amused, obviously not buying our act. "Ms. Walker."

"Boss," I say, acting like it's hard to drag my eyes from my computer screen to him.

"A word?" He walks into his office without waiting for my answer.

I stay at my desk, smiling, smug with the upper hand.

"Um, are you going in there?" Sam asks.

"Eventually." I lean back in my chair, a relaxed pose even if my blood is beginning to surge beneath my skin.

My phone rings. I pick it up and hear Alec's cool voice. "Keep me waiting and you'll see what happens when I make *you* wait. And, kitten, I'm going to love to make you beg."

I slam the phone down.

Because, really, what the hell am I supposed to do with that?

Besides melt into the floor.

Or race in there and fucking jump him.

I swallow and hear the saliva travel down my throat like there are no other sounds in the world. I stand, my face flaming, my skin tingling.

Sam's wearing the superior expression I've just discarded. "Get in trouble?"

"No." And I freaking giggle.

"I *am* going to get this story out of you, you know."

"There's no story." But, because I can't keep the corners of my mouth under control, I turn and step into Alec's office. Not like that helps with facial control, but at least Alec's allowed to know why I'm smiling.

"Close the door." He's sitting at his desk, a smug expression across his face. "Playing games this morning?"

"You're my boss. You're bigger than me. Sexier. I've got to take the upper hand when I can get it."

"I am your boss," he agrees. "And I am bigger than you. But sexier? That's where you're wrong. Let's have a word about what you're wearing."

"I know I didn't dress in anything sexy, but I—"

"Have you seen yourself?" He cocks a brow, his eyes traveling my body, a slow smile parting his lips. "You're sexy as fuck, Teagan. I have half a mind to pull you over this desk right now."

"Then you should see what I'm wearing underneath this..." I aim for a sultry purse to my lips, but my face is so hot, it's definitely red, which messes up the rest of my expression.

He doesn't seem to mind, though, running a hand over his hair, his eyes flashing down my body. "Who needs coffee when you're around?"

"Speaking of, should I get you one?"

"Not until you tell me what you've got on under there."

"Black lace," I say. "And not a lot of it."

As far as exit lines go, it's pretty fucking awesome.

And when I bring him his coffee, it doesn't bother me nearly as much as I think it will. I don't feel subservient. I feel powerful. Especially when he says, "I'd stand to take that from you, but I'm hard as fucking steel right now."

"Hmm," I offer, smug all over again. "Maybe I'll be the one making you beg tonight..."

Another awesome exit line, and before his office door closes behind me, his laughter fills the air.

I call HR to figure out the whole insurance thing, fill out some paperwork over lunch, and before the day's over, I've made a doctor's appointment, after choosing a primary care physician who's *in my network*. The knowledge that I have a network keeps a grin on my face almost the entire day. I make a dentist appointment, too. Granted, my teeth are in good shape because I'm fucking religious about taking care of them—kind of have to be when you don't have access to a dentist for years on end. But I make the appointment.

Because I can.

Alec emails me, even though he's sitting ten feet behind me. *I'm heading out in a few. I'll grab your address from your file and pick you up at seven. Hope you don't have a curfew.*

I respond with, *Ew, don't grab my address from my file. That's so creepy. Stay away from my file, stalker. Also, don't fire me for saying that. Pick me up here*, with Cassidy's address. Then I add—and hit send before I can chicken out—*I only have a curfew if you give me one. For your place.*

Fire you? Not likely. Name a different F-word and my answer might change. Related: will you still be wearing that black lace?

If you're very, very good. Though, on second thought... I'll pick up a new set after work, because I want fresh...everything for tonight.

By the way, I'm only flirting. There will be no F-wording going on this evening, in case you were feeling pressure. Or getting excited. Told you I'm making you wait. (I'll wait as long as you need.)

I'm about to respond when he sends another message. *But don't let any of that fool you into thinking I haven't fantasized about what it'd be like basically every second since I met you. Even when you were Cindy. Especially after.*

And again I don't get a chance to write back because it takes me too long to read his email, and a few minutes later he's breezing between Sam's desk and mine. He turns pointedly toward Sam. "Did you hear from Denise about Monday's schedule change?"

Sam shakes his head. "But I can call your cell phone if I hear from her before I leave."

Alec tells him not to worry about it and slowly turns toward me. "Have a nice weekend."

"See you Monday, boss." But I'm smirking as I say it. And then biting back a giggle when he gives me an *oh, really?* look before walking away.

Nothing can kill my mood. Not a thing. Even when I have to spend the last two hours of my workday filing things in our floor's supply room. Long rows of drawers that pull out into longer rows of dividers—which is my personal hell. It's impossible for me to easily read the labels and everything blurs together and I lose my place nine times out of ten. A lesser girl might break down in tears.

But that girl probably doesn't have health insurance. And she also probably isn't a few more hours away from a date with the sexiest guy she's ever known.

So yeah. *This* girl can keep her shit together.

This girl even smiles while she does it.

Cassidy's eyes widen when she answers her door, and she catcalls me loud enough for her far-off neighbors to hear. "Your makeup—wow. You look *hot*."

"Shut it." I shove past her, but I'm still too high from the rest of my day to be embarrassed. Still too high to let the pictures of Jason surrounding me suffocate me. If I don't look at them, they won't have the chance.

"What's in the bag?" Cassidy asks, and I instinctively crush it to my chest, the plastic crinkling all loud and obvious.

"Nothing."

"It's totally lingerie." She knows me. I've talked about sexy sets before. A lot.

But I was never being honest, and now that I'm actually going for it, I don't want to talk about it.

"Don't you want to wash it first?"

"I don't have time. Can we please drop it? And can you please give me something to wear?"

She motions for me to follow her up the winding staircase leading out of her foyer. "We've got to find something hot enough to match your hair and face."

"Thanks." I blew out my hair, really took my time with it. Now it hangs sleek and straighter than I've worn it in a long time. Put extra effort into my makeup too. Only took me four tries to master the cat eye. Gran told me I look like a whore on my way out, but it didn't cut me as deeply as it could have. I feel pretty. I feel *good*. Which, being here in this house, is saying something. But I'm not letting my thoughts travel that direction. "I was thinking that black top you have, with all the beading on the shoulders."

She shakes her head, not turning around when she responds. "I have a green dress that's going to be fucking killer on you. That's what you're wearing."

I have my doubts about wearing a Cassidy dress. She has bigger boobs; I have a bigger belly. Sometimes shirts work because of the differences in space, but a dress? I can't picture it.

And then she makes me try it on and I can. In a mirror.

Her green dress is perfect. Somehow it isn't too big in the boobs. Somehow it makes my belly look flatter. Somehow I can still breathe in it.

"Yeah. That thing's not going to be staying on you for long," Cassidy says, circling me. "It hits you in all the right spots."

This should make me happy. It really does hit me in the right places. But the thought of the dress coming off—and what it means—makes my nerves ripple uncomfortably under my skin...

Then I remember Alec took sex off the table for tonight, and my nerves relax. A little, at least.

"He's a good guy," I say without really meaning to, my voice way, way too breathless for my liking.

"Oh," Cassidy says, pausing in front of me. "*Oh*. You *like him* like him."

"He's okay," I mumble. Cassidy's my best friend, but—because of it, because of how closely she can look right into me—it's like pushing a boulder uphill to get myself to open up to her. Or, if I'm honest with myself, it's like holding up the immeasurable weight of a secret weekend spent with her brother before he died. He blocks everything else that would maybe come out easier otherwise.

"Remember senior year?" she asks, tucking a strand of hair behind my ear. "I gave it up to Jackson Winters and he dumped me right after—two weeks before homecoming?"

Ugh. That prick. He convinced Cassidy to lose her virginity before the dance so they wouldn't be a cliche, doing it after, but he dropped her literally the next day. He'd been planning to take Cassie LeClaire the whole time anyway. I study Cassidy. "You think Alec's looking for a pump and dump? Because I promise you, he isn't."

"No." She shakes her head emphatically. "I think you're too smart to fall for someone's bullshit the way I did. But remember how you keyed the shit out of the side of Jackson's shiny cherry red Camaro before the dance—and forced me to come back with you afterward, to watch his expression when he discovered it? And he *cried*? And stood up Cassie because of it. And the entire thing was fucking awesome?"

"Yep." The memory makes me smile almost as widely as the actual moment did. It felt good, destroying his car after he'd destroyed my best friend. I swore that day—though it wasn't the first time—I'd never let some asshole dupe me.

"What I'm trying to say is that *if* this Alec hurts you, Teagan, I'll find whatever he treasures as much as Jackson did that stupid Camaro, and I'll destroy it."

I study her harder now, looking deeper in those wide green eyes. "What's with this sudden protectiveness?"

A pale pink sweeps across her cheeks. "You like him. He's not some fuck and fling-away like the others. I want someone good in your life—and if you're finally taking a chance to let him into more than your bed, I want him to be worthy of you."

"I have someone good in my life," I mumble, irritated that she's making me feel more touchy feely than I'd like. Irritated that she's reminding me of all the lies I've fed her—and everyone else. "You. And Vera."

"True." She squeezes me for about two seconds, which is as long as I last in her embrace before stepping away. "You know what I mean, Teag. Your skin is flushed, your eyes are sparkling... It's about fucking time you let a guy in."

"You are exaggerating," I say, ignoring my reflection when she spins me toward her mirror again. "You're trying to make me feel mushy and all that does is piss me off."

She sighs. "I know. But you've got this happiness in your face—I've never seen it there over a guy before."

It's been there, of course.

I need to tell her about her brother.

God. Jason.

The boy I once thought I could love.

The boy I once thought could love me.

The boy who fucking overdosed before I could truly find out.

God. *Jason.*

I open my mouth.

To say what? I once looked at your brother like that? But he swore me to secrecy? And then he died and maybe I should've seen it coming? Sorry? And sorry I've been keeping this from you for almost two years?

Cassidy's head is tilted to the side while she waits for me to speak. I shut my mouth.

I glance out her window, and Miles's town car is pulling into her driveway. "Fuck. He's here."

Cassidy grabs my arm. "Make him wait a minute."

"I'm not making him wait," I say, pulling her with me out into the hall. "I'm not playing games."

"You always play games," she says. Because I've always claimed to. The guilt from lying is heaviest in front of those misled, and I'm about to drown in mine.

"Not this time."

"Not this time what?" Mr. Evans is heading toward the stairs at the same time we are. Fuck. "You look nice, Teagan. Where you headed, honey?"

"Nothing," I say, my face heating. "I mean, nowhere. I'm—"

"She's got a hot date with Mr. Chamber's son," Cassidy teases and I want to punch her.

"Alec?" Mr. Evans blinks. "Isn't he…" *Engaged?* He doesn't have to say the word for it to ring loudly between us. He trails off, making his own assumptions. So this is fucking great. What do I say here? I can't tell him Alec's not really getting married; it's not my secret to share—but I look like a total whore, going out with an engaged dude. *Way to live up to Gran's expectations, Teagan…*

"Mr. Evans, it's not what you think, and I'm begging you not to say anything." How did I not think this through? Embarrassment and regret make good partners in the synchronized swan dive they take down to the pit of my stomach.

"Just be careful, sweetie," he says, his tone deep with warning. "The Chambers family is formidable. And Philip can be a bit of a bear when it comes to his business—which, in his mind, extends to his family."

"I'll be careful," I say. "Thank you."

"I had half a mind to see Cassidy with Alec, once upon a time," he says, his eyes shifting playfully toward his daughter. "Until she met Gangrene, or whatever his name is."

"Dad." But Cassidy smiles through the word, which shows some major progress, if they're joking together. They've had a rough relationship since Jason died.

"Anyway it's not a big deal, we're going to go over some work stuff," I ramble. "Don't make more of this than…" Than what? The thing I'm so clearly trying to pretend isn't happening? Mr. Evans isn't an idiot. "Work stuff, I mean."

"Right," Mr. Evans says, doubt clear across his expression. "He does have some interesting ideas…"

"About small business and tech startups?" I ask, the inkling of an idea blossoming at the back of my mind.

He nods, still frowning. "I've been trying to convince Philip to expand our focus for years now, and the directions Alec came up with are perfect."

"You should team up," I say. "With the two of you pushing for it, Mr. Chambers would *have* to listen, right?"

"Maybe," he muses. "But I'm not sure Alec's the kind of guy I want to get into business with." He gives me a pointed glance.

"Don't misread this," I plead. "He's—"

"Oh, please," Cassidy says, rolling her eyes. "Dad, stop being so overprotective of Teagan. She's a big girl. She can date whoever she wants. And Teagan. Come on. You're not borrowing my dress to discuss work things."

I glare at her. She's not helping. At all.

Probably my own fault for not telling her everything. But I'm so used to lying about this part of my life, I'm not sure how to be honest.

"Don't write him off," I say to Mr. Evans. "Anyway, bye. I'll dry-clean your dress, Cassidy. Thanks."

Cassidy laughs as I flee down the stairs. Her dad stays silent.

Jason's portraits watch me from the wall. And while looking at them doesn't make my stomach hurt the way they used to, I still miss him. And I hate that I'm rushing out of here while his father's judging me for something I can't refute.

Apparently regret and embarrassment were the opening act. Currently on deck, heavy on the board, is self-loathing. What am I doing? I'm an idiot. This will never work. Maybe Alec was lying about Piper. Maybe he's a total player and I'm falling for his bullshit, proving for the millionth time in my life that I'm dumb as a blank piece of paper.

Maybe I'm *exactly* like my mother.

Then I'm outside, and instead of Miles waiting by the car to open my door like I assume he'll be, Alec is striding toward the house. Toward me.

Crisp button-down. Crisp denim. Slicked-back hair and dark, dark eyes penetrating my armor of sadness like an arrow.

Everything else disintegrates into dust in the background.

I smile.

I *breathe*.

I meet him halfway.

CHAPTER TWENTY-FIVE

ALEC SLIDES A hand around my neck, holding me like his palm was created to fit just so. "You look... Wow."

I slide my gaze up to his face, my mouth suddenly wetter than before. "You smell like your soap."

He laughs.

"Or...something that comes off as a nicer compliment," I amend, because obviously he doesn't know what that scent does to me. He doesn't know my knees are turning to liquid and I might slide right into the ground if he lets go. "You look hot."

He doesn't know all I want to do is toss myself at him, wrap my rubbery legs around his waist, lick his mouth...

Oh, God. I'm in so much trouble.

"Thank you," he says, flashing his dimples. He slowly, slowly brings his face toward me, his eyes locked on mine, and says, gruffly, "I want a quick taste before we go."

He kisses the corner of my mouth, his lips lingering against my skin. One second. Two.

I try to remind myself that Cassidy—or worse, her father—could be watching right now. But... I close my eyes, inhaling. That soap scent hits me even deeper and something silky slides through my veins. I turn my face a fraction of an inch, until our mouths are flush, and I trace my tongue along the inner curve of his upper lip.

"Careful," he says, against my mouth. "I only wanted a hint of sugar before dinner, but you keep this up, we won't be eating tonight... Not food, anyway. I can think of something else I'd like to eat." His hand slides down my back, curving around my hip, and the heat of his palm sinks through the fabric of my dress and oh God my knees literally do slip an inch.

I catch myself against his chest, pushing away from him like I meant to do it, grinning, the whispered weight of his lips still echoing across mine. "Whatever. Told you I'd make you beg."

"You think this is me begging?" he asks, holding my chin, sliding his thumb across my lips.

I bite the tip of his finger before I answer, tugging at his skin with my teeth. Hard enough to make him wince a little. "I *think* you said you were driving, like a real date. But it's Miles behind the wheel..."

"I realized we might want to drink." He walks me to the car, opening the door for me.

"How responsible of you." I slide in, greeting Miles, who winks at me in the rearview mirror.

"Though maybe," Alec says, dropping down beside me, "we won't drink quite as much as we did last time."

And I doubt he means to do it, but I'm instantly reminded that I'm the moron who passed out after sharing too many secrets last time, and my mood starts to fall. "Yeah. Maybe I'll stick to water."

My hand is pressed flat against the seat and he runs his fingers over it. "Have I told you how sexy you are?"

"According to my grandmother, I look like a whore, so I guess that puts me somewhere in the middle of your opinions."

"Your grandmother's an idiot," he says without skipping a beat. "I have excellent taste. If I tell you you're hot, you're fucking hot. Understand?"

I stare out my window, watching Cassidy's posh neighborhood slide by, willing my brain to kick out Gran's words, to push away the embarrassment of my past mistakes. He grabs my chin, a little roughly this time, and pulls my face toward him. "Understand?"

And the way he's looking at me, the way his gaze drops to my mouth, the way he wets his own lips, I do understand. I nod and his grip turns to more of a caress.

"So, um, where are we going?" I need him to back away from me. Just a smidgen. Or I might eat him for dinner.

He leans back against his seat, watching me. "Clearwater Heights. I reserved a corner table."

"Cool." I scratch my neck, all casual, like it's not the nicest restaurant in southern Virginia and I've literally never known anyone who's been there—even Cassidy. Then...fuck it. I turn to him, letting my excitement show. "Why a corner table?"

"We'll have the river on one side and mountains in the background on the other," he says. It makes sense. The restaurant sits at the top of a towering business building and is all glass so patrons can look out over the water, or valley, for miles. Or, so I'd assume. And so I'll find out. *Holy shit.*

"Pulling out all the stops," I tease, cocking a brow—and then pausing to consider. "Unless this is a regular night for you."

He laughs. "No. I've only been there twice."

"Oh?"

"And never on a date."

I shouldn't be this pleased. I know better than anyone that it never lasts.

But damn, I *am* pleased. Too much to bother attempting to smother it.

And I'm even more pleased when we're seated in the restaurant and it's exactly as he promised. On one side of us, the river swirls below, and on the other, the mountains rise in the distance.

It's dizzying. It's... "Breathtaking."

"Yes," he agrees, but when I glance at him, he's studying me instead of the view. "You are."

I don't know how to respond, so I turn my face toward the river, watching gentle ripples dimpling the surface. And the sunset. The sky above the mountains darkens from a golden yellow into a bruised purple, stretching over the rolling peaks, and for the briefest of moments I wish I were better with words. Writing, reading. Anything to let me capture this feeling.

The waiter comes, and, after asking permission, Alec orders us a bottle of wine. I don't usually drink it, but there's no way I can't have it tonight. It's red and dry and...the least horrible wine I've ever had. Alec swears it will be delicious with steaks. When our orders are taken, he draws the waiter toward him and says something quietly in his ear.

"What was that all about?" I ask. "You're not having them sing happy birthday to me, right? Because I seriously doubt they do that here." I gesture subtly to the rest of the restaurant. Shimmering accents—on the restaurant decor and most of the women in it. Glistening crystal glasses, and twinkling lights and wedding rings, or earrings, or both.

"No," Alec says. "Wait."

A few seconds later our waiter returns, handing Alec a small bowl that I can't quite see into. Alec tips it forward, though—and I discover it's filled with cherries. I bite my lip to keep from cracking up.

The restaurant's darker now; they upped the ambient lighting as the sun set, and there's a whisper of something classical drifting out of hidden speakers.

And we're practicing tying cherry stems in knots with our tongues, trying not to die laughing.

"This is so not sexy," I say, snorting.

He shakes his head. "You should see your jaw—back and forth and back and forth. It's a lovely jaw, but it's moving as though you're chewing cud."

"Um, did you call me a cow?" I ask, feigning offense.

He backtracks so fast. "No, I meant—"

"Because that's sharp coming from someone who's impersonating a camel about to spit." I giggle, giving up the act, and humored relief relaxes his features.

When my filet arrives, it's almost tender enough to cut with my fork and no knife, and it practically melts like butter on my tongue. "You were right," I say, after swallowing and sipping. "The wine is awesome."

"I'm usually right," he says, sipping his own wine.

I roll my eyes. "Whatever you say, Mr. I Like Spinster Malady."

"Rich, coming from Ms. I Like Demi Jade." He takes another bite. He might've looked funny trying to tie a stem earlier, but the way he chews for real is somehow incredibly sexy. "Let's meet in the middle. Do you like Villain Complex?"

"Who?" I ask, though the name sounds familiar.

"Rock band, kind of alternative, a little indie." He waits for recognition to sink in, and it's hovering right there on the edge, but not quite making it. "They were on *The Sound*."

Oh. Right. Now I remember the name—and why I don't follow the band. "I don't watch reality TV."

"Because of your mom?" He asks the question quietly, but its impact is almost deafening nonetheless.

"What did you say?"

He doesn't drop his eyes, just dabs the corner of his mouth with his napkin. "I looked her up when I learned your real name."

"That's... I mean, that's..." I sputter, unable to force my emotions to words.

"I'm sorry if I crossed a line," he says.

"A line? You crossed an entire ocean." I want to stab him with my fork. Not really, but I can't believe he went behind my back the way he did. "That's my information to share—or to keep."

"When you left that morning, I was desperate to find you. Called the bar, offered to pay for your last name off of a credit card receipt. I went back that evening in case you were there—which I knew you wouldn't be because you hate pool—but you told me all these things about yourself and then left before I could tell you how much I wanted to see you again."

"That doesn't mean—"

"Seeing you again Monday morning was...indescribable. And the second I had the truth of your name, I was crazy for more grounding information on you, things to keep you *real* this time. So I did some digging and I looked her up." He shakes his head. "That logic is ridiculous. Hell, it's not even logic. But you made an impact on me. And I thought I lost my chance to know you."

The sweet sound of a violin plays through the silence between us while he waits for me to respond, and the music tangles around me, tugging at a bitter nostalgia I thought I'd buried.

Part of me feels so betrayed that I'm tempted to walk out of the restaurant, away from him. But... I also understand why he did it. Hell, even if he didn't want to know me, there's still a curiosity that comes with learning someone's mother is quasi-famous.

The problem is, it's embarrassing. The things my mother's known for are...gross.

"*Social Climbing* is only the show she's on right now," I say. "Before that there were others. Three of them. All about rising from nothing and digging for gold."

His eyes never leave my face. "I gathered as much."

"When she's interviewed, she says she doesn't have any family. That she's all alone in the world." I swish the wine in my glass, watching the burgundy liquid roll in circles. It matches the direction of my stomach.

"I'm sorry." He's watching me, concerned. I don't even have to lift my eyes to him to hear his expression in his voice.

"Don't be. I'm not." Anymore, at least. "The first show's producers did a little digging and discovered the existence of my grandparents and came snooping—where they also discovered me. And, in turn, *I* discovered who my mother was. I was sixteen." I take a sip of wine. "My grandparents threatened to sue the pants off the network if they exposed a minor, and so the show let her lies pass as truth." I take another sip. Then I gulp down the rest of my glass. "See? She's a liar. Like me. And she clings to people with money to get ahead. Aren't you worried I'll follow in those shoes as well?" I hate the acerbic edge to my tone, but something in me is cracking. What if I'm right? What if there's a part of me that's attracted to his wealth even if I'm not aware of it?

"You won't follow in her shoes." He says it so simply.

Yeah, because so far she hasn't managed to nab a rich guy, and it seems like I'm actually getting close.

Oh my God.

What the fuck is wrong with me?

"I might already be following." My words are shaky.

"You're nothing like her."

Two minutes ago, I might've agreed with him. Now? Now my thoughts are traitors and I hate myself. "You don't know that."

"My father's had at least four affairs, two of them long-term. My mother doesn't care." He drinks the rest of his wine, too. "And I can tell you here and now I'm not like either of them."

"I'm sorry." I'm always envious of people whose parents love them, but I also always forget that they have Big Things that suck in their lives, too.

"Do you think I'll have four affairs? Do you think I'll sit by idly if my wife cheats someday?"

"You don't strike me as either type."

"And you don't like me because of my money."

In the back of my mind, my mother laughs. *Hook him, sweetie,* she whispers to me. I shudder.

"Here's where you tell me I shouldn't be so sure that you like me." He flashes a grin and I try to follow suit, barely managing.

"Life is fucking unfair," I say, instead.

"And..." Something makes him hesitate and he takes another bite of steak before he continues. "What about your father?"

I study the cream-colored napkin in my lap for a moment, working to drown out the hint of self-pity that threatens to rise. "Don't know him either."

"Did you ever want to?"

"He didn't want to meet me. Laughed when my mother told him she was knocked up—and then disappeared exactly nine months before my mom did. Not a thing on Earth could make me search for that kind of man. I'd rather have no father than *that.*"

He waits, like he thinks I have more to say. Like he realizes it before I do, and suddenly the words come. "There's a part of me that doesn't believe what my grandparents told me. Maybe they lied, either out of spite, or because they didn't want to think about the guy my mom used to propel a disaster—aka me—into their lives. I thought about looking for him for a long time. But I'd rather live with the hope that they're liars and he's not a monster, than find out the truth. That they were honest."

"You'd rather be afraid of the unknown than live with the possible depression of reality," he says. "I get it."

And I think he actually does. "Anyway. Enough about me and my awesome home life. Tell me something about you."

His smile this time is slow to grow, but full enough to meet his eyes. It's on the verge of pissing me off. "What?"

"You're very strong," he says. "Stronger than anyone I've ever met."

"I can't even do a push-up," I say, purposefully misunderstanding him. Then, I sigh. "Thank you, but I don't want your pity. I don't want anyone's pity. That's why I don't talk about this shit."

I also don't want to get mad, but I'm still right on the cusp. I don't like feeling sorry for myself. I don't like anyone else feeling sorry for me. I stab a piece of meat, chewing it into nothingness.

"I don't pity you," Alec says. "I admire you."

It's the first time in my life anyone's ever said that to me—and, even more, he seems to mean it. My throat suddenly feels swollen and my eyes are prickling. I can barely swallow my next bite.

There are too many emotions; there isn't enough *me* to take them all in. I pour myself some more wine, taking a healthy swallow before answering. "And I admire...your ass."

I top off his glass of wine, too, and he takes it, swirling the liquid for a moment. "You don't have to do that with me, you know. Deflect."

"I also don't *have* to be thinking about how much I can't wait to get back to your place," I say. "But here I am, doing that very thing." It's the truth, now that I've said it. Enough talking. I'm ready for some action.

Annoyingly, Alec takes a bite of asparagus. "Tell me about meeting Norris Marshal."

I take a second to transition my line of thinking. "I met him last summer when Cassidy worked at Backbar Amphitheater and Gold Rush Standard came through on tour."

I pause, memories flooding my mind. Cassidy's summer was bananas. Mine was more like a circle. An endless loop of trying not to seem sadder than I should about Jason, and keeping the nasty black hole of anger in check (which rarely worked), and picking up as much overtime as I was able at the salon. But somehow, at the center of that circle, I found Norris Marshal. The one spot that shined brighter for me than anything else, regardless of how short my time of knowing him lasted.

"Norris is this…person-shaped being filled with endless amounts of sunshine." I blush, but it's impossible not to feel a little bubbly thinking about Norris. "That's stupid, I know. But I'm not sure how else to describe him. His wife, too. Like, somehow with one look he got to the center of who I am and wanted to break me free."

"Impossible," Alec says. "You're a maze, filled with twists and turns and *no entrance* signs begging to be cut down." He drinks some wine, his eyes never leaving my face. "And I hope you know I'm up for the task."

Don't blush.

Do not blush.

"It's easier for me to talk to people who don't really know me," I say, immediately regretting the words, certain he's finally going to look at me with pity. Like, *poor broken girl who doesn't have anyone close enough to really talk to. Has to resort to strangers…*

Instead he says, "Makes sense. It's easier to unload on people who can't turn around and hurt you with what they know. And it helps that you already held him in high regard."

"He told me the world was at my fingertips, if I'd reach out to take it," I say, swallowing the rest of my wine. "And that's what I want to do. With you." I reach toward him until his hand meets mine. "Take me home."

He clears his throat. "Are you sure?"

"I want to go to your place, Alec. Take me there."

CHAPTER TWENTY-SIX

ALEC PAYS THE bill, and I don't argue this time. It's probably higher than what I've got in my bank account—the menu didn't even have prices attached to the entrees. I try not to think about it as we take the elevator down and slip into the town car.

Alec tells Miles to play Villain Complex, and as the first strands of music unfurl in the air, I recognize them. I *do* know some of their songs—and like them. Yet another thing I have in common with Alec. Which is weird, considering how different our lives have been.

Before we take off, Miles sets up a tray for us with chocolate-dipped strawberries and glasses of chilled champagne. Alec thanks him, and I try to, too—but all I manage is a nod. I'm starting to get overwhelmed, and the echoes of my mother's laugh are still ringing in the distance.

Alec nudges me with his knee. "We can scrap all this and go get McDonald's sundaes if you'd rather."

His silly offer makes the entire situation easier. I sink my teeth into a strawberry, closing my eyes and moaning when the rich swirl of chocolate and berry plays against my tongue. "This is perfect."

"Almost," he says, and when I look at him, he runs his thumb over my lower lip. "You have a little chocolate right here."

"Did you get it?" I ask, pretty sure there wasn't any chocolate to begin with.

"Not quite..." He moves the tray and leans toward me, pressing his mouth gently against mine, murmuring, "God, you're sweet."

I part my mouth to give him a real taste, and he takes it, his tongue skimming the inside of my lips, teasing the roof of my mouth. I sigh into him, melting against him the best I can with a seat belt across my lap. I break away first, when the car stops at a light. "Let's—"

He pulls me back to him, swallowing whatever else I was going to say. Can't even remember now. Not with the way his mouth is taking control of mine. Not with the way his fingers are tangled in my hair, tugging with that perfect sort of pressure. Not hard enough to jerk my neck back, but firm enough to make my scalp tingle, the sensations shooting down my neck, across my chest, deep into my belly.

Fuck the seat belt.

I unbuckle it, clumsy in my haste, and climb into Alec's lap, my knees at his hips. My dress so high on my thighs it may as well not be there. He slides his palms against my bare skin, his finger grazing under the hem, his tongue forceful in my mouth.

I kiss him harder, taking all he'll give. His mouth is sweet like strawberries, and it makes me giddy that he scooped the flavor out of my own mouth. His palms inch higher, his thumbs pressing into my inner thighs.

Higher.

Higher.

Higher, until they're tracing the lines of my panties between my legs.

"Lace as you promised," he murmurs, dipping one thumb below the fabric.

"Mm hmm." It's the best I can manage because he's tracing places with the pad of his finger that have me unable to do anything other than moan while the most delicious sensation flows along his path.

Miles clears his throat, loudly. "Accident up ahead. Cop cars everywhere. Might want to, um, buckle your seat belts again."

"Oh my God." I fly off Alec's lap so fast it's a wonder I don't hurt myself. I forgot about Miles. Blue and white flash ahead of us in the distance, followed by sirens. I flash a panicked glance at Alec, wondering if he's as mortified as I am, but all he does is grin a wicked little grin—and then lick the pad of his thumb.

Oh my God.

Somehow we make it to Alec's condo without me spontaneously combusting.

Somehow we make it up the elevator—and he remembers to press the button this time.

Somehow we make it through his front door.

But where we don't make it is anywhere else.

He tosses me up onto the foyer console table. The wood presses sharply into the backs of my legs. I part them to give him access and he takes it, sliding between my knees and pressing toward me until there's no space between our bodies. And his mouth...his mouth takes mine, teasing, tasting, biting. He slides kisses along my jaw, down my neck, across my collarbone. His hands are at my waist. Mine are in his hair. I yank his head back up, needing the strength of his kiss again.

I will never not need this.

It's a sobering thought—but it doesn't have enough time to really sink in, because Alec's hands wrap around to my ass and he pulls me toward him, lifting me off of the table. "Told you this was my favorite way to walk," he says, nipping my lower lip. He pauses, though, at the foot of his staircase.

My pumps clatter to the ground. "If I'm too heavy you can—"

"Shut your beautiful mouth." He kisses me to make sure I do, and his body rises and falls as he slips his own shoes off. "I'm having a struggle with my conscience. Do I offer you something to drink—or do I toss you on my bed and show you everything I've been fantasizing about doing this entire week?"

"The second one."

He laughs, maybe because there was not a single moment of hesitation before my answer.

"Don't you dare laugh at me," I say, smiling. And then I kiss him to make sure he doesn't.

He carries me up his stairs, down his hallway—and tosses me onto his bed. Without a chance to catch my breath, he's on top of me, his knees on either side of my hips, his lips trailing along my neck, up my jaw, finding my mouth. His hands drag mine above my head.

I yank from his grasp, pulling them right back down.

In one motion, he flips us so that I'm straddling him. "You want control?" he asks over my gasp. "Take it, by all means."

I only wanted my hands free so I could strip him of his shirt. But I lean down and sink my teeth into his earlobe, whispering, "Good."

I've never felt sexier. And when I lift his shirt, peeling it off of him, the feeling only grows. All because of him, this guy, this sexy, sweet guy with a body harder than iron. Abs like they're carved from marble, and you better believe I let my fingers drift over every hill and valley, the warmth of his skin tingling against my palms.

His hips flex beneath me, and I feel how hard he is, and I shiver because oh wow. *I* did this. I made him this rigid, this thick. It makes me grin. It makes me powerful. I lean forward to kiss his chest, flickering my tongue over his nipples. He groans, his hands tightening around me, his fingers squeezing my ass.

I drag my lips up his neck and over his jaw, loving the texture of his stubble against my tongue. I hold his hands, this time, and pull them above his head. He lifts his chin, capturing my mouth with his, and the kiss is instantly intense. Lips pressing, tongues swirling, whispered breaths between our two bodies.

He threads his fingers through mine and beneath me, his abs go rock solid as he sits up, cradling me in his lap and breaking the kiss a moment later. "I want you in nothing but your lace. And I want to strip it from your gorgeous body."

My stomach jumps. My body is not gorgeous, I almost say. I'd give it a C at best. (And that's probably only because Bobby Fields gave it a D in high school. I mean, I kicked him in the balls so hard I'm pretty sure he still sings falsetto—but I'm not delusional enough to go higher. I'm a realist.) What I say instead is, "How about a little mood lighting?"

He gives me one of his soul-grazing stares, but he doesn't press it. He slides out from under me, lowering the light to a dim glow with a dial on the wall. Needing to gain back some of my momentum, I add, "Lose your pants while you're over there."

He snorts—and drops them to the ground.

"Why," he says, sauntering toward me, "am I not surprised you're bossy in the bedroom?"

I shrug and motion for him to join me, but he curves his own finger for me to go to him at the base of the bed. "Come here."

"And you say *I'm* bossy?"

He grins, his teeth gleaming in the low light, his dimples darkening into sexy shadows at the edges of his lips. "Teagan. Come here. Now." And something in his tone has more than my stomach jumping. My heart. My breath. The blood in my veins.

On shaky limbs, I crawl to him. At the edge of the bed, I rise to my knees and he touches me, one hand on my shoulder, the other on my hip, twisting me until I face away from him. I almost lose my balance in the plushness of his bed, but his hands catch my waist, and when I'm steady, they drop to the backs of my legs, the bases of my knees. He slowly, slowly runs them up the insides of my thighs. I widen my knees and roll my hips back, hoping a finger, or two, will find the spot where I most need to be touched under my dress. Under my panties.

Instead, he drops his hands from my legs, and I bite back a disappointed groan.

"Alec?" slips out of my mouth, though I'm not sure what I'm asking.

"Kitten." He brings his palms to the back of my neck, twisting my hair in his hands, winding it over one of my shoulders—and dropping his mouth on my bared skin, his tongue working along my neck in ways that have my head rolling further to the side.

His lips never leaving my skin, he unclasps the top of my dress and slowly, slowly tugs the zipper down. Inch by inch, past the middle of my back. Slower, slower, below the waist of my panties. When he lifts his head, the air hits my neck, cooling the spot where he's left the slightest trace of saliva against my skin.

"Jesus," he growls, nipping at me once more. "You have the sexiest fucking back I've ever seen, the sweetest skin I've ever tasted, and I never want you in anything but lace from this point forward."

I shiver, and it's not from the cool air on my neck. He jerks the straps of the dress over my shoulders, pulling until the fabric is puddled around my knees. He smoothes his hands along the skin of my lower back, pushing gently, until I'm on my hands and knees.

"Alec?" I ask again, still not sure what I want.

He shushes me. And even still in underwear, this is the most erotic thing I've ever felt, his presence behind me, his palms transferring heat up and down my spine. The dip in the bed when he climbs up, the charged space in the air that hits me when, from behind, he pulls my panties to the side.

The shocked pant of breath that leaves my mouth when he does.

The wetness of his tongue when he trails it along every exposed inch of me.

I can't keep the moan silent this time. I can't keep my hips from rolling. I can't keep this absolute *need* I feel from baring itself. And when he grabs my hips and plunges his tongue straight into me, I make a sound of pleasure closer to a song than anything else.

And I very nearly fall flat on my face.

Too much, too fast.

Or the opposite.

I need *more*.

I twist toward him, and after another dance with his tongue in my body, he allows it, letting me curve my body until I'm on my back and he adjusts himself, one of his knees sliding between my thighs, rising higher, higher up my legs, until I'm close to grinding myself against him for more relief.

"You taste incredible." He licks his lips, wet and shining in the shadows. He shoves his knee deliciously against me and grips my thighs, pushing them wider, wider. "I hope you don't expect me to stop for very long."

I open my mouth, the question I've been wanting to ask finally forming in my mind. I hesitate, a little nervous... A *lot* wanting. "Do you have a condom?"

CHAPTER TWENTY-SEVEN

ALEC HOLDS HIMSELF—holds *me*—very still, his arms all sinew and muscle even in the dimmed light. "I do have a condom."

But he doesn't move.

"Should you get it?" I ask. His knee is between my legs and my underwear is shoved to the side, and it's still taking all that I have not to roll my hips, not to rub myself against him.

He lets one hand drift down my inner thigh, tucking it between me and his knee, his finger dipping the slightest way into me. I moan. I roll my hips.

"Are you begging?" he asks.

And, absurdly, I giggle. "No."

He tightens his grip, harder, harder, one finger—two—slipping into me, then he *clutches* me until I gasp in pleasure. "And now?"

"No." But I'm not giggling anymore. And my hips are rising to meet the movements of his hand. "Actually, maybe I am."

He lowers his face until his lips are at my ear and my entire body flutters, waiting for what I know he's going to say.

Except he doesn't say it. "Told you that wasn't going to happen tonight."

Way more nervous to do it than I should be, I drag my own hand between our bodies, sliding it below the band of his boxer briefs and tentatively gripping him. He picks his head up to watch my face, but I'm much more interested in his. He winces in a pleasure-filled way, and does it again when I glide my hand along him.

"Pretty sure your body disagrees." I'm also pretty sure the long thickness of erection will never, ever fit all the way inside me, but I keep this thought to myself. Because every fiber of my body wants him to try anyway.

His breathing is so satisfyingly ragged, but still he says, "There are other ways to fill our time."

"Alec," I say, as sexily as I can drag out his name. A bit smugly, too. "I'm not interested in your game room right now."

"Neither am I," he says. "I'm going to spend the rest of tonight tasting every single inch of your skin."

His words leave my body a life-sized collection of fiery sparks, filling my skin, filling my mind, filling the space between my legs with the most electric sizzles.

He grabs my hand, pulling it out of his briefs and above my head. I nearly clench my legs around him, desperate to fill the void he left when releasing his clutch.

"Give me your other hand," he says. And I do without even the slightest temptation to fight him on the power imbalance between us right now. In fact, if my erratic heart is any indication, if the way my breath is caught below my throat means anything… If the wetness pooling between my thighs is a sign… He can have all the power. All night.

"Good girl," he murmurs, lowering his mouth to mine. His grip on my wrists is unyielding. His lips are forceful, and when his tongue leads my own in an intricate dance, it tastes of the salt of my body.

"Good girl?" I ask, running my teeth along his lip. "That's not how you want to speak to me."

"If I didn't want to speak to you like this, I wouldn't." His next kiss has so much force behind it, I have no choice but to shut up.

No choice but to give in.

No choice but to *shiver* along the path his free hand traces. Down the inside of my arm, along my ribcage, trailing the cups of my bra— and then sliding under the material. He takes his time, back and forth along my skin, and when his fingers find my nipple, he rubs the pad of his thumb over it until I gasp. He swallows the sound, scooping it from my mouth with his tongue. And then he moves to the other side and brings me to the point of moaning. My nipples are so hard, so full of anticipation, I'm all but pushing myself into his hands.

He releases some of the tension from his grip on my wrists. "Don't," he whispers between sweeping kisses, "move."

But how can I not move with the way my blood rushes under my skin?

How can I not move with the buildup of tension pinging me everywhere, needing his touch?

He lets go, and I bring my hands around his neck, pulling his face harder against mine, sweeping my tongue more deeply through his mouth. He lets me do it, but only for a moment.

He ducks his head under my grasp, breaking the kiss and laughing, a sound somehow full of humor yet also a warning. "What did I tell you?'

"When have I ever taken orders well?"

He grabs my wrists and slams them above my head, his chest over mine, shoving his knee between my legs again, making me writhe. "Start now and I promise you'll be rewarded for it."

He nudges my face to the side with his chin and slides his teeth over my earlobe, his tongue flickering along my skin. I sigh, melting into the bed. "Fine. You win."

"Get used to that," his voice is raspy in my ear. And then he gets to work and I forget how much I want to fight him on it because as long as he uses his tongue the way he does, he can get me to agree to whatever the hell he'd like.

He *bathes* me with his mouth, not missing an inch of skin.

Hands to shoulders, feet to knees to hips, breasts to belly...until I'm fully baptized in the church of Alec.

His tongue is my drug, my addiction, and when I can't stand another moment without more of a connection, when I think I'm going to have to break my promise and use my own hands, he shoves my knees up—and then nudges them apart. His eyes are on mine, glinting in the darkness of the room.

I'm thankful for the obscurity. I might not be able to fully enjoy this in the harsh reality of a world filled with light. In the darkness that yawns over us, when flesh blends with shadow, when my flaws are safely tucked away, it's easier to let my mind free. It's easier to tell him what I want.

"You," I say. And when a hint of amused confusion crosses his features, I clarify. "I want you, Alec. Now. The rest of tonight." *Always*, is on the tip of my tongue, but he slides up my body and captures my mouth in a kiss before I can say it.

He reaches between us again and curves his fingers into me, pulsing them through me until I cry out into his mouth and then sliding them back up my body, feeling me everywhere. Twisting my skin, pulling at me. Massaging me. His mouth never stops moving over mine. Not once.

Always always always reflects its way around my mind like a shattered mirror, like it's the only word I've every truly known the meaning to. And it flashes brighter, a neon glint, when he drags his mouth over my chin, down my neck, across my chest. He tongues one nipple and then the other, until I'm moaning with how tight they are, how ready I am for him, how desperate. My hands twist through his sheets above my head, my legs rise to wrap around him, my feet crossing at his back.

And he's *right there*.

His erection.

So. Fucking. Hard. Pressing through the fabric of his boxers. My hips writhe, and I press myself harder against him until I'm not the only one moaning.

Frustration rumbles up from my throat in a whimper. I want more.

He slides lower, planting kisses along my belly; the friction of his body slipping through my legs is unparalleled by anything I've ever experienced. He hooks his fingers through the top of my underwear and my breath catches.

He slowly, slowly slides the fabric lower, alternating a path of cool air and kisses along my skin as it's bared.

Pushing one of my knees closer to the other, he tugs my panties over my hips and slides them down my legs, down down down over my feet. And they land on the floor in the darkness with a soft rustle.

And then there's silence.

Though is silence the right word when, through the quiet, the air is so charged, electricity crackles deafeningly without making a sound? His hands are at my ankles. They're sliding up my shins. Caressing my knees. Pushing my thighs apart. He flattens his palm against me and then drags it through my wetness.

His fingers press down like piano keys, pressing pressing every note there is to make me whisper, moan, scream his name.

His tongue is on my inner thigh. He's looking up at me. I'm forgetting how to breathe.

Higher, he licks. Higher, his fingers never stilling.

He laps at the crease where my leg meets my hip, and he slides his hands down to lift my knees. I am bare before him, his face is there, and then his breath. Hot. Cool. Hot cool hot cool *hot-cool-hot-cool.*

"Please." I whisper his name, begging. The sampling I had of his tongue inside my body seems so long ago.

And finally, *finally*, so perfectly I almost want to cry, he licks me again. Once. Slow and long, he presses the flat of his tongue against me and then curves it, along me, through me, into me. He shoves his hands beneath my ass, lifting me toward him, onto his face, his mouth, his tongue.

I'm moaning now—maybe have been the whole time, I don't know. I don't know anything except the pressure of his lips and the swish of his tongue as it enters me. Circling into me and out. Again, and again, and again. His face is pressed entirely against me, his nose, even, nudging me, and he twists his head from side to side, pulling me back and forth and... I'm going to fucking explode.

My hands are in his hair. His thick, thick hair; it's soft and glorious and the room is spinning. My legs are around his head and his tongue, his thick, thick tongue is lavishing me in a way I've only ever imagined—and I'm learning quickly my imagination is lacking.

He licks higher, using his tongue to press my skin down flat enough to make my moans grow feral, and his fingers tiptoe into me, slowly at first and then faster, heavier.

Something is building in my limbs.

A light sort of pressure.

It's soft, but full.

Swift, but lingering.

My legs are full of feathers, somehow, spinning, and my belly too. My breath is erratic. My heartbeat, too.

His fingers pump into me. Ruthlessly.

Perfectly.

His name falls again from my lips in a whisper, a sigh. The flutters spiraling through my belly explode into something so much more powerful, dropping like gusts of a tornado, gaining density, gaining speed, lower, so much lower, mingling with the pressure of his fingers, the rhythm of his tongue. His name becomes a chant and my entire body clenches and then *bursts*.

I am grains of sand in a storm made of Alec, scattering in his fierce wind and spinning back. Out to my limits and then retracted. Billow and fall.

But the wind gusts into something even stronger, something *more*, and with one final, unstoppable spiral out, I dissolve into absolutely nothing but a leftover pulse of a girl that used to exist.

And an exhausted Cheshire smile.

CHAPTER TWENTY-EIGHT

I'M SWEATY.
At some point, I reform into some semblance of myself. My skin is slick, damp. *Glistening*.
Then, I notice Alec. Feel him, really. The weight of his head on my thigh, the sharpness of his chin digging into my muscle. His lazy smile takes my breath away.
"Um." I don't know what to say. I'm out of breath, like I've run a marathon. My heart's beating as if that's the case as well.
"Um?" He lifts a brow, amused.
"Thank you?" I mean to say it with less of a question mark, but I'm suddenly a little too aware of our positioning, of how very naked I am, of how high on my thigh his head is... I shift, curving onto my side, facing him, and letting his head slip onto the bed.
His shoulders shake in a silent laugh and he crawls up over me, kissing his way up my body, sweet and silly this time, the intensity of before a nearby memory. "You," he says, between kisses, "are very," kiss, kiss, kiss all the way up to the side of my face, "welcome."
I twist my head toward him, kissing him on the mouth, again tasting the salt of my body lingering on his lips.
"Want some water?" he asks, quite some time later.
"How about a shirt?"

He rises over me, the heat from his body soaking into my own. "And cover all this up? Yeah, right."

"Alec," I say, teasing, both turned on and uncomfortable all at once. "I'm cold."

His expression says he doesn't buy it for a second, but he sighs and rises, striding to a dresser and tossing me an undershirt. I slip it on, pretending I don't suddenly feel awkward. It's soft and smells like detergent and fits me like an oversized trash bag.

At least I'm covered now. I clear my throat. "Water sounds good, actually."

"You still look beautiful," he says. "In that shirt. Out of it. Shit. If I didn't think you'd be terrified, I'd rip that thing right back off of you." He shakes his head, leaving the room.

Leaving me reeling.

I cover my face with my hands, falling onto the bed. What is wrong with me? I just had the most mind-blowing orgasm of my life and now I...what? Am uncomfortable about it? Shaking. That's what I am. Trembly. "Come on, Teagan, get your shit together."

Still, when he comes back to the room, it's as though I've reverted to a teenager and I can't make myself look at him. I reach out for the water, but he holds it hostage.

"Look at me."

My face is so hot I'm almost in pain. "I am."

"You're looking over my shoulder."

"That's definitely not the case." Yes, it really freaking is. "It's dark. You can't tell."

"Come here."

"No. You come here."

He stares me down until I can't keep from looking at him. But even when I meet his gaze, he refuses to come to me.

Well.

Two can play this game.

All night long.

Finally, I'm able to grin. I sit on my heels.

He crosses his arms.

I toss my hair over a shoulder.

He says, "Your nipples are hard and I suddenly fucking love that shirt on you because seeing them push out like that? There's nothing else like it."

"Well your..." Ugh. Why can't I say it? And I'd rather die than reference his erection as his thing again. "*You're* hard. And..." And why don't I have a follow-up here? "God, Alec. What did you do to me?"

"You mean like a few minutes ago? Or... metaphorically?"

There's no doubt my face is neon red even in the dark room. "The second one."

"Pretty sure I've made you like me." He takes a long sip of water. My mouth goes a little dry. And not from the thought of the water. Just... Wow. His body. His thick neck, bobbing as he swallows. His waist is narrower than his shoulders, giving his chest that perfect vee down toward his legs. And his erection. He's so hard it makes me bite my lip almost deep enough to draw blood.

"Is that uncomfortable?" Oh. Right. Because now's the perfect time for words to slip out all unfiltered.

"This?" He gestures toward himself, a wolfish grin flashing through the dark.

"I mean...do you want me to—"

"Stop." He pauses before continuing. "The thought of you touching me in any capacity makes me so fucking hard I could break concrete. But you need a break. So let's lie here for a while. All night. I'll be fine—*he'll* be fine."

"You would do that?"

"Why are you surprised?"

"Because...you're... I mean, you...did what you did and... God, I suck at this. I'm sorry. I *do* like you."

"Ah." He nods, and finally, finally moves toward the bed, handing me the water. "You saved yourself at the end. You were pissing me off for a second there, thinking I'd expect more than you're ready for. But if it's because I fluster you, because you *like* me, then I guess it's okay. Just this once."

But I can't leave it at that. "I'm not selfish, Alec. Or...I am. But I want to please you. It's not fair for me to get all the—"

"*Stop*," he repeats, the word sharper this time. The bed dips when he sinks into it, languidly crawling toward me to press a finger against my lips. "Don't you get it? Your orgasm—getting to tease those noises from you with my fingers, with my mouth, feeling you throb around my tongue like that? It pleases me more than anything I've ever done. More than any blowjob I could ever receive—even from you."

His words bring a glow to me so intense I'm surprised I'm not lighting up the room. "Really?"

He leans against the headboard, pulling me into his chest. "Those noises? The purrs you made—the way you called my name. Christ, Teagan. They'll be on repeat in my memory for a long time. I'm tempted to record you on the next round, so I can play it back whenever I want to, forever."

"Whenever you want to, forever?" I wish I could come up with something more clever than an echo of his words, but I'm too full of a grin. It hits my lips and zooms down the rest of my body. *More than just this summer?* I catch the question before it escapes, but I'm not shocked by how tempted I am to ask it.

His erection is pressing into my back. All I have to do is turn around, twist in his arms, kiss down his body... The thought has me flushing—but something's holding me back. I chug some of the cool water, using the moment to gather my thoughts.

"As perfect as tonight's been," I say, surprised I can admit what I'm about to, "I might have hit my capacity for perfection. I...need a breather." Otherwise, I might explode. Or implode. Or, worse, I might ruin everything. "I'm not great with...too much too fast."

The closest I ever came to letting emotions pile on this fast was with Jason. And that ended before it could really begin. I don't know what to do with happiness when life hands it to me. Not that I can share that with Alec. Not that I should even have the thought right now.

"We have time, kitten." He tugs me tighter against his chest. "I want you to know my body as well as I've mapped yours, but when you're ready."

I don't bite back the next question that thrums through me, alongside all the pleasure rushing with his words. "Are you too good to be true?"

"Are *you?*"

"You're talking to the girl who lied about her name, lied about who she was, got too drunk to offer what she arrived to do—and then showed up at your office with a completely new identity."

He takes the water from me, leaning away for a second to place it on the nightstand and then sliding behind me, nibbling at my neck.

"You keep me on my toes."

"But I—"

"Will you shut up?"

"Don't tell me to shut up!" I grab his thigh, right above his knee, and I squeeze until his leg jerks and he laughs.

"That *tickles*." He digs his fingers into my ribs, and I giggle.

"Say you're sorry," I say, squirming—and resisting the urge to sigh when he slides his hands around my stomach, holding me, making me wish he'd slide them higher... Or lower.

"I apologize," he concedes, a pompous smile in his tone.

"Good. Because I have an idea."

"Oh yeah? I thought we were taking a break?" He grins when I turn to swat at him and tightens his grip around my stomach.

"We are," I say, kind of wishing we weren't... "This is business-related."

"From pleasure to business—isn't it usually the other way around?"

I laugh and twist toward him, loving the pleased glint of agreement in his eye when I tell him I think he should team up with Mr. Chambers.

He talks, excitedly, for a while, and I listen, adding an opinion here or there. But it's hard to focus on business for any length of time because I'm in Alec's bed. Because he's stroking the skin of my arms, the muscles of my thighs. Because he can't seem to keep from dropping kisses along my shoulders.

I slide my hand over the one he's left across my stomach, running my fingers along his skin. It's smooth, but not soft, somehow all guy. His knuckles are covered in raised spiderweb patterns of scarring. I want to ask him what happened, but I hold back. Sometimes people don't want you picking at their scars—visible or otherwise. I sure as shit don't. And I also don't want to risk ruining the night by opening my mouth about it.

At some point, Alec surprises me, pressing a small remote—which plays the audiobook opening of *Dracula* through a few speakers on the walls I hadn't noticed.

"I love this movie," I say, grinning into the darkness.

He kisses my neck, running a hand through my hair. "It's a book. Now keep that beautiful mouth closed."

But I turn my face toward him, stealing a kiss first. "You're kind of cool, you know?"

He grins against my mouth. "I know."

And so we listen.

He asks if I want popcorn, or something else to drink, but I shake my head. "Don't move. Don't do anything. This—this moment right here—I'm tempted to record it, so I can play it back whenever I want to, forever."

A laugh rumbles in his chest and he squeezes me tighter, and pressure from the weight of his arms somehow makes me *lighter*.

There's no anxiety tonight. No tossing and turning and traitorous, torturous thoughts funneling through my mind. There's only a gentle relaxation that comes with the beat of Alec's heart against my back, the soft rise and fall of his chest beneath me. I don't mean to fall asleep so quickly, but I'm out before Jonathan Harker even realizes he's Dracula's prisoner.

CHAPTER TWENTY-NINE

WHEN I OPEN my eyes, dazzled by sunlight streaming across the bed, Alec is watching me.

"That's creepy," I say, but a wave of pleasure washes over me anyway.

He taps my nose. "I missed these freckles last night."

"I had a lot of makeup on," I admit. Then, horrified, I see half of it's smeared across his pillowcase. "Shit—it'll come out, I promise."

He watches me, puzzled until he glances down at the orange-looking stripes across the otherwise stark white. Then, he laughs. "Who cares? I have more than one pillowcase."

"I care," I protest. "Your house is nice. Your stuff is nice. I don't want to make it all dirty."

Annoyingly, he laughs harder. "I like you here. With makeup. No makeup. In my bed. Out of it... Any which way you're here, you make my place a million times better."

Oh God. My brain's not awake enough to respond. My body is, though, trembling in all the right places. Who knew you could be so happy, so *turned on*, so soon after waking up. I sigh—and then I cover my mouth. "I need to brush my teeth."

"There's an extra toothbrush already out in the bathroom for you."

A blush warms my cheeks. "I brought my own."

"How presumptuous," he says. "I brought your bag up earlier." He points to it on my nightstand and rolls out of bed. Still in boxers. Still with abs formed from ridges and valleys.

Still mouth-wettingly appealing.

I scoff. "Like we both didn't know I'd be staying over." I reach out to him. "Come to bed."

He kneels on the mattress, letting me pull him toward me. "Thought you wanted to brush your teeth?"

"I do," I say, deciding in the instant to go for what I actually want. "But you stay right here."

"I was going to make us coffee."

"I have a different method of waking you up in mind," I say, forcing the words out so I can't back down, and slipping out of bed. I tug his undershirt down to cover my thighs.

He watches me. "What is this method you speak of?"

"Use your imagination," I say, "and picture my mouth on your body..." I smile and grab my bag, closing myself into his bathroom.

I'd love to study myself in the mirror, have a truth talk with my reflection. But his serious lack of mirrors issue makes it hard. Still, I brush my teeth. Splash some water on my face. Take a few deep breaths.

Remind myself of the ways he teased my body into bliss last night.

He deserves a turn now, too. And not because of some quid pro quo balance restoration thing, either. I want to start his day with a smile. I want to be the girl he thinks of, the flashbacks he gets when he closes his eyes all day.

I can do this.

I *can*.

Literally, I've done this before. Still. Everything's different when it's with Alec, more nerve-wracking. More significant.

One last deep breath, one last stern glance in the imaginary mirror, and I let myself out into his room. Where he's waiting. On the bed, his hands behind his head, a smarmy twist to the corners of his mouth.

"Christ, you're sexy in that shirt," he says.

"You're halfway decent without one on at all," I say, climbing over to him.

Straddling him.
Feeling him stiffen beneath me.
Oh, Lord.
His grin turns cockier, if that's even possible. And I find it annoyingly attractive. So attractive, in fact, I'm tempted to lean down and lick the corners of his mouth.
I give in to temptation.
And when I rise again, he slides his hands up my thighs, hoisting the undershirt higher, higher, until it barely covers anything. "Well," he says, his gaze steady on mine, "good morning."
"It's about to be."
"Is that so?" His thumbs inch down the insides of my thighs, tracing lines through the center of my body, bringing a cry to my lips. "Ah—there we go. Now it's a good morning."
Focus.
I need to focus.
I force my eyes open only to discover he's not looking at my face. He's...watching. His fingers. Flickering them over me.
Into me.
"*Alec.*" I fall forward, my face tingling painfully.
It feels like the kiss of a gentle breeze compared to what's happening between my legs.
Wet.
Heat.
A sudden desire to let him play with me all morning.
All day. All night.
Forever.
He smoothly slides his hands around me, curving over my ass, and between my legs from behind.
I press my hands beside his face, kissing him, slipping my tongue through his lips, tasting him, biting him gently. "This," I say, speaking against the kiss, my words trembling the way my blood seems to be too, "is supposed to be *my* turn to play with *you.*"
"My house," he says, gnawing on my lower lip, "my rules."
"Is that so?" I ask, ready to play, ready to push. I slide a little further down his body, but his grip tightens between my legs, keeping me from drifting further.
Oh, God.

"Yes. And my rules are simple." He twists two fingers into me, circling, pulsing, making my blood jump. "Nobody comes before you do."

"Wanna bet?" I slide my tongue down his throat, shifting to trail kisses across his chest. He flicks his fingers and my entire body pulses around him.

He sighs, warm and lazy-sounding. "Believe me, I'll be delivering what I promise before you can count to—"

"To what?" I slide my teeth around one of his nipples. I mean to make my way to the other, but, as he groans, he tightens his arms around me, his fingers growing harder, more forceful.

Thrusting into me.

Again.

And again.

A lightness spins through my chest, sliding down my belly, lower to where his hands are playing. I can't control it, can't control the way my limbs are jellying, can't control the whimpers building in my throat, pushing through my lips. "Alec—wait."

But he's pulling my sensitive skin apart, pushing the pad of his thumb against me—somehow gentle, somehow rough—tugging me in circles and my world starts to tilt. Instead of his shoulders, my hands grip his sheets, twisting through the fabric, winding tighter and tighter, matching the sensations that shoot through me.

I manage to whisper, "Not fair," before I come completely apart. Before the warmth pooling between my thighs ignites like a firework finale, *booming* through my veins, through my belly, down my legs, my arms.

Boom, boom, boom.

Boom.

I collapse on top of him, too flushed with pleasure to give him shit for the laughter shaking his chest.

"Told you," he whispers in my ear. "I get my way."

"Shut up," I say, breathing heavy. Enjoying it. Enjoying *everything.*

His hands are on my ass, pressing gentle circles over my cheeks. He moves them up my back, smoothing my skin, up and down and up and down. It's almost enough to lull me to sleep again.

Or, it would be, if he wasn't hard as marble beneath me.

If I wasn't determined to do what I set out to do, even if he beat me to the game.

Lazily, I push myself off his chest, kissing his neck, kissing his jaw, his cheek, his mouth. I dip my tongue through his lips, tasting him, all masculine and mint. "My turn," I murmur, and this time when I lower myself, he lets me go, watching me, a jaunty curve across his mouth.

"You look like a cat who's captured the canary," I say, ducking down to plant kisses along his stomach. "So pleased before I've even gotten started."

"This is just icing, kitten," he says, drawing his hands behind his head. "I've already had the cake—and believe me, there's nothing sweeter than hearing you cry out."

"We'll see," I say, smug. I may be a virgin, but I spent one long, secret weekend with Cassidy's brother before he died, and we made sure... Well, we made sure my tongue was expertly trained to bring out the *icing*.

And when I place my mouth around Alec, I don't hold back.

I grip his thighs. I use my tongue, the gentle edges of my teeth, the back of my throat. The angle of my neck, the sweep of my hair across his abdomen, the squeezes of my hands. My breath, hot and cool.

His hands come down to grab my head, to tug my hair, and his breathing fills the room, ragged and uneven. Harder, faster, his hips rise and fall to meet my rhythm.

I start to hum and when he comes, it's with a roar, and only the thought of watching where my teeth go keeps me from grinning around him.

"Remind me," he says, sometime later, the tenor of his voice a bit hoarse, "to get a standing mirror for the foot of my bed. All I have to do is imagine the view behind you... Your ass in the air, my undershirt sliding up your back, no panties—Christ, the thought's enough to bring me back to the edge. Next time you do this—and please, God, let there be a next time—I want to watch you while you do it."

"That'd be kind of hard, given your fear of all mirrors," I tease without thinking about my words.

His lips fall into a flat line, his eyes lose a bit of their shine. His expression remains poised, but too polite, suddenly. He's shutting down before my eyes. Panic stirs in my chest. "I'm sorry," I say. "I didn't mean to—"

"Nothing to apologize for. Why don't I go make us that coffee?" He gently slides out from underneath me and sits up, stretching as he stands. He glances at me. "Seriously. No worries."

But yeah. Right. He's going for lighthearted and he's so far from pulling it off it's not even funny.

He slips into his jeans from last night, pulling them up, not bothering to button them.

"I'll just…" I motion aimlessly from my spot in his bed. "Get dressed, too."

"You sure you don't want to stay in my shirt? It really does suit you…and my imagination." He winks, and a bit of the balance shifts back between us to what it was before I opened my stupid mouth.

And when I meet him downstairs, dressed in last night's dress—though I may have slipped his undershirt into my bag as a keepsake—he's completely back to himself, handing me a coffee, the scent of bacon sweetening the air. "Eggs or pancakes?"

"Pancakes, obviously," I say, shaking my head. "Do you know me at all?"

"Every curve, every crevice," he says, tugging me into him for a long, slow kiss. I slide my fingers through his hair, sleek and soft. God, I love the access I have suddenly. He's amazing. And not just his hair. I twist the kiss into something heavier. He slips his hands down to grab my ass, pulling me harder against him. "I do love this dress, but I love it even more when it's off of you."

I could get used to this.

He gives a light growl when he releases me. "Maybe instead of food, I'll have more of you for breakfast."

My stomach does a weird hop/twist/turning thing, but I smile, smugly. "Tempting, but you lost the battle when you mentioned pancakes."

It's true, too. I'm starving.

And I love pancakes.

"We can't tell anyone about this at work." I'm surprised I'm the one who has to say it.

His brows rise in surprise, too, like he hadn't considered it. "There are papers we could sign for HR."

"No." I shake my head. "I don't want a bad reputation." Not this time. Not at this job.

"I don't think you'd get one," he says. "But, for now, we'll keep it our secret." He takes another bite, chewing. I could watch him chew for hours, the way his jaw sharpens, the sensual motion of his lips... He catches me staring—and I don't even care. I slide a slice of syrup-saturated pancake into my mouth, still enjoying his.

"The next few weekends, I'll be gone," he says. "Family stuff. A yearly summit in Palm Beach, not to be confused with a vacation, trust me. Vegas for my brother's bachelor party—not," he says, lifting his brows, "that you have anything to worry about. No strippers. Just gambling."

My mouth quirks. Then falls. "Will Piper be at any of these things?"

He shakes his head. "But she does want to meet you."

Boom. A bomb. Right in my stomach. "You talked to her about me?"

"Right before you came downstairs, actually."

"Why?" Beneath the explosion in my system—or maybe what remains now—is a sort of relief. He told her about me. She wants to meet me.

He wasn't lying about not being engaged.

I believed him—I believed in myself enough to believe him, but this seals it.

"Because I told her it's time to break off the engagement. Because I told her I'm falling into something serious."

CHAPTER THIRTY

HAPPINESS IS A glow beneath my skin, so bright, so light, I'm not sure how my feet stay on the ground. I literally can't remember the last time I felt this way. I'm not even one hundred percent sure happiness is the right word. Charged, maybe. Or passionate.

Flushed is a definite. From my head to my toes and all the spaces in between. Aching, too, for more of Alec. His time. His mind. His tongue...

I even say good morning to my grandparents when I walk into their house. Gramps' baggy eyes widen in shock. Gran stares at me like I'm something on the bottom of her shoe.

Oh well. Don't care.

I don't skip up the stairs, but it's close.

I close my door and spin myself onto my bed, staring at the ceiling, grinning like a fucking idiot.

Oh well. Don't care.

My grandparents start to yell at each other below my room, so I put on my fancy headphones from Alec and dive back into my post-apocalyptic vampires. And then I download a book on persuasive reasoning so I can better help Alec with his investment proposal.

I'm still so happy by the end of the weekend, I actually consider canceling my doctor's appointment. I don't, though. I've been through the cycle enough times to know that the darkness always finds its way through. The anger. The sadness. The…blah.

But when I walk into my early Monday appointment—one I still can't quite believe I have, even being here—I feel like an imposter. It's like being sick—and knowing it'll return, but all the symptoms have disappeared right in time for a visit. What if the doctor doesn't believe me?

Guess that's an answer in itself. She'll see how pissed I get if she doesn't believe me and immediately understand I need help. I bite back a snarky laugh. Who knew my anger could be a failsafe…

A nurse brings me to a shabby yellow room and weighs me on an ancient scale and asks a few questions about my visit. I'm up front with her. "Don't tell me what the scale says. And I'm here because I have anger issues and I want pills to make them go away."

She blinks, her pale blue eyes growing amused. "That's not exactly how it all works, but you're on the right track. Dr. Jones will talk to you about all of it."

Dr. Jones turns out to be a chubby man with a sharp gaze. I thought the picture of Dr. Jones on the network's website showed a woman, but I'm sure I mixed it up. I'm tempted to ask to speak with a woman, but find it difficult to say the words. Which is weird, because usually I have no problem with this sort of thing.

Instead, I stay silent and he begins the appointment, sitting on a stool with a thin laptop on his knees, asking me a series of questions. I answer, shortly but honestly, and eventually I slip into feeling a little more comfortable.

Until he asks if I've ever had thoughts of self-harm or suicide.

For some reason, it pisses me the hell off. "*No*. I have anger problems. I get sad sometimes. But that doesn't mean I'm suicidal."

Compassion crosses his face. Maybe it's been there the entire time. Or maybe it's pity. I can't tell, and that pisses me off, too.

"I'm sorry," he says. "I have to ask. And I also have to ask, if you ever do feel those things—will you promise to call 911 to get help first?"

"Yes," I say. "But it's not going to happen. Growing up with my grandparents… If that was going to happen, it would've happened a long time ago."

He opens his mouth, but I can tell by his expression he reconsiders what he's going to say at the last minute, and instead asks, "Do you ever have thoughts about harming other people?"

God. Enough is enough. "Well, I wanted to stab my dinner date with a fork the other night."

And he makes a fucking note on his little laptop.

"Wait—I'm *kidding*. You get that, right? Sarcasm?"

"I get it." He makes another note.

"What are you typing?"

"Tell me why you're here."

"Tell me what you're typing."

"Notes to make sure I don't leave out details that might be helpful with your treatment."

It's almost physically painful not to roll my eyes. He knows why I'm here. I told them when I made the appointment. I told the nurse who brought me here. But all these annoying notes of his are making me feel like I'm skating on thin ice—and he mentioned a treatment, which is my entire reason for coming. So I go with blunt honesty. "I want a drug to help control my anger… And when I get sad. And the way my thoughts spin at night, keeping me up. Sometimes so much I get stomachaches."

He considers me, thoughtfully. "Sounds like maybe you have some anxiety in the evenings?"

I consider him, blandly. "No shit."

"Anger and sadness are often symptoms of depression," he continues as though I haven't just acted like a total asshole, which makes me feel like an even bigger one.

"Okay," I say, trying to keep my tone kinder. I wish it wasn't so hard. "But what can I take to make it all go away?"

"There are several things you can try before we move on to a medicinal approach. Have you tried other methods?"

"Mood journals? Free counseling?" I wait and when he nods again, I say, "I'm not an idiot. I looked up every possible method available to me without health insurance years ago. I tried journaling—but my handwriting pisses me off. I tried books—but reading's a huge part of what started all of this in the first place. Everything blurs together. Instant anger trigger, believe me. I started going to church for free counseling. Didn't help—they tried to bring religion and prayer into helping me make myself feel better. Not against those things, sometimes I halfway believe in God myself, but they didn't do it for me. I can go on and on here, but I promise—if you name it, I've tried it."

Even right now, having to list these things, having to prove to him that I need something stronger, is making me clench my teeth. I have health insurance now. I want a fucking pill that makes me happy.

He makes another note.

My annoyance roars.

But finally, finally, he says what I've been waiting to hear. "There are medications that can help stabilize moods, but—"

"No buts. I want to try."

"*But*," he says with a small smile. "There's no one stop fix-all solution."

"I get it." I lift a shoulder, not to imply that I don't care, but that I know there isn't anything I can do about what he's said. "But anything will help at this point."

"Okay," he says. "I'll recommend a starting dose of fifty milligrams of Zoloft. It's an antidepressant that helps with anxiety too, which may help you fall asleep easier in the evenings. We can see how you do on that, and go from there."

I've waited so long for this moment it actually takes a few seconds for his words to sink in. And when they do, relief is instant; it punches me right in the tear ducts. I blink away the wetness. "Thank you."

"Don't expect immediate changes," he warns. "And start with half a pill for the first week or so, to give your system time to get used to the drug."

I nod, but think *yeah fucking right*. I'm tempted to take an entire bottle at once.

Then, though, I nod a second time, really agreeing. I want to get better. I should follow his directions.

"The Zoloft will help with many of your symptoms, but I also suggest a mild over-the-counter sleep aid for at least the first few weeks because before the medication begins to help, it can enhance a few of those feelings," he continues. "I also recommend that you set up an appointment with our onsite psychologist, Dr. Reyes."

"Psychologist?" My emotions, previously so happy and forward-moving, rebel, scattering in all directions. "Is this because of the fork-stabbing comment? Because I swear I was joking."

"No." He shakes his head. "It's because an antidepressant will help with much of what you describe, but combining it with therapy will make a world of difference."

"Can't I try the pills first?" I've wanted medication for so long—I thought a primary care physician would be all I needed.

"You took the first step in coming here," he says. "You want to feel better, to get better, right?"

I study a painting on the wall, a sailboat, while contemplating his words. "But a shrink? I'm not good at talking about things."

"You've done fine with me."

I wonder if he'd change his answer if he'd been able to hear my thoughts. "You're a doctor and can't judge me."

"Dr. Reyes is trained to listen even better than I am."

Fuck. He has a point. And maybe pills plus talking will help me figure out how to break out of my own mind sooner.

Because, really, the quicker the fucking better.

Even these thoughts are pissing me off.

Which...just...*why?*

Knowing my feelings are ridiculous makes me furious, which makes my feelings even more ridiculous which... Spiral, spiral, spiral. This shit has to stop.

"Fine," I say. "I'll set up an appointment."

"I can do it on my computer."

"Making sure I don't back out?"

"Making sure it's as easy as possible for you to do this," he counters, tapping away. "She had a cancellation, so she has an opening in half an hour. Can you stay to see her?"

I have the first half of the day off. He doesn't know that. I could say no and walk out with my prescription. But...as tempting as that is, I should probably give this a try. I blow air out through my lips loudly, probably rudely, before I respond. "Fine."

CHAPTER THIRTY-ONE

"TELL ME WHY you're here."
Oh my fucking God. If one more person asks me this... "Because you had an opening."
Dr. Reyes looks at me from her faded leather armchair, her expression annoyingly patient.
I lean on the ratty couch she directed me to sit on. "Because I'm starting antidepressants, and Dr. Jones thought talking to you could help in conjunction with that." This is so uncomfortable. Three times today I've had to say what I want. I've had to share that I have issues and I want to fix them and it makes me feel so fucking weak I want to scream.
"You feel angry a lot, sad sometimes, and anxious when you try to fall asleep." She doesn't make me repeat myself again, and I start to unwind. "You've tried non-medicinal methods in the past and have been unsatisfied with their results."
"Tell me something I don't know." I crack a smile. She smiles wider. I start to like her.
"How about you tell me when these things started to happen? Were they all together, or one at a time?"
This gives me pause as I try to remember. "The anger first, I think? It was forever ago—before high school even... Maybe in

elementary school. I was kicked off my soccer team in middle school for my temper. And again in high school." I sigh. "Feels like I was born pissed off, to be honest. Which might be the case, considering my mother barely stuck around long enough to give birth to me. And ignored every attempt I made to contact her when I found out who she was a few years back." Which is so much more than I meant to say.

She waits for me to go on, and when I don't, she asks, "You were raised by your grandparents?"

Deep breath. "Yep. And they suck. And I'd rather not talk about them."

This time, she doesn't respond when I wait, so I grudgingly add, "Right now, anyway."

She continues to wait, but I can play this game, too. Finally, she says, "Dr. Jones left a note that sometimes when you read, things blur together—and this can be a trigger for your anger?"

"Can be? Try always. And mostly anger. Sometimes attempting to read only a paragraph makes me feel like giving up on everything. Which I know is lame. Which makes me pissed off—or, sometimes, sad… Like, blah. Can't get out of bed. Because I'm too old to still have trouble reading. I mean, I don't have bad eyes or anything. I don't get it."

She asks me a bunch of questions about my reading difficulties—and other things I've always struggled with. I'm halfway furious having to think about it all, and halfway relieved to get it off my chest to someone I won't worry about looking dumb to.

"Imagine," I say. "Just imagine being forced to read the same book every day, but the book's written in… I don't know, Ancient Greek or something. But you don't get it. And nobody explains it in a way that makes it readable, the letters are all squiggly and impossible to capture—yet somehow *everyone* else is moving on to the next level of Ancient Greek and you're not and your teachers are getting irritated and your grandparents don't care at all. So you know what happens? *You get passed up.* To the next level. Where you're someone else's problem. Where you're even more confused.

"Even teachers who tried to be positive were all *you can do it, you can do it.* But no. I really couldn't. So I stopped trying. Because I kept passing. It didn't make a difference. And maybe I wanted someone to pick up on it. Maybe I was *dying* for someone to notice. But that was back then. Now? Now I'm fine. I can read at a functional level. All I want is not to have to think about it anymore." At this point, I'm out of breath and out of steam. Dr. Reyes stands and pours me a cup of water from a pitcher on her desk.

"Anyway," I say, embarrassment making my mouth even drier. It helps that Dr. Reyes doesn't allow any judgment to cross her face. "What does any of this have to do with Zoloft?"

She sits back in her chair, her eyes still assessing me. "Were you ever tested for a learning disability, in high school or before?"

I take a long swallow of water, my face suddenly numb. "Excuse me?"

"The way you describe your difficulties reading, and with note taking, is indicative of a visual perceptive learning disability."

Little trembles, a lot like fear, ripple under my skin. I place the glass on her desk. "In English please?"

"The things you're mentioning, the way you answer my questions, leads me to believe you have a learning disability that affects how you understand information that you take in visually, and, often going hand-in-hand with a visual perceptive discrepancy, a touch of dysgraphia—which affects handwriting ability."

"In dumber English?"

She gives me a chastising look. "You have difficulty processing communication that you see. It's easier for you to hear things."

This.

This finally clicks in.

I'm sure I should find this information upsetting. I'm sure it means I'm dumb...but, amazingly, the corners of my mouth refuse to stay down. Those trembles weren't fear. They're *excitement*. "That would explain a lot."

"I can schedule a formal assessment for you; however, I'm not sure you'd find it extremely beneficial. At this point, there's not a lot the paperwork will do for you—and it can be costly. If you'd like to delve in further we can certainly discuss it."

I shake my head, still smiling. "Just knowing what you think, just understanding there's a reason for the problems I've had..." I trail off before I can say that it's enough, because my throat is tightening and my nose is stinging and my eyes are growing wet. "It's enough."

So many memories swirl through my mind. Frustrated teachers. Books unread; tests failed. Handwritten English assignments with more big fat red Fs across the top because they were unreadable. For years, I tried to convince my teachers I wasn't lazy like they all said. Eventually, I stopped bothering. Let them believe whatever they'd like. I stopped caring...

"You must think I'm weird to be smiling," I continue. "And I'm sure later I'll be doing the opposite, when it sinks in that I'm dumb. But knowing there's something legitimately—*medically*—wrong with me? It's...*freeing*."

"A learning disability doesn't mean you're dumb, Teagan," she says. "I have no doubt you're a capable, intelligent young woman—especially given how you're reacting. All this means is that you process things differently. That you might need different avenues to help you when you need to read something, or write something."

"Like audiobooks?" I ask, thinking of listening to *Dracula* on Friday night, of *The Passage*, of the other books I've listened to ever since Alec set me up with the app for my phone.

"Exactly."

But... "That won't help me at work, though. And, as much as I love listening to stories—I need my job. I want to succeed." Wow. Saying it makes me understand how true it is. I want to succeed. I want to be Denise. Or higher.

"There are tools that will help, though. There are text-to-speech readers available. Or, if you don't have access—increasing font size, say in your email folders, may help. Perhaps you can request a laptop to take notes on at meetings, as your handwriting troubles you."

Imagining it all is...thrilling, to be honest. "Oh God, that would help me so much."

"Because you're an adult, Teagan, for much of this you'll have to be your own biggest advocate. Do you feel comfortable asking your boss, or the HR department, for some of these aids?"

Alec's face flashes through my mind. He's already helped me so much without realizing it. "Yeah, I do."

She nods. "Good. I'll give you a printout before you go, listing some of the available options to consider."

"Does this mean I'm not actually depressed?" I ask. "That I'm just dumb?" I smile wider, so she'll know I'm joking (mostly).

"Not dumb," she repeats, anyway. "But much of what you describe sounds, on the top, like clinical depression. We can delve a little deeper for the rest of the hour. There is frequently a link between the two, learning disabilities and depression. Does depression run in your family?"

The urge to smile is gone. "I don't know my parents, and my grandparents would never admit something like that." And this time, I find myself telling her everything. Never knowing my father. A mother who claims I don't exist and who's returned, unopened, every letter I've ever sent. The words tumble like drunk gymnasts from my mouth, and I let them.

So we talk.

And we talk.

And we talk.

I'm more candid, more *open* with Dr. Reyes than I've ever been with anyone.

We talk about what it means to be realistic and to stay honest with myself. I tell her I'm always honest with myself, not mentioning my mirror reality chats. She says that's good, that I've been helping myself—but when I'm feeling down, I need to be careful not to be too hard on myself.

"Depression can make people see themselves through a distorted lens," she says.

I laugh, a little bitter. "Trust me, I'm way harder on most other people than I am myself. That's a huge part of the reason I'm here. To be nice."

"Are you sure it's not yourself you need to be nicer to first?"

"Aren't you supposed to tell me if that's the case?"

She smiles. "We can determine it together. However, I do have another client scheduled in about five minutes. So perhaps we can start here next time."

"Next time?"

"I'd like to see you once a week," she says. "We can drop the regularity after the first month, but it's beneficial to start therapy with an accelerated frequency at first, especially in combination with medication."

"I would come that often," I say, surprising myself with the truth. "But I started a new job last week. It's half an hour from here, so lunch breaks are out, too." And I know from the office hours listed on their website that they're not open late enough for me to get here after work.

"I understand. But I would like to schedule quarterly check-ins then, will that work?" When I nod, she continues. "And in the meantime, I'd like for you to consider a therapy site called Straight Talk No Jacket."

I laugh at the name and she twists her mouth, admitting she doesn't love it, though the wordplay is clever. She explains it's an online counseling center, where I can speak with licensed therapists via video chat. "They don't take insurance," she warns. "But it's affordable—and sometimes insurance companies will offer reimbursement. I'm happy to write a referral on your behalf."

I can't stop nodding today. It's...weird. I'm used to the opposite. "I'd appreciate it."

And so I walk out of the building a changed girl. A prescription in my pocket. A small amount of understanding for all my years of failure. A sort of hope I'm not sure I've ever encountered before, one that brings a new outlook, a positivity toward the future I *know* I've never had.

Today is going to be a good day. The truth of it is beating with every pump of my suddenly full heart.

CHAPTER THIRTY-TWO

WHEN I GET to work, I walk straight into Alec's office. "You made them give me health insurance, didn't you?"

"Hello to you, too," he says. "I missed you yesterday—why didn't you return my text?"

Because, like a total lame-ass, I couldn't think of a clever response to *Hey kitten*. I was too focused on my looming doctor appointment.

"Tell me." I can't believe I didn't put it together sooner.

"It depends on if you'll be pissed at me or not." He offers a faux-nervous grin, and it makes me laugh.

"Thank you," I say, literally never having meant the phrase more than in this moment. I have pills in my purse. I have my first Straight Talk No Jacket appointment booked for two weeks from now. And actually being *heard* at the doctors' office today—by three different people, no less—makes me more hopeful than...ever. "You seem determined to change my life."

Then, because all of a sudden the air is filled with too much cheesiness for me to allow, I add, "Or maybe I'm still reeling from Friday night."

"You aren't the only one. When I close my eyes, I hear you purring, moaning. I can hear it when you speak now—those perfect little noises are right there waiting to be coaxed out of you."

I open my mouth, but find I'm too self-conscious about my voice to actually speak.

"Jesus, kitten, watching you... You have no idea..." He breaks off, cringing. "Shit. I have a meeting in ten minutes and I'm halfway to wood just thinking about Friday."

"So," I say, grinning, "I shouldn't ask you to remember what it felt like when I had you in my mouth? When my hands were gripping your ass? Your balls? My tongue flickering over you—"

"Teagan," he groans, leaning forward. "If you don't stop, I'm going to break a hole through the bottom of this desk."

"Let's not flatter ourselves, Alec. You're big—but nobody's got that sort of reach."

His laugh booms through the room. "Trust me, kitten. You give me all the reach in the world."

I drag my tongue over my lower lip, loving the way his eyes track the motion. "I'll leave you with this then." I lean over his desk to whisper closer to his ear. "I can still close my eyes and remember your flavor. And I'm desperate for another taste."

I exit his office high from the strangled noise my words force out of him.

And I giggle when he leaves late for his meeting, his expression pointed when he passes my desk.

Sam also shoots me a telling look. "What gives? Seriously. I need to know."

"I got a funny email," is all I say. He rolls his eyes.

I take my first Zoloft the next morning, breaking the small oval pill in half, like Dr. Jones suggested. I know I won't magically be super happy, but a tiny part of me can't help wishing maybe I'll be the first person ever to be affected that way.

All I feel, though, is a little spacey a few hours later. Sleepy—but not so much that it affects my work. Or my ability to flirt with Alec—thank God.

Most of the week passes much in the same way.

Reading long emails still really fucking frustrates me.

Filing still makes me miserable.

And it still takes me literally days to decipher notes I take during meetings. Which pisses me off more than everything else combined. Well, not including the fact that Alec hasn't asked me out again, and I've been too chickenshit to do it myself. It's so much fucking easier to take initiative with people who buy my act than it is with someone who sees through it the way he does. Actually, it's not that he sees through it—he doesn't even let me start the play.

Whatever.

Maybe the pills are kicking in, or maybe it's my own mental state feeling relieved because I'm at least taking pills that will help, but even when I'm pissed off, I only snap at Sam like fifty percent of the time.

Alec's out of town for the weekend—so I spend most of it in my room, listening to books and maybe, possibly, starting to fall for my boss for real. Because he gave me books. He gave me health insurance. He didn't run away from my crazy. Any guy who does all that seems like he'd be worth loving. At least a little.

Or maybe it's specifically because he's Alec. All I have to do is picture his face, imagine the timbre of his laugh, the weight of his hands on my body, and I start to melt. My body's ready for another interaction with his—so much so that I'm constantly in a state of anticipatory tingling—but he pushes on my heart, too, making it feel swollen beneath my ribs. His presence is there, on the sides of my neck that tighten when I can't fight a smile. In the tapping of my fingers when I'm counting down the hours until I see him again. Through my mind in the late hours of the night, while I toss and turn.

By Monday morning, it's clear. I've got it bad.

That sneaky motherfucker snuck his way into more than something physical, into feelings that travel under my skin like a lifeline. I'd give him a piece of my mind about it, if only I could stop grinning long enough to do it.

The next week, we're slammed.

Well, Alec is slammed. It's business as usual for me and Sam. But Alec is in constant meetings and out of the office half the time, and I hate it. I keep waiting for him to ask me out again.

I keep telling myself *I'm* going to ask *him*.

I keep chickening out.

Miss you, kitten, he texts me toward the end of the week, while I know he's meeting with his father.

Who is this again? I respond, smiling.

Don't act like I haven't heard you purr, he sends back. And a second later: *Can't tell you how much I'm dying to do it again.*

Oh, this must be Alec. Sorry. Hard to keep track of all my suitors.

You better be joking.

And if I'm not?

Sam snatches my phone out of my hands, and I whirl around in my chair. "Give that back."

"No. No way." He dances away from me, holding my phone out of reach. "You have a secret—and I know Alec's involved. If you won't spill it... I'll have to dig for it myself."

I'm up and in his face without thinking about doing it. "Give me my fucking phone."

"Teagan—come on."

"Ask me for my stories," I hiss, "and I might give them to you. But don't you take my shit. Don't you go digging where you have no right. *Give me my fucking phone.*"

Someone clears their throat, and I turn, realizing we've made a bit of a spectacle for the rest of the office. People are staring, people are smirking, people are avoiding my gaze. And good for them, too, because I'm ready to fucking roast anyone I catch looking.

"I was only joking." Sam shoves my phone into my hands, as the rest of the office begins to filter back into their regular routine. "I wouldn't really go through your phone."

"How the hell would I know that?" I ask, softening my tone when I notice how red his face is.

I...have issues with my privacy. Probably something to discuss with my therapist. But all I had growing up were my secrets. My life. I could share it with whom I chose—a select few people, and mostly just Cassidy. Sometimes Jason, but never all the way.

In fact, Alec knows me better already than anyone else ever has. I can't decide if that's sad, or if it means something more.

I sigh and walk to Sam's desk. "Here." I drop my phone in front of him, text messages opened. Alec's most recent one reading, *You're my only one if that makes a difference.*

"You're his only what?" He scrolls up through the conversation. "Suitor?" He glances at me, his eyes wide. "Okay, first of all, who the hell even uses that term anymore?"

"Don't be a dick. I couldn't think of what else to call it."

"Date. Boyfriend. Paramour. *Lover.*" He ticks off his fingers as he names all the words. So annoying. "Pick one. This is not the 1800s, Teagan."

I snatch my phone from him. Again. "And this is why I don't tell you things." It's why I don't tell most people things.

"Don't be all huffy," he says. "The more important thing here is—"

"*Huffy?* Now who's using outdated terminology?"

"Point made." He grins, but only for a moment. "But what about his fiancée?"

"Wipe that judgment from your tone," I say, quietly, glancing out to make sure nobody's paying us attention. "It's not what you think."

"You're not sleeping with him?"

"Well, no. But also, his situation with Piper... It's not my call to share, but..." What am I doing? I wanted to open up to Sam, but I can't do it by giving away a secret that isn't mine to share. "You know what? Forget it. I can't talk about it."

"No way. You have to dish, Teagan."

"This isn't some fucking reality TV show drama for you to sit back and munch popcorn with."

"Let me rephrase." He scratches his lower lip, hard enough I'm nervous he'll draw blood. "I'm in a huge fight with Ty, and I could use a distraction. And as *bitchy* as you are, for some reason I kind of like you, and I wouldn't mind getting to know you past that annoying exterior."

He's eighteen and talks like he's thirty. And I don't know whether or not his words piss me off. "Is this where I punch you or where I hug you?"

"How about don't touch me at all," he says. "You scare me."

A laugh expands in my throat, throwing itself from my lips. But it barely cracks a dent in his wounded expression, and I add more sedately, "Tell me what happened with the boy-toy."

Apparently, Ty doesn't want Sam to meet his parents. Which Sam would be fine with—except it's because Ty doesn't want to introduce a guy to them until he knows things are serious.

Sam's been under the impression they've been serious for months.

"Oh, honey," I say, wanting to cross the space between our desks again, but holding back because I know better than anyone what it's like to not want the pity that comes with physical comfort. "He's a moron."

"Too bad that doesn't make me want him any less than before." Sam stares at his computer screen, but I'm pretty sure his world's too bitter right now to take in much of what he sees.

"What are you going to do?"

He drops his face into his hands, smearing his words. "I don't know."

I mentally run over my bank account, knowing the balance down to the penny. I get paid tomorrow, which means I can splurge today. Or, at least, offer to buy the kid a meal. "How about I take you out to lunch, and you can tell me more—or not. Whatever. But let's get out of here, get some fresh air, get some—"

"Okay." His smile trembles when he looks at me, and he seems so young, so innocent. He's not that much younger than I am, but at the moment it feels like we're eons apart. Or maybe it's because he's wearing his emotions across his face and I keep mine trapped in my teeny, tiny heart.

I wish I hadn't been such a bitch to him before this.

I wait for self-loathing to set in, for anger to snap in my veins—and it *does* happen, but…it's muted. My mind manages to box up the self-loathing, pushing it away, and my blood quickly reduces to easy waves instead of tsunamis. Easy to ignore.

My smile doesn't tremble at all.

I wear it all the way up to when Alec strides toward us, his shoulders tense, his arms tight at his sides. He greets us, but his words are as stiff as his body language. Granted, his eyes soften when they land on me, but he doesn't linger, heading instead into his office, shutting the door slowly, with so much control I can tell it costs him.

Sam's chair squeaks when he swivels toward me. "Need a rain check on lunch?"

I'm already standing. "Give me ten minutes."

"Take as long as you need. I don't have much of an appetite anyway."

"We'll fix that," I tell him. And then I step into Alec's office.

CHAPTER THIRTY-THREE

INSTEAD OF SITTING behind his computer, Alec's slumped in a chair at the table in the corner, tapping—slamming—a pen up and down and up and down on the table. His suit jacket's strewn across his desk. His leg's jumping so hard the table's shaking.

"What's wrong?" I cross to him, intending to take a seat next to him, but he grabs my wrist, fast as a snake, and yanks me into his lap. "Alec!"

"What?" His question is surly, his tone raw. His thighs tense beneath me when he shoves his chair back further from the table. "The glass is frosted. Nobody can see us."

"They might be able to see one blurred shape at the table now, instead of two," I say, struggling—and failing—to escape from his arms.

"Nobody's paying that close attention. If you want me to stop, tell me. Otherwise, let me fucking touch you. I need to fucking touch you." He sinks his teeth into my earlobe, clamping a hand down on my thigh, forceful enough to make me jolt.

Deep down in my belly.

"HR probably frowns on this," I say, while also giving in, turning my face toward him and leaning back against his shoulder. "Did the meeting go badly?"

"You could say that." He pushes his nose into my neck and when he lifts his face he trails his tongue along my skin.

I shiver. Hard. And a longing unfurls between my legs, so full, so strong I'm tempted to widen them, to see what he does. But he's unhappy. And he's not getting out of talking this easily. I keep my legs where they are. "Upset client?"

I can't imagine that's it, though. A dissatisfied client wouldn't have Alec so tense his ab muscles are practically concrete against my back. That wouldn't have his shoulders so rigid it's a wonder he's not bursting through his shirt.

"Bullheaded father," he says. He's quiet for a moment, staring past me, but his thoughts swirl through his expression, so I wait for him to settle on the ones he wants to share. When he does, his words come out spiked as hammered nails. "He turned down my proposal again. And was pissed I don't want to let it go."

"Why didn't you tell me you were meeting him about that?" I ask, shock mingling with annoyance in my tone, in my gut.

"I wanted to tell you when I'd done it. Made it happen on my own." He works his jaw, his expression angry—but not with me. It costs him, I can tell, to admit defeat.

And his reasoning helps to melt my annoyance. "I'm sorry."

"I was captain of my lacrosse team in high school. Undergrad, too. President of my fraternity my sophomore and junior years—and my business fraternity now. In almost every aspect of my life, I'm a *leader*. I take charge. Yet my family... Jesus. I can't believe how much I roll aside to give them what they want. I've done everything my father's ever asked of me, everything Grandfather's ever demanded. A puppet, dancing whichever way they pull my strings. Pathetic."

I cover his hand with my own, needing a connection, hoping the contact will push the truth of my words into him. "Not pathetic. At all. And if they aren't pleased with how hard you work to make them proud, maybe it's time to cut some of those strings."

"Funny," he says, squeezing my fingers. "I was thinking the same thing. There are other investors I can go to."

"Or, you could talk with Mr. Evans," I remind him. "If the two of you joined forces on this, your dad would have to listen. He respects you both."

"He respects Brad, yes. Me? Not so much." There's not a single thread of self-pity in Alec's tone. Only a dry sort of acceptance.

I start to hate his father. But not everyone's family is as fucked up as my own. Maybe he deserves the benefit of the doubt, for a little while longer, anyway. "Maybe he'll respect you more if you don't give up."

"Maybe," Alec says. "But it's not only the proposal he's upset with me about."

"What happened?"

"You." He says the word so simply it takes a moment for my breath to disappear from my lungs.

"You told him about—"

"No." He shakes his head, nuzzling it against the side of my neck in a way that's probably meant to reassure me, but doesn't. "I mean you make me want to cut some strings, Teagan. But I've needed to cut them for a long time anyway."

"Okay...?"

"I told him Piper and I are ending the pretense of our engagement. He had opinions about it. Insistent opinions. He wants me to wait. Says it'll be bad for business right now. Says..." The size of the breath he takes pushes his chest against my back. "It doesn't matter."

It does, though. Discomfort rolls through my stomach like lava. "He has a point. It's stupid to throw away something that benefits your families on a whim. We've barely known each other a month."

But instead of looking relieved that I'm giving him an out—his expression darkens. "You're kidding, right?"

"Alec, I—" I freeze when he slides his hand up my leg, pushing my thighs apart. I tighten my hand on his to keep him tame—but he's a million times stronger than I am and drags both our hands under my skirt until he's cupping me against my underwear. Until *I'm* cupping his hand, while he cups me against my underwear.

"Um..." I can't remember how to breathe, how to say no, or why I'd even want to.

"This is not a whim. *You* are not a whim." He lays his palm flat against me, holding it still, heat transferring from his hand to my body. I start to pull my hand off of his—but he grabs it, covering it with his own, and presses it back against me. Pressing me...against myself.

I will not squirm. I will *not* squirm. "You can't know that."

"Yes," he says, curving his finger—and mine—over my panties, making me, damn it, squirm, "I can."

"How?" I mean to sound derisive, but he's using my own finger to tap out a rhythm beneath my skirt, and the word comes out in a whimper instead.

Tap, tap, tap. He leans closer to me, the pressure increasing, his mouth directly next to my face. "Because..." he says. *Tap, tap, press.* "You've been the first thing on my mind every morning since I met you."

Tap, tap, slap.

Oh my God.

I should tell him it's the same for me. He deserves to know.

But I can't make the words come.

"Show me what you like, kitten," he says softly in my ear. "Teach me how to touch you."

I swallow past the rise of nerves in my throat, past the flutters of excitement. "You've already proved yourself an A-plus student."

"This time I want a guide." He slides his thumb beneath the edge of my underwear, lifting it from my skin. "Show me."

"I can't." But there's an electric spark striking under my hesitation, telling me not to stop. I like this, touching myself for him.

"You can." He pushes against my hand and I let him, both our fingers creeping beneath my underwear. I'm wet already, no surprise, and *aching*.

"Alec," I beg. I always beg with him. For things I can't name. Somewhere in the back of my mind it annoys me, but the rest of my body's too turned on to care.

He reverses our hand positioning again, sliding his beneath mine. "Show me."

He's begging, too.

I can't believe I'm fucking doing this. What if someone walks in?

I twist my neck toward him to ask, but change my mind at the last minute, capturing his mouth with my own in a sharp, biting kiss, pulling at his lower lip with my teeth.

"I like this," I murmur, deciding on the spot to fucking go for it.

I press his finger, one, then two, into me.

"And this." I press his palm against me, showing him the pressure I like best. "Hard. Like this."

"You're so wet, so warm," he says, his voice rough. "So fucking sweet. You have no idea what that does to me, feeling you respond to me."

"Maybe I'm responding to *me*."

"Even fucking better." He picks up the pace, the pressure, the...everything, making my hips roll forward, so I can press myself harder against his fingers—against *our* fingers— moaning. "Shh," he teases. "Can't be too loud in here, kitten."

He tugs my skin, pulling it apart, and when he masters the rhythm I best respond to, he takes it on solo because I'm beginning to shake so hard, I need both hands to grip the table in front of us.

He shoves my underwear all the way to the side, dragging his fingers across me at the same time, making me gasp. The air hits me coolly and then his hand is back against me, and I swear to God I want to weep at the tumbled, erotic mix of sensations.

"Do I have it right, then?" He hooks one finger into me, sliding it, twisting it, hitting my spot—and new ones that turn my gasp into another moan. And another. And another.

He bites my mouth this time and yanks on my tongue with his teeth, pulling back with a pleased little smile, forceful enough to travel fluidly through me, a lightness twining with all the heat.

He's grown hard beneath me, pressing through his pants. When I shift my hips directly over him, he shudders and grabs my hip with his free hand, shoving me more roughly against him. "The things you make me want to do..."

"The things I want to let you do," I say. Grinding, grinding, while his fingers never stop fondling me, pushing into me, slipping along my slick skin.

The air is syrupy between us, weighty and fluid and sweet, and when he flattens his palm against me—pressing down harder, harder, pushing in another finger, deeper, deeper—I tingle so powerfully it's almost painful, and my head loses a battle with gravity, falling back to rest on his shoulder.

He lets go of my hip to rub his hand up my stomach, over my breasts, caressing, squeezing, tugging at my nipples until they're tight and sticking out through the thin fabric of my bra, of my shirt.

"You like this?" he asks, and when I nod, biting back the volume of the moan building in my throat, he captures my chin and tugs my face toward him. "I want to watch your face when you come."

The warmth of self-consciousness floods my cheeks, but it's nothing compared to the heat between my legs, and I don't look away. I bite my lower lip, my hips rocking, his wrist twisting.

We're in his office. We're supposed to be *working*. He's fucking me with his fingers so hard I can't keep from crying out.

This is so wrong.

I fucking love it.

He watches my face, his own so smugly intent it's almost enough to drop me over the edge. But it's more than his expression... It's this entire moment.

It's electrifying. And not because we aren't supposed to do this here.

It's this thing between us—between his hand and my body, between my heart and his mind; it's all connected and it *sizzles*. My breath is coming in little moans. My eyes close and my head starts to roll again, but he yanks my chin back in place, the short, demanding motion tipping me over the edge.

I've never been held so captive; I've never been regarded with such warmth.

His eyes are bright and determined. His fingers are quick and hard and demanding.

My body is trembling out of my control, and goose bumps rise along the base of my collarbone, a whirlwind sensation whipping through my body, spinning so fast I lose my breath.

"Look at *me*." He tightens his grip on my face, and when I open my eyes he's staring at me so intensely, my belly constricts and releases so fast, with such a physical blow, a cry that's more like a pleasured sob escapes my mouth.

And then it's not just my stomach pulsing. It's everything, everywhere. An orgasm funnels through me, taking up the space where my stomach used to be and slamming me lower, lower, until my legs squeeze shut around his hand, which he never stops moving.

His fingers nimble and fast, exploring me, his thumb pressing, pressing, smearing me in circles, while he whispers, "Fuck, that's it, Teagan, let it go, let it go," until I do. As quietly as I can, which is to say, not that quietly at all.

He releases my chin, sliding his hand up my face and into my hair, yanking my head to the side to capture my neck with his mouth and his foresty scent invades my senses, intensifying everything.

His fingers don't stop, tugging, piercing, twisting until there's not an inch of me left unexplored and then he starts again a second time, a third, and pressure like a deluge beats first in my chest then floods into my belly.

"Good girl," he growls, and I go completely under, lost, lost to the final crash of the orgasm. I squeeze my eyes closed—and, *oh God*, my mouth, to prevent any overly loud moaning—and it's like there's an entire ocean inside my body, whipping through me to the rhythm of his fingers in wild, biting, pleasure-filled waves, crashing, *swelling* through me.

Eventually, it slows, flowing more like water pushed by a breeze, lighter, lighter, until all that's left is a hollow, glowing memory of the motion that rocked me only moments ago.

Even still, I tremble.

Tremble.

Tremble.

CHAPTER THIRTY-FOUR

WHEN I FINALLY open my eyes, the light of the office somehow shocks me.

And then...

I nearly slide right off Alec's lap.

He locks his arms around me, keeping me from slamming into the table.

Holy hell *I may never be able to walk again.* My limbs are made of liquid, sloshing everywhere. I wonder if people heard me come. I tried so hard to stifle myself, but... I glance out at the office, but everything's so blurred I can't tell if anyone's looking.

"That was so fucking hot," he says a second (minute, year, century—who knows, who cares?) later, pulling me tighter against him.

"My clumsy ass?" I ask.

"The way you drenched my hand and moaned my name," he says, tossing a big ball of heat right back between my legs, holy hell.

"Oh... That..." I slowly, subtly pull my underwear across my still-exposed skin, doing my best—and failing—not to shiver in the process. When I'm covered, I stand, turning to face him, the table at my ass. Guess I can stand after all. But what I can't do is find the right words to respond with.

He runs his palms up my thighs, over my skirt this time. Which is a bit of a letdown—although I doubt I could handle a second round. He smirks, knowing exactly what I'm thinking. "If I thought you could handle another go, I'd bring you back to my lap. There's nothing I'd like more than getting to keep my hands on you—in you, the entire day. Fuck. I want you, Teagan. In every way. I want you."

I shiver again. And then... *Why?* I almost ask. Because I don't get it. But I'm still glowing, and I don't want to burst this bubble. "You want me...on my knees?"

"Stop." The word is quiet and deafens me all the same. "Don't purposefully twist my meaning into something less."

"I'm saying—"

"This is why I've worked so hard to keep my hands off of you recently." He stands, too, stepping away from me, toward his desk. "Don't you wonder why I haven't invited you back over?"

"Maybe." Yes. "Don't you wonder why I haven't asked *you* over?"

"I know why you haven't. It's for the same reason."

"Which is?"

He sweeps his jacket off his desk and shrugs it on, making the everyday motion sexy as hell. "Because, sweet Teagan, *I* know what this is between us. But I can't have you, not in my house, not in my bed, until *you* know it, too."

"I know what this is," I say.

"Tell me."

But I can't make the words come. Maybe I don't have the answer. Maybe I'm scared. Instead, I twist the silver picture frame on his desk... It's a toddler. Cute little girl. "Um. Do you have a kid?"

I don't know why the thought shocks me so much—but his expression drops down to something dark and he shakes his head. "That was my sister as a child."

"You have a sister?"

"Had." He closes his mouth and tells me more with his eyes than anything else that the conversation is closed as well.

"I'm sorry," I say, my heart twisting, an autumn leaf dropping from my chest, falling, falling.

"You still haven't told me what this is," he says.

I search his expression, but it's calmly unreadable.

"See," he says when I hesitate. "You can't."

I'm not sure which is more frustrating, my inability to articulate what it is between us, or his annoying determination to make me. "Why does it matter so much?"

"Pride, maybe," he admits with a shrug. "I want all of you, Teagan. Your body. Your mind. Your heart. And until you're ready, I don't want to take the risk." I open my mouth, but he speaks again first. "And let's clear the air about it because I know you won't tell me if you're thinking it—I'm not talking about sex."

"What if I want to talk about sex?" Because, suddenly, I do. "What if I want to do more than talk about it?"

"What if I want to invite you to my brother's wedding?"

"What if you didn't avoid my questions?"

"What if you said yes to mine?"

"Come on," I say, exasperation pushing my tone into something sharper than I intend. "Your dad's pissed that you want to break it off with Piper. You think he's going to allow your *receptionist* on your arm at your brother's wedding? When is it?"

"My assistant, not that it matters. Next weekend—and who cares about my dad?"

"Next weekend? Are you nuts?" Even if this were a good idea, I can't find a dress that fast. And, more importantly, "*I* care. And I'm pretty sure deep down you do, too."

He strides toward me and grabs my hands. "That's the thing. I don't. I've spent my entire life coasting along the path they chained me to. But I'm changing. *This* is changing me. And they need to know they can't control me anymore."

"I don't want to be used as a slap in your family's face."

"You're not a slap to them—you're a prize, a treasure, for me. I want to see you all dolled up and spend the night imagining what you're wearing underneath. I want to dance with you, to watch you whirl on my arm, and to catch you, all night. I want to taste the champagne toast still on your tongue when I kiss you."

It makes my head spin, everything he's describing. "God, what are you? A poetry major?"

"Don't snark your way out of this."

"Don't fill my head with fairy tales. I'm not your Cinderella."

"No. You're a kitten with a mighty roar." There's not a trace of mockery in his tone. I'm not sure how he does it. "Fuck Cinderella. This is our own story."

"*Fuck Cinderella*? Now you've gone too far." I try to smile, but it falls limply across my lips, dissolving into something closer to a frown. I'm...dazzled. He's stunned me with this sudden bout of intensity. "I'm not going."

"Because you don't want to—or because you're scared of my father?"

"Does it matter?"

"To me? Yeah."

"I don't want to get fired. Getting in the middle of a family battle when your father runs this company? It's not smart."

He laughs, a bitter sound, and trails the backs of his fingers down my jaw. "Don't you get it, Teagan? This thing between us? It guarantees you won't get fired. My father'd be setting himself up for such a huge lawsuit."

And immediately, I see it. If Alec tells his father about me—I'll keep my job.

For the *worst* possible reason.

The lava, long settled in my stomach from earlier, erupts in flames. "I don't want to blackmail my way into keeping my job." I slap his hand away, the sound ringing through the room. "And I'm pretty fucking offended that you think I would."

His sigh's so heavy, it sounds like it's attached to the weight of the world. "Do you hear yourself?"

"Do you?"

"Give me a little more credit." He laughs again, as sharp as the last time, but not as harsh. "We both know you'd never do that."

"Then why would you mention it at all?" I don't know what to do with my hands. He's standing here in front of me, one hand in his pocket, all casually cool, and I'm looking up at him like, I don't even know what. A moron. "Back up, would you? I can't think with you this close."

He lifts an amused eyebrow, taking a step back, and with distance between us I really do find it easier to sort through my thoughts.

"Thank you." I offer the words grudgingly.

"My remark about my father had everything to do with my frustrations with him and absolutely nothing to do with you." He reaches for my hand, stopping an inch short until he sees the permission in my expression. "Will you at least consider saying yes?"

As if any girl could resist the way he weaves his fingers through my hand, so gently—after I know how rough he can be with them? After very specific parts of my body are still halfway on fire from the way he hammered them against me?

"Will Piper be there?"

"Her whole family will be—but I can ask her to stay home. She might appreciate the time away from her family, away from mine..."

"No." I wait to feel nervous over attending the same event as Piper and her family, but I don't. Probably because I won't be going. "I thought we agreed to keep this secret—bringing me to a wedding kinda blows any sort of cover."

This stalls him. "I want to say I don't care, because for me, I don't. But I don't want to make things uncomfortable for you."

"Thank you," I say, annoyed at the disappointment running through me. He's being considerate. I should appreciate it.

But I don't.

He grins a cocky grin, like he can read it in my expression, though I'm trying so hard to keep it blank. "You want to go."

I do. I really do. "No, I don't."

"Say yes," he says, all demanding.

"I'll think about it," is all I'll promise, letting my gaze wander the office to avoid the pressure to give in.

"I get what I want, you know. Might as well say yes now." His smirk widens when I scowl at him. It'd be annoying if it didn't bring out his dimples. If it didn't fit the features of his face perfectly, all angles and smooth skin.

"I'll *think* about it." I turn to leave because I'm discovering that sometimes being near Alec, speaking with Alec, touching Alec, stirs things in me too...*full* to handle. I need space. Before I exit, I glance back. "But don't get your hopes up."

It's a weird thing, though, that my own hopes are raised. Not sure why. But the moment I step out of Alec's office, I'm buoyant.

All the way through lunch with Sam—who didn't seem to hear anything from Alec's office, or is too polite (or scared) to mention that he did.

All the way through the rest of the day.

All the way home, and even after that for a while, too.

"It's because he's totally falling for you," Cassidy tells me later, on the phone, her voice annoyingly confident.

I search for a way to argue against her point, but come up blank. "Shit. I mean, I wouldn't say he's *falling* for me. But he cares for me. Enough to upset his family by bringing me to his brother's wedding. You're right."

"Wouldn't be the first time."

"Keep telling yourself that." I scratch at a piece of chipped paint on my ancient cheap-o desk, the small familiar thrill when it lifts from the wood mingling with the much, much bigger thrill of the realization that Cassidy has a point.

"Doesn't change the fact that I can't go."

"Oh, come on. You know you want to go."

I roll my eyes hard enough she might actually see me through the phone. "No shit. But I don't want to lose my job—*or* keep it because I spread my legs for Alec." My stomach literally rolls with my words. I hate cheapening what's between us. "Not that that's all it is," I say, quickly.

"I *knew* it. You're totally into him, too."

"Whatever." Suddenly I feel like the exposed piece of my desk, her words scraping at the cheap paint I usually cover myself with. "That's not the point."

"No, but it's *a* point. And a pretty big one, too."

"You're not helping."

"Go to the wedding," she says. "It'll be huge and fancy and perfect. How can you pass that up?"

"You mean how can someone like me, from the slums, pass up the opportunity for a ritzy evening?" My tone would slice a lesser person into millions of slivers. Not Cassidy, though. I have no doubt she's rolling her eyes almost as hard as I was a second ago.

"You're impossible."

"So are you." A smile works its way through my tone, because she's driving me nuts—but I don't want to rip her head off like I usually do. "Anyway. Where are you off to this weekend?" She travels almost every weekend for her travel blog.

"Uh..." She pauses for a moment, probably in shock because I neglected to blow up at being called impossible. I can't blame her. I'm a little surprised myself. "New York, there's a small indie film festival right outside the city."

Part of me wants to tell her about the Zoloft. She'd want to know. But she'd also be *too* happy for me. And as much as I love her, I'm not ready to come clean. About that, or the learning disability, or...being a virgin. Still, when she asks, so casually, about how Alec measures up in bed, I can't lie to her.

"I'm keeping this one to myself" is all I say, fighting a wave of irritation that she'd ask like that. Like sleeping with Alec would ever be some easy offhanded thing to do or talk about. This irritation surprises me. It's my fault she doesn't know sex is a big deal for me. I'm the one who spent years letting her think—*leading* her, and everyone else, to think—I bang basically anything that moves. Funny, at one point I felt like it gave me so much power.

It no longer makes sense to me. All I feel is regret for not being happy with myself as I was.

"You have it *so* bad," she says.

This time, I don't deny it. I'm done lying about my romantic life. Right now. But I move the conversation on to other things because I'm not ready to come all the way clean about everything else. Not yet.

When we hang up, I still don't know what to say about the wedding. I stare at my ceiling the rest of the night, conflict eating up all the space in my brain that's otherwise become reserved for listening to books.

In the morning, I know what I'm going to do.

CHAPTER THIRTY-FIVE

I'M NOT GOING to the wedding.

I don't want to risk my fledgling career. Denise came to mind a few times during the night—how powerful she is, how efficient, how she runs meetings without breaking a sweat—and if I fuck it up with Alec's family, I may never get to be her.

Hell, I may never get to be her regardless, but I don't want to stack the odds higher against me.

I can't go. What I can do, though, is revel in how hard Alec tried to convince me to change my mind yesterday.

I mean, he really tried to change my mind.

And told me he wanted me.

Like, not just in bed. Which—even if that was all—would still be more than anyone's seen in me in a long time. But he wants more.

And he can have it.

He thinks I don't know what this is, but I do now. I get it.

I leave my room, ready for work, with this grin that my facial muscles are growing all too familiar with. The Alec-inspired grin. Both annoying and wonderful.

He'll be pissed when I tell him no, but I'm not worried. Because he cares for me—enough not to end things over my decision. What's one missed social event? And, plus, maybe I'll sweeten my answer with…a trip down south, under his desk.

Yum.

My breath skips a few beats, imagining it. I want him in my mouth.

I want him in my life.

And instead of scaring me, this *thrills* me.

Enough to have me practically hopping down the hallway to the stairs—I mean, obviously I don't hop, but still. I haven't even had the urge to do so since…elementary school?

That urge to skip disappears real fast, though, when I get to the stairs.

Because Gramps is lying at the bottom of them, prostrate.

Panic chainsaws through my throat, but I breathe past it. He probably got drunk last night, couldn't make it up the stairs and passed out there.

But the rationalization doesn't keep me from sprinting down the stairs, splinters scouring my palm against the bannister.

"Gramps?" I nudge his face. Nothing. I shake his shoulder with enough force to bruise him, turning him onto his back. Nothing.

"What the hell are you doing?" Gran says angrily from the steps behind me. I didn't hear her approach, but she doesn't startle me. I'm too numb in the moment. This can't be happening.

I slap Gramps' face…

And he wakes up like a fucking caged animal, yelling and thrashing—and nailing me right in the damn cheekbone. So hard my ears ring.

"Goddamn it, Teagan." My grandmother's words float to me like they're filtering through cotton.

I shake my head. "What?"

He's on his feet now, bellowing and still swinging and staggering to the couch, falling over the armrest and snoring immediately.

I'm numb on the inside.

Not the outside though. My cheek hurts like a bitch.

"Frozen peas in the freezer if you're going to complain." Gran's voice comes through clearer this time from her perch above me in the stairwell.

I spin toward her, spitting, "Did I say anything?"

"I see you rubbing your face, like a timid old man could actually do any damage." She's looking at me like I'm a piece of trash, and the steel in her tone is stronger than any compactor.

Thankfully, I'm used to it. "He fucking clocked me. No shit I'm rubbing my face. It hurts."

"See? Complaining." She pats her hip, probably for her pack of smokes, forgetting she's in her nightgown. "If you'd left him alone, your face wouldn't be smarting now."

I blink. I blink again.

I blink like the wipe of my eyelids on my eyes will somehow cover my ears as well. "Are you kidding?"

"You know what he's like when he's drunk."

"Yeah, he's an idiot. Clumsy. Not violent." I've never been hit before. No matter what else my grandparents have done to make me miserable, they've never been physically abusive.

Five more months. I have to hold on for five more months, when I'll have saved enough to be comfortable on my own.

But... I can't keep waiting.

Maybe it's the Zoloft. Maybe I'm changing at my core anyway. Maybe it's a combination—but whatever it is, I'm looking around the place I've always grudgingly called home, with fresh eyes. Peeling paint. Stacks of cigarette butts shoved in ashtrays on end tables that wobble next to sagging furniture. The hole in Gramps's sock and his disgusting yellowed toenail sticking out of it. Not that I didn't notice how gross this place was before, but for the first time, it's too much to stand. Getting out is more pressing than saving money.

"How have we lived like this for so long? It's vile." The question is more for me than her, because I can't believe I have.

Saving money is a valid reason, but maybe it's not the room I'm seeing with fresh eyes. Maybe it's the truth in my heart. Saving money is also an excuse to stay in place. And it's not cutting it anymore.

She pats her hip a second time and grunts, shoving past me and grabbing an old butt from a side table, lighting it. "Don't you insult the roof I've kept over your head. You're no better than we are."

"Yes," I say, allowing this truth to sink all the way in—for me, for her—before I continue. "I am."

"Get out of my house." She points toward the door.

A bitter laugh escapes my mouth. "That's it, though, isn't it? This is your house. Never mine. Never a home."

"Show some gratitude," she says, sneering so hard I can't figure out how the cigarette's not falling from her lips. "We took you in when—"

"Nobody else wanted me," I recite tartly. This line's been thrown at me so many times it's on permanent repeat in the back of my mind most days. Louder on the bad ones. "Why are you such a nasty person? Why are both of you this way? What did I ever do to deserve this?"

You were born, I hear her thoughts as loudly as if she speaks them. *You were born and your mother—the one person we actually loved—left because of it.*

But we don't talk out loud about my mother here, and so she doesn't say the words. And if she has another response, I don't stick around for it. "I am better than you," I repeat, walking to the door. And, before I close it on my way out, I add, "Or, at least I'm on my way."

It takes a few moments on the road until I notice how hard my hands are shaking. It takes longer than that to figure out exactly what it is I'm feeling.

Fury.

Reckless with it, I text Alec at a red light. *You want to use me to slap your family, go ahead. I'm in for the wedding.* Because I'll be using the event to slap my grandparents too. Fuck them for thinking I'm not good enough. God. Fuck everyone.

Let's skip over the part where I remind you I'm not using you as a slap to where I tell you I'm thrilled you've accepted my invitation. I'll be smiling my entire flight to Vegas.

Right. His brother's bachelor party. He won't be at work today.

I'm taking off today since you aren't there.

A pause, and then: *Playing hooky while the boss is gone. I like it.*

Shit's not always about you. I hit send and then hate myself for it.

He calls me and I clear it, because what the hell can I say after that?

He calls me again and I answer because I know. "I'm sorry."

"What's wrong, kitten?" His tone is low and tender enough to make a sliced onion cry.

Not me, though. "Fight with my grandmother. Pretty sure she

threw me out. Pretty sure I was leaving either way."

"Go to my place. I'll have Matthew give you a key."

"Um…" My mind circles his words like a vulture. His huge condo. I can see myself there. It's tempting. It's too tempting. "No. I have somewhere else I can stay." Probably.

"You sure? I kind of enjoy the thought of you in my place. In my bed. In my T-shirt again…"

Don't pass up such a golden opportunity, my mom's voice invades my conscience. So I say, "Have a good trip. I'll see you Monday," and I hang up before he can say anything else.

Before *she* can say anything else.

CHAPTER THIRTY-SIX

CASSIDY'S IN NEW YORK, and even if she wasn't, I don't want to stay with her. I can't be surrounded by the echoes of Jason without going crazy. Also, I'm pretty sure Mr. Evans is disappointed in me for going out with Alec.
    It's Vera's place I drive to. She likes her sleep, so I doubt she has any classes scheduled this early. I'm assuming I'll catch her before she leaves. I huff it up the stairs to her apartment, and I lift my hand to knock right as the door opens and I find myself face to face with a brown-haired guy who looks familiar, but I can't place him.
    "Oh. Hello," he says, his tone as surprised as his expression.
    "Slinking out at eight a.m.," I say, giving him the look that feels right at home across my face. Disgust. "Classy act, dude."
    He cocks his head to the side, his own expression cooling. "Actually—"
    "*Teagan.*" Vera walks up behind him in tiny pajamas. "Quit it with the third degree." She slides a kiss on his cheek from behind, gently prodding him out the door, past me. "Have fun in New York, Jeff."
    His eyes slide over me when he turns to take one last look at her. "See you when I get back?"
    "Call me." Her smile's wide, but it doesn't reach her eyes.

Then he's gone and she's ushering me inside and I'm watching her cute little butt in these shorts tinier than underwear and wishing, not for the first time, I had a nicer ass. "You wear those shorts around any guy, they're going to beg you for another round."

"I wear these regardless of whether I'm sleeping alone." She drops into a seat at her dining table, back to a half-eaten bowl of Cheerios. "And speaking of sleeping, I was planning on getting back to it, so why are you here?"

"I'll leave," I say, ready to turn around, but she holds up a hand to stop me.

"No," she says, her mouth full of cereal. "Stay. Sorry. I'm tired and Jeff…makes me tense."

"Why was he here?"

She gives me a cynical expression. "Because he's also kinda helpful at relieving tension."

"Where do I know him from?"

She spoons more cereal into her mouth. "He's a roadie for Gold Rush Standard. You met him with me last summer."

"*That's* it. Guess he has some free time with Luca James in rehab?" I snort. The poster boy for the anti-drug movement had everyone fooled. Especially Cassidy. She almost lost Gage last summer when she went off gallivanting with Luca. She still beats herself up for what she did—even though she and Gage are annoyingly happy. Personally, I think they're a stronger couple now because they know how miserable they are apart.

And let's be real. Who *wouldn't* run off with the sexiest rock star alive if they had the chance?

Although, I think of Alec and… I'm actually not sure I would. Granted, I don't have the offer on the table, so who knows? Plus, Cassidy was all fucked up from Jason's overdose.

She ran away with a rock star to deal with her grief. Mine took my natural inclination toward bitchiness and set it on a steroid cycle. Pretty sure she got the winning hand in that fucked-up card game.

"What?" I ask Vera, who's waiting for a response to something.

"What happened to your face?"

I touch my still-tender cheek. "Long story."

She waits, a pointed expression on her face.

I sigh. "Gramps. But it was an accident."

She watches me a few seconds longer, as though trying to weigh the truth of my words.

"I swear. It wasn't on purpose." I wave away the box of Cheerios she offers me, taking a seat across from her. "How was your mom's visit?"

"Weeks ago," she says, snapping in a very un-Vera-like way.

"I started a new job, Ver. I've been busy, if you're pissed I haven't checked in sooner."

"You had time to talk to Cassidy. Even stopped by her house before a date."

"Your mom was here then," I remind her, but it only makes her eyes flash.

"And I could've used a break."

We can keep going down this rabbit hole of sniping, or I can apologize... Which, oddly enough, doesn't make me want to murder her for considering. "I'm sorry. I should've called you."

"You don't have any—" She cuts herself off, brows furrowed. "Wait. What?"

"Believe *me*, I'm not repeating myself," I say, grabbing my phone from my bag and placing it on the table. "And before you keep grilling me, don't forget—these things work both ways."

She stares at me like I've grown antlers. And then, surprising the hell out of me, she giggles. "I'm itching to fight with someone and I would've bet millions you'd be an easy target to practice with—and yet, here you sit, all calm. Way to ruin my ability to be irritated. Who are you and what have you done with Teagan?"

"I didn't know you had the ability to be irritated to begin with," I say, reeling inside from her words. She's right. I should be an easy target for verbal sparring—but I bit back my desire to punch out. And apologized instead.

A grin yanks my lips apart, and despite everything shitty that this morning started with, happiness looms in my chest like an overfull balloon. I was nervous I'd feel different taking an antidepressant, but I don't. I'm still me—but I'm also a version of myself I can actually almost stand.

"How's this?" I ask, loving the way her eyes are all wide at my expression. "I'll tell you something I haven't told Cassidy. Or anyone."

She leans forward, her elbows on the table. "Like you have to really ask a journalist if they want an exclusive?"

"Calm down, Ms. Journalism Major," I say. "This is so far off the record it's like pen and paper have never been invented."

"Obviously," she says, huffing, offended. "I'm just so glad you're actually ready to open up to me about something—anything."

"Do you want my story or do you want a box of tissues for the tears you seem about to burst into?"

"*There* she is," Vera says, her voice dripping with the smile she's trying not to wear. "That's the Teagan I love."

"You care about me. You love me. I mean, my God. You're smothering me."

"Watch it, or I will." She points beyond me to her living room, the furniture all dressed with hot pink pillows.

"Death by girly-ass pillow? I literally can't think of a worse way to go."

"Just shut up and tell me what's going on with you."

So, I do. I tell her about the Zoloft. And about the learning disability. And it all comes out so much easier than I expect.

And Vera doesn't even blink. I couldn't ask for a better reaction.

"Visual perceptive learning discrepancy," she repeats, slowly. "My best friend from high school had an auditory processing discrepancy... I wonder if they're similar." Then she shakes her head. "No—probably the opposite. He has to write everything down—or read instructions rather than hear them."

"Yeah, I'm the opposite," I say, agreeing. "I need to hear things."

"And you feel like knowing that about yourself makes life easier?"

I nod. "Don't get me wrong, life's not perfect. Hell, I'm here because Gran kicked me out of her house. But, I handle situations better now than before. And knowing *why* things aren't always easy for me helps."

"Obviously, you'll move in with me," she says, all nonchalant.

Some of the tightness in my chest unravels. "I was going to ask if you wanted a roommate."

"Yes. Please," she says, excitement lighting her face. "I've been so lonely since Cassidy moved out."

"But Cassidy's fun," I remind her. "And I'm—"

"A total bitch sometimes," she says. "I know. But I could use someone like you around, helping me toughen up a bit. I'm sick of people seeing all my fluff and no substance."

I gesture toward her pink pillows. "You kind of set yourself up for it."

"I'm allowed to enjoy girly things and still kick ass."

And to this, I have no comeback. "True. I got paid today. I can give you rent and a deposit." I'll be back to pennies in my account afterward, but...worth it.

She stands, dumping her bowl in the sink. "Please. My mom pays for this place. I don't want your money, just your company."

"I'm not going to live here for free." I stand too, leaning on the table.

"The only things I actually pay for are cable and internet. You can split those bills with me."

"I'll pay them fully," I counter.

"Fine. Then with my extra cash, I get to take you out to dinner once a month."

I definitely have the better end of this deal. "I love you too, you know." Ugh. My stomach twists. Pills or no pills, this fluffy girly stuff is so not ever going to be my style. "Don't get used to hearing it."

"Hearing it this once'll keep my soul lighter than air for...gosh..." She slams a hand dramatically over her heart. "*Years*, at least."

"Shut up," I say. "Show me my room. Then you can go to sleep."

"Do you need to get your stuff from your car?"

This deflates a bit of air from my bubble. "I didn't think to grab anything when I left. I was too mad. And I really don't want to go back there." Then, though, I discover the perfect Band-Aid. "But I got paid today. And I'm skipping work. So I'll go buy new things for now."

"In that case," she says, "fuck sleep. I hear the word shopping and I don't even need coffee anymore."

I glance around her apartment. Splashes of pink and black and gold. Feminine and bold. "You do have an eye for pretty things. Maybe you can help me find a dress."

"For what?"

"Get changed," I say, grabbing my keys. Springs Corner won't be open yet for the best shopping, but we can hit other, less expensive stores for necessities like underwear and a toothbrush first. "Then I'll drive. And I'll tell you all about Alec in the car." I use my palms to push up from the table and wince at the pain. I forgot about the splinters on the banister in my haste down to Gramps earlier. "Also, do you have tweezers I can borrow? I've got a few slivers of wood to pull from my palm before I do anything else."

She brings me tweezers—and rubbing alcohol, which stings like a motherfucker. But other than that? My day finishes a hell of a lot better than it started. I end up with the things I'll need to survive the next couple weeks, plus several cute new pairs of pajamas, almost as tiny as Vera's—and a fucking amazing dress. And the bruise on my face fades so much by the end of the day, I bet it'll disappear by Monday and I won't have to answer any stupid questions about it.

I can't believe Gran kicked me out.

I can't believe how *relieved* I am to be away from there. Well. Yes, I can.

Mostly, though, I can't believe how lucky I am to have someone like Vera in my life to make it all so much less horrible than it could be.

Cassidy, too. Who knows better than to offer sympathy even all the way from New York when I fill her in on everything. All I get is a series of texts making plans for all the girls' nights we'll have in the future.

And drinks. Lots and lots of drinks.

CHAPTER THIRTY-SEVEN

ON MONDAY BEFORE work, I borrow Vera's laptop for my first online therapy session. Vera fixes me with a stern expression. "You break that laptop, I break you. *Capisce?*"

"Being tough only works if the other person doesn't know you well enough to know you're full of shit."

"Oh. I guess that's why you're not scary anymore." She lets her features fall into the closest thing to smug I've seen her wear.

"Blah, blah," I say, waving my hand through her words. "You'd still be scared if I wanted you to be." She starts to retort, but I'm running late, so I cut in before she can, gently patting the laptop in my hand. "I promise to take care of your baby."

"Have a good appointment." Vera loved the idea of an online therapy site. If mine goes well, she's going to sign up, too. Knowing I'm not the only one who could use someone professional to speak with makes it easier for me to close myself in the guest room—or, *my* room now—and log on to the site. While I wait for the video component to load, I pull my headphones from Alec out of my purse, connect them to the laptop, and slide them on. By the time I'm done, my therapist is logged on as well.

Dr. Wú looks like she's in her late thirties and has a friendly face. She's thrilled the Zoloft is working already. "So many people have to try different combinations to find something that helps," she says. "It's easy to get discouraged—I'm glad you won't."

"I've been wondering if it's partly a mind over matter thing," I admit, leaning against the headboard, cringing when it squeaks. "Like I know the pill should help me, so taking one every day puts me in a better mental place before it even takes effect."

"I'm sure that helps," she says, a strand of hair falling forward when she nods. She tucks it into place. "I went over your questionnaire last night, so before we go over that—is there anything in particular you'd like to speak about?"

That damn questionnaire took me hours to fill out. And I'm sure it was riddled with spelling errors and incomplete sentences and...whatever.

My mind flashes to my grandparents. Who raised me on permanent thin ice.

To my mom. Who never wanted me.

To a blank spot where my father's face would be if I knew what he looked like. Which is stupid to wish for because he never wanted me either.

My throat strangles itself when I try to find the words to bring him up. "No. I'll let you lead, if that's all right."

She tucks more hair behind her ear and takes the conversation in a direction I'm much more comfortable with. "How have you been dealing with Dr. Reyes' suggestion of a possible learning disability?"

"I haven't really been dealing with it," I admit. "It's nice to know, but the thing is I don't want my life to be about depression. And I definitely don't want my life to be about a learning disability."

"It doesn't have to be," she says, glancing down from the screen for a moment. "Is your life about having red hair? Is your life about enjoying horror movies?"

"Those aren't the same."

"They're a part of who you are."

"Still. Not the same."

"Would you say you've felt much of your life *has* been about your anger?" she asks.

The answer is simple. "Yes."

"You wrote on your questionnaire you believe that anger stems from depression and your learning disability. Which means, by addressing them, you're fighting the thing that's made you most upset. Maybe having days where your life is about those things is preferable to the days in the past when it's seemed to be all about anger. Because you're treating all of it now."

"I don't want to think about it all the time, every second of every day."

"And you won't. But even with Zoloft, even with therapy, some days, your life will be about your depression. But some days it won't. That's the way this illness works. The good news is you're helping yourself now—and hopefully we can maintain things so that *most* days it's not at the front of your mind."

"I need some time to swallow that," I say. "I get that it's true. I knew it coming into this. But...hearing it so black and white is a lot to chew."

"I understand." She glances down again at something off screen before saying, "Then let's move on to some of the ways you can best help yourself."

Uncertainty has its grips in me, though, sliding doubts under my skin. Maybe therapy is stupid. Maybe Zoloft is stupid. If I can't get to a place where I never have to think about depression, what's the point? My mind is forceful enough to move the thought to my mouth. "What's the point?"

"You can do nothing and let your depression bring you lower and lower—or you can fight it and let it make you stronger in the process."

I appreciate that she didn't miss a beat, didn't need clarification. "Tell me how to help myself."

She wants me, it turns out, to more actively deal with my learning disability.

I'm not surprised. One of the reasons I selected Dr. Wú was for her description on the website. She specializes in depression—and learning disabilities. Also drug use and career guidance and grief counseling. While the time that's passed since Jason's overdose has really helped me heal, I could probably use a bit of retroactive grief counseling anyway.

I thought Dr. Wú and I would be a good fit. And she's starting to make me think I was right.

"Self-determination is important when you learn differently than others," she says, her words easy and mild-mannered enough to keep me from feeling bad about myself for being different. And she goes on to discuss the different aspects of self-determination.

Understanding myself and the ways I learn differently and how it all might affect my performance in daily life. Setting goals to keep myself on track with the ability to complete tasks. Learning from my experiences, tweaking and improving processes as time goes on, to make my career—my life—more manageable.

"Eventually," she tells me, "it will all become second nature. So you won't be living it every day. Or, rather, you will be, but you won't be so aware of it. You'll have set the stage for your own success."

I can't decide if the work ahead of me makes me excited—or full of dread. When I mention how sometimes I confuse the two, how sometimes I should be thrilled, but get angry instead, she tells me it's common.

"Sometimes depression or anxiety can make it hard for your body to understand what you're feeling," she says. "Your system can mistake excitement for anxiety, or regret for anger. But this is part of self-awareness, and knowing these things will help to temper them."

Our session's up after that, but I set my next appointment before closing out. Because while she makes it all sound so easy, I'm sure the moment I'm out the door today, I'll forget it all. Or twist it. Or think of a zillion questions about everything.

Funny thing, though. When I step out the door, I don't forget it all.

I drive to work reliving the conversation. Helps that it was face-to-face and I didn't have to read anything.

Which is a strength I should focus on. I hit the brakes, skidding to a stop behind the car in front of me, which is doing the same thing. Ugh. Traffic. But I have a good memory. If I hear something, I understand it a lot quicker than if I read it.

I should ask for a tape recorder for meetings, instead of taking notes. Or whatever the modern equivalent is for a tape recorder. Suddenly, excitement dances in my stomach. And this time it doesn't feel at all like dread.

"They're called voice recorders," Sam tells me later, as we start our computers. "But you don't need one."

"Actually, I do," I say, snarking a little because ugh. He doesn't get to tell me what I do or don't—

"No, I mean you can get an app for it on your phone."

"Oh." I offer my cringe as an apology. "I can't believe I didn't think of that."

"Here." He spins his computer screen toward me. "These are the top-rated ones."

I can't read them from where I'm sitting, and I lean back like I'm too lazy to get up. "Tell me which one I should get."

He studies the selections for a few moments and rattles off the name of the one he thinks will be best for recording meetings instead of personal thoughts or dictation.

"Where's Alec?" I ask, glancing at the clock. "He's late."

"He's out until Wednesday for his brother's thing in Vegas."

"Till *Wednesday?*" A whine forces its way into my tone. Yuck. But I didn't realize he'd be gone so long.

Ugh. Now I miss him.

"Yes. So that gives you two full days to catch me up with what the hell is going on with you two."

I pull my phone out of my bag to download the app Sam named—and, obviously, to avoid answering him. But as if on cue, a text from Alec buzzes in my hands. *What are you wearing?*

I bite back a laugh. *I'm at work, weirdo. Nothing to see here.*

You're always worth looking at. I need a visual.

What are you even doing up right now? Isn't it before 6 am over there?

Haven't been to bed yet. Caught up in gambling. And then maybe a comic book or two. Send me something for sweet dreams.

Nerd. I shake my head, but I also hike up my skirt. Just a few inches. Just showing a bit of thigh. And I send him a picture of my knees.

Jesus. Can't want to spread those gorgeous legs again. And a few seconds later: *I need to see your face.*

And because he makes a grin start all the way in my chest before it travels to my lips, I give him one. It's harder to take and Sam snickers when he catches me, but I'm too happy to care.

How are things at home?

New home now, I write, wondering how to send a tone through text message so he'll know I don't want to talk about it.

Are you all right?

I send him a picture of my middle finger.

A minute passes, and then Alec responds with a picture. His face, his hair all spread out and messy on his pillow, smudges of shadows under his eyes, but a smarmy twist to his mouth. *You didn't ask, but here I am anyway.*

Send me something a little lower, I respond, my fingers shaking with the sudden flash of hunger for him. And when he does, the image comes in of his bare chest, sculpted abs, the start of his happy trail...and the rest of him covered by a comic book. I take a closer look just in case—but all I get from it is the name of the comic book. *Silver Surfer.* I crack up because he's such a nerd, but nothing about his reading tastes keeps me from taking another look. And another. And that flash of hunger erupts into something much, much stronger.

Have to turn my phone off, I say. *Otherwise I might combust. Hurry up and come back to me.*

I do turn it off, too, because I'm not sure how I won't spend my entire day staring at those photos. And I swear the deep timbre of his laugh reaches me all the way from the other side of the country.

I'm eating lunch in the break room when Denise walks in. She acknowledges me with a quick nod and half a smile before hightailing it to the coffee pot. Which, thank God, I've refilled. She adds creamer and sugar and without even waiting for it to cool, chugs.

"Thank God for caffeine," I say.

"Back-to-back-to-back meetings all day—all week. I'd be dead without it." She fully smiles this time. "You're Teagan, right? Alec's assistant?"

"I am." It's like a high school crush, the sort of thrill that jumps through me because she knows my name. I place my fork carefully on my plate, not wanting another bite of salad in case it gets stuck in my teeth. "And you're Denise?" As though I haven't had her name tattooed in my mind from the first meeting she ran. But it doesn't do me any favors to play dumb. "I mean, I know who you are. Sorry. Nice to meet you, Denise."

Awesome. Rambling on top of wishy-washiness. Her expression's amused, and she leans against the counter, not speaking. Probably waiting for me to keep adding feet to my mouth. I should go back to my salad.

Then I remember Dr. Reyes telling me to be my own advocate.

I stand, instead, to face Denise. "I wanted to tell you that... I think the way you run meetings is brilliant. And it seems like you're brilliant in every other area of your job, from what I hear in those meetings anyway."

"Thank you." Her amusement turns to something else. Surprise, maybe?

I don't know how to take it, but I keep going anyway. "And Alec's leaving at the end of the summer to return to Harvard..." This gives me pause. I haven't been focusing on it at all—but now my stomach's dropping with the weight of an eighteen-wheeler. He's leaving... I'm staying.

"And?" Denise prompts me with a kind, but firm, tone.

Right. Take it one thing at a time. *Deep breath. Eye contact. Don't wipe your clammy hands on your skirt... Whoops.*

"And I'm not sure what my responsibilities will be when he goes, but if you ever need an assistant—or any position that would give me the opportunity to work for you—I would love the chance."

She takes a long glance around the break room. "This place has been a lot cleaner the past few weeks—are you responsible for it?"

Now it's easy to look her square in the eye. "I am."

Sam's squeamish about cleaning up after other people, but even at its messiest, the break room is practically sterile compared to my grandmother's house. So I clean it, and he organizes the supply room. It works. And now, I'm even gladder for it.

"I already have an assistant," she says. "But I like your initiative. I'll see what I can do."

Her words keep me floating through the rest of the day—and the next one too.

Then Alec doesn't return on Wednesday.

My grandfather's doctor had to go out of town, he texts me. *I'm on babysitting duty the rest of the week. But I'll be there to pick you up Saturday. Can't tell you how much I'm looking forward to seeing you... Touching you...*

I shiver when I text him Vera's address and tell him I hope his grandfather feels better soon—and that I'm sorry he has to miss work.

It hits me a few minutes later—Alec is a good person. Down to his core.

He's demanding and arrogant. He's got more talent in the tip of his tongue than I ever knew was possible—definitely more than any other guy I've ever known. And his family's got some serious issues...

But through it all, he's good. His heart is good. He's the kind of guy who'll miss work to spend his days with his sick grandfather—who, let's be real, seems like a total asshole.

I *admire* Alec.

I'm going to miss him so much when he's at school. I'm not sure how I'll function. The thought makes a fist in my stomach, clenching so tight I stop breathing. It hurts. The thought of being without him hurts.

Fuck.

I tap my fingers against my coffee mug so hard it sloshes onto my desk. I wipe it up with my hand, too distracted to do much else.

I don't want to run away. I don't want to push him away.

These are the things that usually define who I am.

I'm changing. And he's part of the reason why.

CHAPTER THIRTY-EIGHT

VERA HELPS ME get ready for the wedding, and the more she grins the harder I frown.

"You're allowed to be excited, you know." She tugs another strand of my hair around her curling iron.

"How the hell am I supposed to be excited when I can barely breathe?" I press my hands into my stomach as the lid of the toilet, where I sit, digs into my tailbone. This is stupid. I never should've agreed to go. "His pretend ex-fiancée is going to be there. He told his family he's bringing me. His father. His *grandfather*." I wish I'd never texted him to ask if his family knew. I wish he'd told me how they reacted, so I had a better grip on what to expect, but he's too *Alec* to do that. Too polite. Too considerate of my feelings. Which pretty much tells me all I need to know about how his family took the news. Oh, God. I can't do this.

"So what? It's not like they wouldn't know you were there when, you know, *you show up with him*." Vera doesn't get it.

"So his family doesn't like me." Which, okay, *might* not be true—but I can't imagine they're thrilled, considering I'm the reason he broke off his perfect, business-favorable engagement. "I've never met the fiancée—ex-fiancée. Ex-pretend-fiancée. Whatever. I haven't met her—so it's been like she doesn't exist. But she *does*. And it's weird that I'm going. And to the rest of the world, I'm a fucking cliché. Like he dumped her for his secretary."

"When have you ever cared what other people thought?"

"His dad's the CEO of my company," I say, seething because I have to explain. "What he thinks of me matters."

"Then don't go," Vera says, laying the curling iron down on the sink. "If it's such a huge mistake, back out."

"Maybe I will." I stand, irritation wrapping around me tighter than the curls she's created in my hair. I start to stride out of the room—but I catch a glimpse of my reflection from the corner of my eye and...

Wow.

"Vera," I breathe. "What did you do to me?"

Her reflection regards mine smugly. "Not much. Just played up on your features a bit."

It's so much more than that.

My eyes are huge, and my skin glows. My cheeks are softly rose-tinted and my lips are halfway parted, pretty and pink.

"You're a fucking genius," I say.

"Tell me something I don't know." She puts her hand on my shoulder, pushing me toward my seat on the toilet. "And imagine the final product when you're actually in the dress."

I let her guide me, because now I'm imagining Alec's face when he sees me for the first time in a week, all done up. And when I have my dress on?

How can I pass up the dress?

I imagine how it'll feel to dance with him, to let him kiss the champagne toast from my mouth.

He's worth this.

How can I pass *him* up?

Short answer: I can't.

I don't want to.

I won't.

So I let Vera finish my hair and add one final coat of mascara. And then I put on the dress. It's long and burgundy and instead of clashing with my hair, it complements it. The material starts with a high neckline and drops all the way down to sweep the ground behind me. One long slit goes almost all the way up to the top of my thigh. There's beading along the shoulders and the back is open halfway down my spine, barely covering the sexy low-back bra I bought to go with it.

"Whoa," Vera says when I step through my bedroom door into the living room.

"Right?" I twirl. "I've literally never been this fancy. Ever."

"I was going to beg you one last time to let me dust you with glitter." She holds up her bottle of it with a guilty expression. "But you don't need it. You're perfect."

"Considering I practically went into debt for this dress… I hope I make an impact in it." I couldn't pass it up. The second I laid eyes on it, I knew. And it fit. And it was perfect.

And it still is.

With timing that is, of course, impeccable, there's a sharp knock at the door.

"He's here," Vera hisses in a whisper.

"No shit." Panic is a funny thing, squeezing my windpipe. "Where are you *going?*"

She turns on her way to her bedroom. "This is your thing, your moment. I'll meet him again some other time."

She gives me a thumbs-up like a fucking nerd and then tucks herself away in her room.

I fill my lungs with so much air I can't believe they don't pop. Then I slowly let it all out.

Then I open the door.

Alec.

He looks at me and his smile is a carnival ride, dropping my stomach with the force of suspended gravity. His eyes drop down and then rise against me, slowly, slowly reaching my face. "Damn, kitten."

But while he's noticing me, I'm noticing him. And… "Damn, Alec."

He cuts his tuxedo like it was invented solely to fit around him, all sharp and elegant.

His hair's slicked away from his face, and his smile's blinding. "You are so fucking beautiful."

"Do you want to come in?" I ask, flustered and gesturing to the rest of the apartment behind me. It's disconcerting to be this turned on while in formal wear, while standing in a shabby doorway. "For a drink?"

He swallows, but I don't think it's because I've offered a beverage. "If I come in, we won't be making the wedding."

"You mean," I say, a grin tugging at the corner of my mouth, "you'd have me waste this dress? Vera would be—"

He grabs me and yanks me to him, crushing his mouth over the rest of my words. His hands curve around my back, his fingers trailing my exposed skin. I hold his shoulders, not sure if it's for my own balance or to keep him in place. His tongue is gentle at first, sweeping through my mouth, growing more demanding.

He tastes like mint and whiskey.

He smells like soap and leather.

He feels like home. Like trust.

I slide my hands up his neck to hold his face, my own lips more insistent than his.

He cups my face, too, then gently breaks the kiss, which, however disappointing, is probably a good thing considering how fast I'm breathing.

"I've missed this. I've missed you," he says. And with his next words, he takes my breath, tossing it away like it's nothing. "I'm addicted to you, Teagan. I crave you when I don't have you. I crave you now that I do. You're the sweetest drug I never knew I needed. I will never not need you."

"Alec..." I stammer over his name.

"You don't have to say anything," he says. "I wanted you to know—needed you to know. I'm yours. However you'll have me. I'm yours."

"If I wouldn't ruin this dress, I'd be jumping you right now. You get that, right?"

The grin that splits his face is dazzling. "If you wouldn't kill me for it, I'd be forcing the issue anyway."

"I'd like to see you try." Words come easier now that we're back on familiar ground.

He holds out his arm. "Shall we?"

I take it. "Let's."

At any other time walking down a concrete stairwell in muggy Virginia summer heat might feel ridiculous in formal wear, but...nothing about standing next to Alec looking the way he does is ridiculous.

The only thing that's ridiculous about the situation is when we step into the parking lot and I discover a huge, long limo waiting for us. The limo's not the ridiculous part. My mother's voice in my head is. The one that tells me I've made it. The one that cackles at the way the sun shines like diamonds against the car's exterior. She's as smug as it is humid outside.

I try to drown her when Alec hands me a tall flute of champagne inside the limo. He sips a glass of whiskey, watching me.

With the second flute, I finally succeed. The coolness of the air conditioning settling over my hot skin helps too.

"How's your grandfather?"

"Irritated," he says. "Irritating. On bedrest, but still well enough to destroy me at chess."

"Comic books, chess... What's next? Model airplanes?" I tease, but my tone is weak. He's rich. He's smart. He's cutting a tuxedo like nobody's business.

He's a fucking catch and a half.

I wish he wasn't.

"What's wrong?" Alec asks, concern dampening his features.

"Nothing. This is perfect," I say, stronger this time, putting my empty glass down across from us and taking his face in my hands. "How could anything be wrong?"

"I know you're lying," he says. "But you look like you're about to kiss me, so I'll let it pass. For now."

If I were my mother, she'd kiss him fiercely, recklessly, really driving home the point of how much she wanted him.

I kiss him sweetly, teasing him with my tongue and keeping my lips gentle over his. He's the one to pull me tighter against him, to press our mouths harder together. I let him.

I revel in him.

I'm going to spend the rest of the night doing the exact same thing.

CHAPTER THIRTY-NINE

WE KISS AND kiss and kiss so long my mouth goes numb. And then we kiss some more.

But my mother won't shut the fuck up, laughing in the back of my mind.

I'm the one to break away because my brain's about to split in two. I'm going crazy.

"I'm in therapy," I say, suddenly panicked. Because who doesn't love a good mood ruiner? "I have a shit-ton of issues. Like, I was practically in love with Cassidy's brother—who overdosed almost two years ago—and I never even told her."

Comprehension filters through his gaze. "You're talking about Brad's son. That was an awful situation. I'm sorry for your loss."

"Well..." I struggle to come up with something else to say. "Whatever. It was a long time ago. I don't know why I brought it up." Of course I do, though. To ruin the moment. It's my super special talent.

Alec studies me, hawk-like in his expression. "It's good. That you're still in therapy, I mean."

"So you agree I need therapy?" I ask, challenge rising in my tone, moisture rising in my eyes. I watch out the window across from where we sit, letting the blur of the landscape distract me until it defeats the sting of tears. Of course he thinks I need therapy. I'm nuts. I broke off from kissing him to talk about a dead boy I used to almost love.

"I think most people would benefit from therapy," he says, calmly. "And maybe while you're there you can figure out how to stop trying so hard to push me away. I'm not going anywhere."

"I doubt you've ever been to a shrink," I say, unable to stop myself. Literally. I try to bite back the words, the bitterness they're laced with, but they come tumbling out anyway.

He drags a hand across his face, not meeting my eyes for a moment. But when he does, his expression is both full of steel—and, somehow, vulnerability. "You see these scars?"

He raises his fist toward me and extends his fingers, slowly, the web of scars stretching across his knuckles, over his fingers, and down the back of his hand.

"I'm surprised you've never asked about them," he says, his voice steady.

I force my eyes to his. "I figured if they were something you wanted to talk about...you would."

"Well," he says, a twisted, disarming smile across his lips, "here you go. This is what happens when you punch a mirror with a cabinet behind it. You don't just bust up your knuckles, but your entire hand. Bled enough to end up in the hospital. Three times."

I grab his hand, which is starting to shake, and I pull it into my lap. I want to kiss my way along his scars, I want to take away this thing that still causes him so much pain.

"You went three times?" I hate the thought that comes to me. "For that one mirror, or were there others?"

He doesn't answer, but he looks away, and that tells me all I need to know.

"Why?" I ask, hoping it's okay to ask.

"I had a twin," he says, still not looking at me.

"Your sister?" I remember the picture in his office, of the toddler.

"She died in a car accident when we were seventeen. Sh-sh-she..." He clears his throat, tightening his fingers in my grip almost painfully. "She called me for a ride home, but I told her I was busy. Which I was. Trying to work my way into some girl's pants." He pauses, remembering, regret piercing his features. "So my sister got in a car with her drunk ex-boyfriend. And neither of them made it out."

"I'm so sorry," I say, knowing the words will never be good enough, but needing him to hear them anyway. I've never understood more clearly than now why Alec doesn't use his looks and his money to bang a bunch of chicks. I have no doubt that night pushed him far, far away from that path—if he'd ever been on it to begin with. "That must've been horrible."

"I imagine it wasn't pleasant," he says; for the first time his tone comes out with a bite to it.

"I meant for you—"

"I know what you mean." He shakes his head, breathing out with a shaky gust of air. "Sorry."

I run my thumb over the back of his hand. "That's why you don't have mirrors…anywhere in your place."

It's not a question but he answers me anyway. "For a long time, I couldn't stand the sight of my reflection. Not when she never got to see hers again. We weren't identical—but we were close enough. I couldn't see me without seeing her. I couldn't see me without looking at the person I let die."

I understand him completely. Sometimes, from certain angles, Cassidy resembles her brother so strongly I can't look at her.

"It's not your fault," I say, my heart slowly deflating between my ribs, struggling to beat, like it's having trouble breathing. "You know that, right?"

"I do, because of therapy." Breath shudders through him. "My slightly bedraggled point is that I've been in therapy for the better part of a decade. Even my therapist sees a therapist—says it's good to cleanse the mind even if nothing's hurting it at the moment. That's why I still go."

"I'm sorry," I say. "To bring this to surface on a night like this one."

"Let's not apologize anymore tonight." He shrugs off my words, his eyes still far away. "It's a celebration for family. If she can't be here physically, she at least deserves a space in my mind."

My mouth twists when I try to fight the sour thought that pushes through. I look away, but he sees it first.

"Tell me," he asks. "Have I freaked you out?"

"No!" I turn toward him so fast my neck cracks. I rub it, confessing what I wish I didn't have to. "I was thinking... You want your missing family in your mind. I can't keep my mother from ruining my thoughts."

"I'm—" He starts to apologize, catches himself. "Parents have a way of haunting us whether they're here or not."

"For the longest time I wished mine would be here to haunt me," I say, my words much more casual than their definitions to me. "Now I wish they'd stop altogether."

"Your father too?"

"Nah. Too hard to listen to a voice I've literally never heard." My breath shakes out of me. "God. Kiss me again or something. Let's get this limo back on the party trail, yeah?"

So he does, and we do. And by the time we pull up to the wedding, I'm breathless with the way I need him.

Even the scene unfolding outside the windows doesn't hold a candle to my awe with him.

To call the house we're pulling up to a mansion would be to severely undersell it. It's three mansions stuffed into one and you can see it from about a million miles away, which is about how long the driveway is. It's a hotel of a house. In fact... "Is this a hotel?"

He laughs. "This is my grandfather's estate."

"Well holy shit." I throw a hand over my mouth. "I can't talk like that here, can I?"

"Kitten," he says, grabbing my hand and lowering it. "You talk however the fuck you want. You don't need to change a thing about yourself for my family. Don't be nervous."

I'm not so sure that's true; not with the way my stomach's down near my feet right now. Dread's a heavy bitch. I flash back to the way his grandfather told me to get out of his hospital room. The way his father's eyes slid over me like furniture.

That was a family emergency, though. This is a celebration. Different atmosphere. Right?

Ugh. Why do I doubt it so much?

But...

I have Alec.

And he has me.

And it's enough for that block of dread to crumble at the corners, my stomach righting itself. "I've never put much stock in people being better than me because they have money," I say. "I think I'm nervous because I..." I stutter, having to clear my throat. Why is this so hard for me? "Because of how much I care about you."

"I *know* I'm nervous now because of what I feel for you."

"Guess that makes us even then," I say.

"Even?" He laughs, his eyes dancing as he pulls me from the limo. "Not a chance, kitten. You topple me."

CHAPTER FORTY

THERE'S NO WEDDING party, Alec tells me when I ask if he's supposed to be doing something for the groom right now. "They want to be alone up there. Didn't even do a rehearsal dinner, which really pissed off my grandfather, because it was the one event he could've participated in, if he'd hosted it at his house like he wanted."

Right. Because he's on bedrest. Relief is a cool breeze against the smarmy heat in the air. His grandfather won't be at the wedding. One less person for me to worry about.

"Tell me about your brother," I say.

Alec laughs but there's not much humor in it. "Mark is three years older. A *perfect* fit for my family—which is to say he's a fucking snob—even if he went to medical school instead of following in our father's footsteps. It's literally the only way he's ever rebelled, and nobody made a big deal out of it because, you know, the prestige of having a fancy surgeon in the family has a nice feel to it."

If I didn't know him better, I'd miss the bitter undertone beneath the dryness of his words. "It's kind of romantic," is all I say, though. "Just your brother and his bride in front of all their friends and family. Like they'll be in their own world."

"It's mostly because Candace used to date his best friend. It'd be awkward to have him up there."

"But why not have you at least?"

"Mark wants the spotlight all on him. And I don't mind—not when it means I get more time with you on my arm."

I blush because he's looking at me so intensely he's impossible not to believe. He leads me along the path around the side of the house to where the music is pouring through the air, and I stop short as we turn the final corner.

The scene splayed out before me is immaculate.

Lights twinkle everywhere. Beautiful people do, too. Throngs and throngs of them. There's a trio of musicians down the way from us, playing their triplet of string instruments with tunes light enough to make a person feel like floating. Beyond that soothing sound is a chorus of laughter, a clinking of glass, the summery chirps of crickets. A mingling of aromas twists pleasantly through my nose; spiced citronella, grilled meats, and the musty vanilla scent of tobacco—the fancy kind that goes in pipes or is from cigars, miles away from the cigarette butt stench I'm used to.

The lawn before us is so immaculately manicured I'm tempted to bend down and get grass-level. I bet there's not a single strand that isn't perfectly even with the others. God. This plantation, the enormousness of the house and the land stretching out beyond it, makes it surreal that my grandparents' house is within a half an hour of here. It's like there's no way that other, less shiny world actually exists, and I start to realize why rich people seem so lost in their own lives.

My palm goes slick in Alec's hand; I don't think I can do this. I turn, and he's already watching me, amused. So I lift my chin, and I pull him forward.

A few steps in, my bravado shivers a little, and I let him take the lead. It's beautiful, this place, and it's taking every ounce of my will not to feel like an outsider. That's not how I roll. Not now, not ever.

The entire scene is draped in elegance. We head toward a huge open-roofed structure, the skeleton of a tent made for thousands of people. Hundreds of strands of twinkling lights crisscross overhead, a roof of stars that glimmer so brightly they should be blinding, but somehow aren't. Clusters of candlelit lanterns hang here and there, suspended with metal twine tied to the high sides of the structure.

I keep my hand tightly in Alec's. There are so many people here—hundreds—I don't want to lose him in the crowd. Tables and tables and tables line the way, surrounded by silk-swathed chairs, and centerpieces featuring lit candles of different shapes and sizes, in varying shades of ivory and cream. And crimson rose petals scattered around each arrangement.

"Is this where the ceremony will be held?" I ask.

"The ceremony's in the barn." Alec points off a ways to a red building in the distance.

"Chambers," someone calls behind us. And when Alec turns he pulls me with him until we find the voice. A startlingly handsome guy about Alec's age—surrounded by a group of other similarly gorgeous people. Alec's fraternity brothers from Harvard, it turns out, and a few from his lacrosse team. And their dates.

"We'll catch up a little later," Alec says after introductions. "I promised Teagan a tour of the property."

He tugs my hand, but I stay put. It's sweet, what he's doing. He knows I'm not comfortable, but these are his friends, his people. They're no better than me, even if I have to remind myself of it every other second. And...if he loves them, I want to know them. So I smile and I try really freaking hard to bring it all the way up to my eyes, and I say, "You can show me later. I want to hang out with your friends."

"I like her," says one girl, pulling my hand from Alec's. She smiles at me, her eyes—almost as dark as her skin—shining. "Let's get you a cocktail, yes?"

I like her right back—and follow her without a backwards glance, even if the weight of Alec's gaze is heavy against my back while I walk.

Amara is my new friend's name and she—and her other friends—love tequila.

"I can't," I say, waving away another shot. I want to stay sober tonight. For after the wedding, for the things I want to do with Alec. For the things I want him to do to me... "Liquor messes with my medication." I'm not even sure I'm lying. I should probably check on that.

"Buzzkill," one girl slurs, but Amara tells her to fuck off—a split second before I'm about to. Instead, I grin wildly at both of them.

"I was worried you would all be snobs," I confess, the words slipping smoothly from my mouth, probably an effect of the two shots I haven't waved away.

"We were worried Alec would bring Piper," another girl confesses right back.

"Not a fan?" I ask, my face suddenly feeling numb. This, however, has nothing to do with the two shots and everything to do with Piper.

The girl looks at me like there's no question about it. "Are you?"

"I've never met her." I shrug, speaking casually, as though my stomach isn't inching down toward my feet.

She's nice. She wants to meet me, I remind myself.

She'll skin you alive, Sam once said.

Why, *why*, didn't I say yes when Alec said he'd ask her to stay home?

Because I'm a fucking moron.

"Anyway," I say, turning to a girl whose name I've already forgotten. "Tell me how you all know each other."

The sun's beginning to set, though it's doing nothing to cool the air, when Amara asks me, "How do you stand it?"

"How do I stand what?" I grab a glass of water from a passing waiter, sipping it, enjoying the chill as it slides down my throat.

"Piper?"

This again? I want to snap. "He wants me," I say, instead. "That's all I care about."

"So it doesn't bother you that she's with Alec right now?"

My head turns so fast it's a damn miracle I don't lose my balance. I see them immediately. Laughing like old friends. Or lovers. He sees me almost as quickly and motions for me to join them. But I can't stop staring at Piper. She's in a dress that clings to her curves like second skin and she's...hot. Like, even *my* pulse trips over itself a little looking at her. Smoking body? Check. Long, dark hair and full lips? Check. Wide eyes that, even from here, look green, with streaks of jet black eyeliner out to there? *Check.*

I was not prepared for this. For her.

Alec signals me over again.

This time, Piper's gaze follows his gesture until her eyes meet mine. Her laugh falls away like a boulder shoved straight off the edge of a sharp cliff, and her expression darkens—right down into hatred.

The hush around me is suddenly much louder than the conversations were a moment ago, as though people are collectively holding the same breath, waiting for our inevitable confrontation.

Because *I* know their relationship was fake—*unless it's all been a lie*, but I close my mind to that annoying little doubt because I trust Alec—but everyone else here thinks it was real. Alec must realize this the same time I do because he winces. Hard.

Shit.

Double shit.

Shit times infinity.

We should've talked more about this. Like, a *lot* more.

But my feet move their direction, because I've never been one to back down from awkwardness. I've never been one to back down from anything involving a possible confrontation. I don't think I'm built that way. Like with the whole fight or flight thing, my instincts choose fight every time.

Alec leaves Piper and strides toward me, grabbing my hand, murmuring, "I'm so sorry we didn't plan this out a little better ahead of time."

"A little better?" I ask, my words loud against the echoes of his. I lower my voice. "You told me to trust you."

"I'm an idiot," he says. "I forgot to figure it out with you girls."

And then we're there.

And then she's whispering, "Play along," before saying loud enough for anyone within hearing to catch, "You *bitch*."

And then she's dragging me away. Her hand's tight on my wrist, but surprisingly not tight enough to hurt—as much as she looked like she wanted to cause me physical pain.

"Piper. Let's be adults about this." Alec's matching us stride for stride, and I'm not sure if he's playing along too or genuinely concerned about her theatrics, but I shake my head at him. I've got this. I don't need a knight in shining armor, even for a fake confrontation.

He falls off after a few more steps.

I try to pull my wrist from her grip, but she doesn't let go, pulling me along behind her.

This is growing embarrassing. People are watching, and Piper is clearly in control. Maybe it's an act, but I'm not okay coming out the loser, even in a play. My heel sinks into the grass and I stumble, yanking my arm from hers. "Hold the fuck on."

She whirls around, glaring. "Do not make me cause a bigger scene here. I will if I have to—but you'll regret it, I promise you."

Just an act. This is just an act. Just an—oh, fuck it. "How about don't make *me* cause a bigger scene?" I can't keep from adding a power-balancing, "*Bitch*." Her lips twitch, which makes it hard to keep mine steady. "I get that your feelings are hurt, and I'm sorry for it. But this is a wedding, for fuck's sake. It's not about *you*. Or me. Or even Alec."

Someone behind us laughs, covering it with a cough a moment later.

Piper starts to smile a split second before she catches herself, and giggles rise in my chest. *Whoops*. We can't lose it here, not after everything. So this time I take her wrist, this time I drag her toward the house, hissing, "Let's talk in private."

We go through an entrance a few feet beyond the string quartet and the second the door closes behind us, she whirls to face me. "That was perfect."

CHAPTER FORTY-ONE

"THIS IS A fucking meet cute if I've ever seen one," I say, trying to pretend I'm not dazzled by the foyer we walk into. All marble and a domed ceiling that must reach the clouds. One huge arched entryway leads out into a room the size of a ballroom. Hell, I crane my neck to peer in, discovering more marble flooring, multiple crystal chandeliers, bigger than my car, hanging from the ceiling, maybe that's what it used to be. Now it's furnished with gleaming gold-lined furniture and fancy rugs and the air even smells rich, like cotton and leather and something someone like me can't even bother trying to name. I'm too poor.

And this isn't even the main entrance, either. God.

"A meet cute?" Piper laughs and her entire frame shakes. "That was ridiculous. I haven't even been thinking about how we'd play this. Don't get me wrong—I've wanted to meet you, but I've had my own shit going on and... This slipped my mind. I improvised."

"And chose to go with over-the-top dramatic?" I ask. Then, panic laces through my ribs. "Alec's grandfather's in here somewhere—we need to get the hell outside." I remember how cold his eyes were when he kicked me out of his hospital room. I can't imagine how much worse it'd be to get caught in his house.

She laughs again, carelessly this time. "Oh, please. Old Man Winter's up on the fourth level playing chess with Dr. Greenwald. He acts sour because he can't come to the party, but trust me. He's loving life."

"Loving life? He had a stroke," I say, my tone dry enough to make her lips twitch.

"That old brick's got more years left in him than I probably do."

As relaxed as she is about it, my own panic loosens. "Was the scene out there really necessary?"

"Obviously." She gives me a curious stare, like she's uncertain why she has to explain any of it to me.

"Why? There are thirteen different ways we could've done this." Thirteen's a bit of an exaggeration, but... "You tried to make me look pathetic."

"I have a reputation to uphold." She twists a long curled strand of hair between her fingers, her tone bored. "Especially as *the jilted ex*, it's expected that I'll make drama. You gave it back better than I'd ever dreamed, too... Not that I'm surprised. Alec told me you were a firecracker."

I should probably be offended by that, but there's too much else to process first. "You didn't look that great yourself—isn't your entire family here?"

"They expect it more than anyone." She smoothes invisible wrinkles from the stomach of her dress and adds as an afterthought, "Shit. I forgot to check if any of them were even watching." As though she *wants* them to have been watching.

That doesn't add up for me. "Aren't you people all about class and civility?"

"There's one thing my family puts above even that." Now she studies me, long and hard enough to make a lesser girl shake. "Alec really didn't tell you, did he?"

"Tell me what—that your relationship was fake? He did." I take a few steps past her toward a table in the middle of the entryway. There's a vase full of flowers and suddenly I'd rather study them than her. But she doesn't speak until I do.

She twists her head toward me, a considering expression crossing her features. "My life would be so much easier if I could feel it for him. He's the epitome of a fucking catch."

"Guess it's a good thing you don't, as he seems to feel whatever *it* is for me." There might be some sort of weird friendship thing blooming here, but she doesn't get to assume Alec would be with her if she wanted him.

"Easy, tiger. He fell hard for you the first night he met you. I'm saying—"

"What, exactly?"

"That it'll be hard to find another beard as genuinely awesome as he is." Her mouth curves into a snide smile and she waits, waits for it to click in.

Click. The word *beard* settles into place in my mind. "Oh."

"I hear you met Kelly on the elevator?"

"Who?" I'm thrown for a moment—and then I remember. The first night I met Alec, the scene in the elevator with the girl I assumed he had history with. "The blonde asshole chick?"

Piper beams. "That's basically the best description I've ever heard of my ex."

Kelly is Piper's ex. Oh my God, *now* I get it. "You're a lesbian?"

"Let's go ahead and use the term queer, if we have to use one at all."

"Okay..." I give my mind a moment to catch up with what I'm learning. Alec never even hinted... "You like girls, and your family doesn't know?"

"I sometimes like boys too, but not as often," she corrects and then laughs, though it comes out more like a verbal representation of a sneer. "And my family definitely knows."

Click. The final piece falls into place. "They don't support you. You have to marry a man they approve of to get your inheritance."

"Bingo." She laughs again, this time more delighted than bitter. "I can't believe Alec didn't tell you."

"It's your secret, not his," I say, remembering him telling me something similar. "*I* can't believe you're telling me now."

"Oh, honey. I'd tell the world if I could—I'm not ashamed. But I want that money. And my best friend is half in love with you, which means we'll be in each other's lives. Might as well be honest."

Well who knows what to say to something like that? "Um. Sorry to fuck up your cover operation."

She shrugs. "My parents were breathing down my neck, and Alec has a savior complex where I'm concerned. It was never going to be the real thing—and there'll always be a guy somewhere out there who'll pretend to fuck me if there's a nice fat check in it for him if he gets me down the aisle." Her eyes soften. "It was nice Alec didn't care about the money. For a little while I got to be with someone who wasn't using me the way I was using him."

"That's... I mean, your family would really make you—"

"They're awful." Another shrug. "And for some reason I still love 'em. And anyway, Alec bought me time. I solidified my straightness to appease my family for at least...a year, or more. Who knows? Then I'll find someone new. Quickie wedding. Grab the cash when I'm of age. Quicker divorce. Voila."

She's so casual about it. Not even a flicker of resentment passes through her eyes. I'm...at a loss for words. "How old do you have to be to—"

"Careful, by the way," she says, gesturing toward the door. "Most of them will accuse you of wanting him for his money," she warns. But the way she looks at me tells me it's more than a warning, it's a test. And a stop sign to my questions.

"The first time I picked him up," I say, using my tone to warn her right back, "was in a seedy pool hall. I had no clue he was wealthy. Believe it or not, the fact that he's rich makes me less inclined to be with him."

"Believe it or not," she says, "I believe you. Alec's not dumb enough to fall for anyone less."

"You were there, weren't you?" I ask, suddenly realizing the truth. "When Alec... When his sister died, and he went through his difficulty with mirrors."

She blinks, and I know I've surprised her. "Not when he broke any of them, but every time after. Of course I was. Why?"

"He mentioned once that he owed you a lot. But your situation now makes it seem like you're the one who owes him." The bite of a blush stings my cheeks when I mentally replay my words. "Not that you owe him anything, I mean. Just that—"

"We're friends. Closer than siblings," she says, with an easy smile. "We don't owe each other anything. It's not about that. You're perceptive. Every minute I spend with you shows me exactly why he's falling for you."

"We should get back to the wedding," I say. "Before they send in the troops." Before she talks about Alec falling or being half in love again. Or before I drop to my knees and beg her to repeat it all, word for word.

"Nah," she says. "They're all out there pretending our little unpleasantness never even happened. They'll gossip like hungry puppies over brunch tomorrow. Old Man Winter"—I crack up at her nickname for Alec's grandfather this time—"made it clear he has a strict no-house policy that most of them are too scared to break. But you're right. Pretend you hate me for a little while out there, okay? And in a few weeks we'll *come out*," she snickers, "as the friends I can tell we'll be."

CHAPTER FORTY-TWO

ALEC APOLOGIZES AGAIN, but I brush it off. Things with Piper...well, they went pretty perfectly. We head over to the huge red barn for the ceremony. It's lit with twinkle lights like the rest of the property seems to be and it smells of hay and gardenias. It's as elegant as the rest of the setup with a more rustic tone. The center aisle is lined with burlap and lace.

We sit in the front row, and I've never been more nervous about anything. Mark is standing in front of everyone already. He looks like Alec, but in a slicker sort of way. Shorter hair. Smugger expression. Not as attractive as the one Alec usually wears. He grins at Alec and tips his head to me before his eyes slide away. Guess we're officially introduced.

The seats behind us fill quickly—and before I know it, my nerves are standing up so straight they're about to pass out, because Alec's father is ushering his mother down the aisle to take their seats. Next to ours.

Alec's father greets me with a smile, but it falls flat in his eyes. He exchanges a long, unreadable glance with Alec. Well, not that unreadable. Pretty sure under the bland surface of his expression lies a layer heavy with disappointment.

I'm going to have to fucking *shine* at work. There must be an audiobook out there on how to impress your boyfriend's father when he's also your gazillionaire boss...

Alec's mother's smile doesn't reach her eyes, either, but she offers me her hand anyway. "Nice to meet you, Teagan."

I don't know why it shocks me that she'd know my name. Of course she does. Alec told her when he announced I'd be his date tonight. And I have a feeling Mr. Chambers has been bitching about me ever since. I wrap my hand around hers, giving a small shake. "This is a beautiful wedding."

"It reminds me of my own," she says, a bit of her sour expression relaxing. "We were married here years and years ago."

"It must've been as magnificent then, if not more so," I say, proud of myself for sounding so... I don't know, able to carry on a respectful conversation, maybe? I'm also filled with a melty sort of relief that this moment is way less stressful than I'd imagined it would go. Rich people and their civility. They might loathe me, but it's barely discernible right now.

"You're sweet," she says, and before I can respond, the music changes and everyone stands.

Candace, the bride, is gorgeous in a dress that accentuates her thin frame and a sheer veil edged in lace trailing down her back and along the rose-lined aisle. Through the veil, her skin is dark and dewy, and her eyes are round and excited. She's luminous with the glow of someone in love, and it strikes something deep inside of me.

"She's stunning," I whisper.

Alec agrees. "Wait till you meet her. She's so nice it's almost painful."

"I thought you said she was the wrong girl for your brother?"

He shoots me a look, and I realize maybe I'm whispering too loudly. But everyone is craning their necks, focused on the bride—and Alec, the only one looking at me instead, cracks a smile. "She is. Mark is the one who doesn't deserve her."

My gaze darts to his father for a moment, the salt-and-peppered back of his head. I wonder if Mark's a chip off the old block when it comes to monogamy. I turn to Mark next, but his expression is so excited it's contagious. Whatever Alec's reasoning is for not thinking he deserves his bride, right at this moment, he definitely seems enamored.

The ceremony is short, and Alec's mother cries through the entire thing. Politely, of course, dabbing at her eyes with a silk handkerchief. Mr. Chambers doesn't show any emotion at all. I wonder if he's thinking of his own wedding. Or maybe he's biding his time to get back to his mistress.

Gross.

Maybe I shouldn't worry so much about impressing him. Maybe my goal should be to impress Denise enough that she wants me to work for her—regardless of whom I'm dating. Perhaps in spite of it, actually. I get the sense she'd be less than thrilled to think I'd sleep my way up the ranks of the company.

Shit.

But, I look down where Alec's fingers are twined with mine... He tightens his grip, rubbing my hand with his thumb. Oh, well. Let Denise think what she will. Let anyone think what they will.

I'm not giving this up.

That's my girl, my mother whispers. In my mind, I stab her with a kitchen knife. In real life, I slide my hand out from under Alec's. When he gives me a puzzled look, I scratch the back of my neck.

I'm not sure if I hate myself or my mother more right now. Giving a big old *fuck you* to both of us, I place my hand back on Alec's.

Because, really, fuck my conscience.

We follow the newlyweds out of the barn for dinner—surf and turf so delicious my new goal in life is to be rich enough to eat lobster every night—and then dancing. They cut a cake taller than I am and more delicious than anything I've ever tasted. Except lobster.

I don't drink much, just a glass of champagne, and Alec doesn't either. But he does kiss me after the champagne toast. He does dip his tongue into my mouth, searching for traces of the bubbly drink like he promised he'd do, making me drunk with how much I need his tongue on other spots of my body, *in* other spots of my body...

And we do dance.

We dance for what feels like hours—and also only the blink of an eye—under the twinkling lights, and though we're surrounded by miles of people and a six-piece cover band, we're in our own world.

Giddiness is its own sort of drug and I'm so high on it I don't know how I'll ever come down. I can't stop laughing, and when he asks me what it's about, all I can tell him is, "You."

A moment later, he's laughing with me.

And still, we dance, his hands on my waist, running along my spine, sliding down my arms to spin me out and back again.

Eventually I have to beg for a break to get some water. The fans placed discretely around the reception may be keeping the area cool despite the muggy summer heat, but I'm freaking parched. And starting to sweat. And I'd rather not be gross for...after.

I'd be embarrassed with how quickly I gulp down the ice water Alec brings me, but he downs his just as fast—and goes for another round without my having to ask.

"You're pretty fun," he says, pulling me in for a quick kiss. "Not that it's new information for me. But you know how to show a guy a good time."

"You think this is fun," I say, nervous my next words will make me blush. "Wait till later."

"Later?" he asks, his head tilting, a curious—and maybe hopeful—smile stretching across his mouth. "What do you have in mind?"

"Everything," I say. "I have everything in mind."

He goes still. So very still. Still enough that my own grin rises uncontrollably in the sweetness of the silence between us.

"Tell me what this is," he says, finally.

"Same answer," I say, easily, honestly. "This is everything."

"You figured it out," he says, and before I can agree, he pulls me in for another kiss. This one much better than the last. His lips are slow over mine, lingering—and simmering beneath their gentle graze with a heated passion I can't wait to tease fully out of him later.

I break it off because, well, one of us has to or we're going to end up naked in front of all these people. From the corner of my eye, I see Piper heading toward us. She notices me at the same time and winks before she glares, turning on her heel and heading the other direction. I laugh. She's good. Could be an actress.

Behind her, though, is Mr. Evans. He sees me and doesn't break stride, coming straight over. My stomach clenches at his approach. I knew he'd be here and wondered when we'd run into him. Usually,

I'd seek him out. But usually I'm not with someone he disapproves of me being with.

Still, his face is a mask of polite pleasantry as he reaches out to shake Alec's hand. "You're looking well," he says. "And Teagan, my girl, you are close to upstaging the bride."

I knock his hand out of the way when he offers it to me and hug him instead. "Where's Mrs. Evans?"

"She wasn't up to it," he says, motioning to the dance floor and surrounding area. "Crowds."

He doesn't need to explain further. I know they've come a long way in their grief since Jason's death, but Mrs. Evans still isn't much for celebrations.

"How'd the Berkeley Group meeting go?" Alec asks, smoothly steering the conversation elsewhere.

Mr. Evans' eyes light up. "Please, tonight's no time for business. But we've come up with something you'll love."

"Berkeley Group?" I ask. "Why is that name familiar?"

Alec only winks at me, though. And Mr. Evans says, "I'm hoping you'll let me steal Teagan away for a dance?"

"Like Alec has any say in the matter," I say, taking his hand. "It's time you let me see that jitterbug, Mr. Evans."

The band has other plans, though, switching to something slower. Mr. Evans shrugs, a charming little disappointment across his face, and pulls me in for a dance better suited to the music.

"I told you to call me Brad," he reminds me.

"I grew up with you as Mr. and Mrs. Evans. It's a hard habit to break."

"Use whatever you're comfortable with, but you're like family to us, honey. Seems a waste to use such formal titles."

Like family to us.

No crying tonight, I remind myself, but I have to change the topic of conversation before I lose it. "I understand if you don't approve of me being here with Alec, but—"

"He told me the truth about his...irregular relationship," he says. "I'm sorry I misjudged you. You know, I always sort of hoped you'd end up with our Jason." He pauses, his eyes going dark for a moment before his expression clears. "But it's clear you deserve someone who'll stick around. And judging by the way Philip's son's eyes follow you, he's not going anywhere."

The way he implies Jason chose not to stick around hurts me. I tense in his arms, waiting for the gale force of grief to slam into me—but it doesn't come. Instead, I'm able to relax and keep my steps in line with his. "I miss him... Jason," I add, though the clarification's unnecessary.

"Every minute of every day," he agrees, and his easy admission eases the sting of his censure toward his son. It must be hard, to have so much anger mingling with all that love. No outlet for it other than the passing of time.

I think about Jason while we dance in silence. I really think about him. About what I felt. And I think... I think it's been easy to pin my broken hopes on a boy who died almost two years ago, because I didn't have to move forward with the thing that scared me most: finding someone like Alec. Finding someone who makes me feel like I deserve everything my grandparents spent their lives showing me I didn't.

And that's... Well, that's some fucked-up shit I'll have to bring up at a future therapy session, because I'm done thinking about it for tonight. With his usual impeccable timing, Alec asks to cut in, and I swing myself easily into his arms.

"I couldn't stand watching this dress and everything in it spinning to the turn of someone else's hand," he says. And then he spirals me beneath his own like a ballerina dancing in place on a jewelry box.

"*Berkeley Group,*" I say, smiling when it hits me. "They're one of the startups you want to invest in."

The corners of his lips curl up. "Mr. Evans thought it might work if we invested in one company to show my father what sort of success we could have—and then branch out to others."

"Smart. Why didn't you tell me you'd teamed up with him?"

"I was waiting till it was a done deal. I wanted to watch your face light up—though what it's doing now is better than anything I'd imagined. Now," he says, with a grin that can't possibly top my own, "no more work talk." He pulls me in close and then shoves me out, whirling me in circles.

"What was your sister's name?" I ask after, breathless from his spin, hastily adding, "If you don't mind my asking?"

I've been wondering, and I don't know why I haven't asked before. Maybe because I've never been so sure of him—of *us*—as I am in this moment. I can ask him anything.

I'll tell him whatever he wants to know.

"Elodie," he tells me. "Her name was Elodie and she was the only thing this family ever got right—until we didn't." A shadow casts its web across his eyes for the briefest of moments.

I open my mouth, but he spins me again and when he yanks me back to him, it's to crush his lips against mine, kissing me so hard I can't seem to remember to breathe. It makes me dizzy.

He makes me dizzy.

And then he spins me yet again.

"How much longer do we have to stay?" I ask when he sweeps me into his arms and sways me in an easy rhythm. I rise on my tiptoes to get closer to his ear. "Because if you like my dress, what's underneath is even fancier."

"They already cut the cake, and the limo's on standby," he says so quickly I laugh. "We can leave whenever we want. Which, for me, is right fucking now."

CHAPTER FORTY-THREE

WE MAKE IT almost all the way to the side of Alec's grandfather's mansion when his father swoops in—I swear—out of thin air to stand before us. Yeah. So I guess on top of being super rich, he's a freaking wizard, too.

"It hurt your mother to watch you walk out without saying goodbye," he says to his son, completely ignoring me. He's not even sweating like he ran to catch us. Maybe he's able to ride air like a speedboat...

Oh, man. This is not the time to giggle. I barely catch one slipping up my throat.

Maybe if I release it, some of the sudden and unwelcome fear in the pit of my stomach will leave, too.

I try to disentangle our fingers, but Alec only pulls me closer to him. "I'll see Mom tomorrow. She looked busy before."

Mr. Chambers' eyes flash, but I speak before he can. "We should've said goodbye. I'm sorry—it's my fault. My..." Oh my God, I want to lie and say my stomach's bothering me or something but I stand here gaping instead, unable to bring myself to do it. I...don't want to lie to him. What the fuck is wrong with me?

"Your...?" Mr. Chambers prompts me to go on, and I want to swallow my tongue.

"*We,*" Alec says, saving me, "will go say goodbye now."

"Why don't you go ahead," Mr. Chambers responds, holding out an arm to me. "I'll keep your *assistant* company."

My instinct is to look at Alec, to beg him with my eyes to protect me. My reality is that I've always protected myself, and I'm not going to stop here. I place my free hand on Mr. Chambers' arm, right as Alec says, "Not a fucking chance." He looks at me like I'm crazy when I step away from him to stand with his father. "What are you doing?"

"I'm..." What am I doing? I take a breath to steady myself and inhale the thick scent of cigar that lingers on Mr. Chambers. "Discussing things with your father while you're gone."

Alec studies me, and I see clearly in his expression how much he wants to stay. But I also see the moment he reminds himself that I can handle things. I see the respect that sharpens his focus—and then the irritation when he turns his gaze to his father. "We spoke about this."

Before Mr. Chambers responds, I say, "Y'all spoke about me? Well, Alec, you go on and say goodbye to your mama, and I'll let your daddy give me all the details." For some reason my sarcasm comes out in a syrupy, forced Southern accent, which is embarrassing but somehow feels fitting, too. My stomach is a twisted knot of brambles, but I refuse to let it show on my face.

Alec opens his mouth, but I jerk my head toward the sounds of the wedding around the house. After one long glance at his father, he leaves, promising, "I'll be back in less than a minute, swear to God."

I allow myself the few seconds it takes him to disappear around the corner before swallowing and readying myself to face his father.

"He's too good for you." Mr. Chambers speaks first, angling his body more toward mine, towering over me the way his son does. Though I feel absolutely nothing like what I do when I'm faced with Alec's height. Instead of tingles, there's only a fierce sense of intimidation. Not that I'll let him see it.

I drop my hand from his arm. "If you didn't believe that solely because of how rich you are, I'd agree. He is too good for me. Not because I grew up with nothing, but because he grew up with *everything*—and still managed to come out with a kind heart."

"I can't fire you," he says, steepling his fingers over his stomach. It's startling, the resemblance of his all-business tone to one I've heard his son use. Startling the way the shapes of their face match, the angles of their jaws. "But I can make sure you hate your job."

I start to slide a finger beneath the high neck of my dress—because it's suddenly itching, and I need a bit more room to breathe—but I stop myself, because, no. Fuck that. It's rare that I'm grateful for how much practice I have being a bitch, but in this moment, I've never been happier to have the spine I created.

"You sound like a villain in a movie," I say. "But you raised the boy who became the man that Alec is. So I know you're not a bad guy. You love your son. And I love my job. So good luck making me hate it."

I probably wouldn't recognize the glimmer of respect that shines in and out of his expression if I hadn't seen the identical flash on his son's face a second ago. So, I understand the game now. Direct honesty is the way to win with Alec's father. I ask, "You're worried I care for Alec because you're rich?"

"I know where you came from. Of course I am."

"Where I came from?" I want to laugh. Or maybe cry. Mostly, I don't want to understand him the way I do. But I say, "Yeah, I get it. You're right to worry. Sometimes I worry about the same thing, about whether or not there's a small part of me subconsciously attracted to Alec's wealth." This time, I've shocked him—his eyes go wide and then way narrow. And I almost smile. "But if I had to live out of a cardboard box if it meant getting to be with your son?"

He nods, barely, waiting for me to go on.

I take a moment longer to consider my answer, wanting to make sure I speak the truth. "Hell, I'd live out of a shoebox if I had to."

"Really now, Miss Walker." His expression says he doesn't believe me, but his tone is amused. "A shoebox?"

I don't miss his use of my name. It's a step up from my work title. Score.

"Yes. A shoebox. And let me tell you something else, too. Alec knows better than anyone—the first time he does something to *buy* me in any way? I'm gone. Not that he ever would, but I will never be the type of girl who wants to be kept." *I'm not my fucking mother,* I almost say. "And that is why I love my job. I want to make something of myself. Trust me, you won't have an employee who works harder. And if I need to sign something with HR to date Alec—or I don't have to work for Alec... If that makes this situation better, I'll work for someone else who needs an assistant. Or a second assistant. Or anything." Oh, God. I can't shut up. "I'm a quick learner. Well, okay, no I'm not. But I'll put in extra time and ef—"

"You should quit while you're ahead." While he doesn't chuckle when he cuts me off, I swear there's one beneath his stern tone.

And then, wait... "You think I'm ahead?"

"I think we can table this discussion for another time."

"Because it's inappropriate to discuss business like this at your son's wedding? Or because...you might be starting to like me?"

"A little of the first, nothing of the second. But I won't meddle in Alec's personal life—"

"More than you already have, you mean?" Oops. I really need to learn to shut up.

His nostrils flare. "*And* I'll have HR go over the paperwork with you if you choose to continue a relationship with him. Other than that, time will tell if you're able to impress me at the office. I'm aware you had a hand in the way he reshaped his proposal."

It's not exactly a compliment, but considering what Alec and Mr. Evans put together seems to be working, I take it as one anyway. Plus? *Time will tell.* The best phrase I've heard all night. Well, no. Alec's said some pretty fucking awesome things to me tonight, too. But this is somewhere toward the top five at least. Mr. Chambers is leaving the door open for me to be successful even if I stay with Alec.

"Thank you," I say, right as Alec rounds the corner.

He looks me over, then his father. "You're both still standing?"

I laugh. Mr. Chambers, not so much. But whatever.

"I was worried," Alec says, glancing between us a second time. "At first about you, Teagan. But the more I thought about it, the more I realized it was you, Dad, who I should be afraid for."

I want to kiss his face off. I want to jump him here, in front of his father and the stars in the sky. I want to fast-forward through time until the moment he's above me, in his bed, pushing himself inside of me for the first time.

Oh, holy hell. I cannot fucking wait for the rest of tonight. I've never been so sure of myself. Or of him.

Mr. Chambers sighs and pulls a cigar out of his jacket pocket. He steps a few feet away to light it, and doesn't say anything else. Clearly, he's still disappointed in his son. But I wonder if the disappointment's really a test, something to force Alec to prove how much he wants me. Maybe this is a game Mr. Chambers plays with everyone.

Maybe Mr. Chambers is a chess player like the rest of them...

Alec looks at me and shrugs. I shrug back. I guess we've been dismissed.

But, oddly, it kind of feels like the opposite.

CHAPTER FORTY-FOUR

"YOUR PLACE OR mine?" Alec asks, following me into the limo. "I have to tell the driver."

His question gives me pause. I hadn't considered that I have a place we can go back to now. But... "Yours."

Because that's how I've been picturing it. In his bed.

Plus, at his place we'll be alone.

And, seriously, I can't stop thinking about his bed.

"I'd ask if you're okay," he says, "But I already know you are. The second I walked away, I realized you would hold your own."

"Your dad's intimidating as hell," I say. "But we reached an agreement—well, I think we did, anyway. What..." I try to hold the question back, but I'm too curious. "What did you discuss with him about me?"

Alec rolls his eyes toward the ceiling of the car. "He told me it's inappropriate to date you because I'm your superior. I told him I'd look for a new job, now or after graduation, if it bothers him that much."

Wow. "Alec—"

He shuts me up with a kiss.

I pull away, smiling. "Okay. Point taken. No more talking about your father. There's only one thing I want to focus on the rest of tonight anyway—and you know exactly what it is."

"I do." He slides a hand over my lap, dipping his fingers between my knees. "I'm right there with you, kitten. Believe that."

The limo ride takes for-fucking-ever. Somehow, we fill it with light conversation. Did I know Alec wants to start his own firm someday? Did he know I never had a middle name? Did I know Norris Marshall's putting out a solo album while Luca James is in rehab? We spend the most time on this last one because holy shit, no, I didn't know that, and I'm fucking pumped for it.

But I'm trembling on the inside. With nerves. With anticipation. With hunger.

He offers me a drink when he gets to his place, but that hunger's roaring something fierce and I don't want to waste any more time, even on a water. I shake my head and I take his hand and I pull him up the stairs, down the hall, into his bedroom.

This, however, is where I pause, where my nerves are louder than my want. Because his bed is exactly as I've been picturing it. Like every other time I've been over here, but suddenly it feels larger. More intimidating. White, fluffy, and intimidating. A snort chokes out of me, slicing my throat with its sudden unexpectedness.

"You okay?" Alec's hand is on my shoulder, his grip tight.

I turn to him and the second our eyes meet my doubts drip away. I pull up on my toes to kiss him. "I need to splash some water on my face."

He tilts his head toward the bathroom doors. "You know the way."

That I do. What I didn't know though, is what to expect when I opened the doors.

A mirror. Huge and framed in dark wood, hanging behind the sink.

I spin around to find him watching me, amusement plastered on his face.

"But you...?" I trail off, unsure of what I'm trying to say.

He gives the most endearing shrug. "I like the way you look at me sometimes. Kinda made me want to see myself again."

I cross to him in three steps, wrapping my arms around him, sinking into his chest when he returns the hug. Even if I hadn't learned his history, I'd have known this was a big deal. Knowing what I do now? This is more than big.

It's gigantic.

"You're one of a kind, you know that, Chambers?" I glance up at him to see the amusement doubled on his features.

"Actually, I do, Walker." He lets me go and spins me toward the bathroom, slapping my ass through my dress. "Now go splash that water because I've got a craving for a taste of your sweet neck, and if you aren't back soon I'm coming in after you."

I close the doors behind me, laughing, and run the water. Not wanting to ruin what's left of my makeup, I wet a washcloth and gently dab it along my forehead and under my chin, wiping away some of the humidity still lingering there from earlier. I almost run it under my arms, too, but I can still smell my deodorant, so I leave them be.

One last glance in the mirror, where I think I'll need to take a deep breath or do something to steady my nerves…but I don't. I'm not nervous in a way that needs reassuring. All I want is to be with Alec. And so I step through the doors, and I make it happen.

He's standing pretty much where I left him, jacket off and bowtie hanging loosely around his neck. He's still in his shirt and vest and he cuts a sexy fucking picture, all swank and steam. I walk straight to him, and I kiss him, hard. He breaks away, laughing. "Feeling feisty?"

"Feeling a lot of things," I say, my hands drifting down to unbutton his vest—and then up to slide it off his shoulders. "Ready to feel even more."

He takes his bowtie the rest of the way off and I unbutton his shirt, stripping it away from him, too. He does his belt, I do his undershirt.

"Fuck." I can't keep my hands from smoothing over the ridges of his abs, the slopes of his pecs. "It's like you're carved from stone."

"Feel a little lower, and you'll know it's true." He slides his feet from his shoes and yanks at his socks, one at a time. I take his advice and unbutton his pants, my fingers grazing his erection as I slide the fabric lower.

"Yep." I nod, fighting a blush. "Your...cock certainly feels rock hard."

"You said it," he says, laughing, his eyes dancing. "Look how far we've come."

"Not far enough," I say. "But we're about to change that."

The rest of his laugh falls away and he sucks in a breath. "If you're—"

"Don't you dare ask me if I'm sure," I warn. "I wouldn't be here if I wasn't."

He's silent for a moment, long enough to make me squirm. Then he spins me around and pulls my hair away from the side of my neck, whispering against my skin, "Then it's my turn to undress you."

He licks the side of my neck, long and slow, edging his teeth along my skin in the same path—and I nearly sink to my knees at what it does to me, sparking things all the way down through my toes.

"I'm not turning the light off," he says, his tone laced with steel.

"I don't want you to," I whisper.

He stands behind me, so close the heat from his body soaks through my dress.

He unzips me, deliberately, with care.

He lowers my dress, sliding it down my arms, running his hands over my skin, guiding the material lower, lower, and he swallows when it drifts below my back, exposing the underwear I'm wearing for the occasion.

"White lace this time?" he asks in a strangled voice.

When I bought them, I figured, with a smirk, it would be appropriate. You know, white for a virgin and all? But hearing the worship in his tone, I don't care what white represents anymore. I only want to have him speaking with this reverence toward me for the rest of forever.

He drops to his knees behind me, pulling my dress with him. I step out of it and he gently wraps a hand around my ankle, pushing against me until I widen my stance. My stomach catches at what he must see—these panties don't cover much. I twist toward him. "Alec—"

But the expression on his face stops me. "Let me cherish you," he says, his voice low, steady, his hands traveling up over my calves. He closes his eyes and rests his forehead against the back of my leg. He trembles, and dips his tongue against my skin.

His hands caress the backs of my knees.

I face forward and grab the edge of his dresser. Maybe I've been feeling my own trembles—they're growing stronger now, making my legs shake.

Maybe we're trembling together.

His palms carve the shapes of my legs, the curves of my ass. He slides his fingers under my lace and another deep intake of his breath fills the air, like a sweet symphony performed only for me.

"I want to take my time," he says, and I'm not sure if it's to me or to himself. He runs gentle kisses along the tops of my legs, his hands slide around the fabric covering my hips, dipping lower, touching me. He vees his fingers through my flesh, spreading me in a way that makes me tingle so hard I nearly fall over.

My own sigh shudders out into the silence of the room.

"I need you, Alec," I find myself saying. "I need you to get up. I need you to kiss me. Because if you don't, I'm afraid I might cry, and I don't understand it—but it's there. Please. Kiss me."

He stands, smoothing his hands up my body, curving them around my waist as I spin to face him. "I'll kiss you," he says, cupping my face, "anytime you ask me."

"Then do it," I say, half a smirk climbing my mouth. He places his lips over mine before the full thing can form.

This kiss is not like our previous kisses. There's something more. Something in the pressure of our mouths against each other. Something in the promise of his tongue when it glides through my lips to dance with mine.

We walk toward his bed without breaking the kiss. But when it's there, hitting the backs of my legs, he stops, and he looks at me, a question in his eyes.

I give my answer in a simple smile. "I'm happy," I say. "Truly happy to be here with you, like this, right now."

I used to think happiness was a fragile thing. Something to be protected. But this...this is something to be displayed. To be shown. And so I slide back onto his bed, and I pull him with me.

CHAPTER FORTY-FIVE

THE FEATHERY COMFORTER covering Alec's bed swishes as we edge backwards along it.

He pauses above me, the muscles in his forearms like twisted ropes. "I need you naked, Teagan. I'm nearly in pain with wanting you."

"I need you naked," I say, lifting up on my elbows to drag a kiss across his mouth. "I need you inside of me in the worst way, Alec. Soon."

"Soon," he agrees. "But not quite yet. Let me look at you, first."

Anticipation races up and between my ribs, tightening around my heart, but I nod.

He slides the straps of my bra over my shoulders, gently tugging them down until my breasts are free from the cups. He pauses, just looking at me.

I prepare myself for the wave of embarrassment, the urge to cover myself...but it doesn't come. And I get it now, I finally understand. I wasn't ready for this before.

This time, I don't reach for the light switch when he removes my bra completely, tossing it away. This time, I'm not mentally nitpicking my body or wondering if he is. All I have room for in my mind is him. This moment.

Love.

So much it's almost painful between my ribs. So much all the breath leaks out of my lungs and is vacuumed up into my heart. Because that's where everything is at the moment.

Love.

And maybe it's a trick of the light, or the pull of my own emotion, but I swear it's reflected straight back at me on his face. In his caress.

He slips his fingers under the hips of my underwear, and I lift my body to allow him to pull them down. Over my thighs. Past my knees. Along my shins. Slowly, slowly.

All the way off.

I've never been this naked with another person.

And I don't mean without the clothing.

He rises onto his knees and pauses, a sheepish twist to his mouth. He thumbs the waist of his boxer briefs. "Yes or no?"

Conviction is an anchor in the space between us, when I say, "Yes." Then I rise onto my knees as well. "But I want to do it."

I love the way he swallows when I hook my fingers into his waistband. I love the way he shudders when I trail my wet mouth across his collarbone and down his chest.

I love the way he bucks his hips when I free him from his briefs, his erection rigid, so full from wanting me.

There's a drop of wetness at his tip, and he trembles when I run my finger over it, looks pained when I slide my finger into my mouth to lick the taste of him from my skin. Salty. Tangy. Alec.

I shove him backwards, onto the bed, so I can climb over him. So I can slide my lips over his erection, tease him with my tongue until he's groaning and grabbing my hair, weaving it into his fists.

I trail my fingers up the muscles of his thighs; I cup him and massage him. My tongue flirts, flickering around his head, and when his grip tightens in my hair, I slide him down into the back of my throat, twisting my face from side to side, never relaxing my hands, not for a moment.

He bucks his hips against my face, and I know he won't last much longer. The thought makes me giddy.

But he surprises me, letting out a strained sound that's half a roar, and sitting up. He slides out of my mouth, and I glance up at him to complain, licking my lips.

"Come here." He speaks before I can, and yanks me to him. In a maneuver the most skilled gymnast would be impressed with, he lies back and spins me until I'm positioned over his face, looking at his legs—and his tongue *plunges* straight into me.

Holy hell.

I lean forward, my hands on his chest, my head arched back, my knees inching further apart, flattening myself against his mouth, giving him access to every inch of me. And he takes it.

He licks me from front to back, leveling his tongue against me and then rounding it through me, into me. He nuzzles me with his nose and trails me with his teeth, *sucking* me, breathing on me, into me.

His hands splay across the cheeks of my ass, kneading them, spreading them, pulling me down with more force against his face. His tongue is all the way inside of me, mapping every part of me, and I bite back a scream that would bring his entire condo down.

He dances his fingers higher along my back, pressing lower, lower until I dip my head down and swirl my tongue around his erection again.

It's hard to concentrate, though, and I'm starting to pulse against his face, while his hips are jerking him further into my mouth. I rise on my knees to take him at a better angle, but he yanks my hips back, slamming me onto his mouth again, and I swear to God he's got the longest, strongest, most demanding tongue in the world. My nerves are a line of dominoes and he's brushing it against them, knocking them down in a million rippled effects.

He holds me in place, devouring me. If my stomach were to jerk any harder than it is, I might implode into absolutely nothing. Even my breathing quivers.

I add a hand along his base and stroke him while I suck.

He goes completely rigid. In my mouth. Beneath my body. He turns his face, gently biting the inside of my thigh, murmuring, "Hang on, kitten."

But I don't want to hang on. I want to bring him to the brink. I want to push him over the brink so hard he *flies*.

I suck energetically. Faster. Rougher.

He matches my speed, my pressure with his tongue and soon it's me at the brink, me about to lose control, me moaning around him.

He clamps a hand on my ankle and, in one breathtaking jerk, I find myself under him, face-to-face this time.

I'd pout but I've lost my ability to command my features. I'm too light, too full of spinning. "Alec..." I trail off when he slides a hand between us.

"Do you feel this?" he asks, pressing two fingers into me, curling them mercilessly until my chin tips up and my neck arches, and I let out a sound of pleasure I've never made before.

"That's me. *I* do this to you." His tone is intense. And smug.

"You do." My words are weak, too filled with pleasure for any real weight, and they flutter from my lips. "I never knew why I was waiting. But now I do. I was waiting for you."

His eyes narrow and his chest expands with the breath he's holding. "You have no idea what it means to hear you say that. No idea."

He flickers his fingers and I moan again, my body beginning to pulse. "Hold on," he say, easing his fingers out of me. Again, I want to pout but I'm too invested in the moment, too fully aware that everything here is leading to something bigger.

He smoothes his hand up my body again, until it rests between my breasts. "Do you feel this?" Now he taps his fingers, damp from my own wetness, against me, in the rhythm of my heart. "Do you?"

I nod and wind my legs around him, needing to feel him between them. Needing...something. More. But he holds his body away from mine, his eyes never leaving my face. "I want this," he says, *tap, tap, pause.* "I want all of it."

"Take it," I say. He can have whatever he wants from me, as long as he gives me what I need. I've never experienced this clawing sort of ache, etching itself into every inch of me. My body is quivering, begging me to beg him, but he speaks before I can.

"Don't tell me to take it," he rasps. "Tell me I have it."

"You have it. You have everything." The words tumble out so easily, so smoothly... For the first time, I realize how much of me he truly possesses. He dug his way through every wall I've ever raised and now there is only him, only Alec.

With my words, something in his expression relaxes, like a sigh cascading over his features. And finally he lowers himself between my legs, allowing his erection to slide through the wetness waiting there, and I nearly come undone with no more than the feel of his tip, nudging me open.

"Do you want me to get a—"

"No." I shake my head, wrapping my feet more securely around his waist. I don't want a condom. I only want him. Alec, unsheathed, inside of me.

And like he's reading my thoughts, he pushes himself into me. Slowly.

A tight, throbbing pressure fills me as I stretch around him, and I'm not sure if the pain or pleasure that comes with it is greater. The noise that falls from my lips is full of both. He pauses. "Am I hurting you?"

"Almost as much as you're pleasing me," I say, my teeth gritted. "Don't stop. All I want is to feel you everywhere."

He pulls away, and I gasp at the lack of contact but before the sound is finished leaving my mouth he's back. Inside of me. His entire head, pushing through me, *into me*.

And then he pushes harder, further in. I gasp again, this time...a little more pain. But I tighten my ankles around him before he can pull out. "Don't stop," I repeat. "I knew there would be pain. That doesn't keep this from being the most meaningful moment of my entire life."

His eyes soften; he wants to stop. I can tell by the tense set of his shoulders, by the worry in the muscle ticking in his jaw, that hurting me destroys him. Piper's words flash through my mind, the ones about him being half in love with me. I believe it now more than ever.

"I won't stop." He shifts his hips forward another inch. And another.

The more he gives me, the more I want. The more the pleasure pulls ahead of the pain. I grab his ass and I pull him toward me, but he locks his stance without budging.

"I need you, Alec," I say. "All the way inside of me."

"Teagan..." He stares at me, into me, and he crushes his mouth against mine, breathing heavy, and when I open my mouth to accept his tongue, he pierces me, pushing all the way inside.

I moan, and I hold him, digging my nails into his back. My body yawns around him, spreading to allow him a full fit.

It's uncomfortable—but it's also amazing. There's not a single nerve in my body that wants him to stop.

"Teagan," he says again, his whisper right at my ear. He kisses my neck, he says my name. I turn my face to capture his mouth with mine, needing him to kiss away the discomfort. He uses his mouth, his tongue, his teeth. He runs his hands along my body, lightly, forcefully, everything in between, and my back arches, and I ache for more.

Yet, the inside of me is tender and tense.

But I breathe deeply and discover undercurrents of pleasure running beneath the surface. The more I focus on them, the stronger they grow, whirling, flooding, *rushing*. And because of the way the sensations surge through me, I notice how still Alec is against them.

He is still. So, so still.

When I open my eyes again, he's watching me with a sort of tenderness I never knew existed before this exact moment. Part of me dissolves under his gaze, a brick I'd stacked against emotion deep in my soul that I will never, ever get back. But, in this moment, I don't want it anymore anyway.

I'm not sure which of us is more surprised when a tear slips down my cheek.

"It's okay," I say when he starts to speak, concern etched into his brows. "It's because I'm *happy*." The last word quivers as I speak it, and another tear escapes, slipping sideways down my other cheek. I keep my gaze steady on his, but soon my vision is too blurred to see clearly.

He's done this to me. He's found the center of who I am, and he's set it spinning.

Me.

I am spinning.

In love.

Alec kisses me again, feathering his lips over mine and whispering sweet nothings against my mouth and across my cheek and into my ear, and he slowly, slowly rocks his hips back.

Then forth.

Back.

Then forth.

And small blossoms of pleasure unfurl, growing and growing until my mind is unable to focus on anything else.

My hips start to rock too, and soon the way I dig my fingers into his back is a sort of mindless pleasure rather than to ward off the pain of moments ago.

We move together fluidly, his stomach and chest easing over my body as he thrusts. Soon, I'm bucking my hips to meet his force, because it feels *good*. Better than good, with every moment, every motion that passes. He pauses here and there to combine our mouths in sweeping kisses, but our bodies never slow for long.

Except for once.

Except for when he goes still again, pressing his forehead to mine and closing his eyes. I roll my hips, needing to continue the beautiful friction, but he shakes his head against me and whispers, "hold on," so strangled, I'm oddly tempted to giggle. Oddly tempted to press on and make him lose control. But I don't want the moment to end, so I hold my body motionless the best I can.

A moment later, he loses a bit of the tension from the way he holds himself, and when he opens his eyes there's a wicked gleam in them.

He pushes up on his knees and, before I'm expecting it, he pushes all the way into me—at a different angle.

An angle that has him ridging deeper into me, knocking every nerve down along the way.

An angle that has him hitting a new spot at the depth of his drive, one that makes me shiver uncontrollably underneath him.

And then he reaches between us, rolling me in his fingers, pressing me in circles until I'm begging him not to stop, never to stop... He slams into me again and again and again and a wildness builds in me, my hips rolling, rolling, needing to reach a peak I never thought I'd find tonight. Not my first time.

But Alec is determined. And there's sweat on his brow.

I want to lap it up with my tongue.

I settle for his mouth though, pulling his face to mine, slipping my tongue through his lips, clawing my hands through his hair, down his back, to grab his ass and pull him harder into me.

And harder.

He responds in kind, slamming so hard into me my head slides halfway off the bed. Instead of stopping, he thrusts again and lowers his head to pull a nipple into his mouth. He doesn't hold back, sucking as hard as he's fucking, as hard as he's tucking me between his fingers, and I can't bite back a cry. It rips out of my lungs and fills the room, and I wrap my arms around him, holding on, holding on and somehow starting to fall without actually falling.

He's grunting, and I'm spiraling down around him in the no-longer-steady room. Flashes of heat span out from between my ribs and twist lower, lower in the both familiar and also achingly new sense of a looming orgasm. I tighten, tighten, tighten around him with so much force he loses himself too, and we're thrashing and moving and swimming in each other.

I don't know who finishes first. All I'm aware of are the echoes of pleasure writhing through every single part of me. They're so intense I lose track of all else and when I come back down, Alec is panting over me, his dark hair tangled and sweaty against his forehead.

My heart is slamming in my chest, and I am tingling from head to toe. Trembling, too. And when Alec collapses on me, I discover I'm not the only one.

"*Fuck*, kitten." His voice is hoarse, and he slips out of me—and the loss of him there makes me whimper. His shoulders shake when he laughs, burying his face in my neck.

I love you, I want to say, but don't.

"Come here." He tucks an arm under me and rolls us to the side, folding me into his chest. I let him hold me, because I've never felt so cherished, so *safe*.

For a while, a long while, there's nothing but the sounds of our breathing and the racing of our hearts. I hear the way his pounds in his chest as clearly as I feel my own.

Another set of tears well in my eyes, though these I'm able to blink away. Mostly.

I thought... I thought it would be real, raw even, with nothing separating us. But it turns out the lack of a condom has nothing to do with why the moment is so raw between us. This goes so much deeper than that.

"You know me for exactly who I am," I say, leaning away to study his face, tugging my fingers through his damp hair, treading them down his back. "And I love that you do. I've never..." I clear my throat. "I've never felt this way."

He kisses me, slowly and smoothly, before he says, "Neither have I."

CHAPTER FORTY-SIX

I'M NOT SURE when we fall asleep. Sometime after we discuss pancakes for the morning, and sometime before I tell him I love him. Because I chicken out repeatedly on that front.

When I open my eyes, the first things I see are his hands, wrapped around my own. One of his arms is thrown over me, the other under my neck. Spooning. I've never done it.

I never want to stop.

His chest is hot against my back.

He's got morning wood between my legs.

It makes me grin.

It makes me want to do wicked, wicked things.

Until my mom's whispers twist through my mind. *That's right, sweetie, that's how to keep him hooked. Spread your legs, and he'll do the same with his wallet.*

I've never scrambled out of bed so fast in my entire life. Alec cracks an eye, stretching—totally uninhibited by his nakedness, by the thickness of his arousal. "Get back here," he grumbles, reaching out for me. "I can't stand one moment without you in my bed."

"Gotta pee." *Gotta pee?* What the hell is wrong with me?

But I dart into the bathroom and do it anyway, hanging my head in my hands. Really, what is wrong with me? How do I get my mother out of my head? How do I keep her from ruining this?

I love him. That love has *nothing* to do with his money...right? So why the hell is my stupid make-believe mother still taking over my thoughts?

I wonder if Straight Talk No Jacket does emergency Saturday sessions.

Then I think of my last session. Self-determination and self-knowledge. Maybe those things don't only have to apply to my career. Maybe they can help me here, too.

Alec raps on one of the doors. "I'll start breakfast."

And I love him more now than I did a second ago. He wanted me back in his bed, but he knows I need some time. He's not pressing me.

Still, it's another few minutes before I can let myself out of the bathroom. I smile when I notice the undershirt he's left on his bed for me.

I slip it on, and then, after a moment of silence to make sure my mother has nothing left to say, I head downstairs.

Alec's mixing batter in nothing but boxer briefs, and he looks fucking delicious.

"What's going on in that head of yours?" he asks, a knowing look across his face.

God. He can read me like a book.

Better than I can read an actual book...

Ha.

I'm so punny.

I take a deep breath, surprised to be more nervous about this than I was about sleeping with him last night. Self-determination, I remind myself. And self-knowledge. I know what scares me, and I know I want to be honest with Alec. Because that's our thing.

And I don't want to lose him.

I open my mouth—right as my gaze falls on a familiar folded piece of clothing. Cassidy's blazer. "I forgot I left this. Why do you still have it?"

"At first, I didn't know how to find you to return it." He levels me with a look that'd pass as stern if he wasn't smiling so wide with the memory. "Then...it was my safety measure. If all else failed, I had a reason to talk to you one last time."

He shrugs like it's no big deal. But it is. It's a really big freaking deal, and it makes me melty all over, knowing he didn't want to give up on us from the start.

"Score, there's fifteen dollars in the pocket, I think. Coffee money!" I smile when he laughs. "What happens when you go to Harvard in the fall?" I ask. It's not the thing I wanted to say, but it's one of the things I've been afraid to bring up. So I guess it counts.

He looks surprised—and then aware. "You think this is a summer thing?"

"I don't know what to think." I know what I *want* to think...

"This is more than a summer thing," he says, serious and tender. "I've got one more year there. I'll come back all the time. And you can fly out on the weekends. If you want, I mean."

"I'm not sure I have the budget for that," I say, quietly. But I offer him a smile, anyway, because he clearly hadn't even thought about the end of the summer, like the possibility of us being over hadn't entered his mind. And I love him for it.

"I'll fly you out," he says, like it's so simple. Like it doesn't make my stomach sour.

"I don't want you to fly me out. I mean, I do. But... I'm nervous that part of me likes you because you're rich." There. It's out in the open now.

"Because of who your mom is?"

Because she's in my head. "For one thing. But also. You're rich. I'm poor. Isn't that how these things work?"

There's a long pause before he responds. "Is that really what you think? Really how you define me?" His jaw clenches. I've hurt him.

"Wait—hear me out, okay? I don't *feel* like what I feel for you has anything to do with your bank account." I reach halfway to him, but he moves away. Understandably. Heartbreakingly. "But I have my mother's genes. And she chases bank accounts like dogs chase balls. With zero discretion. And you're rich. And you're pretty. And it makes me nervous."

He doesn't say anything and the silence between us is a balloon full of tension growing closer, closer to popping.

"You know what—can we go back to a few minutes ago and start over? Forget I said anything?" Because...because what if this has nothing to do with his money and *everything* to do with my mind finding a way to hold on to my mother's voice, since it's the only interaction I'll ever have with her? How did I never pick up on this before? Instead I, what? Have been using her as an excuse to keep myself from being happy with Alec?

No. Not an excuse, a valid reason. What I said to him is true—I do have her genes.

But, still. Maybe there's more to it.

This...is something I might need more time to digest.

And later—because right now Alec's expression is so grim, my stomach clenches. I want to fill him in on my epiphany, but I don't know how to put it into words that don't make me want to punch myself in the face. Then he asks, "You think I'm pretty?"

And the balloon of tension I thought was between us bursts into laughter.

"You know you're pretty," I say, thrilled that I've somehow found my way to this guy who's so easygoing, who lets me be a little neurotic—and then let's it all go. "I..." *love you.* Why can't I say it? "I... I'm starving. Hurry up with those pancakes."

But when he turns from me, toward the stove, I have an idea.

I'm going to set something up for us. Something special. So when I tell him, there'll be no doubt it's true. So when I say the words he won't wonder if they're a part of the euphoria that comes with how perfect last night was.

"You've got a nice ass," I say, admiring the way his briefs shape it. "God, even yours has more shape than mine, all flat." I sigh, all dramatically.

He leaves the batter on the counter, striding toward me, a devilish grin across his pretty mouth. "You do not have a flat ass, you beautiful idiot. You have a gorgeous ass. I could kiss every inch of it. In fact, get that sweet ass over here so I can do it right now."

And when I shriek, attempting to run away, he captures me with the grace of a lion springing on its prey. And he makes good on his word for the rest of the morning.

We never do get around to those pancakes.

CHAPTER FORTY-SEVEN

I TELL ALEC I want to take him somewhere next weekend. He asks for details, I refuse to give them. So he thinks it's a surprise—which I guess it will be—which puts extra pressure on me to figure out where the hell I want to take him. It needs to be special.

Clearwater Heights comes to mind. But to get reservations there before next year I'd need to be...well, Alec. And that place is so far out of my budget it's about as available to me as Mars is, which is to say I'd pretty much need to sell a spaceship to afford it.

I almost ask Vera if she has any ideas. But... I'm not ready for her gooey-eyed response when I say the L word.

I almost ask Sam for an idea at work. But... I kinda want this to come from me. And Sam's busy trying to decide if he's going to forgive Ty—who's begging for another chance—while also stressing out about leaving for his freshman year at Brown in a month.

A month.

That's how long I have with Alec. Should I be panicking?

Because I'm not.

Maybe this is how love works. Maybe love gives us faith that things will work out. And even if they don't, my life is better for having him in it.

Holy shit I'm a sappy motherfucker these days.

For obvious reasons, it's difficult to avoid Alec at work. And not like I really want to avoid him, but I'm so tempted to blurt out my feelings every time I see him, I find myself cleaning the break room a lot. And I take over the supply room for Sam to keep me away from my desk. It really does help me to pass a shit ton of time, considering I have to read labels for specific things, like types of pens and printer paper and a bunch of crap people leave wherever they please. Things people without a learning disability could sort in ten minutes or less. It's annoying, but I know I have options to make it easier. I'm choosing in this instance not to use them because the entire point is to keep me out of Alec's line of vision for a little while longer.

Because when he looks at me, even if I'm not facing him, I swear to God I can feel it.

On Wednesday, he calls me into his office.

"You," he says, leaning against his desk, all forced casual and still sexy as fuck, "have been avoiding me. Should I be worried? Is it the HR stuff?"

"No," I say, my eyes widening. I'm such an idiot, giving off mixed signals. I take a few steps toward him, then I stop when the words try to bubble their way up my throat. I am not going to tell him I love him at the fucking office. "I'll sign the papers whenever they send them."

"Then talk to me. What is it?"

Oh God, he's going to trap me with this annoying habit I've developed of being honest with him.

But there is one truth that might get the job done without my having to tell him *everything*. "This job's important to me. Being around you makes it hard to be competent because all I want to do is jump you when I see you."

"I get it. I can't look at you without wondering what you're wearing under your clothing. You've ruined me," he says, with a smile.

Warmth. Straight between my legs. Flutters, too. I cross one ankle and lean against the door, hoping he can't see right through me. "*See*. This is what I'm talking about! How am I supposed to stay professional when you say things like that... When you make me *feel* things like this?" *Also? I love you.* I want to shout it so bad I literally bite the tip of my tongue.

"So you're saying you want to keep it professional on business days?"

"No—but also yes." I hope my expression shows my chagrin. Because, "Believe me, Alec. Even right now I'm having trouble"—*not telling you I fucking love you*—"not begging you to bend me over your desk. But this is the sort of thing HR will definitely not approve of, regardless of what we sign."

Plus, honestly, I feel the weight of necessity to do a fucking awesome job here. Nobody knows better than I do that I'll be under Mr. Chambers' scrutiny for the foreseeable future. I don't want a reputation as the office flirt or to be seen as a girl who screws her way into keeping her job... Not to mention the fact that, while Zoloft seems to be helping, I'm well aware how quickly a person can slide back into depression—and losing my job, or my reputation? Yeah, I've got firsthand experience with those triggers.

"Screw HR." Alec wets his lips and shoves off his desk, taking one deliciously menacing step toward me. His nostrils puff out in a small flare when he takes a breath, and his face is so full of desire, my mouth goes wet. Aaaaand there go any thoughts about the possibility of depression. Damn, he's fucking hot.

"Alec," I say, pleading—though whether for him to let up or keep going, I'm not sure.

"Fine. I'll behave," he says, "But on the weekends you belong to me. With me."

Four more weekends, I estimate, before he goes to school, and my stomach tenses. "Starting with this weekend," I say. "Friday night. Don't forget."

He gives me a blandly amused look. "I'll be thinking of it every hour at least, and yet somehow I'll remain professional." His expression sharpens into something much less bland and a lot more dangerous and he takes another step toward me. And then another. "Unless you stand here for one second longer."

I want to take him up on it. I want to bounce myself off this door and straight onto him. He glances at my mouth, and I run my tongue over my lips, and...

"I—" I cover my mouth with my hands before *love you* can follow. And I hightail it out of his office.

Time passes excruciatingly slow. I'm aware of Alec every second of every minute, like this whole being professional thing actually makes me want him more even if I'm the one who set the parameters.

At one point he's just standing there, down the aisle in front of my desk, at someone else's desk, and he's drinking a bottle of water. I watch him tip the bottle to his mouth. I watch the liquid travel down his throat.

My own mouth goes so wet I wonder if it's possible to be overhydrated.

And, because I swear he came complete with Teagan-mind reading capabilities, his eyes slide over to mine, and they freaking twinkle because there's no doubt he knows what I'm feeling.

I spend a lot of time cleaning the break room.

I catch him looking at me too, sometimes, with this speculative expression, like he's...nervous. I try to keep my hopes from pole-vaulting, but they leap right out of my reach—because maybe he wants to tell me he loves me too.

On Thursday, I figure out what I want to do.

Nothing fancy. I can't afford it—and it's not me anyway. And I want the moment I tell him to come straight from who I am.

Which means peanut butter and jelly sandwiches, hard ciders, and chips. Lake Imperial and my picnic basket, the one I made in middle school. Maybe the blanket I made, too, to spread on the grass. We can skip the picnic tables. I'll take him to a spot I know doesn't get much traction. We'll be alone.

It might not be much, but it won't matter to Alec. We'll have the lake and the setting sun. We'll have the fireflies and the chirping crickets and birds overhead. We'll have each other and I'll tell him I love him.

Oh my God. This is too much. I'm so...ugh. What has happened to me? I turn to Sam, typing away at his desk. "Hey."

"What?" He doesn't bother looking over. I envy his multitasking abilities.

"Say something annoying."

This gives him pause. He looks at me, his expression unsteady. "Uh, why?"

"Because I haven't been irritated in a while and I need to make sure I still can be. You're usually good at it—so give me your best shot."

His mouth twists in that cocky teenaged smug sort of way we all lose the ability to master once we hit twenty. "You had VPLs yesterday."

"I had what?"

"Visible panty lines."

Yep. Turns out I can *definitely* still get pissed off. "You're such a little shit. Why didn't you say anything? Why did you even look?"

"Sorry. They were noticeable." He at least has the decency to blush, even if his mouth stays in the smug twist from before. "Also sometimes you talk out loud while you type. It's annoying."

"*You* are annoying." I throw a pen at him and the nib leaves a black mark on the chest of his shirt. He looks from it to me and the expression on his face is so bewildered, I burst into laughter. "Guess it's your turn to walk around with something embarrassing for people to stare at all day."

It doesn't occur to me to apologize until later. But the fact that it registers at all...well, I'll call that progress. Even more so when I actually do it.

Another thing that doesn't occur to me until later is that in order to have the picnic I want, I have to get my things from my grandparents' house.

Fuck.

CHAPTER FORTY-EIGHT

I TAKE FRIDAY off of work, texting Alec that I'm fine but I have to deal with some personal stuff. I swear, I have to stop calling out. Alec may be cool with it—but he won't be my boss for much longer and I need a better track record. Especially with Mr. Chambers probably looking for reasons to get rid of me. Plus, I only get fourteen days off *a year*.

But today... Today I'd be a waste of space at work. Today I need to focus on dealing with my grandparents.

Ugh. It's too early to think about them. I'm going back to bed.

Alec calls me a few minutes later, and my voice is still groggy when I answer. "The sun is barely up. I was so close to falling back asleep."

"I'm taking off today too, to be with you," he announces. He doesn't sound groggy at all. He sounds awake, alive. Even wired, maybe. "Let's do your personal stuff together."

I sit up, rubbing sleep from my eyes. Yum. An entire extra day with Alec? I'm tempted. My entire body's tempted, if the tightening in my nipples is any indication. The warmth in my belly. The wet between my thighs...

But I say, "Go to work, boss. I need to do this on my own."

"Sounds serious."

I shrug, laughing silently at myself when I remember he can't see it. God, I need coffee. "I'll tell you about it tonight. I'll text you where to meet me."

He's hesitant before responding. "Are you sure?"

I'm touched when we hang up, because I think he was able to read the nervousness in my voice.

I *am* nervous. I have to face the people who raised me with as much care as they might have given a fucking slug. I need to get my basket and my blanket—and, hell, most of my other stuff while I'm at it. But this might be the last time I ever see them, and there are some things I need to get off my chest.

Just...not first thing in the morning.

Brunch in an hour? I text Cassidy. *My treat.*

How about breakfast now? she responds. *We're leaving in a couple hours for North Carolina.*

Kelsey's Diner, I say. *And you can bring Gage if you have to.*

She brings Gage.

I want to be annoyed, but he makes her happy.

And he's a nice person.

And... I'm not sure why I want to be annoyed anymore.

They walk toward the table, Cassidy all blonde and curves, Gage all sharp-featured and disheveled. Even in a sallow old diner, they shine. Ugh.

She hugs me. He hugs me. And, add the fact that he smells awesome to the list from before. Not as good as Alec, but close enough.

Cassidy drops into a seat, but Gage stays standing. "I've got some lyrics to work through. Thought I'd give you girls some alone time, cool?"

A grateful smile widens my lips. "Gig tonight?"

"Yeah. Then some much needed beach time." He leans down for a quick kiss from Cassidy. "With the sexiest bikini chick in the Outer Banks."

Cassidy rolls her eyes, but her cheeks are prettily pink and there's a smile in her tone. "You haven't met Quinn yet."

"Doesn't matter." He tweaks her shoulder, nods to me, and then heads off to his own table. A moment later he's lost in his notebook, scribbling away.

After a waitress takes our order, Cassidy levels me with a stare. "What gives?"

"What do you mean?" I aim for an innocent tone, but my pitch is way off.

"I haven't heard from you this early in the morning since we were in high school and you were texting me not to pick you up because you were ditching."

"Those were the days." My words feel almost as crooked as the smile I'm trying to come up with. "Are you excited to see Quinn?"

I don't quite understand why Cassidy cares enough about her roommate to visit her. The few times I've been down to North Carolina to see them during their school year, Quinn's been...distant, to say the least. She hides in her room and barely responds when Cassidy tries to make conversation. I wondered if she was shy, but Cassidy said no, that she'd drastically changed this past year, growing secretive and kind of moody.

I would never be friends with someone like that, but...then again, I can't be surprised Cassidy would be. She's friends with *me*, after all...

Maybe it's her calling, collecting all of us rejects.

"Teag. Out with whatever you're holding back." Her expression softens. "Is it Gran? Is she still bothering you?"

"No. Yes—she's part of it. But..." I find my shrug comes easily. "I'm going over there after this to get my stuff, and then I'll be done with her—with both of them—for good."

I expect Cassidy to ask if I'm sure that's what I want, the eternal optimist that she's always been, but all she says is, "Good. You're better without them."

Relief shudders through me in a laugh. "Anything is better without them."

"Do you want me to go with you?"

"No," I say, meaning it. "I need to do this on my own."

"You're really okay about it?" She studies my face, and I nod. I can tell the moment she believes that I'm telling the truth because her own stance relaxes. "You get to turn a whole new page. Ugh—and you get to do it living with Vera. I'm so tempted to move back in—how much fun would that be?"

"Awesome," I say, imagining it. "Though then she couldn't sneak around with that Gold Rush Standard roadie from last summer."

"The one she made out with last year?" Her mouth parts and her eyes go wide and—oops—I guess she didn't know.

"They're doing quite a bit more than making out if the noises in her bedroom a few nights ago were any indication." Guilt shoots little arrows my way for sharing Vera's business, but it's not like Cassidy wouldn't find out eventually anyway. "Have you heard from Luca?"

"Nope." Cassidy's jaw tightens. "I told him to burn my phone number last time he called."

"No such thing as forgiving and forgetting, huh?"

Her eyes burn with anger. "He wrote a song as his apology. I forgave him long before that. But how can anyone fucking forget when that song's played like every five minutes?"

I glance at Gage, erasing something in his notebook. "Does it bother him?"

"Not anymore." Some of the tension drains from her expression. "At first it did, but...he says he's confident enough in how much I love him not to let a stupid song bring us back down. And he says he'll write me millions of songs, so who cares about one fading pop artist." She shakes her head, laughing.

I'm a little swoony myself. "He's halfway decent."

"I sometimes feel like I don't deserve him." She twists to look at him, and like he senses her movement, he catches her eyes, grinning a lopsided smile. She's wearing the same one when she turns around. "But all I have to do is look at him and I'm better. Better than better."

The waitress drops off our food. I use the interruption as an excuse to ask what I really want to know about.

Okay.

I open my mouth to ask about the first time she told Gage she loves him, but something else comes out instead. "I slept with Alec."

She blinks at the change of pace, and then her features twist into something pleased, something greedy, and she rubs her hands together. "I want the details—was it amazing? I can't believe you waited this long."

"Believe it," I snap. "And not just with Alec either."

"Not just with Alec?" She tilts her head, considering my words—and then her eyes light up. "Holy shit—did you have a three-way?"

"God—*no*. What is wrong with you?"

"What's wrong with you?" she snaps back this time. "It's not like you've never said you wanted one." She shovels eggs into her mouth, chewing angrily.

"I was a *virgin*," I say, angrier even than the motions of her jaw. "I'd never had sex. And you can wipe that shocked expression off your fucking face because if you were any kind of friend you'd already know this."

"But you always... I mean..." She slowly lowers her fork to the plate in front of her, eggs forgotten. "Why would you always say—"

"Because it was fun. It was easy." It was making myself the thing my grandmother always said I'd be—but defiantly, like *in her face* defiantly. Like her words never hurt me, never bothered me. "And you never even questioned it. Never even stopped to wonder why I was spreading my legs for everyone I came in contact with." My voice is sharp enough to slice someone—it's like I *am* my grandmother right now. God. Antidepressants have definitely helped to stem some of my mood swings, but I still have so far to go along the self-improvement path. I fucking hate lashing out like this. *Hate*.

"First of all," Cassidy bites out the words, "even if you had been sleeping with the guys you said you were—why would I judge you for it? You want to be ashamed of your imaginary sex life—go ahead. But don't put that on me."

"I..." Damn. I can't believe I'm fighting a smile. "You grew some claws this year, huh?"

"Kinda have to with you as my best friend." She's not ready to smile yet. Which makes me lose the battle with my own—it forces my lips to curve, and even wider when she glares at me.

"I'm sorry I lied," I say.

"I'm sorry you ever felt the need to."

I push my pancakes around. "It was never about you, or not trusting you. It was... I don't know how to explain it. My mind's a fucked-up place sometimes."

"Tell me something I don't know," she says, her words drier than the Sahara.

"You should be careful what you ask for," I say. "But it's too late to take it back now."

And I tell her everything else, too.

And we talk for hours.

And she's late leaving for the Outer Banks. But this, I don't apologize for. Because we needed these hours.

"How did I not know you had feelings for Jason? I was so blind," she says, squeezing me into a huge hug.

"It was kind of a whirlwind. It happened so fast, somehow we noticed each other at the same time, and there were a few weeks of flirting. He... He didn't want me to say anything until we knew what it was, so we spent that weekend together—but I didn't hear from him again after, so I thought he'd changed his mind. And then he was...gone." I wrap my arms around her, ducking my face into the hug so I don't have to see the tears that shimmer in her eyes. "I'm sorry."

"Don't be. Please. I'm sorry there was no closure after your weekend together, but I'm glad it happened," she says. "I'm glad he had that weekend with you. That he knew happiness with you. Before he died."

Before he died. Before he died. These are such horrible words, and my heart splinters all over again. I don't care whether or not we would've ended up together; nothing changes the fact that Jason should still be here today.

He died too young. And over something so stupid.

There's a question Cassidy's too nervous to ask—I feel it in her stance, and I answer anyway. "I never saw him using drugs. I never knew."

I want to tell her I'm nervous he was using around me and that I didn't pick up on it. I want to tell her I've spent more nights than I can count sleepless over wondering how I missed the signs, or if I could've prevented his death. But I don't. I let it rest. Because my fears aren't facts, and transferring them to her won't do any good. And because I feel closer to her than I have in ages. The distance has been all my fault, but it's starting to close and that's what matters most.

Well, that and getting my shit from Gran.

Double fuck.

CHAPTER FORTY-NINE

THERE'S A SHINY black truck with new tags parked in front of my grandparents' place. I pull up in my ancient clunker and sputter to a stop right beside it. The sight makes my stomach twist, but I'm not sure why.

Actually, maybe I do. If Gramps has a new truck...is that where my payments have gone? Rather than to water bills, he stashed them away for the down payment?

Irritation starts to simmer in my gut, but I smother it. Why should I care about cold showers when I'll never have to take them here again? I'm letting go of this place today. Of them. Of everything from my past.

I ignore the truck and I take the few steps up to the front porch. And my fucking house key doesn't work when I try to open the door.

They changed the locks.

Well, fuck this.

I bang on the door until my hand feels tender. I kick it a couple times, too. I'm about to break through one of the screened windows when Gran finally opens the door. "Oh. You."

"You changed the locks?" I don't meant to sound so hurt, but my voice is smaller than usual and, instead of anger, a confusing sort of sadness fills me.

"You left."

"You told me to."

"Eh. You're old enough to look after yourself now." She glances over my shoulder.

"Expecting someone?" I *almost* manage to laugh—my grandparents literally never have company—but the mangled sound makes it as high as the base of my throat before it fades. I brush past her. "Don't worry. I'll be gone in a few. I need my things, and then I guess this is over."

I wrinkle my nose against the ashtray stench that assaults it. The stink seems worse now, but maybe that's because I was used to it for too long. I take the stairs, skipping the broken ones and avoiding the splinters of the handrail, and there's a certain sort of elation that begins to fill me when I remember this is the last time I'll ever do it.

Because if something goes wrong with rooming with Vera, I'll live in my car before I come back here. I'll sleep under my desk. I don't care. Anything is better than this.

I stuff most of my clothing in a duffel bag. I grab the basket, pulling out my baby blanket and holding it against my chest. Only for a moment. It's a bit more worn than I thought it was, but maybe that'll add to tonight's charm.

Gran's still watching outside when I return, bag and basket in tow. "Where's Gramps?" I ask.

"Trading in my car." She's sucking on a cigarette and...for the one moment while her cheeks are hollowed, I notice how the years have aged her. She's bitter, always has been, but maybe that's the life she was dealt.

Her answer makes a bit more sense about the truck—maybe they traded in both their old cars for it. I glance at it out the front door. "Guess I won't get to tell him goodbye."

Her snort puts a horse's to shame. "Guess not."

Considering the last time I saw him he hit me—unintentionally doesn't make it that much better—I can't say I'm too upset about it.

"Do you blame me?" I ask quietly, my stomach tighter than a dead man's noose.

"For what?" Her words are more warning than question, and still she watches out the front screen. Hot summer air pulses through the grating, sticky on my skin. Her shirt is damp under the armpits and beneath her breasts.

"For my mother leaving." My clarification is quieter than the question was.

The answer's always been implied, but I've never had the guts to ask.

Now she swivels her head my direction, and if looks could kill...

I wave my hand in front of her monstrous expression. "I know, I know, mentioning mommy dearest goes against rule number one. But... I don't care." What I do care about, however, is the way my voice cracks. It doesn't stop me though. "I want an answer."

Still, she doesn't respond.

"What is it?" I pause, waiting for my throat to stop constricting. It takes longer than I'd prefer. "Do you have some... I don't know...some long lost fear? You can't let yourselves love me because you're afraid I'll leave you like she did?"

For a moment, I can't read her expression. The type of tension that's actually hope runs its way along my ribcage, like mallets over a xylophone, lightly at first and then, after the reality of the moment sinks in, hard enough to snap. Because this is it. This is the moment I've always feared, always craved.

In the deepest, most hidden parts of my mind, the rest of the conversation goes like this: *Love you?* she'd ask. *Of course we love you. But your mother broke our hearts, and it's too hard to show love after that. You look so much like her it's sometimes painful.*

In reality, she begins to laugh, which is interrupted by series of hacking coughs. "When did you get this needy?"

I press harder. "Is that it? You raised me to be hardened against needing things, or people, because she left you and you didn't want me to ever go through what you did?"

She drags on her cigarette and the soured twist to her face takes regular contempt and makes it a little bitch. "What the hell sort of sissy shit are you talking about?"

A part of me wishes I wanted to tear at my hair.

A part of me wishes I wanted to scream.

A part of me wishes I wanted to do anything other than offer the quiet smile that I do.

Because that would mean I hadn't given up, that there was still some sort of hope for a semblance of a relationship with the only relatives I know. But it's over. Has been for a long time. From the very beginning, honestly.

"Thank you," I say. "I needed to hear that."

Tires crunch over gravel and a new truck—delivery, this time—pulls up to the house. And I watch, stunned, when a man uses a dolly to haul two boxes from the back. A new washer and dryer.

There is a thought slamming its fist at the door of my mind, and I am doing everything I can to keep it out. Double lock. Triple lock.

But this thought... It cuts through those locks with a chainsaw and comes through anyway.

"Why did Gramps trade your car in?" I ask, a hot, tingling sort of pain dancing along my skin.

"To make room for the new one," she says, her tone slow and steady, like I'm an idiot for asking.

"For the new truck out there?" Please, please be for the truck.

"No." She smiles a brittle smile. "That's his. Mine's a station wagon."

"A...new station wagon?" Oh God. Oh God. "Where did you get the money?"

Her smile goes from brittle to gloating in no time at all. "A friend of yours, actually. You seem surprised."

My heart.

My heart.

There is a piece of barbed wire circling my heart, and my stupid fucking heart is twisting back and forth, like the wire is a Hula-Hoop. And it's *shredding* me.

"Alec," I say. "He gave you these things?"

Where is my breath? I clutch my stomach and bend at the waist. I'm so close to falling to my knees I almost give in and do it. But I don't think I'd get up after. And I have to be able to leave. That was my entire reason for coming.

But I wasn't expecting this.

"Why?" I ask, the word dropping like an anchor, pulling me down, down, down with it.

"Guess you'll have to ask him." And after a few beats of silence, mine full of shock, hers full of gloat, "Told you you'd end up like your mama," Gran says, her cigarette breath making me gag. "Least when you spread *your* legs, we reap the rewards rather than just the consequences."

Just the consequence. That's what I am to her. To both of them. I'm not their grandchild. I'm not their blood. I'm the mistake my mother made and didn't want to face. They were stuck with me.

They never loved me.

Never bothered trying to.

This is actually what I came for. To learn the thing that will give me no regrets about never seeing them again.

And now I have it.

And now I can leave.

I do it without a backwards glance.

And with a heart dead in my chest.

CHAPTER FIFTY

PERCHED ON A picnic table with the orange setting sun rolling over the water before me, I slap at a mosquito after it's had a few seconds of ankle blood. It's probably the tenth in the past five minutes. Guess I forgot citronella candles. Or bug spray.
Guess I forgot pretty much everything.
Guess I don't really care.
My anger's only ever been a scorching thing. So this coolness coursing through me is difficult to understand. Difficult to feel. Or maybe it's so cold it's made me numb.
The headlights of Miles' town car come into view, and in the back of my mind I wonder if I should be nervous. Shouldn't my stomach jump?
Shouldn't I feel something?
Anything other than empty?
Because if that's the case, I'm failing.
Even Alec's familiar stride through the park toward me only brings the smallest twinge.
He's smiling.
He's smiling, even when he knows what he's done.
Huh.

Guess I can feel pain after all. It hits in the weirdest spots. Beneath my belly button. Along my collarbone. At the base of my throat.

I'm not sure what he sees in my expression, my face alone is still too numb for me to understand, but whatever it is, he falters as he gets closer, his smile vanishing.

"Aren't you going to ask me what's wrong?" I ask when he doesn't.

"Let me explain—"

"Did you know I wanted tonight to be special?" I say. My voice comes out like a song, teasing with a bitter edge.

"If you let—"

"It needed to be," I say, talking over him. "Because I wanted to tell you I loved you."

Surprise washes the edges from his expression.

Pleasure follows, and he steps toward me.

But uncertainty comes next, and he goes still.

"Yeah, it's confusing, isn't it?" I laugh. It twists humorlessly through the air. "Thinking you know something and then realizing you don't."

"You spoke with your grandparents." He's not surprised, just clarifying to fill the silence.

"I've had all day to think about it—and, maybe it's because I'm slow," I pause, swallowing past the lump of torn pride in my throat, "but I can't figure it out. Were you trying to make peace with them for me?"

"N-no, I—"

"Because that is never, ever going to happen. I went there today to get my things and to cut them completely free from my life. To cut *myself* free from them." I study the water for a moment, steeling myself. My insides seem to be swaying with the gentle ripples. Soon, too much time passes and I have to look at him again. It nearly kills me. "I didn't realize I'd have to do the same with you."

"Don't say that." His eyes dart between mine, like he's searching for a way to replace the meaning of my words with something else, something less set in stone. Panic loosens his features, tightens his stance.

But anger is a zipper trying to close my ribcage, making me choke. It hurts. Every part of this hurts. "I am so fucking stupid. I thought...when you called me this morning you seemed nervous—I thought it was because of me. I thought you were reading the anxiety in my tone. But you weren't. You were nervous for yourself, because you knew I'd find out what you'd done."

"You were always going to find out," he says. "I would never keep that from you."

"When did you go to them?"

He doesn't say anything, guilt wringing the truth from his expression.

"When?"

"Tuesday."

I stare at the setting sun until my tears clear. "You did keep it from me then. All week."

"Because I knew you wouldn't agree to it."

"Oh, right." I scoff at him and grip the picnic table so hard a splinter slides into my palm. Guess I was always going to get a splinter today, no matter how hard I try to avoid them. "Because you know better than me. I'm just a little woman and you're the big man who gets to march around beating his chest and making decisions over my head when I'm too dumb to know any better."

"You know that's not me." His tone is level but there's an entire ocean of anxiety beneath it.

"The Alec I *thought* I knew would never, under any circumstance, go behind my back and to the people who literally never showed me any love in my entire life and reward them with shiny, new, expensive toys."

"Hear me out," he says.

"Oh, I'm going to," I say. "You get to say your piece—that's the only reason I didn't cancel tonight. And then I get to say mine. And then we get to go our separate ways."

He winces and the pain in the shadows etched across his face makes my heart shred itself all over again. "You told me you didn't believe what you'd been told about your father."

My soul goes still as stone. "I told you I had childish hopes that maybe he wasn't a total monster."

"I wanted to give you the truth," he says.

Not just my soul now—everything is still. The lake. The crickets. The air. "And?"

"They were lying. The moment your grandmother asked how willing I was to make it worth her while to tell the truth, I knew they'd lied to you about him." He steps toward me, thinking I'll need him to hold me or shatter with the news, but I've reached my full shock capacity for the day and this… This is so big it will take me a lifetime to understand.

Still, a question rises from my gut, from a place I can't keep it back. "He's not a monster?"

"I can't speak for the kind of man he is," Alec says. "I wanted you to be able to choose whether or not to look into him, or contact him. But I can give you the number where he can be reached. And I can tell you…he never knew your mother was pregnant."

My father never knew he was my father.

My father…

I start to laugh. Just a few whispers of a humorless sound, really. And when Alec's expression drops to absolute sympathy-laden concern, I laugh harder.

And then I go quiet.

I feel it happen.

I feel my mind open to his words. I feel my mind sweep them inside and guide them into a very faraway corner, one I rarely access. I feel my mind lock them away to keep them safe until I can process them.

I wonder if this is what going crazy feels like.

Because all I feel is an icy calm.

No.

Wait.

Rage.

Rage I'm unused to, because there's no heat in it.

My rage is an ice storm, and Alec's caught out in the cold.

"How dare you?" My tone is dry ice, my words, raspy, scraping my throat. "Am I supposed to be *grateful?*"

"No, I n-never intended—"

"You can't just throw money at things to fix them. You can't—"

"Yes, I can," he says, finally snapping, and I've never wanted to punch someone more than I want to punch him right now. He shakes his head at what he sees on my face. "Not the important things, Teagan. I know the things that matter most can't be purchased. But them? They don't matter. You matter. And you deserve to know who your own father is."

"Stop." I throw my hand up like it'll do anything to block the word *father* from my ears. "You don't get to talk to me about my father. Don't you understand?"

"You know what I understand?" he asks, his voice suddenly so quiet I have to strain to hear him. "I understand that I love you. That I started falling the moment I met you. That it's real, it's there, and it's not going away. *That* is what I know more than anything I've ever known. I never intended to hurt you."

All week, this is what I've been dying to hear. I've hoped beyond my wildest anything that he would return the words I was so giddy to offer him.

Now they're the last things I want to come from his lips.

"You know nothing," I say, bitter with the truth of it.

Heartbroken.

Heart-kicked-out-of-my-chest.

Heartless.

"You don't love me. If you did—you would know I value my ability to act on my own behalf. You would know I can't *stand* when people go behind my back. For anything, but especially when it comes to my family life. I almost kicked Sam's ass the other week when he took my cellphone without my permission. And this? What you did? I don't give a shit about your intentions. Your *intentions* are the very reason I'd never be able to trust you again."

"Teagan—"

"Piper was right." I almost laugh again with this realization. How did I miss this before? "You have a savior complex." My world starts to crumble, finally, with the weight of my anger and my sadness, and I stand from where I'm perched before I crumble with it.

"Piper?" he asks. "What are you—"

"You're trying to save me. You've *been* trying to save me." I can't breathe. I am trying to pull air into my lungs but they've been crushed by my sudden understanding. "Audiobooks. Making sure I have health insurance. This thing with my grandparents. I can't *breathe* without feeling you somewhere in my life."

Oh my God.

I've been like my mom all along, letting him make my life better.

And with this, my world is no longer tilting.

It's disintegrating. I have no footing because it's no longer there beneath me.

Dust. All I'm left with is dust.

My face crumples a split second before tears run razors across my eyes. "You turned me into my mother," I manage to gasp out before I sob.

"You're nothing like her." He strides toward me, all furrow-browed and concerned, and sweeps me into his arms and holds me against his chest and... I let him.

I let him because I want to remember the feel of him, the scent of him.

I let him because I can't stem my tears, and I'd rather press my face against him than let him see them.

I let him because I need to walk away, but I'm too weak.

"Tell me how to fix it," he says, his voice a jagged mess.

"You don't get it." Finding the will to step back is like looking for an unburned sliver of wood after an all-consuming bonfire. But I dig, and I dig, and I find it. Even if it still burns me. "You took the one thing I based my entire life on and crushed it."

"Teagan." Panic makes a knife's edge out of his voice. He drops to his knees, gripping my calves, looking up at me, the destruction of the entire world in his eyes. "D-don't do this."

"I'm not doing it. You did." I swallow, my throat so swollen with a fresh batch of tears I almost choke. "You can't fix this. There's nothing to fix. It doesn't even exist anymore."

And it turns out I'm not too weak to walk away after all.

CHAPTER FIFTY-ONE

I LOOK BACK, because of course I do. Numb or not, I can't leave without turning.

Alec's no longer on his knees, but he's still facing the water, his hands fisted at his sides, his shoulders rigid. He's all shades of black and white, a silhouette against the last few moments of sun, and a hairline fracture splits beneath my sternum and races out like a crack in ice, spreading in rivulets through my chest, across my ribs, down my spine.

I have to get to my car before I fall to pieces.

I have to make it home.

Miles is smoking a cigarette, leaning against his hood.

He smiles.

Then he frowns.

He asks a question.

I give an answer.

I make it to my car.

I make it to Vera's.

And then I don't remember much.

CHAPTER FIFTY-TWO

PANIC IS A red-hot branding iron shoved straight into my stomach. I sit up in bed, gasping, sweating, trembling.

The burn of my reality scorches until I double over in pain.

Besides me, Vera snores, softly, almost prettily. Did she come to bed with me? I have a vague memory of stumbling into my room and her hands cool on my hot, tear-streaked face.

Did she help me change into my new pajama set? I honestly can't remember.

I slip quietly out of bed, knowing sleep is done for the night, but less than a minute later Vera's joining me in the living room, rubbing her eyes. "What time is it?"

"Three thirty."

"Want me to make you some tea?" she asks through a yawn. "Making some for myself."

I don't like tea, but I nod. Maybe it's time to start liking tea. Maybe tea will make me calmer. Maybe tea will keep Gran's careless, laughing expression from swiveling on repeat through my mind.

Vera makes us tea.

It's fucking gross.

It's so gross I spit mine back into my cup. The moment the last of the liquid passes my lips, though, I keep them open and I tell her everything.

My tone is dead, the way I'm trying to keep my insides.

"Wow," she says, and her eyes glint, wet with tears. "I couldn't really understand what you were saying when you got home. I'm so sorry, Teagan."

"Please don't be emotional," I say. "I don't want your pity."

"There's a difference between pitying someone and hurting along with them because you care for them," she says, but the rebuke is gentle.

"I have trouble feeling the difference," I say, calmly. "So I'd prefer neither."

She sips her tea, also calmly. If she's struggling to compose herself, I can't tell. And I'm grateful for it.

I'm grateful for her. I don't have many friends, but the ones I have are worth more than millions.

"I texted Cassidy," she says. "She's coming back in the morning. I figured you could use both of us right now."

Oh. Great. Now I'm going to end up the emotional one. I take another sip of my tea. Spit it out again. "Gross."

"If I was going to look at this like a journalist—detached and professional," she says, looking at me expectantly until I nod. "I'd divide this into four parts and tackle each one separately."

"Four parts?" I ask.

She counts off on her fingers. "One. Your grandparents are horrible people. You always secretly longed to discover a shred of decency in them and you've had that longing smashed to smithereens. That might take some time to process, but ultimately, it's not surprising. Two. You have a father out there who doesn't know you're alive."

"Stop." I stand. I pace. I clutch my stomach. "I'm going to throw up."

"Breathe," she says, rising to stand with me. "Deep breaths. You're not going to throw up. That's the hard one. I had to say it to get it out of the way. The rest will be easier."

"I can't think about..." I pause, panting like I'm out of breath. I *am* out of breath. "I'm not ready to deal with that one."

"Fine," she says, her tone stern rather than placating. It helps ease a bit of air into my lungs. "Three. Alec took your trust and twisted it. He—"

"Twisted it?" I tilt my head, wondering where her faulty logic comes from. "He demolished it. He—"

"Is in *love* with you." She sips her tea again. "He wanted to give you something that matched the depth of what he feels for you. He did it the wrong way."

"You're wrong," I say, but my words are weak.

"As dumb as his actions were," she says, "he did them for the right reasons."

Instead of snarking at her, I rub my eyes, furiously, willing the threat of tears into submission. "Who needs therapy when you're around?"

She cracks a tentative smile, and I can't match it, but I don't bite at her for it, so she pulls me back to the couch and sits closer to me this time. Just an inch. Just close enough to place a hand on my knee. "And here's the fourth part: You love him, too. You love him and he loves you, and nobody in the world can ease your hurt better than he can right now."

"I have you," I remind her stubbornly. "I have Cassidy, coming all the way back from the beach."

"You have us," she agrees. "But he's the first person you trusted enough to tell these things to. He's the one you want by your side. He's the one who can make right the wrongs he's done. If you want to let him. And we both know you do."

I want to push back harder, but I don't. Because she's speaking the truth, my truth, a feeling in my gut I haven't been able to name.

"Or," she says, her tone suddenly aces and spades lighter than before. "There are a dozen eggs in the fridge. We can take 'em and throw 'em at your grandparents' fancy new cars. I'm always happy to go that route with you, too."

Finally, finally, I laugh. It's a small thing, this laugh. Short and without much energy, but it's there. I didn't force it.

And beneath it is a steadiness that wasn't there before.

"I love him," I say. "But he hurt me, in the worst way he could."

She opens her mouth, but looks away, and it's closed when she faces me again.

"Don't you have something to say to that?" I ask.

"Don't you?"

"You sure you don't want to switch your major to shrink-hood?" She lifts one meticulously groomed brow. It's her only response.

"Fine. Whatever. Clearly, journalism suits you." I sigh, and then I give in. "I should forgive him. Because I love him." The more I say it out loud, the clearer my answer becomes. "And because he didn't *mean* to hurt me. And sometimes intent matters." I pick up my own tea, sipping. And, of course, it's still disgusting. I put it down. "I don't want to talk about my father, but I will when I've had time to process it. And I wouldn't have that option if Alec hadn't done what he did. I might even be grateful when that time comes."

Oh my God. Relief is a splash of cold water shocking my system. It's like being reborn, right this instant, from someone who's always quick to rise in fury—into someone who's also now quick to forgive, quick to understand that sometimes things aren't black and white. *Even* while my feelings are still so bruised. So raw.

I'm usually the best grudge-holder I know. This moment, this realization that I don't have to be... It's jarring. In the *best* way.

"What else?" Vera asks, her eyes all wide and happy. The entire atmosphere is changing, no longer as heavy with my pain—it's tightening with anticipation.

"He makes me happy when he's not being a fucking idiot." A honey-like smoothness melts slowly through my chest, down my arms and legs. I've wondered if my mother's voice is in my mind because I can't help clinging to any interaction with her, even imaginary. But Alec gave me the means to have an *actual* interaction with my father. "I need Alec. I don't want to be without him. I'm going to go get him."

"In the morning?" she asks, covering a yawn. "Because I'm happy to snuggle the rest of the night with you."

But I'm wired. I couldn't sleep right now if I superglued my eyes shut. "I'll text you later."

She yawns again, this one stretching out over her grin. "Go get him."

I'm going to. I'm not even changing out of my pajamas first. I grab my bag, and I open the door to go to Alec.

He's already here.

CHAPTER FIFTY-THREE

ALEC IS SITTING in the landing of the concrete stairwell of Vera's apartment. His head's resting against the wall, and his feet are on the ground, his knees pulled up. His eyes open a second after I open the door.

It'd be nice if my emotions didn't tend to get completely snarled together so I could tell what exactly I feel right now. Excitement, I think—but maybe it's dread. I think maybe I'm happy, too, but my entire system's been under so much strain the past few hours, everything has a hollow tinge to it.

"How long have you been out here?" I ask, and turn to see if Vera's witnessing the same thing I am.

She seems in complete control of her emotions, grinning wide enough to break her face in half.

"I wanted to give you this," Alec says, his voice hoarse, and when I look at him again, he's standing, stepping toward me. He hands me a folded piece of paper. "I brought you your father's information, if you want it."

My breath catches in the steel trap of the word *father*. Just because I've come around to the idea of possibly interacting with him doesn't mean I'm ready to address it yet. "You could've texted me."

"I wanted to hand you something solid."

"You wanted a reason to come here." I almost smile. It's like Cassidy's blazer. But this is so much bigger than that.

"I would've been here even if I'd texted you."

"Why?"

"To tell you I'm sorry." He grabs my hand, covering it with his. I try not to sigh at the contact, at the way it steadies me in such an unsteady situation. Vera was right. I need him.

"I should've told you everything from the beginning," he says. "I thought if I surprised you... But I know you better than that. I wasn't thinking things through. I'm sorry I hurt you. I'm more sorry than you'll ever know." He lets go of my hand. It drops to my side, the folded slip of paper still between my fingers. "But you deserve to decide whether you know your history. I had the means to get it for you. I won't apologize for that."

"I..." I glance back for the comfort of Vera's support, but she's gone, the door to her room closed. I can do this. It's not *weak* to give in, even if my pride still manages to protest. But I know now, there's a strength in the ability to let go of anger. So I say, "I won't ask you to apologize for it."

Shock makes a fresh playing field of his face, erasing some of the divots left from our earlier fight. A fresh determination rises along the sidelines, too. "I won't lie to you, even to make things right. I learn from my mistakes."

"Good," I say, relief making my voice softer. It's the best thing he could've said. "Do you want to come in? Because there are some things I need to tell you."

"Yes. Because I have a few things of my own to say. And this time you're going to listen to them."

Still, he waits for me to motion him inside. When he crosses in front of me, though, he stops and takes my face in his hands and he kisses me. Without permission.

But he didn't really need it anyway.

I cling to him.

He yanks me tighter, lifting me off of my feet.

His mouth is hard, merciless.

So is mine.

One of us relents, I'm not sure which, but after a few moments, the kiss changes. Stretches. Expands.

Softens.

A tremble begins in the center of my chest and ripples out. Down my arms and up my neck.

I pull away before I begin to cry.

"I'm not going to apologize for that either," he says, placing me gently on the floor.

My laugh is watery at best. "I'd use my knee to hurt you if you did."

He sees it now, that I'm leaving the possibility for *us* open, and his entire body loosens, one vertebrae at a time. He follows me into my bedroom.

I close the door behind us, while he takes in the room.

"It feels weird that this is my first time here," he says.

"I haven't been here that long." I still have my father's information in my hand. I'm still not entirely ready for it. I might not be for a while. I slip it into a dresser drawer.

I'm…comforted to know it's there.

Alec paces my room, checking out Vera's various decorative touches and knickknacks on the bookshelf. "So this is where you sleep without me." Now he faces me, though we're both far from the bed in the center of the room. "Every night we haven't spent together the past week has been a mistake."

"I'm not sure I agree," I say, hating the words. Hating the truth.

"If we'd been together this week, maybe I would've seen how stupid I was—"

"Not because of that," I say. "I mean, yes, that too. But…" I stop, gathering my thoughts, taking a few deep breaths. "I'm depressed, Alec. Not just right now because I'm sad—but clinically. And I have a lot of work to do, righting myself and dealing with the shit I've avoided dealing with. I've only taken baby steps so far, and I don't know what the future holds in that regard."

"You're treating it," he says. "That's what matters. Depression isn't something to be ashamed of—and it isn't something that should keep you from having the future you want."

He's right. I know he is. "Even so… The other issue is that I also don't know how to be with you without becoming like my mother. All she's ever wanted was a man with a pretty face and huge bank account. I hear her, goading me on toward your wealth. She's in my thoughts. Which means those are my thoughts."

Maybe I'm not one hundred percent convinced that's why she's in my mind, but the fact is, the direction of her voice when she speaks to me is always about his money. And that will always bother me.

"Those aren't your *thoughts*. They're your fears," he says, his face relaxing, like it's no big deal. "That's a different thing."

His words shine a beam of relief through me. He's right again. *My fears are not facts.* But...still. I can't keep from saying, "Even if I'm not actively with you because you're rich... You have more than I do, Alec. This will never be equal."

The change in him, the shock across his expression, then the furious understanding, is startling. Suddenly he's the angry one, and I have to fight the urge to drop my gaze when he comes toward me. He drags a hand across his face, his eyes bright and livid. "Of all the stupid—"

"Watch it," I warn. "I'm the only one who gets to use that word about myself." Which I'm trying not to do anymore.

"Of course *you're* not stupid. But, Jesus, Teagan. *Think*. What about what I get from you?" He shouts the question, his raised voice shocking me all the way through my core. "Did you ever consider that? Did you? So from me, you get fancy meals and restaurants. A few flights out to Boston. Big fucking deal. I could shower you in money and it still wouldn't tip the balance in my favor. You inspire me. Do you have any idea what that's like? I refused to cave to my *father*—for the first time ever. The one place in my life I've never felt comfortable taking charge, and you pushed me to do it anyway with the proposal. I didn't give up because of you. And because of it—and for so many other reasons—I won't give up on us, on this. You make my life better."

I don't know what to say to that. I hadn't considered that I might bring anything to the table. I hadn't considered I might not need money to make things between us equal. And he stood up to his father about *me*, too.

"Listen to me." He grips my shoulders, not too rough, but not too gentle either. His voice is broken though, his expression worse. "I am so much better than the person I was before I met you."

Actually, I discover, I know exactly what to say. "Alec, I—"

"Think of every obstacle we blew to bits before us. Your fake name. My position above you at work. My fake engagement. Teagan, we can get past this. I will spend every day for the rest of time making it up to you. I will never go behind your back again. And if you can't believe it right now, I won't blame you, but give me a chance. Let me show you." His voice breaks right down the middle. "Let me love you."

I grab his chin, not too rough, but not too gentle either. My voice is strong, steady. "You done?"

"Depends on your answer." His face is purposefully blank, and I finally realize it's what he uses to hide fear. He's afraid of what I'm going to say. Which makes me speak so fast, I almost trip over the words.

"Well, *before* you spoke over me, what I was going to say is this..." Deep breath. Look in his eyes. Memorize what they do next. "Alec, I love you."

Glassy. That's what happens next in his eyes, they go a little glassy. Or at least I think they do. I don't have more than a split second to study them before he's kissing me. Gently. Smoothly. His hands are pressed against my lower back, pulling me toward him. I slide my palms up his face, along the scruff of his jaw, into the mess of his hair. It's almost as soft in my fingertips as his lips are against mine.

This kiss is a languid thing, almost lazy, though one of us is shaking against the other.

I'm surprised to discover it's him—his arms are shaking around me.

"What's wrong?" I ask, breaking the kiss. "You're trembling."

"To keep myself from crushing you," he says, holding himself very, very still. "Hearing you say that stirs things in me that would frighten you."

"Bet you're wrong." I step away from him, smiling as suggestively as I'm able. "Try me."

"I will." His eyes fall to the bed, then back to me, and my breath begins to stretch for the marathon that it senses is coming.

I take another step away. "Why are you still standing there?"

"Because I need to get this right first."

I lift a brow, not as easily as Vera does it, but somewhere close. And I fight a smile because I know him. And I know what he's about to say.

He doesn't disappoint. "I love you, Teagan."

"Oh, that?" I affect as bored a tone as I can. "That's old news."

His grin is quick, sharp and infectious. He closes the distance to me. "Your turn."

"For what?" I blink up at him, all innocence.

"Say it again," he demands.

"You're bossy." I fight a smile as wide as a yawn.

"Say it again." His voice is lower, and there's a muscle twitching in his jaw. He tightens his grip.

I squirm in his arms, purposefully rubbing myself against his body. "You can't tell me what to do outside the office."

"Let's play make believe." He walks me backward toward the bed. "This is my office." When we get to the bed, he yanks me around and pushes me forward onto my hands. And nerves start to synchronize in my belly. The hottest flash of longing zapping them all in a row. "And this," he says, his hands at my waist, holding me in place, "is my desk. And if you don't tell me what I want to hear, I'm going to keep you bent over it and tease the words out of you."

I snort, and though unladylike, it releases an entire flock of giddy relief. We're *in love*. We're about to have sex, and he wants me to tell him I love him again first. "Now you're tempting me not to say it."

He leans over me, his scruffy chin rubbing against my shoulder, and he nips at my earlobe. "What if I promise to tease you anyway. Will you tell me before I do?"

I push us up from the bed and twist around in his arms, because I want to face him when I say the words. It takes about a year and a half for my mouth to release its grin to let them out. "I love you, Alec Chambers. And I'll say it whenever you want me to, forever."

His expression darkens in this delicious sort of way, and he kisses me, biting my lower lip before he pulls away. "Again."

"I love you." I jolt when he draws my camisole down, his thumb grazing my nipple, his pupils going wide in his dark, dark eyes.

"Again." He pushes me back until I catch myself on the bed, and he pushes himself between my legs.

"I love you."

He bunches the fabric of my tank top in his hands and *rips it*. The sound tears through the room, and my shirt splits right down the middle. Now he drops his gaze, and I do too, to my stomach. It quivers, and my breasts rise and fall with the quickening of each breath I take.

"That was *new*," I say.

"Again." He drops before me, taking his time, dragging his hands down my body, roughly, perfectly. He bites my stomach. He growls against my skin. He pauses at my pajama shorts, looking up, with a steady, commanding gaze. "I said, again."

"I love you." Somehow I get the words out even without any breath left in my lungs. He pulls my shorts down. Underwear with them. And once he's dragged the fabric down to the floor, he slides his hands up the insides of my legs, pushing against them until I widen my stance and I think I'm going to fucking die.

"Again." His gaze holds mine so intensely my entire body starts to spark, and his fingers are touching me, tickling me, pulling my skin apart. "Tell me."

"I love you." This comes out barely a whisper, and before I've finished speaking, he licks me. Long. Slow. His tongue rolling over me in a way that forces a moan from deep in my chest. He doesn't drop eye contact, and the slow swivel of his face against me nearly makes me collapse. With one hand, I twist the comforter between my fingers, and I grab his hair with my other, gripping his head while his tongue slips, slips, slips through me.

He pauses, purposefully breathing hot air over the sensitive flesh spread before him, and I yank his hair so hard it shocks him. His mouth twists in a wicked grin.

"I want you inside of me," I say, panting. "I need you."

"Say it."

"I love you." I match his grin. "Now please fuck me."

His quick intake of breath makes me laugh—and then he levels me with a look so intense, I forget to breathe.

"I love you so fucking much." He says it like a threat, like a promise. He says it like it's everything. And he's rising now, trailing his tongue along my skin. The room is filled with the sounds of my breathing, finally remembered, and with the clanking of his belt buckle coming undone, with the rustling of his jeans as he shoves them down his legs. He pauses for the shortest moment to rip his shirt off.

"I love you," he says, kissing me, lifting me and tossing me on the bed and easing himself over me. "I love you."

"Listen here," I say, grabbing his face and returning the lip bite from earlier. "I'm all for your manhandling tendencies in the bedroom, but let's establish some ground rules. *I* get to be in charge sometimes."

In a move I'm quite proud of, I wrap my leg around his and roll us until I'm on top of him. And, okay, he probably helps it along, but a girl can enjoy her moments regardless. He glances between our bodies, his wicked grin widening. "You want to ride me, kitten, believe me, you'll get no complaints."

A lesser girl might flee at the size of his erection, but the thing is...I've never been one to back away from a good challenge. And this? It's the absolute fucking best.

"Kitten?" I ask, dryly—though it thrills me to my core that he still calls me this. "Let's see which of us is the first to purr."

I wrap one hand around him—and lick my lips when he jerks against my palm. I lift on my knees, and I lower myself over him, *onto* him.

He moans, and when I begin to rock my hips, falls silent, the look on his face one so full of pleasured intensity my entire body shivers to have it directed at me.

Or...

Maybe I shiver at the way he feels inside of me. Hard and slick and huge. He *fills* me.

When he thrusts himself harder into me—faster, too—I grab the ridges of his ab muscles to steady myself, and I slam my hips over him, back and forth and side to side and *holy motherfucking hell* I've never felt so good in my entire life.

And then he reaches out to grab my breasts, flickering his thumbs over my nipples in the rhythm I ride him with until they're so tight against his caresses I bite my tongue to keep from begging him to pinch them harder, to help ease some of the way he's made them ache. He does it anyway.

"I love you," he says.

And he says it again, fiercer this time, as he slides his hands down my body, down, down, all the way down, to use his fingers against me.

With me.
Against me.
With me.
In circles.
With varying pressure.

Until that pressure sinks through to the core of me, expanding in my belly, hot and fierce and spinning.

Until my head falls back, and I grip his thighs and discover how much deeper he can go from this angle.

Until I'm crying-whimpering-moaning his name, which maybe makes me the first to purr.

But it's not long till he's the first to roar, so I'm pretty sure I'm the winner.

If these things need keeping track of.

Pretty sure they don't.

But it doesn't keep a smug smile from my face anyway.

Until he kisses it off of me, and we start all over again.

CHAPTER FIFTY-FOUR

WE SLEEP MOST of the day away. And when we wake again, he slips into me with a sigh that twists into a moan that twists into another roar.

And then again.

And then I tell him I have to take a break for at least twenty-four hours. "I'm still getting used to this," I say, sinking my teeth into his shoulder. "I'd like to be able to walk tomorrow."

His laugh is loud and rich, and he pulls me against him, and we doze some more.

When he next opens his eyes, I'm sitting on the edge of the bed, fresh from a shower. The sheet of paper containing my father's contact information is in my hand, still folded.

"You want to talk about it?" he asks, rising to wrap his arms around me.

"No." But in his arms, I instantly relax, and I speak about it anyway. "What if...what if he's a convict. Or worse? What if the number's wrong? What if he doesn't want to hear from me?"

"But what if he does?" Alec asks.

And that one question changes everything.

I stand and I slip the paper back into the drawer, closing it.

"You aren't going to call him?"

I shake my head. "Maybe tomorrow. Or maybe in a week. Or a month." I turn toward him. "I need a little bit more time to adjust to the fact that he's out there and to the possibility that he might want to know about me. As long as you'll hold my hand when I do."

"I'll hold your hand anytime you ask." He rises, crossing to me and kissing me. "And plenty of times when you don't."

"Go shower," I murmur against his mouth, glowing. I start to step away, but he holds me at an arm's length.

"Listen," he says, his expression serious enough to twist my stomach. "Last week, you brought up me returning to school, like you thought this could end when that happens."

"But you reassured me," I say. "I don't think that anymore. I get it. I was—"

"I need to know you *really* get it," he say, running his thumbs over my collarbones, making me start to tremble—again. "This—you and me?—this is it for me, kitten. One year of school between us and then I'm home for good. Or we can go wherever you want—wherever *your* career takes you. Us, I mean. Because it's you and it's me and it's final. Do you understand what I'm saying?"

"That you love me," I say, the corners of my lips rising so high they feel like they're halfway up my cheeks. "That you want to love me forever."

His eyes soften, they dance, they blink...and when they look into mine again, they're full of pleasure. "I *will* love you forever."

When I close my eyes, I can envision the outline of our future. The details are blurry, but his shape and mine—they're together through it all. I don't know how I got so lucky. I don't know how *we* got so lucky.

But it happened.

I kiss him. I kiss him hard. I kiss him sweet and soft. I kiss him and kiss him and kiss him until there's no way he'll ever doubt my response. "Same goes, Alec."

"Good," he says, biting my lower lip. "Just so we're clear."

"Crystal."

After one more lingering kiss, he slips into the shower, and, when the grumbles of my stomach grow louder than the leftover euphoria in my mind, I head out of the room to fix us something to eat.

I walk straight into a room of my friends. Cassidy, Vera, Gage...

They're all looking at me with expectant, shit-eating smiles.

"What?" I ask, ignoring the matching smile that's tugging so hard at my own mouth.

"We weren't sure if you were ever coming out," Gage says, sipping a beer.

"We also weren't sure exactly what sorts of sports you had going on in there," Cassidy adds, wrapping me in a hug. "Sounded intense. Did you score?"

I open my mouth to make a ballsy sort of statement—and then I shut it again and head to the fridge for a hard cider. There's an array of Mexican food on the table, and I dig in, ignoring their protests and demands for information. I offer a plate to Alec when he steps out a few minutes later, shirtless, with wet hair. He looks as shocked as I felt when I realized we had a bit of an audience waiting for us.

I think it's the first time I've ever seen him embarrassed.

And, because of it, I can't stop giggling. All the way through introducing him to Gage, and re-introducing my best friends.

Later, when an unfortunately *shirted* Alec is bouncing quarters in cups of beer with Gage, Cassidy nudges me. "Okay. Now you have to tell me. How was it?"

"Sorry I made you ditch your beach weekend," I say.

She waves my words away. "I think Quinn was relieved for us to go, honestly. She had some of her own stuff going on. Now. Stop stalling. I want details, Teag. Come on." Her words are teasing, playful. Then she pauses, considering. "God. Sorry. It's none of my business. Old habits and all…"

I tell her I don't mind her question and she doesn't need to apologize—who could blame her for being curious? Especially with all the tall tales I've spent the past few years telling. "But you know… I'll keep it to myself all the same." I glance at Alec, pressing my lips together to suppress a smile. Because what we do in the bedroom? Hell, what we do anywhere…

It's all ours.

And there's something really fucking special about that.

He catches me the next time my eyes wander his way, and he mouths, "I love you."

I mouth it right back.

I've never known such happiness.

ACKNOWLEDGEMENTS

There are not enough thank yous in the world to send everyone who helped to make this book what it is, especially:

Katy Upperman, Alison Miller, Elodie Nowodazkij, Elizabeth Briggs, and Tracey Neithercott. You girls are brilliant writers, and I'm blessed—*beyond* blessed—to have you in my corner. That you made the time to read this so quickly and so thoroughly during your busy lives means so, so much to me. And your feedback was (as always) invaluable. (And Liz—*thank you* for the title!) And thank you, Cindy Thomas, for your unwavering encouragement.

My spreadsheet girls. As always, thank you for keeping me on track!

My hideaway girls. You guys are the fucking best.

All the readers and bloggers who've been so wonderful along my author journey. Especially Silvana Reyes from Hopeless Book Lovers & NA Source—and everyone in Riley & Crew. You guys give me such huge heart eyes.

Stephanie Parent. Copyeditor extraordinaire. Thank you!

Cait Greer. For all your paperback formatting—you're the best, and someday I'm totally going to hug you.

Sarah Hansen of Okay Creations. For yet *another* lovely cover.

Nelson. For talking about equity firms with me, and for helping me find the time to write.

Sweet girl. For just being your sweet, sassy, hilarious self. I love you.

ABOUT THE AUTHOR

RILEY lives in Northern Virginia and spends most of her time with her characters, playing with her toddler and husband, and pretending she knows how to be an adult. Former dancer. Current writer. Lifelong lover of accessories, books, and the beach. And cats. Can't forget the kitties, of which she has two.

Visit RileyEdgewood.com to contact Riley!
She loves hearing from her readers!

@Rileyedgewood
Facebook.com/rileyedgewoodauthor

Made in the USA
Lexington, KY
19 March 2016